Silver Blades
Book One

Lisa Mortara

Foil Books

Also by Lisa Mortara

Snow Blind—a sequel to Silver Blades

In the Shadow of the Eiffel Tower

Registered with the U.S. Library of Congress

Foil Books

Cover design by Lynne Pierce
Cover photos by Lisa Mortara
Upper back-cover photo: in the distance, the Mole Antonelliana, signature building of Turin, Italy

Remembering the Silver Blades
Fencing Club

and fencing buddies Ric and Matt

1: Unworthy of a Spy

Erika Rivoli squinted into the northern Italian mist, cold clamping down on her like wolves' teeth. Compared to sunny San Diego, Asti's November weather still unsettled her. An ocean, a continent, a world separated her from her balmy hometown, and yet it was a distance she desired— distance from those bastards in the CIA, and not least from *the accident* that haunted her still.

She could barely navigate her way through the dense alien fog, and upon reaching the arched stone porticoes of Piazza Alfieri she ducked into the Cremeria café. Normally she would have continued on to the Reale for her morning cappuccino. But after two weeks of living in Asti she knew that today was the waiter Mas1simo's day off. Massimo, who invariably acknowledged her with a polite smile and a bit of small talk, was about her age, twenty-four, and the Reale seemed less inviting without him.

In the Cremeria she stuffed her gloves into her coat pockets, her copy of the *Times of London* wedged under one arm. In the warmth of the café, with its fragrance of rich, perpetually trickling espresso, her frozen muscles began to unstiffen. *Ahh*, she sighed to herself, looking forward to relaxing with her coffee and newspaper.

She unbuttoned her coat, glanced around for a table, and almost collided with a waiter juggling a tray of beverages. The tray remained aloft but one of the cups slid to the edge, sending a splash of coffee onto a petite elderly woman heading toward the exit.

"*Oh, Signur!*" the woman cried in the local dialect.

The waiter stared at the lake of liquid on his tray. "*Scusi, Scusi!* I don't know what happened."

The woman glared at him. "Just get something for my coat."

A harsh voice for such a small woman, thought Erika. She looked from the woman to the waiter to another observer, who also stood cocooned in winter layers, which not only included a stocking cap but a scarf covering part of his mouth. "Sorry," the man said to the waiter in Italian. "Didn't mean to jostle you." His bright brown eyes shifted to the old woman. "Can I help?"

The waiter, an old guy himself, returned an embarrassed frown. With his free hand he produced a clean cloth from the pocket of his white apron and offered it to the distressed woman. "Take this, Signora..." His tone was imploring, as if the woman were some kind of dowager empress. She even looked imperious, her skin as white as the fog outside. And though she seemed frail, she snatched the cloth and wiped droplets of coffee from her fox-collared coat with aggressive strokes, all the while emitting little grunts of irritation. The handles of her purse started to slip from her thin left wrist. As Erika moved to help, her own bag began to slide off her shoulder. The man with the barely-visible face reached out to the woman. "Allow me, it was my fault." His dark eyes were dancing, youthful like his voice. The woman relaxed, held out her arm, and in one fluid movement her purse slid off her wrist into the man's hand and out the door with him. Erika's eyes flew wide, the waiter's mouth dropped open, the signora let out a shriek.

Oh my God. Erika clutched her own purse and dashed for the exit, the old woman and the waiter hurrying after her. She felt she'd been part of the mess and needed to do something, at least follow the thief and alert others in passing.

"Stop him!" The old lady's arms flailed as she and the waiter exited the Cremeria after Erika.

"I can't see a damn thing!" said the waiter.

Erika made out a faint figure at the end of the arcade and rushed after it, gripping her purse to keep its strap from slipping again, her other hand clinging to her newspaper. Stepping off the curb into the street brought the blare of a horn; the car, lights dim in the smoky mist, swerved around her. She gasped and sprinted across the narrow strip of asphalt, slinging her purse bandolier-style across her chest.

She was now entering the City Gardens with the thief's silhouette at the limit of her vision. She picked her way along a sinuous paved path, then felt an eerie softness under foot. Something grazed her face—cool, light fingers. Another gasp escaped her before she realized she had drifted onto grass and that the caress she felt was only that of a feathery evergreen.

She stepped back onto the paved path and stopped. Now, not even a wisp of the purse-snatcher's silhouette remained. Which way to go? Suddenly aware of the frigid air biting her hands and neck, she tucked the newspaper under her arm, buttoned her grey wool coat, and pulled her gloves back on. No point in going any further. She turned and retraced her steps as best she could. With a sour expression she scrutinized both directions of the street she'd crossed and returned to the arcade, slowing in front of the Cremeria. Having failed to catch the thief she would not go back in there. Or maybe she should...otherwise the old lady and the waiter might think her a partner to the purse-snatcher, racing out to join him...No, she decided, she didn't feel like reporting her failure to catch him, and so she continued on to her usual café, the Reale.

"*Buon giorno*," said Piero as she entered. Like his younger colleague, Massimo, the barista Piero always bade her Good Day. "Cappuccino, as usual?"

"*Sì, grazie,*" Erika answered with more distraction than politeness. She took a seat at a table and dropped her *Times* in front of her. It wasn't until Piero brought her coffee that she quit staring into space and unfolded the paper, dated 9 November 1977—yesterday's issue since delivery from London took an extra day. Still, nothing could hold her attention after the morning's fiasco. Her gaze drifted towards the café window, out at the floating white vapor into which the purse-snatcher had vanished.

Why had she not guessed his game? She should have been alerted the minute he admitted to jostling the waiter's tray, especially with his head swathed like a Bedouin's. She didn't even suspect the thief's offer to hold the lady's handbag. He had beaten Erika to it, and she had even fumbled with her own purse while clutching her newspaper. And if that weren't enough, the pine branch in the gardens had spooked her and slowed her down. *Not at all how a spy should act.*

The thought made her shake her head bitterly. Well, she wasn't a spy...*though she should be*. Weeks of interviews and tests at CIA headquarters in Langley, Virginia, had culminated in the dashing of a dream. "Sorry, Miss Rivoli," read their brief letter, "we regret to inform you that we won't be able to employ you for field operations, though you could always apply for a position with Radio Free Europe." *Radio Free Europe*...blathering propaganda across the airwaves all day. *Not what she'd had in mind.*

About a month after her rejection she left for Italy.

Erika looked down to find the edge of her unread *Times* crumpled in her right hand. *Time to go*. She grabbed her purse, pulled out her Italian lire, and dropped the correct change on the table next to her unfinished coffee. She left, still toting the *Times*, though outside the Reale she scowled at the newspaper. She should have left it and her own cumbersome purse with the waiter in the Cremeria to prevent the items from slowing her pursuit of the thief.

She walked to a small trash receptacle under the porticoes and aimed the *Times* at it. Then she changed her mind. Why toss out a paper she enjoyed; it would be just as fitting to trash her purse.

Gradually her anger slackened as she considered where to go next. She didn't want to return to where she was staying before noon. Her body gave an involuntary shiver. Not a day for an aimless stroll. She puffed out a sigh and headed through the soggy fog towards corso Alfieri, the thoroughfare of Asti's historical center.

Indecision: it could very well have sunk her with the CIA, she reflected, feeling once again the hot stab of disappointment at the agency's passing her up. All those multiple-choice questions—about a hundred per exam, some presenting scenarios whose connection to the ability to perform spy work seemed obscure—had set her to second-guessing.

"What would you do if you were walking down a sidewalk and happened onto a large boy kicking a smaller boy?"

A: walk on by

B: intervene forcefully

C: tell him to stop or you will call the authorities

D: look for a phone and call the authorities directly

At that desk in Langley she had sat chewing her lip and flicking her fingers over the choices, finally choosing answer B, because you had to be tough and unafraid in the CIA, right? Really, she had no idea what they were fishing for with that question, or in any other of the series of exams she took over a five-day period.

As Erika drifted down corso Alfieri she passed another arcaded complex on her right. A lateral walkway led to a little nest of shops. A Longines boutique, a travel agency, and the Manhattan Institute crouched in mist under the low, right-angled porticoes. Erika didn't enter the complex. No, she would be returning there this evening to her job at the Manhattan Institute, a language school. A "black job," as the Italians would call her under-the-table English tutoring.

As she continued down the narrow street a car next to her sounded its horn, a light toot of warning before rumbling past over the cobblestones. *I see you, no need to frigging honk!* With that, she decided to head home. Enough waffling—indecision was unworthy of a spy!

2: Red and Black

The CIA had ordered Erika to tell no one about her prospective recruitment. Not a word about the tests, the interviews with psychologists, psychiatrists, agents. "Your parents can know but that's it." Erika had not even informed her parents of her week at CIA headquarters in Langley. To anyone concerned, she was out of town visiting an old friend.

Naturally she had kept silent about failing to get into the CIA. Not out of deference to the "Company," but to hide her status as a reject. As for Erika's present sojourn in Italy, she had told family and friends that having minored in Italian and spent many summers in Italy, she would now look for a job in the country of her heritage—the original home of her immigrant grandparents with whom she had spoken Italian nearly all her life.

Plus, if she could somehow redeem herself, maybe even prove the CIA wrong...

She was bilingual, fairly athletic, and even a bit daring if she did say so. Wasn't that what they were looking for—a combination of brains and physical fitness? It had seemed so, for they were the ones who'd invited her to Langley.

She thought of her polygraph test at CIA headquarters. A middle-aged fellow had administered it, jovial on the surface though his gaze was annoyingly oblique at times. "Don't be afraid to answer 'yes' when it comes to a question about trying marijuana," he'd warned with a friendly smile. "We wouldn't get any young agents if dabbling in pot was a disqualifier."

She appreciated his attempt to put her at ease, though

being wired-up from torso to fingertips hardly felt relaxing.

"Just breathe calmly and answer without deliberating. I'll be asking the questions; no one else will come in."

Erika sat in a padded chair with the examiner behind her at his desk. She couldn't see his machine or score chart, but she listened keenly to its mechanical workings.

The man cleared his throat. "I'm going to ask you a series of questions that you'll only answer 'yes' or 'no' to. Some may sound ridiculous, like, 'Are you fifty-years-old?' Don't be thrown, just answer truthfully. Are you ready?"

She swallowed and nodded.

"Is your name Erika Christine Rivoli?"

"Yes."

"Are you from San Diego, California?"

"Yes."

"Did you go to college in New York City?"

"No."

"Have you ever traveled to a communist country?"

"No."

"Have you ever had a friend or a family member who espoused communism?"

"Yes." *Damn it*—did she say that weakly? She thought she perceived a slight swish from the machine, and now there was a pause.

"Have you ever had any contact with a foreign intelligence service?"

"No."

"Have you ever had a sexual encounter with someone of your own sex?"

"...No." *Shit*, the shock of the question had made her hesitate. Another pause.

"Have you ever smoked marijuana?"

"Yes."

"Have you ever tried LSD?"

"...No." *Swish-scratch. Christ!*

She had coasted downhill with the rest of the questions, thank God. But still, *her lie about the LSD*. Why hadn't the guy warned her about that question? She might never have tried LSD if not for her unsupervised adolescence. And since *the accident* her parents had only distanced themselves further.

Erika's pulse ticked up, just as it must have beneath the cuff squeezing her bicep at the moment of her polygraph lie, which caused the needle to scratch a long black zigzag. And yet the examiner had told her she passed; but what did that mean? If they had nailed her lie about the LSD, wouldn't they have wondered about her character? Or might the CIA have expected selective honesty, something undoubtedly practiced by its field agents?

Her thoughts swiveled back to the purse-snatching as she climbed the two flights of stairs to her cousins' flat where she was staying. The thief's laughing eyes—*yes, he was mocking us all!*

She rang the bell and waited. She didn't have a key and hadn't asked for one. Despite great kindness and generosity demonstrated by cousin Elsa and her husband Angelo Marengo, a childless couple in their late sixties, she considered this living arrangement temporary.

"Ciao," said Elsa, opening the door. In the entryway Erika immediately engaged a pair of *feltri*, two squares of sewn padded wool on which Italians glided to avoid scuffing up tile or hardwood floors. Italians didn't pad around the house in their socks. "Since both you and Angelo are home early," continued Elsa, "we'll have lunch now."

Erika shot her cousin a quizzical look as she skated after her on the *feltri*. "Angelo's home early too?"

"Yes, and he's restless with the news about the latest Red Brigades attack in Turin. He can't stop ranting so I've forced him to the table."

Another attack! Erika tossed her coat and scarf on the bed in her room, the name *Red Brigades* stinging her like an elusive wasp. The Red Brigades were just one, though the most infamous, of a variety of communist terrorist groups running amok in Italy. Apart from Italian efforts to combat them, there had been the CIA's interest in taking Erika on to infiltrate cells of Italian communist youth. She had looked forward to the job, later feeling it had been snatched from her.

Distracted by Elsa's announcement, Erika abandoned the *feltri* and headed for the kitchen to hear Angelo's account.

Elsa's husband never forgot his *feltri*. "Have you heard?" he asked Erika as he shuffled alongside the table, one of his navy-blue suspenders hanging off the shoulder of his white dress shirt. "The Red Brigades have struck again."

A lock of grey hair dangled over his furrowed forehead above a bulbous nose and luminous blue eyes that looked perpetually surprised. His short body reminded Erika of a football standing on end, and the whole effect normally made her grin to herself. But not today. She took a seat at the table and gave him her full attention.

"Three of them in balaclavas," he said in a gravelly voice, rising with drama, "shot a bank guard in the kneecaps with Kalashnikovs. The guard's in the hospital and the bank's cleaned out."

Erika pictured the guard in front of the bank's entrance, poised with his own machine gun. Such guards were stationed at banks all over Italy, including in Asti. So far the town hadn't been hit, but who knew...and who knew how the CIA would have planted her undercover in Italy. *If only they'd had the good sense to hire her*.

"Sit down, Angelo," insisted Elsa, removing her husband's napkin from his top plate so she could serve him *albese*, a raw, ground veal dish, cured with olive oil, salt, and lemon juice, which Elsa prepared daily at Angelo's request.

Still grumbling, Angelo sat, freeing his arms completely from their suspenders in order to tuck in. Elsa sat with them just long enough to consume the first course then rose to bring the minestrone from the stove. Lunch was the highlight of the Marengo household, long and leisurely—the table set with triple plates for three courses and glasses for both mineral water and wine. An increasingly tedious event for Erika after two weeks. Of course she appreciated her cousins' hospitality and the Italian they spoke with her, but today she couldn't suppress her restlessness.

"Anything specific about this terrorist bunch?" she asked Angelo.

"The usual vicious, subversive punks. Turin's a nest of communist extremists. Red gangs galore. Last month, before you came, a group called the Armed Proletarian Squads threw Molotov cocktails into a discotheque—a young student burned to death." Angelo gave a guttural growl and poured himself another glass of Barbera.

"If Mussolini was still around," said Elsa, dabbing her mouth with her napkin, "he'd mop this lot up in no time."

Erika had heard these sentiments from other Italians, including her own grandfather who had been Elsa's uncle. Tall with short, elegantly-coiffed grey hair, Elsa exhibited the pale stately air that prevailed among the elders of the family.

Angelo winked at Erika. "Elsa would like *Black* terrorism back in government. Those hooligans throw Molotovs just like the Reds, remember?" he said, glancing at his wife then turning back to Erika. "Again, last month in Turin, one of those right-wing idiots beat a guy into *albese* on the sidewalk for carrying a leftist newspaper."

True, Italy roiled in revolt. The CIA had expressed fear that the country's democracy could topple.

Elsa stood to fetch the chicken and Swiss chard from the stove. As she filled their plates she said with a stern frown, "A man like Il Duce would permit *no* terrorism, Red or Black."

Angelo cocked his head and threw her an amused smirk. "I know, and the trains would run on time and laws would be enforced—"

"No more Moroccans would get into Italy—" Elsa added.

"The Southerners wouldn't be up here either," said Angelo to Erika with another wink.

"And there would be no weeds along the roadside…" Erika finished.

Angelo and Elsa looked at each other then laughed good-naturedly.

"My grandparents told me," said Erika with a shy grin, "that under Mussolini not one blade of stray grass ruined the country's picture-perfect landscape."

Elsa's expression softened. "We miss your grandparents. Since they died you're the only one from America who keeps in touch."

Erika nodded then looked away. A marble pillar of her life had come crashing down when her grandmother died at the beginning of this year, her grandfather having passed away four years earlier. They left her a small sum of money, and Erika had thought it a fitting tribute to spend it on a plane ticket and a fresh start in Italy.

Angelo poured Erika more wine. "It's true. When your grandparents used to visit before the war things ran like a Swiss clock. But those days are gone. Now we have Red terrorism, Black terrorism. They say the Asians'll arrive soon and then it'll be the Yellow Brigades."

"The Reds are worse," Elsa insisted. "The Blacks are striking back in protest."

"I guess they're called *Blacks* because of Mussolini's Black Shirts," said Erika.

"Yeah, but they're thugs and imbeciles all the same," said Angelo. "What do you expect when no party in parliament is worth a damn."

"People take to the streets," Erika answered. *Either*

overtly or covertly.

Elsa pointed to Erika's plate. "Don't let your lunch get cold."

After they finished their cheese, fruit, and coffee, Angelo took out a cigarette and offered one to Erika. She didn't smoke much, sometimes after dinner or while indulging in a drink with friends. Today she accepted one of Angelo's unfiltered Nazionali as she sank back into thoughts about her grandmother. If she had been alive when *the accident* in America had taken place things might have been easier...

Angelo and Elsa retreated for their daily siestas. Elsa would be napping for at least two hours and Angelo until five, sometimes six o'clock. Practically the whole city closed shop between one and four, which left Erika with little to do but join them in some down time.

She took Angelo's newspaper, *La Stampa*, to her room. She considered going out once the shops reopened, but what was there to explore in the soupy fog? Bad enough she would have to navigate it this evening on her walk to work.

She lay on her twin bed, propping herself against the headboard. The room served as a spare bedroom of sorts, but mostly as a repository for Elsa's overflow of *stuff*— stacks of clothes, linens, crocheted doilies, and whatnot. Erika's sparse wardrobe lay squeezed into a large armoire with more of Elsa's clothing. The house was cramped all around, with a separate formal dining room but no American-style living room. The "living" took place in the kitchen, with a couch and the only television. Elsa and Angelo owned the modest building they lived in, and if they hadn't rented out the other six flats, they could use one purely for the storage of Elsa's plethora of clothes and knickknacks; Erika was sure that Angelo would just as soon throw most of it out. He complained about the clutter, mostly about the potted plants occupying various corners of the flat. Once Erika had seen him pour leftover coffee from the Moka pot into one of them. He'd slipped her a sardonic smile and grunted, "It's good for them." Erika didn't comment that she'd heard coffee *was* actually good for plants.

She kicked off her shoes and flipped through *La Stampa*; no news of today's bank attack, for the paper had been printed beforehand. She did scan an article about a Red Brigades jewelry heist in Rome the day before, then dropped the paper on the Oriental rug next to her bed, once more musing about where in Italy the CIA might have sent her. She slid down flat on the bed and fixated the ceiling's crown molding, blowing out a long sigh and rubbing her forehead with the heel of her hand. She would probably never know what had definitively scuttled her with the agency. So for the time being she would be patient, tutoring English at the Manhattan language school from five to eight in the evening, Monday through Thursday. Hardly cloak and daggers (unless you counted the risk of being an undocumented worker) but enough to keep her in modest spending money while Elsa and Angelo temporarily housed her.

As she drifted off to sleep, the scratching of the polygraph machine sounded in her mind, etching fantastically the motto she had seen on a wall in the CIA lobby: *...Ye shall know the truth and it shall set you free.*

She woke with an anxious start, plagued with subconscious guilt for napping rather than *accomplishing something*. But she couldn't help dozing off again, having slept in mere shreds and patches the night before; and most nights, for that matter, since the *accident* back in San Diego. She sucked in a deep breath, clenched her teeth, and blocked the memory of that disastrous day from her thoughts. Her mind couldn't bear to relive it, although occasionally, and only for a split second, she wondered whether her rejection by the CIA might have had something to do with it.

"*Basta*," she said at last. "Enough." She checked her travel alarm clock on the night table. Almost four o'clock—might as well get ready for work.

3: "Nights in White"

The fog turned colder and more confounding that night, swallowing light from street lamps and car headlights as Erika walked to work down Asti's main street, corso Alfieri. She stuck close to the façades of the buildings to avoid getting run down by a careless driver, for she was treading on a non-raised sidewalk, a pedestrian walkway simply designated by a different design of stone to distinguish it from the street's cobbles. She gave her purse a squeeze, better to keep it building-side after what she had witnessed this morning.

"*Che tempo schifo*," came a male voice from the murky sea in front of Erika. Then a man and woman emerged walking arm and arm. As they passed her, Erika felt like sending the rejoinder, *Yeah, the weather is crap, especially when you come from sunny San Diego.*

This was her first winter in northern Italy and the occasional summers she had spent here with her grandparents had sorely misled her. By November lows could sink below freezing, and the damp cold seemed to swell with the fog to invade her very core.

She shivered, pulling her scarf more tightly to her neck as she entered the open shopping arcade that hosted the Manhattan Institute. Here danced a mist tinged yellow from the lights of the shops.

She nodded at the uniformed guard in front of the Longines boutique. Gripping his short machine gun, he always gave a stiff nod back. She passed the travel agency. Through its picture window, white light illuminated metal and Formica furniture. A poster of a beach and palm trees beckoned—*could be the Caribbean, Polynesia, or even southern California.* Erika's thoughts swayed to birds of paradise and giant Mauritania fig trees, the scent of pepper trees in her previous neighborhood and things that bloomed all year round, the world she had left behind. With no regrets.

The entrance to the building housing the Manhattan Institute, which specialized in English language studies, stood in a recessed area of the arcade. Erika opened its glass-and-metal door and climbed the stairs to the first floor where she greeted Rossana, the secretary.

"Are there any students yet?"

Rossana, a woman about Erika's age, removed her glasses and rubbed the bridge of her nose. "Could you have a seat for a moment, Erika?"

Erika paused, then sat at the worn mahogany study table opposite Rossana's desk. Here was where she wrote assessments of her students' English-speaking skills.

"I've got a bit of bad news...the school's closing down next week..."

Erika stared at her.

"And since today's Thursday..." Rossana gave a helpless smile.

"It'll be my last evening?"

"I'm sorry, Erika. They've been struggling to keep this location open...it was a decision from above and I didn't even find out for sure until yesterday."

Erika shook herself from her astonishment, noticing Rossana's reddening complexion. "It's not your fault," she assured her. "You're probably out of a job too." She gazed in dismay past Rossana, feeling her chair had been kicked out from under her.

Rossana leaned forward, sliding a hand across her desk toward Erika. "Listen, I might be able to help you. There's a Manhattan school in Turin—bigger with more students.

And with the people we're turning away who'll probably flow to Turin, they might need to hire more tutors. I could call and recommend you..."

Erika stood up slowly. "How would it work for me in Turin? Here no one asked if I had a work permit..."

"I'm sure it's the same. These schools need native English speakers. Plus you've got an Italian surname that's native to this area, and you live here. The job would be the same, conversing with students, modeling pronunciation, judging their English skills."

Erika gave a couple of hopeful nods just as the door opened.

"Ciao, Erika!"

"Ciao, Silvia." Erika's smile felt wooden. She wondered if her student had been alerted to the school's closure. "Come on," she said, leading the way down the hall to the classrooms. "Let's get started."

Three students came for lessons that evening and none seemed to be aware of the school's closure. Erika wanted to mention it—at least say goodbye and tell them about the Manhattan Institute in Turin—but it would be awkward if they hadn't already been informed that this was effectively their last evening with her.

When it came time to go home she stopped at Rossana's desk. "When were you going to tell the students?"

"I've been giving the news as they leave." She shook her head and raised her palms. "I'll phone the ones who still don't know."

"You're telling them about Turin..."

"Of course. You can pick up your final payment next week, and tomorrow I can call Manhattan in Turin for you."

"Thanks. Do you think I'd get the same hours?"

"Probably more. Turin has about a million people. You'll have to commute, it's about half an hour by train."

"I'll take the train up tomorrow and put in my application."

The train. Attached to electric wires it glided rhythmically, a subtle metallic *clu-clung, clu-clung* reverberating from the tracks. In her compartment Erika drew on a cigarette as she contemplated the barren countryside beyond the vapor-streaked window. Brown trees. Brown land. Muddy sky...

"Would you put that out, please?"

She turned to face a woman whose presence she hadn't previously noticed.

"No smoking, Signorina," added a bald man who wagged his index finger at her.

Erika looked around in disbelief; she'd thought she was alone in the compartment. "But this is a smoking compartment..."

"No, you're mistaken." Another passenger, this one a bespectacled woman with the air of an old schoolmarm.

From where were these people mushrooming?

She was dreaming, yet somehow aware she was in a dream...."Signorina!" Rossana from the Manhattan school appeared next to Erika.

Tap, tap, tap. The sound came from above her. She twisted around and frowned up at the metal bars of the luggage rack. A stubby-looking man in a black suit sat there, dangling his legs over the side. When he grinned she observed a stereotypical Italian from an American sitcom, slick black mustache and gold tooth gleaming. He bent over and flashed a picket sign at her: SMOKING EXTREMELY FORBIDDEN.

Erika glanced down at her fingers and found her cigarette had vanished.

Bang, came a noise from the corridor. She turned towards the door. *Bang!*

Voices rose in unison from the crowd in her compartment. "*Oh, Signur!* What's happening?"

Erika squinted at them, they all seemed to blur together. Her gaze flicked back to the luggage rack. The little

Italian was gone but his sign came tumbling down on her lap. DO SOMETHING! it now read.

I have to wake up. She exerted the muscles of her mind, but it was like trying to drag herself from an extraordinary force of gravity. She couldn't pull herself out of the dream.

Another *bang* from the corridor.

"Help, someone's got a gun!" came a plea from the blob-crowd in the compartment.

Erika went to the door and inched it open. Multiple figures in red and or black balaclavas were advancing down the corridor with pistols, shooting through the glass of random compartment-door windows. She jerked the door shut and drew the curtains, then reached for the picket sign. Instead she found an épée in its place, its tip broken and jagged. Then all went quiet except the musical *clu-clung* of the train. She assumed the en garde position and rotated the damaged but deadly weapon. The door slid open. She lunged...

And woke with her heart hammering. She clicked on the lamp next to her bed, knocking her alarm clock to the floor. "*Jesus!*" she said, retrieving it with a shaky hand.

Two a.m.: she had slept for only about an hour—another "night in white," as sleepless nights were called in Italian. She returned the clock to the bedside table and dropped back onto her pillow. Images of the dream revolved in her mind like a spinning mobile. *Would these nightmares never end?*

She rubbed her face to clear her thoughts. *The accident:* the fencing accident, to be precise. She had gone to therapy after the tragedy, but none of the sessions had helped. And when the psychologist asked her if she might envision taking the sport of fencing up again, it was the last appointment Erika made.

She turned off the lamp and diverted her thoughts to Rossana from the Manhattan school, whose cameo appearance in the dream was no doubt connected to anxiety over the closure of the school and the end of Erika's income. For the umpteenth time she cursed her rejection by the CIA, recalling that one of the agents who'd interviewed her had briefly popped up as a passenger in her dream. She reflected back on the meeting with him and a female agent in a hotel room at the harbor in San Diego. Both were at least in their late thirties. The man had taken the lead, his air outgoing and glib, while the woman sat back with what seemed weary indifference. Her hair hung long and straight, streaked with tired grey as well.

"As a field agent," the man had explained, "you'll make friends with communist youths and become their comrade to gather information. At any point if you're ordered to drop them, you'll do it. It can't matter how fond you might have grown of them or that they might be in danger. You'll have to be disciplined enough to follow orders and leave them behind."

Erika remembered glancing at the woman who sat in one of the three chairs; the woman simply looked away as if to convey, *I'm tired of this business and I don't care whether you get hired or not.*

The man made up for it. "Do you think you could handle that kind of work, Erika? His tone was enthusiastic, his smile winning. She longed to join the team.

"Yes," she answered, "my nerves are pretty solid. I used to live with a friend who was afraid her ex was going to break into the apartment at any time. One night the burglar alarm went off and when I went to her room she was shaking with her revolver in her hand. She handed the gun to me and we waited for the police. No one ended up being in the house but I was ready to shoot if I had to."

The agent's brows rose. A flicker of interest flared in the woman's gaze.

"Listen, Erika," he said, "it's likely you will never use a gun in the CIA and we're not looking for people who are trigger-happy—"

"I don't mean I *wanted* to shoot somebody...I was just prepared to defend us..." *Shit, had she blown it?*

No, it turned out that she was passed along to the weeklong tests in Langley. The man invited her for a drink after the interview, just the two of them. In the hotel bar he acted like a regular good-time Charlie. Lots of laughter and talk of movies and sports. Just one small detail rang odd about him. Erika sensed a strange shallowness behind his eyes, as if only a quickly-calculating brain resided there. When he smiled he flashed charm without depth, something opaque. Curious, but not off-putting. Still, Erika did wonder what might have occupied that space between eyes and calculating brain, once upon a time.

She rolled onto her side in bed. The fact was that she couldn't manage to release her yearning to be an undercover agent who traveled the world, speaking foreign languages, unearthing secrets, and *making the world safe from communism.* She didn't actually buy into the red scare. Maybe she would just like to help rid the world of malignant groups, be they left- or right-wing terrorists. The thought made her turn back to her dream: the black and red balaclavas represented Fascists and Communists, and the little Italian stereotype probably harked back to her growing up blond-haired and blue-eyed, with many people expressing wonder at her Italian origins.

She tried to empty her mind and fall asleep, despite a tingling sensation that had started up in her head. It wasn't new, this nighttime web of white electricity that she could at once feel, see and hear in her mind. She turned onto her back again and stretched all five-foot ten inches of herself until her feet hung off the bottom of the bed. Then she reached for her lamp, gingerly this time, and turned it back on. Where had she left the novel that wouldn't fit on her nightstand?

A clang sounded outside her room as if something metal had hit the kitchen tiles. She heard swearing. "*Dio faus!*" It was Angelo. She sighed and wrenched herself out of bed.

4: Little Paris

Clu-clung, clu-clung. Erika was riding the train, for real this time. She had sunk into sleep, rousing only slightly when her head would slip off the brown vinyl headrest with the swaying of the carriage. At the sound of her compartment door sliding open she whipped to full attention.

"*Buon giorno*," said a man who entered and closed the door.

Erika nodded as he sat in the seat nearest the door, suited and carrying a leather briefcase. Crisp-looking businessmen seemed to dominate the passenger traffic on the nine-thirty train to Turin.

Erika, on the other hand, felt like she had a pile of books stacked on her head, her neck straining to keep them balanced. She had slept no more than three hours last night and her eyes ached. The clanging outside her bedroom had turned out to be the aluminum Moka coffeepot crashing to the floor in the kitchen—Angelo, determined to make coffee in the middle of the night after sleeping all afternoon. He didn't excuse himself for the noise, choosing instead to invite Erika to join him. Rather than count sheep or red and black ski masks, she had accepted and now she was paying for it. She felt as flat and flaccid as pizza dough when it was paramount that she present her perkiest, most enthusiastic self to the Turin branch of the Manhattan Institute.

She massaged her cheekbones and gazed out the window at the skiff of snow on the landscape. It had come in the night, dissolving the imprisoning fog. Still, a greyish-white sky remained, confining, cage-like.

The commuter in her compartment lit a cigarette. They occupied a non-smoking compartment, but in reality hardly anyone bothered to complain about smoking on Italian trains, at least not in second-class carriages where Erika traveled. On the limited funds her paternal grandparents had left her she had no money for plush seats in first-class. She hoped they would have admired her pursuing a life here. Their son, Bruno Rivoli, couldn't care less about Italy.

Bruno: hard to imagine such a quintessential Italian name wasted on an individual in denial of his heritage. Erika's father went by his middle name *Alan* and had christened his two children *Erika* and *Keith*. The three names did not even exist in the Italian language. Not that names mattered all that much, but Erika couldn't understand why her father had turned his back on his roots.

Alan, the all-American, never talked about his travels in Italy as a nineteen-year-old with his parents. The year after the family returned in 1950 he married Cheryl Wheeler, a perfect American specimen who claimed lineage going back to colonial times. By high school Erika had quit addressing her father as *Dad* and had started calling him *Bruno*, partly to irritate him, definitely in disdain of his mania for all things American. People assumed she got her blond hair and blue eyes from her non-Italian side, despite the glaring fact that her mother (and brother) had brown hair and eyes. No, the fair genes came from Italy, and Erika was certain her father considered the light coloring a boon— and one more reason to go by Alan since Bruno meant *brown* in Italian.

The train glided into Porta Nuova, one of Turin's several stations, this one architecturally resurrected after the bombardments of World War Two. Erika got off and channeled through the crowds whose voices and footsteps echoed off high-vaulted ceilings and marble floors. Frigid air slapped her face as she exited and began the ten-block walk to the Manhattan school. She wasn't familiar with

Turin's public transportation, though if she landed the job she would definitely learn tram and bus routes.

The long walk down corso Re Umberto allowed her first glimpse of Turin outside its historical center, the latter famed for castles and palaces. Here, she passed lines of trees on the sidewalk, their branches slim and naked in November, save for the odd stubborn yellow leaf. She passed a bank, its presence pre-announced by a uniformed guard with a sober grip on his black machine gun. Soon after, she found the Manhattan school's multistoried stone façade, entered the building and took the stairs leading to a space similar to that of the school in Asti. This foyer was more spacious, with a worn leather couch accompanying the table and metal shelves full of dictionaries and books in English.

Here also was Rossana's counterpart, stationed behind a mahogany desk, telephone and typewriter at hand. The woman looked Erika over impassively, waiting for Erika to initiate a greeting, which she hastily did. "*Buon giorno*, I'm Erika Rivoli, here about a tutoring job...maybe you've heard from Rossana at Manhattan in Asti where I used to work... she was going to phone this morning..."

As Erika ran out of words, the woman lifted a set of dark brows that contrasted with her blond hair, the latter bleached, no doubt.

Erika shifted her weight under the woman's appraising gaze. She reckoned she was dressed professionally enough in her turtleneck sweater, wool skirt, and tights...

"Yes," the woman finally responded. "Signorina Dotta called this morning. Too bad about the closure of the Asti school." She gave an impersonal sigh and left Erika standing, though an empty chair sat next to the desk. Unlike Rossana this woman was plump and well into her thirties, and Erika sensed she enjoyed wielding petty powers, like keeping people shifting from foot to foot.

"So you're American..." the woman went on. A veneer

of boredom seemed to vie with a spark of interest.

Erika nodded. "I've got a bachelor's degree—"

"You're a native English speaker, that's what we care about."

Erika cleared her throat and wondered whether the woman had any other expertise than rudeness.

"At any rate our director is leaving for lunch at eleven-thirty, perhaps he might see you before he goes. Wait here." The woman eased out of her chair and swayed leisurely down the hallway.

Erika sat on the edge of a chair at the big table. She wouldn't get too comfortable; she had noted another private language school, the British School, in Elsa's copy of Turin's phonebook. She was mulling over that option when someone entered the lobby. A young man, with an unlit pipe in his hand.

His eyes scanned the room, lighting on Erika. For an instant he held her gaze with a slight frown, then a faint smile took the frown's place before he placed the pipe between his teeth and shed his overcoat. He shot a glance towards the corridor down which the secretary had gone, then he sat at the table across from Erika and removed the pipe from his mouth.

"*Buon giorno*," he said casually. "Are you waiting for someone?"

"The secretary. And you?"

"My session starts later but I came early to see about changing my schedule."

Erika nodded, noting a sprightliness in his brown eyes—intelligence, a hint of humor, perhaps. And of something else...something familiar. She vaguely recalled meeting someone with similar dark wavy hair, although she didn't remember any young person smoking a pipe. And his pause when entering...maybe he'd seen her before as well.

She was about to say something when a slow, heavy clicking of heels down the tiled corridor signaled the return of the secretary.

"Signor Barbasio has time to see you before he leaves. Down the hall, third door on the right."

Erika rose and thanked her. As she headed for the hall she caught the young man's smile again and returned it. Maybe he would still be there after her interview.

Instead he was gone when she came out; considering her more immediate concerns she wondered why she even cared. Apart from that vague air of familiarity, the pipe interested her and the fragrance of loose tobacco wafting from him. Erika's father used to smoke a pipe, when he was younger and they got along better. The scent of pipe tobacco almost made her yearn for those days.

Back outside, her thoughts returned to her interview. Signor Barbasio had said he would get back to her about a job. He would have Brigida, the secretary, call her with his decision on Monday. Erika shook her head at the thought of Brigida as a potential colleague, and Barbasio had hardly impressed her either. His tone was tepid which matched his pale, almost frail looks for someone who couldn't be over forty; he was probably one of those Italians who kept their windows shut during the sweltering summer for fear of drafts. At least he had nodded soberly when she'd informed him of her university degree and tutoring experience in Asti. Why he wouldn't make a decision right away (he had admitted they needed to hire someone) she didn't know, unless he was obliged to interview a set number of people.

As Rossana in Asti had surmised, this boss did not bring up the work permit business. That she would need a legal document to be employed in Italy never entered Erika's naïve head before leaving San Diego. She had only happened onto the subject in conversations with some of her students who discussed working abroad. She hadn't revealed her "paperless" status to anyone, and the idea of applying for documents after the fact did not seem wise. All in all, if her employers didn't care, neither did she.

She had written down the address of the British School but hesitated after taking it out of her purse. Would the Brits ask for work papers? Would they even tolerate an American accent? Better for now to wait for the call from the Manhattan school.

It was only one o'clock when Erika arrived back at Porta Nuova train station. Not knowing when she would finish up at the school, she'd told Elsa she wouldn't be home until late in the afternoon. She checked the railway schedule: a train departed from Turin for Asti about every hour. So rather than rush back to Asti only to hang around the house and stew about her situation, she would get a bite here and stroll around "Little Paris."

The city's nickname derived from its castles, palaces, and balconied baroque buildings. And yet the Turin of armed bank guards and nests of Red and Black terrorists couldn't escape her thoughts. She wanted to learn more, and for that she could ask Ivan Rivoli, her second cousin and an avowed Communist. He lived in Asti but worked in Turin. She wondered if the CIA had discovered both his and his parents' leftist affiliations, hence Langley's polygraph question about whether she knew any Communists.

Maybe having dodgy cousins had contributed to her rejection. She wondered whether any of her cousins had received a visit from inquiring strangers. She wouldn't ask, for it would only raise curiosity about her. She did have a pointed question for Ivan, however, which she would ask tomorrow night, when they were to leave Asti and spend the weekend in the country. Did his group of pals include a guy with brown wavy hair, a scintillating smile, and a pipe?

5: Red Country

"Why did they have to call him *Ivan*?" complained Elsa. "A communist name." She was washing dishes after dinner while Erika remained seated at the table with Angelo, waiting for Cousin Ivan to arrive.

"It's actually Russian for *Giovanni*, I think," said Erika. "*John,* in English. So it's a Christian name." She immediately left off, feeling pedantic and a touch disrespectful at practically correcting Elsa, who cleaned up while Erika sat idle. Yet there was no room at the sink for two and Elsa liked to manage her own kitchen.

"Then why didn't they just name him *Giovanni,* like normal people?" Elsa took the rubber nozzle attached to the end of the faucet, twisting it to rinse the sink. "The priest who baptized him was not fond of the name, I can tell you that."

"Ooooh, Ivan the Terrible!" said Angelo, winking at Erika. "The boy's twenty-four years old now. Don't you think it's time to get over his name?"

"It's not just his name, the whole family are communists."

Angelo gave a dismissive wave and rose to skate-shuffle on his feltri over to the window. He clicked on the outside light and looked out the drapes at the wrought-iron enclosed terrace. "No more snow, but some fog's returned." He glided over to the television to change channels. "When's he coming, anyway?"

Just then, the doorbell rang. "Here he is," said Elsa, dropping her dishtowel on the counter and striding, head high, out of the kitchen and down the hall to open the door.

As she rose to follow her, Erika noticed Angelo stub out his cigarette in the soil of one of the potted plants on the floor. "Good fertilizer," he quipped, and tossed the butt in the trash under the sink.

Before Erika could catch up, Elsa was ushering Ivan back down the hall and into the kitchen. He exchanged handshakes with Angelo and kisses with Erika.

"Coffee?" Elsa asked him.

"No thanks, we're meeting friends. Are you ready?" he asked Erika, before turning back to Elsa. "We're staying over at my parents' farmhouse tonight, did Erika tell you?"

Elsa gave a skeptical nod. "Will your parents be there?"

"No, they're busy."

"Leave them be," said Angelo. "I'm sure they don't intend to waste the weekend with old people."

Erika gave an embarrassed little sigh. "Well, thanks for dinner," she said to Elsa, retrieving her overnight bag from the couch.

Elsa walked them to the door. As elder cousin to both Erika and Ivan, practically old enough to be their grandmother, she aimed another look of subtle reproach at them before saying good-bye.

"She doesn't approve," said Erika, as they jogged down the stone stairs.

"She's sixty-eight, you've only got to nod and smile and then ignore her. Don't you do that with your parents?"

"I wasn't even living with my parents before I came here. They don't bother with what I do."

They reached the ground floor and Erika made sure the heavy wooden door shut solidly.

"Lucky for you," said Ivan, as he unlocked his car. "They're not hovering Italian parents."

"Yeah, I suppose," Erika agreed, shrugging.

They sped out of the neighborhood in Ivan's white Fiat 127. He didn't pursue the topic of parents, for which Erika was grateful. Ivan knew Bruno and Cheryl Rivoli only superficially, having met them on a trip to the States four years prior. On the other hand, he'd known Erika's grandparents all his life through the couple's many trips to the old country; and yet Erika doubted he'd ever mentioned his enthusiasm for communism to them. She hadn't even realized the extent of his communist sympathies until this year.

"So who's this friend of yours we're off to see?" she asked.

"Nadia Regis. Her grandparents have a country house not far from here. They won't be there, though."

"Is it like your country house in Pautasso?"

"I don't know, this is my first time visiting there."

"All these country houses, you'd think everyone's rich here."

"Well we're *not*. Most of them are farmhouses passed down for generations, like my mother's."

"I know. It's still an attractive situation."

"It's our culture."

Ivan accelerated when they reached the outskirts of Asti, shifting through the gears as though he were torturing them, squeezing every bit of oomph out of the sub-compact.

"Let's have some heat," Erika said. "It's freezing."

Ivan obliged, but the air that sputtered out was lukewarm at best.

"How long have you known her?" asked Erika.

"Nadia? A few months. She works in import-export like me, only at a different firm. Her English is better than mine."

"I was thinking about your friends. The other day I ran into a guy in Turin who looked familiar, like someone I might've met in your circle. A little older than us. His profile reminds me of a Roman bust. Dark wavy hair, dark eyes. Smokes a pipe..."

"Nobody I know."

A ways out of the city, the road grew tortuous, but

Ivan's foot held fast as they wrenched around narrow curves through the dark countryside.

"I don't know where I could've met him, then," said Erika, testing the vent. "The air's gone cold—what's going on with the heater?"

Ivan felt the air on his side. "The car's old," he said, and whipped the lever to the off position. "Heat works for fifteen minutes then stops."

His pronouncements led to harder acceleration and as they rounded a bend, rubber screeched and Erika grasped the hanging passenger handle. Faulty heating, no air conditioning, no radio or cassette player: "Looks like it's time to buy your Alfa GTV," she said.

"Not going to happen with the job I've got." He turned the blower back on and warm air spewed out. "A miracle," he muttered.

Erika basked in the warmth, smiling at Ivan's sarcasm. They had hung around together since her first summer visit with her grandparents when she was seventeen.

"How'd you meet that Roman, anyway?" he asked

"I don't know that he's Roman. I just know I've seen him before, I ran into him in the lobby of the Manhattan Institute in Turin." Erika shivered. "Hey, the air's gone cold again."

"*Cazzo*," Ivan swore, and shut the heat off again.

Erika gave a snort. She always found that obscenity as expressive as its English counterpart, *fuck*. Even more colorful as it referred to the male sex organ.

"So why the Manhattan school in Turin?" asked Ivan, as he threaded the car higher into the hills.

"They've closed the one in Asti."

"Oh...I'm sorry. Well, if you end up in Turin you'll find it a much more exciting city. We'll be able to meet there."

"Is the train commute okay?" In Italy, gasoline was triple its cost in the States and Ivan, like many dwellers of Asti who worked in Turin, drove his car to the station, rode the train, then took two different trams to reach his office.

"Makes for a long day but you get used to it."

After several wrong turns Ivan found the road that led to the long driveway his friend Nadia had specified. They turned in and followed it down into a hollow, to a paved courtyard where they parked in front of a two-story house. The house appeared attached to another structure but it was too dark to determine anything else. *If I had to find my way back here*, thought Erika, *I'd be screwed*.

Nadia Regis swung open the front door and swept them into the living room, giving both Ivan and Erika kisses on the cheeks though she was meeting Erika for the first time.

"How's work?" she asked Ivan. "No, don't tell me—who wants to talk about it on the weekend? Your cousin Erika's as tall as me. Amazing, then again she *is* American. Lovely you could come, Erika. And this"—she indicated a man standing behind her—"is Flavio Moretti, up from Rome and working in my office."

In the pause that finally arrived, Erika shifted her gaze from this tall, perky friend of Ivan's, to the Roman, Flavio. Unlike the Manhattan-school student, he looked nothing like a classical Roman bust. This man struck Erika as nothing short of exotic: wavy black hair hanging almost to his shoulders, olive skin contrasted with keen blue eyes and high flinty cheekbones—all he needed was an Arabian horse and a scimitar and she could see him thundering out of the nineteenth-century Caucasus.

She and Ivan shook hands with him. He granted smiles to both of them and then focused on Ivan. "You and Nadia both have Russian names. I like them."

"My parents are leftists," Ivan said, flushing slightly.

"Communists?"

"Mm," Ivan affirmed.

"Sorry," said Nadia. "Ivan told me you were American and we know how communism's viewed in the States."

"I've got nothing against the Italian Communist party,"

Erika assured her.

"Erika knows we're not Stalinists in Italy," said Ivan, shifting his weight and stuffing his hands in his pockets.

"But we're not diluted socialists either," Nadia emphasized. "Why bother with Pink when you can go pure Red."

Though hardly shocked, Erika felt surprise. People talked politics often in Italy yet they didn't usually barrage you with their views before you even sat down, especially if they'd never met you before. She wondered at this reception.

Then Nadia placed a hand on her arm, suspending the chatter. "What kind of host am I?" she said, as if reading Erika's thoughts. "Come sit down, you two. And Flavio, you're my co-host this evening, so help me get drinks." She motioned towards the living room furniture, then withdrew to the kitchen with Flavio in tow.

"Is Nadia always this intense?" Erika whispered to Ivan, as they took seats on a faded brown sofa placed against a side wall. "I mean, I like her..."

"We both enjoy discussing these things. Flavio too, evidently. Interesting individual..."

"Yeah, they both are." Erika glanced around the room. Closer to the kitchen sat a square table with four chairs, nicks in their wooden legs. The tile floor in front of them was chipped in a couple of areas too. She wondered if Nadia's grandparents had lost their ambition to keep the place up. She didn't see any photos of them or anyone else, but noticed a portable tape deck sitting on a credenza next to the dining table.

"They're pretty enthusiastic," she went on. "*Going pure Red*...next jump, the Red Brigades?"

Ivan smirked. "Don't be silly, we're committed to the Party, that's all."

"French champagne, a yacht in Portofino. Let's see, what else does an Italian Communist aspire to?" Erika winked at him.

"You don't understand the *Italian* Communist Party...never mind," he muttered, as Nadia and Flavio reentered the room with a tray of glasses and a bottle.

"We're back. *Pick your poison, kids,*" Nadia said in exaggerated American English. Her voice, a touch husky, was not unpleasant—sexy even, matched with the plunging V-neck sweater that hugged her tight jeans.

Flavio waved the bottle of Four Roses bourbon. "I'm having whisky."

"I'll have the same," said Ivan.

Nadia grinned at Erika. "Is whisky too strong for us girls? I have other stuff..."

Erika gazed back, fascinated by Nadia's rough sensual exuberance. "Definitely not."

"Then whisky all around! Bring a couple of chairs from the table over near the couch, Flavio, so we can all get cozy." She set the tray of glasses on the table. "Oh, I forgot ice—be right back."

Flavio, sinewy in build, lifted both chairs easily and set them at either end of the sofa, turning them inwards toward Erika and Ivan. He returned to the table, poured a couple of fingers of whisky into each of the four glasses then came back to sit in the chair nearest Erika. "So where are you from in the U.S., Erika? Your Italian's good."

The compliment didn't hurt from this fellow who kept reminding her of a Caspian prince. His eyes appeared more green than blue now as he observed her with a sparkling smile. Like Nadia he looked older than Ivan and Erika, probably in his thirties to Nadia's late twenties.

"I'm from San Diego," she replied. She gave a shy smile. "My grandparents emigrated to the U.S. from Asti, and as long as they were alive we spoke Italian."

Flavio leaned forward, combing his rippling hair back from his forehead with his fingers. "I'd like to visit California."

"So would I." Nadia was back, shaking a bowl of ice like a pair of maracas. "Let's make this a proper American whisky."

She plopped ice into the glasses of bourbon and brought them on the tray to her guests. When she returned the empty tray to the table she pointed to the cassette player on the credenza. "Now for music. Any requests?"

"Is that your grandparents' machine?" asked Ivan.

Nadia blinked as if distracted. "No, I bring it with me when I'm here."

"What would you like to hear?" asked Flavio, focusing back on Erika.

"Um..." She looked at Nadia. "Do you have any Mina?"

"Good taste." Nadia opened the top drawer of the credenza. "Ivan likes her too."

"I *love* Mina," said Ivan with a dreamy look.

"Who doesn't?" Flavio agreed. "She's practically the Italian flag."

Nadia was sifting through her cassettes, making clicking sounds. "I know I've got her somewhere...Here we go—*Minacantalucio*."

Once she got the music started Nadia began dancing her way back to the group, drink in hand. Flavio smiled at Ivan and Erika, his gaze lingering on Erika.

They all sat talking about Italian singers and musical groups. Erika hadn't even finished her whisky when Nadia suddenly declared: "Time for a top-off. *Can't go dry*," she added in exaggerated English, and hopped up to fetch the bottle.

Maybe Nadia was already tipsy, thought Erika, draining her glass so it could be refilled.

Having made the rounds with the bottle, Nadia said, "Now who wants to dance? Flavio, help me push the table out of the way."

Flavio slid out of his chair, and after doing Nadia's bidding, slipped an arm around her waist and started moving to the music.

Nadia waved Erika and Ivan over. "Come on, you two!"

She's hyper at the very least, Erika thought, not feeling quite ready for the dance floor. But Ivan was already on his feet and beckoning her. She took a large swallow of bourbon and set the glass on the floor. A burning rushed down her esophagus, followed by a tingling throughout her head and body when she stood and let Ivan pull her into the group. To the Latinish percussion of "Il nostro caro Angelo," Nadia sashayed to the wall, clicking a switch to extinguish the ceiling light and leaving them silhouetted in the low glow of a shaded lamp on the credenza. She gyrated back and threw an arm around Erika, then moved on to Ivan, roughing up his hair before dancing back to Flavio.

They danced to the end of that side of the cassette, Erika, by now, in thrall to the rhythms. When the cassette clicked to a stop she could barely cease her momentum. Nadia flipped it over and restarted it, then snatched up her cigarettes while Flavio retrieved the whisky. They all finished their drinks and let Flavio refill their glasses. Nadia cranked up the volume and they danced and smoked and drank, juggling glasses and cigarettes and arms that draped round one another in bacchic revelry.

When the slow number "29 settembre" kicked in, Erika decelerated enough to feel her heart thumping and her hairline prickling with sweat. Nadia and Flavio slipped closer to each other, her arms looped around his neck. He whispered something to her and the two of them moved to the table to set their glasses down.

"Don't mind us," said Nadia, "we'll be back in a bit. Make yourselves at home in whatever way you want." Holding hands, she and Flavio wobbled towards the stairs. As they started their climb Flavio glanced back. Erika thought his eyes were narrowed, though it was too shadowy in the room to tell.

She and Ivan looked at each other. Ivan shrugged and

went to the table. "We're out of bourbon, I'm going to look for something else in the kitchen. Nadia did say to make ourselves at home."

Erika gave a distracted nod and flopped down on the couch, musing tipsily at the retreat of their hosts—perhaps a little rude, though not strange that a couple would break off from a party to be alone...

"Erika?" Ivan called in a singsong voice, swinging a bottle of Ballantine's as he came out of the kitchen. He set it on the table. "I'll be right back after I find the bathroom."

She shook her head—"I'm smashed enough"—then sank down against the cushions. While Ivan was absent the song "L'Aquila" came on. She closed her eyes and let the music seep into her, as vapory and melancholic as the dark night outside. The bass and the swift sharp violin strokes exuded a mystical mood that reminded her of "Papa was a Rolling Stone." And now that the excitement had ebbed, a familiar, heavy hollowness returned to weigh on her.

Ivan reappeared, bringing the bottle with him to the sofa.

"I've changed my mind," Erika said, extending her glass. She picked up her pack of Marlboros and offered him one. Ivan smoked MS's, the in-brand of Italian cigarettes, but took one of her Marlboros. They were more expensive, though as infrequently as she smoked, Erika didn't really care what one brand cost versus another. She had been carrying this pack around for almost a week.

They settled back and let the perfect pairing of smoke and spirits further infuse their senses. When she finished her cigarette she doused the butt in her ice and set the glass on the floor. She relaxed back, eyes closed, head lolling onto Ivan's shoulder; his blue cashmere sweater felt soft to her cheek. She didn't give a damn about the CIA or the Manhattan school, or anything else. When her eyes opened Ivan's face was only inches from hers, his hazel eyes rimmed with red. He was boyish-looking for twenty-four and he was her second cousin, but at that moment he appealed to her and apparently she did to him, for he leaned in and kissed her. Erika's back arched and she pulled him to her.

6: Smoke, Mist, and Mirrors

The next morning Erika gazed out of Ivan's farmhouse window, mulling over the mist both outdoors and inside her aching head.

Almost nothing seemed right in Italy. The gleaming green of summer woods, orchards, and vineyards had mutated to brown, leaving a skeletal landscape that shifted in the fog, a murkiness only to be outdone by the confusion of the previous night.

If Nadia and Flavio hadn't returned to the living room, who knows how far she and Ivan might have gone in their drunkenness? As it stood, they accomplished some pretty heavy petting. Her face burned and her headache ticked up a notch when she pictured Nadia and Flavio walking in on them. "Oh, sorry!" Nadia had blurted.

During the sobering drive back to Ivan's house not a word had passed between them. After they'd let themselves in, they each mumbled good night and retired to separate bedrooms.

Now it was nine in the morning and while Ivan still slumbered, Erika stood in the living room rehashing the events of the evening.

After surprising them, Nadia and Flavio had discreetly turned their backs while Erika and Ivan composed themselves. Nadia resumed her effusive chatter and Flavio his air of detached observer, although they hadn't spruced themselves up much before returning from the bedroom, or wherever they'd been. Their hair still rumpled, Flavio with a shirttail hanging out, it seemed they wanted to announce their bout of passion. Something seemed pat about it, or had they just been eager to get back and check on their guests?

Well, she would see. On balance she did like them.

Her thoughts turned to the Manhattan school in Turin, with another day and a half before she would hear about the job. She reconjured the scene at the school, with Brigida the Germanesque bureaucrat at the reception, the pallid, ambivalent Signor Barbasio, and that wavy-haired guy, the familiarity in his eyes still clinging to her like a sporadic itch. She thought of his black pipe, then of her father's brown one; how as a small child she would snuggle with Bruno on the couch, the cozy, sharp-sweet scent of wood and spice floating above her.

Then she had turned four and her little brother Keith was born. When Keith reached the age to join Little League and tinker on projects with Bruno in the garage, Erika witnessed the birth of an exclusive father-son club. When Keith turned ten, the bonding expanded to hunting trips with Bruno's friends—girls unwelcome.

Hunting: had that been the beginning of the informal estrangement between father and daughter. Mechanically she hummed the theme to *Peter and the Wolf* as she continued to peer through the glass at the bleak landscape. What joy she'd felt as a five-year-old, sitting in Daddy's lap as they listened to Sterling Holloway narrate the fairytale. She would picture herself as the little blond Peter of the Disney film, toting the popgun through the hills next to her father. One day this should have become a reality, but no— that joy would belong to Keith. The years filed by with Bruno offering Keith part-time employment in his building enterprise while Erika's interests turned towards Italy and fencing, a sport boasting panache and singularity.

She forced her thoughts away from all that, back to the dark-haired, pipe-smoking stranger at Turin's Manhattan school. She had to admit she found him attractive and wouldn't mind seeing him again, if only to ask if he remembered crossing paths with her somewhere else.

She opened the front door of the farmhouse, stepped outside to test the day, and was met by the scent of damp, decaying leaves mingling with the icy mist—a death smell one had to accept in these northern climes if the rebirth of spring were to be expected.

As she turned back to the house, the village church bells sounded and she stopped to listen to at least that one thing that stayed the same year-round. Their clanging must have woken Ivan, for when he came downstairs he not only complained about them but snapped at Erika for standing with the door open. He hugged his pajama-clad arms as he made his way to the kitchen. "Bloody bells—someone ought to bomb the church."

You could join the Red Brigades and do it yourself. She didn't voice that joke, she didn't wish to say much to Ivan at all. She regretted the previous night's indiscretion and wanted to make sure their relationship returned to its solid cousinly plane. She hoped he felt the same since she valued their friendship over all else they shared. Deep down she blamed booze for getting the best of both of them.

Judging from his grumpiness it appeared he agreed. After making caffè latte for them both he sank into silence at the table. Neither of them touched the biscotti he had automatically placed on the table. As for Erika, the thought of food this morning almost brought bile to her mouth.

While Ivan was upstairs getting dressed, the phone rang. "Could you get it?" he called down to her.

It was Nadia, inquiring how they were.

"Fine, fine," answered Erika, flushing a little and relieved Nadia couldn't see her. "Thanks again for the fun evening...loved the music and dancing."

"We did too. Adored your company. In fact Flavio and I were thinking we'd like to get together with you again...maybe all four of us could meet this afternoon."

Considering the out-of-sorts atmosphere in Ivan's

house, Erika thought a bubbly Nadia just what might be needed. "I'll check with Ivan but I'm sure he'll be onboard."

"Good, we're thinking of the Cremeria in Asti—Piazza Alfieri. Do you know it?"

"...I do," Erika answered with a disconcerted smile. *I was there chasing a purse-snatcher only two days ago.*

"About three?"

"Okay. Unless Ivan calls you back we'll be there."

"Fabulous! *Arrivederci, carissima!*"

Erika hung up, her gaze lingering on the grey telephone. *Carissima:* did Nadia already consider her such a *dear* friend? And of all places to meet!

She turned as Ivan descended the staircase, dressed in chocolate-brown wool slacks and another cashmere sweater, this one a rust-colored turtleneck. Her cousin's enthusiasm for clothes surpassed her own. But he was Italian, after all.

As for a reprise of Nadia and Flavio's company, he responded tepidly. "We'll meet them but I'm going to call Nadia and tell her not until four." He lit a cigarette and walked to the window to look out. "Don't want to seem we're at their beck and call. I'll tell them we're having lunch with relatives, so we'll be late."

"Okay..." said Erika, watching Ivan blow smoke at the window. It was close to one o'clock and she looked forward to getting out of the house. "We can lunch like Americans and grab a sandwich in a café before we meet them."

Ivan nodded distractedly. His moodiness lasted through lunch and continued while they killed time ambling about Asti in the cold. At ten past four he deemed it fashionably late enough to move the car to Piazza Alfieri. As they got out and headed towards the Cremeria, Erika slowed, eyes narrowing at the archway of the portico leading to the café, her first visit there since her failure to catch the purse thief. The old lady would probably never patronize the place again, though the unfortunate waiter might remember Erika's running out without returning. At least she hadn't had time to order anything.

As she followed Ivan through the glass and wooden doors she eyed everyone she passed. Waiters strode to and fro but she didn't recognize any of them. Only Nadia, who from the back of the room rose to wave at them.

By the time they reached the table Flavio was on his feet too. "Pleasant to see you both again." His eyes swung from Erika to Ivan, his gaze holding Ivan's for a lingering second.

Erika wondered at the greeting, almost formal considering the revelry of the night before.

"*Signori*," the waiter addressed Ivan and Erika after they sat. Erika was facing the wall and his reflection appeared in a gilded mirror.

"We're drinking hot rum punch," said Nadia.

"I'll have the same," said Erika.

Ivan ordered coffee with grappa, and the waiter left.

"When it arrives, drink your punch slowly," Flavio warned Erika. "There's more rum in it than anything else."

"Takes the edge off the cold," said Erika. "In San Diego we might be drinking tropical rum mai tais."

"If we were only there right now." Nadia gave a dreamy sigh before turning a placid smile on Ivan. "So did you have a nice lunch today?"

"Typical Piedmontese fare." Ivan slipped Erika a significant look.

"*Fritto misto,* no doubt," Nadia said to Flavio. "One of our characteristic dishes." She walked her fingers up the back of his head and down again to tickle the nape of his neck. "Lemon fritters, sausages, breaded veal—you'll have to try it soon."

Flavio caught her hand and gave it a little squeeze, then let it go as he focused on Erika. "I've just started sampling local dishes, there's so much to learn about this region. You probably know more than I do."

Again his exotic look gave Erika pause. His scraggly

black hair hung forward, reminding her now of an image she had seen of Franz Liszt leaning over his piano. Though Flavio had the accent he did not come off like the classic Roman on television—loud, pushy, gesticulating. He reminded her more of the classic Piedmontese stereotype, "courteous but reserved." In this case, the perpetually animated one was Nadia, the Northerner.

The waiter arrived with their drinks, steam rising from Erika's glass cup like smoke from a fire just getting going. She took a sip of her grog then drew on the cigarette Ivan had lit for her. The current of smoke curling upward reflected in the mirror. From the mirror Erika could observe the room receding back almost to the entrance, and once more she cursed her slow reflexes when taking after the purse-snatcher. No chance in hell of *his* returning.

As more swirls of smoke meandered in the reflection, she again recalled his eyes, dark and dancing...and a pipe...no, that was the wavy-haired guy at the Manhattan school. No... *yes!* Erika's pulse skipped a beat. The eyes of the Manhattan student and the thief were one and the same!

7: City of Light, City of Darkness

Or could she be mistaken about Paolo Lorenzi? Erika eyed him slyly as he sat next to her at the Formica table. For not only had she landed the job at Manhattan in Turin, the suspected thief had presented himself for one-on-one tutoring in her Tuesday, two p.m. class. Same wavy, collar-length brown hair from last Friday. Same prancing clever eyes she remembered from the Cremeria.

He had referenced a schedule change on Friday when they'd met in the Manhattan school's lobby, and once recovered from the initial shock of his presence in her classroom Erika used that subject to get started. "So, did you get the hours you wanted?" she asked him in English, once they'd gone through the preliminaries.

He had registered surprise at seeing her again, nothing extreme, merely a raising of the brows at the coincidence. Now he sat resting his elbow on the rectangular table, chin propped on one fist, as relaxed as if they'd been working together for months.

"Yes," he said, smiling, "I'm here afternoons now, so I have time in the morning for my personal projects."

Projects...what might they be? His English seemed proficient, his delivery smooth. *What else might he be good at?*

"To tell the truth," he went on, "I also wanted a new teacher. I need to improve my accent, my idioms, lots of things. And I would prefer to learn a pronunciation more American."

She could tell he had learned British English, but of course his Italian accent shone through. "Well, your English

47

is already pretty good, so I hope I'll be able to help you."

"Thanks." Paolo sat back, his smile broadening. "Before you, I had a teacher with a Scottish accent—not always easy to follow."

Erika returned his smile, her eyes following the line of his nose, the only other feature, besides his eyes, that had been completely revealed at the Cremeria. The bridge was high, she recalled, just like this guy's. If he was the thief—and she was increasingly leaning this way—he did not act the least bit self-conscious. Was that to dispel any suspicions on her part, or maybe even to challenge her? Taking a seat right next to her when he walked in exhibited boldness. Maybe he hadn't recognized her, though he should have, considering she'd remembered him with much less to go on. She recalled his slight frown when they'd first locked eyes in the Manhattan school lobby...

He was watching her now in the pause she'd created, eyes inquisitive, head slightly atilt. "Usually I just dialogue with the Scottish teacher..."

"Right," said Erika, focusing back on her tutoring. "Maybe *converse* is better."

"That's what we did."

"Yes," she said with a chuckle, "but I meant *converse* is the verb you need. *Dialogue* is used more as a noun."

"You see?" he said beaming. "How my English needs improvement?"

Their laughter rose then trailed off as Paolo opened his notebook.

"Okay," Erika said, proceeding the way she normally did with new students. "Tell me about yourself."

"I have a degree in architecture, though for now I conduct my own research on the occult in Turin's buildings—the projects I had mentioned."

"Sounds fascinating."

His eyes sparked at her interest. He leaned in, knees close to hers. "I'm glad. Now that you're my teacher you might hear much about it."

Erika felt a growing heat in her cheeks; a part of her wanted to edge away from him, but she stayed put. "I'll look forward to it," she said, again sensing he might be issuing some kind of challenge.

"I wish my father had interest for my studies." He sat back with a frustrated sigh.

"Doesn't he?"

"He thinks I should work with him as salesman in the Lavazza coffee company. Or find a regular job in a firm of architecture."

She didn't ask why he wasn't working for a salary in his chosen field, but she did wonder whether he'd complained about his father to his former teacher. It all seemed rather personal. This might have been a perfect time to call his bluff and ask, *Does your father know about your other additional activities?* And she just might do it sometime soon, but for now she would let Paolo Lorenzi, crackerjack purse-snatcher, reveal what he chose.

Erika's schedule at Manhattan in Turin added up to six hours a day, from two in the afternoon to eight in the evening, Monday through Friday—over eight hours per week more than at the Asti school. Enough, she hoped, to allow her to rent a place in Turin.

"Not a good idea," said Elsa, sitting at the table while Erika ate her late-evening dinner. She and Angelo had long since finished, and as Elsa kept Erika company, Angelo sat in a kitchen chair watching television.

He glanced at Erika. "Haven't you heard what happened in Turin today?" When Erika didn't respond he widened his already owlish blue eyes and turned his chair to face her. "They shot the assistant director of *La Stampa*. Multiple times in the face, *Dio Santo!*"

Erika set her fork down as Angelo handed her an extra edition of the Turin newspaper, dated 16 November: *Carlo*

Casalegno, ambushed on the way into his building by the Red Brigades, now in critical condition in the hospital...

"This is the first time they've attacked a journalist," said Elsa.

Erika swallowed hard, picturing the gruesome image of a man's face ripped apart by bullets. "It's horrible," she said, "but I'm no journalist; they wouldn't target me."

Elsa tapped the table with her index finger in rhythm to her staccato delivery. "All it takes is to be in the wrong place at the wrong time—"

"And a stray bullet whizzes by," Angelo finished.

Erika could have pointed out the trivial odds of getting shot accidentally in a city of a million people, but she thought it best not to argue with her hosts. Besides, she wasn't afraid of getting shot. And it wasn't bravado talking: as for the specter of death itself...well, she'd been intimate with it. *When you've already committed the ultimate taboo...*

Her gaze had drifted and Elsa asked her if there was anything wrong. Rousing herself, Erika looked back at her cousin. She felt bad about Elsa having warmed up dinner over two hours after she and Angelo had finished. Sometimes it was ten o'clock before Erika sat down to eat, depending on how fast she could leave the school and catch transportation to the station in order to take a train back to Asti. She had tried convincing Elsa to let her prepare her own light supper, only to meet her cousin's insistence on keeping a tight grip on her kitchen.

Definitely time to find a place of her own in Turin. She could ask at school, though the only person she saw on a daily basis was the secretary Brigida who continued to keep her nose in the air. Or, she could approach Nadia Regis, who'd invited Ivan and her to her party and lived in Turin...

Early the next morning, hoping to catch Nadia at home, Erika walked to the SIP, the telephone office where she preferred to make her calls rather than racking up more bills for Angelo and Elsa. Dawn had broken and buildings exuded the fresh sharp scent of rain on stone. After last night's rain, Asti was rinsed and polished and finally *visible*. As she entered the short lane where the SIP was joined by a pizzeria, a cinema, and a small record shop, everything seemed more spacious, more welcoming, under the cracks of blue showing through the clouds.

Inside the SIP, she pulled out the work number Nadia had given her. The clerk took it and assigned her a booth, where she could make her call in privacy, then pay for the minutes used when finished—nice and tidy.

"Ciao, *bella*," chirped Nadia. "Wonderful to hear from you!"

Another term of endearment though they barely knew each other. It didn't bother Erika, she kind of envied Nadia's extroverted ease. Erika told her about her new teaching job in Turin and its hours, then invited her to meet for lunch one day.

"I could do it today...the rest of the week I've got meetings and things. Let's see, I've got from twelve to two, if you can make it in time from Asti..."

"Oh," Erika said. "Sure...great...you've got two hours, then?"

"This is Italy, *cara*, land of long lunches. I could even slip out early, and if we don't dawdle over our food we can take a walk afterwards."

Erika rang off, called Elsa to tell her she wouldn't be home for lunch, then left for the station.

She met Nadia in Piazza San Carlo at eleven forty-five, and once greetings were exchanged, Nadia charged into tour-guide mode. "This is one of the most famous squares in Turin," she said, sweeping a hand towards the tall ocher-tinted buildings, their façades and balconies elaborately sculpted. Like Piazza Alfieri in Asti, arched porticoes formed a base under which cafés, shops, and restaurants abounded. In Turin, however, the scale of richness and elegance was grand.

"Remember," said Nadia, "Turin was the first capital of a united Italy. The original parliament building is near here." She started walking, then stopped, her eyes bright. "Oh, and this is where they filmed *The Italian Job*, all those Minis racing under the porticoes!"

They settled into a restaurant, and Erika sensed an opportunity to ask Nadia, the Communist, about the shooting of journalist Carlo Casalegno by the Red Brigades. Erika shook her head. "From what I've read, Casalegno was a reasonable man who condemned both left- and right-wing terrorism."

"A tragedy," Nadia agreed, her gaze turning distant. Then her smile returned. "Tonight there should be a rally for him right here in this square, so let's keep our spirits up—the morale in the city is low enough right now."

True, thought Erika. Almost everyone she had passed on her walk from the train station to the piazza looked stricken. Some shops were closed in protest. Even their waiter's demeanor was grim.

But Nadia made up for it. Throughout lunch she chattered on about history, art, movies, until she noticed that Erika had finished her meal. She gave a sheepish smile and speared her last tortellini. "Okay, we should move on."

From there, Nadia marched them to Turin's medieval castle. Despite her dominance of the conversation, Nadia's knowledge was so impressive that Erika hadn't yet brought up the subject of rentals in Turin. She let Nadia enlighten her about shopping as they walked down the stylish via Roma en route to the castle, with Nadia proudly pointing out Hermes and Chanel (*like a good Communist*, Erika commented to herself). But the morning's glimpse of blue sky had ended, to be replaced by a marbled grey-and-black vault. By the time they reached Piazza Castello thunder boomed above, and cars rumbling by on the cobbles shone dim yellow lights.

Nadia grabbed Erika's arm. "Let's hurry before it starts to pour."

Erika quickened her pace, marveling at the hybrid castle: one side indeed medieval, with austere towers, replete with arrow slits and a moat; the opposite side, a baroque palace with classical columns, statues, and tall windows radiating light and enlightenment. It sat enthroned in the middle of a piazza-intersection with traffic charging around it. Standing on the sidewalk next to the schizophrenic structure, Erika felt something somber and latent stir inside her, like the vibration of a barely perceptible earthquake. She'd seen the castle before but never experienced this sensation of something shifting within her. "It's like one side looks to the future and the other to the past," she said uneasily.

"Like the god Janus," Nadia agreed. "The medieval side's well over a thousand years old. Some say it's a center of ancient energy, a sort of white magic." She glanced at Erika with a shrewd smile. "If you believe in that stuff."

"Do you?" Erika asked.

Nadia shrugged. Or maybe she shivered; the wind was whipping up as she and Erika made the rounds of the castle.

"I'd like to hear one of my student's views on that subject," said Erika.

"And how is the teaching going?" Nadia asked.

"Fine, only I'd like to move here to avoid the commute, find a small studio. Was your flat easy to come by?"

"Mine's got one bedroom, but studios are out there to be had. I'll ask a friend of mine who knows about housing in the city. He's one of the people who like to discuss the different energies in Turin. White magic in this square, 'black' in Piazza Statuto."

"Funny," said Erika, "this is the second time this week I've heard about the occult in Turin. It's something totally new to me."

"And yet it's notorious here. Goes back hundreds of years—alchemists and people who practice both white and black magic."

"*Well...*" Erika responded, mildly intrigued. "The student I mentioned is an architect who's doing research on Turin's occult buildings."

They'd stopped at the castle's medieval side and were peering into the deep grassy moat.

Nadia looked up. "What's his name?"

For a moment Erika hesitated, picturing architect Paolo Lorenzi moonlighting as purse-snatcher. Then she obliged.

Nadia blinked, and blinked a second time. Finally she said, "Same as my friend."

The wind was tangling Erika's hair, and now her thoughts as well; a dual chill embraced her. Icy droplets began to fall. She pulled up her coat collar. "I forgot my umbrella," she muttered, as Nadia and she continued to watch each other.

Abruptly Nadia tightened her green wool scarf and reached into her purse. Out came a compact umbrella. "Here, we'll share it. Let's get back to the porticoes."

They crossed the street against the red light, wind driving rain sideways at them. "This way," said Nadia. "We can have a quick coffee over by the Rinascente department store."

They ducked into the café, Nadia stuffing her umbrella in the holder by the door. Erika took a distracted look around: wood-paneled walls were decorated with framed posters of turn-of-the-century advertisements. They claimed a table and peeled off their coats and scarves. On the wall above Nadia hung a poster for an herbal ad, featuring a man with a red bulbous nose with plant foliage doubling as hair.

"Art nouveau?" Erika commented, surveying the prints, not knowing what to say next regarding Paolo

Lorenzi.

"Turin's full of the style, and full of coincidences," Nadia said with a faint smile. "It seems you and I know the same Paolo Lorenzi."

Erika nodded. "When did you meet him?"

Nadia pulled out a pack of cigarettes, shaking a couple of them free. After taking one she extended the pack across the table.

Erika took one and leaned in for a light. She sat back.

Nadia drew slowly on her cigarette, settling into a stare that lengthened with the stream of smoke she blew. Then her face snapped back into its usual friendly smile. "I've known Paolo for a while. He's a fellow Red."

8: The Handbag of Matilde Fassino

The second hand of a wall clock ticked forward mutely as Erika was seated on a wooden bench in the waiting room of Porta Nuova station, her train for Asti due to leave at nine-fifteen p.m. Further down the bench, a middle-aged woman, bundled to the chin in a high-collared coat and scarf, picked through her purse, emitting little impatient sighs while eyeing the clock from time to time. A young man across the room slouched on his bench, overcoat hanging open as he indulged in a Mickey Mouse comic book, the corners of his mouth occasionally twitching in a smile. He too cast random glances at the clock. Station time appeared to trump watches.

Only Erika sat staring at the wall, consumed with a triangle of sorts that had obsessed her since she'd left Nadia: A) Paolo Lorenzi and Nadia were fellow Communists, B) Paolo was an architect, C) Paolo was a purse-snatcher. The three components knocked around her mind like billiard balls. *Even if "A" might be reasonable, with Reds galore in Turin, "B" did not jibe with "C". She could hardly accept an architect doubling as a fly-by-night thief targeting old ladies.*

The young man stood up and Erika glanced at the clock: five past nine, time to board. On the way to the platform she continued to reason, *Paolo Lorenzi would either have to be off in the head...*or, she thought, loosening her scarf as she climbed into the train, *Somehow the purse snatching was connected to something else, such as "A."*

Still, why stoop to something as low as robbing a frail, elderly woman?

The train raced through the night. Alone in the lit compartment, Erika observed her warped reflection in the window, superimposed like a cubist painting against the black of the night. Almost everything about her life seemed surreal these days—the fog that never lifted for more than a day or two, the occult that Nadia had talked about, armed guards everywhere. Erika had not mentioned Nadia's relationship with Flavio during this afternoon's outing, and with the excuse of the rain, Nadia had begged off visiting the former parliament building, electing to return to work. Still, she and Flavio were a strange pair. And now Paolo Lorenzi had joined the bizarre mix. She would see him for tutoring tomorrow and ask the architect about housing in Turin...and perhaps about other things.

The purse. It reared in her mind as soon as she woke the next morning, for she had dreamed of it sitting on the wall of the Dark Age castle's moat. Erika was trying to climb from the moat to reach it, clawing the rain-sodden grass that kept sliding through her fingers.

The purse, she repeated to herself, getting out of bed quickly to get ready. She would drop by the Cremeria this morning, just to ask a few questions. She imagined Paolo Lorenzi, eyes gleaming as he regaled Nadia with stories of his research. Erika wasn't quite ready to challenge him about the handbag, but she could use Turin's fame for the occult to further her probe of him this afternoon.

She walked into the Cremeria, newspaper under her arm the way she always started her mornings. A young, white-aproned woman strode back and forth from espresso machine to cash register, working alone behind the bar. Although Erika had expected to see the waiter from the week before, she took a seat anyway and ordered a cappuccino. She spread out her *Times of London*—November 18th. It wasn't yet December and it was getting colder by the day.

Before long the door opened and rattled shut. A thin, mustached man, slightly hunched, walked towards the bar. He took off his hat, and wispy grey hair appeared, which he smoothed down. Erika remembered this comb-over, and pictured the waiter trying to sooth the ire of the elderly lady with the coffee-stained coat. She snatched up her bill and headed to the bar.

The man was unbuttoning his coat and asking the girl behind the bar to hand him an apron.

"I'll pay for my cappuccino now..." Erika said, looking pointedly at him.

He motioned to the girl. "She'll take care of it."

Erika pulled out her lire and placed the banknotes in the plastic tray next to the cash register, one eye trained on the old man as he started to move off. When her change was returned, she followed him. "Um, sir, I don't know whether you remember me..."

He turned around.

"I was here last week when an elderly woman got her purse stolen..."

The waiter frowned, his grey mustache twitching as he studied her. "Ah, you were here that morning..."

"Yes." Erika drew herself up. "After the thief took her purse I followed him, but the fog was too thick to see anything..."

The old waiter sighed and gave Erika a weary smile. "A miserable day all around. Yes, I remember you. You left the café and I hoped you would catch him." He shook his head. "It was a disgrace for the Cremeria."

"Well, I feel partly responsible," said Erika, "and I've felt bad ever since..."

The waiter peered at her.

"If only I'd gotten to her purse before that criminal did."

"Oh Signorina, no use second guessing things like that. That day all of us were made fools of."

"I hope the woman's all right. Do you know her name?"

"Of course, everyone knows who Matilde Fassino is."

Matilde Fassino, Erika repeated to herself until she was outdoors and well past the café. She took a piece of paper from her purse and jotted it down. A name, that was all she had, but it still excited her. So much, she almost forgot the errand Elsa had asked her to do. She halted about a block from the house and began a jog back to the butcher's where she picked up the veal for their *albese*.

"Sorry," she said when Elsa opened the door. "I got hung up and had to go back for the veal."

"We'll have to hurry," said Elsa. "You only have an hour and a half before your train. I'll prepare the *albese* another time."

Too bad for Angelo, who expected the savory veal dish every day. Erika could hear his chair scrape the tiles before she entered the kitchen. He never lifted a chair. In the middle of the night, when she lay awake, she often heard the chair's groans through her closed door as it was dragged across the floor.

"No *albese* today?" he grumbled, as Erika took her seat at the table. He plucked his cloth napkin from its pewter ring, gave it a dramatic shake with his tobacco-stained fingers, then tucked it into his dress shirt.

"You can have it tonight," said Elsa, easing into her place at the table near the stove.

"Sorry again for being late," Erika said pointedly to Angelo.

He responded with a grumble, whose tone suggested her apology was grudgingly accepted.

She watched him reach for a stalk of celery and drop it onto his plate, then for a tomato which he examined before slicing. Erika handed him the olive oil then selected her own vegetables for her salad. As Elsa cut up some raw fennel in her plate, Erika finally asked, "Do either of you know who

Matilde Fassino is?"

Angelo was energetically salting his salad, while Elsa drizzled a few drops of vinegar on her fennel. Both of them paused to look up.

"Everybody knows of her," Elsa answered. "She's one of the richest women in Turin."

"What about her?" said Angelo, stabbing a slice of tomato.

"Someone snatched her purse when she was in the Cremeria last week."

"*Oh, Signur*," said Elsa. "Was she hurt?"

"No, but she had an awful shock."

"Did she report it?" Angelo asked. "I didn't see anything in the papers."

"I don't know." Erika paused, thinking it better not to reveal she'd been present, so as to avoid being asked why she was only mentioning the incident today. She said, "Evidently, some guy grabbed her purse from her while she was leaving the café, then fled with it."

"Brazen thieves!" said Elsa.

"Humph," Angelo grunted. "Did he think she'd have millions in her bag?"

"Who would carry around that much?" said Erika. Millions of lire equaled thousands of dollars.

"It doesn't matter if all you carry is lipstick, said Elsa. "Scum like that will knock you to the ground for your purse."

Erika narrowed her eyes in contemplation. So was her student deranged, or was Paolo Lorenzi out for something *specific* in that handbag?

They finished their salads in silence, Angelo tearing a corner off his bread and mopping up the oil in his plate. After he popped the bread into his mouth, Erika asked, "How wealthy *is* Matilde Fassino?"

"Who knows?" said Elsa, rising to clear their plates then setting a pot of bean soup on the table.

"Rich enough to own a huge villa up on Superga," said Angelo.

"Superga?"

"A high hill overlooking Turin," Elsa explained. "There's a magnificent church there where all the dukes of Savoy are entombed. A very chic area."

Erika's fascination continued. "Is she an aristocrat or something?"

Angelo gave a cynical chuckle and arched a wiry eyebrow. "No. She's a loaded old lady whose banker husband made a fortune during the war, and not altogether honestly, let's say."

The Second World War, he meant of course. Italians referred to it as *the war*; unlike the Americans, they'd experienced no other war since.

Erika hadn't time to pursue more about Matilde Fassino with her cousins, but on the train to Turin the wealthy widow and her purse rode along in her thoughts, not least because Paolo Lorenzi would be her first student of the day. Could Fassino have withdrawn a bundle of bills from a bank, with Lorenzi somehow in the know? After which he staged the spilling of the coffee to steal it? *The spilling of the coffee*...why not just grab the purse and run? Elsa had mentioned purse-snatchers who shoved women to the ground to rip their bags from them. Not only had Paolo Lorenzi not harmed Matilde Fassino, he hadn't even touched her. Did he see himself as some modern *Red* Robin Hood—slick, flamboyant, a mocking poster for his cause?

9: Black Angel

This time at the Manhattan school, Erika waited for Paolo to take a seat before casually rounding the teaching table and placing herself opposite him. Let him start talking about the architecture dear to his heart, then she would drop Nadia's name into the conversation along with the housing issue.

That was her plan as they proceeded through pleasantries and small talk, while Paolo readied his notebook and pen. So far he hadn't smoked in their sessions, perhaps out of respect for the teaching environment. Even in the school lobby he had held the pipe unlit, fingering it and chewing it as her father Bruno often used to do. She felt an urge to see Paolo smoke the pipe, to observe his pose, to get a whiff of his particular tobacco as it burned...

He jolted her from her musings. "Nadia Regis called me last night...I believe you know her. She says you're looking for a place to rent here in Turin."

She gazed at him in wonder. Nadia must have called him as soon as she got home yesterday, in what Erika could only reckon was eagerness...perhaps urgency. "Yes," she responded. "Nadia's a friend of my cousin's. How do you know her?"

"Oh, I've met her around..."

In Red circles, you mean. She kept that to herself.

Paolo smiled. "I think you say, *small world.*"

Erika acknowledged the cliché with a nod, returning a faint smile. Might he now be aware that she knew he was a thief *and* a Communist? "It's true," she said. "I *am* looking for a flat."

"And I happen to know a lady who has a mansard to rent. *Mansard*," he repeated. "You know, one of those flats at the top of buildings below the roof..." He frowned, searching for the right word in English.

"Attic apartments with dormer windows. I'd only need a studio space—a *monolocale*," she specified in Italian, "with a bathroom."

"Ah, *studio*," he repeated, nodding while jotting the word on the graphing-paper squares of his notebook. "The mansard flat I know of has a cooking corner and a bathroom. Very small but not expensive."

He sat back, arms folded proudly with this inside knowledge. His wide-set brown eyes expressed warmth, and a strange candidness. Did he really not give a damn about what she knew about him? Her thoughts wheeled back to the Cremeria...maybe he truly didn't recognize her.

He continued to observe her placidly, and a tingling inside made her glance down at her own notebook where she kept data on her students. "Could I see the place?" she asked, slowly looking back up.

"I could show you after you finish here," he said, placing his arms on the table and leaning in.

"Tonight?"

"Why not?"

She scrutinized him on the sly: she *did* need a place to live, and yes, she itched to figure him out. "I work till eight, so I'd have to meet you there."

He waved that suggestion away. "I can drive you. When I leave I'll call the owner and tell her we'll come this evening, if she's...*disponibile*."

"*Available*," Erika translated mechanically, her mind calculating. "That's generous of you, but the inconvenience..."

"No bother. We could eat something after, unless you must return to Asti early."

She stiffened.

"Nadia told me you live there," he explained.

Nadia—how much had she told him about her? Well, at least Nadia knew him and the secretary would see her leave with him. "I won't be in any particular hurry to get home," she said.

"It's an appointment then?"

"A *date*."

"*Date*. See how helpful you are!"

Erika's last tutoring session of the evening had finished and she stood contemplating Paolo from the hall. He sat in profile at the communal table in the lobby, his black pipe lit this time. Chin tilted slightly upwards, he held the pipe with his thumb, index, and middle finger, the way one balances a wine glass from the bottom. As Bruno used to do years ago before he quit smoking, she noted with a fleeting sense of curiosity.

His overcoat lay on the back of the chair next to him, but his camel-colored wool scarf remained looped around his neck in a loose, casual knot. Stylish, sophisticated, she thought as she took in the whole of him; a debonair thief from a classic old movie.

"You don't mind that I smoke?" he asked, as he rose to greet her.

"Depends on your tobacco." She tilted her head and gave the air an exaggerated sniff followed by an approving smile. "Holds promise."

"*Holds promise*. I like that expression. Speaking of that, I cannot *promise* to show you the flat this evening. The signora will not be home. But we could look at the building...and still have dinner." He rocked onto his toes, then back onto his heels, his smile eager.

"I'd like that," she said, having already phoned Elsa about being late.

"Good. There's a pizzeria in via Garibaldi where the flat

is located. And if you don't mind, we can continue to speak English."

"Fine with me."

She watched him in the dark as they walked to his car. Bundled to the chin in coat and scarf he looked almost as obscure as that morning in the Cremeria. No stocking cap tonight and his wool coat was navy blue, whereas the coat in the Cremeria might have been black, she wasn't sure...

A block and a half down the sidewalk they arrived at a dark Alfa Romeo GTV—the very model coveted by Ivan. Flashy car for an unemployed architect, thought Erika. Did he need to steal to maintain it? The car was nicely equipped inside as well, with a radio and five-speed gearshift, and a large ashtray where Paolo laid his spent pipe.

They pulled out into the wide thoroughfare of corso Umberto, slicing through the darkness. "I think you'd like living in via Garibaldi," he said. "Many shops and cafés, a short tram ride to the Manhattan school. And the flat is between Piazza Castello and Piazza Statuto, the heart of the historical center."

"Mm," she murmured, her focus remaining on the road and their route.

"Plus it's a very famous zone. They say via Garibaldi connects the centers of white and dark energy in the city."

Here we go again with the esoteric. Erika perked up and turned towards him. "Nadia mentioned something like that," she said. "Piazza Castello, the source of white magic..."

"And Piazza Statuto, the source of black magic—or energy, some people would rather call it." He glanced at her. "That is, if you believe in that kind of thing."

"Nadia made the exact same comment," said Erika, smiling to herself.

"Anyway, I'll show you the Piazza. It's close to the flat and we can park there."

When they pulled into the square Paolo cut the engine

but left the headlights on. "You've never been here?"

"No, just to Piazza Castello," she said, squinting through the light.

"You'll have to come in the daytime. For now we can profit from the streetlamps to see a very interesting monument."

Take advantage of, Erika mentally corrected, though this time she let it go.

Paolo pocketed his pipe as they left the car to enter a yellow haze of streetlight. There, a pyramid-shaped mount came into view. It looked like jagged rocks with statues stuck to it.

"What is it?" asked Erika.

"A monument to the men who died building the Fréjus railroad tunnel to France," Paola said through puffs of frosty vapor. "Completed in 1871. Can you see their images on the rocks?"

She could: men sculpted in what seemed white marble, two looking as if they'd expired, their limbs splayed out in exhaustion; others looked to be trying to climb the jagged mountain, or to just hang on to it.

"Some say it is supposed to show the human sacrifice in the endeavor," Paolo explained.

"Others believe it symbolizes the triumph of reason over—how do you say—the brutal forces of nature? At any rate, most people think it is the ugliest monument in Turin!" Staccato puffs spewed from Paolo as he laughed. He pointed upwards. "This is what has fascination for me, though. See the bronze statue at the top?"

Erika craned her neck and squinted into the delicately-dancing haze. "A black statue...an angel?" she said, identifying a set of wings.

"Yes, but not an ordinary angel. Look at his head—can you see what's on top?"

"... A star?" she guessed.

"A *pentagram.* And something else about him is

66

strange."

Erika continued to study the angel but couldn't distinguish much.

"He faces via Garibaldi," Paolo explained, "which leads to Piazza Castello."

"Center of white magic..."

"Correct," declared Paolo, hands on his hips. "Black magic challenging white. Not everyone believes it, of course. Some say the angel is only a symbol of the *genius* that was needed to construct the tunnel. And yet, with his pentagram he looks towards Piazza Castello—and not the other way, towards France and the tunnel of genius. Anyway, you need to see it in daylight."

He was right. Darkness brought on uneasy feelings. She felt a chill, as if something invisible was breathing frosty air at the nape of her neck. She shrugged the irrational thought away and pointed at the angel. "Is he why the square is considered the center of dark energy?"

"Not entirely. This monument is modern, respect to Turin's long history."

"You mean *relative* to Turin's history."

"Yes, thanks. Anyway, dark energy goes back thousands of years in this place. I'll tell you about it on the way to the flat."

As they locked the car and left the square, heading down via Garibaldi on foot, Paolo expounded. "Before they built the monument there was a guillotine in Piazza Statuto, from when the city was under Napoleon. And a few streets over, there used to be a huge Roman necropolis. So in ancient times it was a zone already considered, how do you say...*infausto*."

Erika thought for a moment. "I think that would be 'ill-omened', or something like that."

"Exactly. They crucified people there and buried them, along with others executed throughout the years. Do you see that street sign?"

Erika narrowed her eyes as they crossed the street. When she got close enough she read aloud, "Corso Valdocco."

"*Valdocco* goes back to the Latin, *vallis occisorum*— valley of the killed." He grinned at Erika. "A little *macabro*, no?"

"*Macabre*," she said, returning a crooked smile. "And you're trying to sell me on this neighborhood?"

"Oh, please excuse me! I get sometimes *carried away*, I think you say in English." He swept out an arm. "See, this a busy commercial street—*very modern now*!

True. Shops abounded, of course shuttered at this time of night, but cafés and restaurants emitted a cozy, inviting glow, boosted by the streetlamps. The *other,* this dark energy Paolo spoke of, was superstition arising from historical events. Still, the black angel made her feel strange, as though he had breathed that chilly air down her neck...She shook herself and asked where the apartment was located.

"A block down, on the left, right before the pizzeria sign."

The apartment building was one of several at this end of via Garibaldi, all with three floors above ground level and dormer flats jutting from their roofs. He pointed out the dormer flat that could potentially be hers. Again, she couldn't make out much in the dark, and so they moved on to the Pizzeria Garibaldi next door.

Pods of animated diners made Erika feel even more confident about the neighborhood. She ordered a Four Seasons pizza, Paolo a classic pizza Margherita, and as they ate and drank beer, Erika steered the conversation back to Turin's occult, partly out of curiosity but also to show she had no fear of such superstitious things.

He told her of Turin's fame as part of an international triangle of both black and white magic. "Turin—Lyon— Prague for the white magic; Turin—London—San Francisco for the black."

"San Francisco—*really*?"

Paolo shrugged. "Nothing that can be proved, still these things obsess many people."

"But not you?"

"No, I *study* them. These ideas, the buildings and monuments they are associated with, make part of Turin's..." He scratched his head then gave a helpless sigh. "I'm losing the vocabulary."

"*Character?*" she suggested. "Turin's *character*, and your English is pretty good, by the way."

"Thank you." His eyes glittered. More than ever they mirrored his look that morning in the Cremeria.

After their meal, Paolo's black pipe rested in his hand, the way you hold a brandy snifter, thought Erika this time. It wasn't just how he balanced the pipe; Paolo's hands themselves reminded her of her father's— finely muscled, sinewy-strong. She thought of Bruno's pipe rack, how he preferred a certain brown pipe trimmed in black, and a tobacco that produced woody scents.

Paolo's smoke gave off spiciness. She liked breathing it and fancied it a part of everything about Paolo she found different from Bruno: dark eyes, longish wavy hair, his enthusiasm for things unique about Turin. At one point Erika took a drag from her Marlboro and their individual streams of smoke entwined.

Erika snapped back to attention. "So did the signora say what time I could visit the flat tomorrow?"

Paolo tapped his forehead with the stem of his pipe. "I almost forgot—she said to come anytime in the afternoon. We could meet there..."

Erika watched him for a moment, then said, "I'd like to thank Nadia too. Maybe we could get together with her for a drink afterwards. Tomorrow's Saturday, she might be free."

Paolo hesitated, nibbling on his pipe's mouthpiece in

distraction, his gaze reflecting indecision.

"I'll call her," pressed Erika, pleased to observe Paolo ill at ease for once. She hoped Nadia would be free and willing to meet them.

At last Paolo agreed with a nod, and his roguish smile returned. A *Red* smile, Erika mused, realizing she might have to play the Red herself to unmask Paolo the thief.

10: Little White Illegalities

Once more, it turned out that Nadia was free to meet for drinks. Nadia seemed ever willing to please, Erika observed as she lay awake staring into the dead of the night. She never talked about her insomnia, a defect no one need know about, and which some might construe as a weakness. The CIA, for example. The day of her physical exam at Langley they presented her with a list of conditions next to which she marked *yes* or *no*. She checked the *no* box to most everything, including sleep disturbances and was thankful the question did not come up in the polygraph test. She felt in perfect health, other than occasional migraines (which she also neglected to mention to the CIA physician), a residual effect of a car crash she had suffered shortly after the fencing accident.

Tonight she had woken abruptly, a rush of anxiety coursing through her like a hot Santa Ana wind. Times like this she suspected the fencing accident as culprit but always tried to steer her thoughts clear of that minefield, which could in turn bring on the migraines. Better to focus on something else, such as her date with Paolo tomorrow. After inspecting the mansard flat, she and Paolo would meet Nadia, and Erika would watch the two Reds interact. More than ever, she wanted to discover Paolo's motive for stealing Matilde Fassino's purse, increasingly suspecting a link to his communist activities. And if she did obtain a confession of the theft from Paolo? Would she report it to the police, only to have him deny the admission? She sighed, freeing her hands from the bed covers and resting them above her head on the pillow. Why did she care about all this, anyway?

The shame of being duped in the Cremeria—proof that the CIA might have been correct in rejecting her? The mystery and the attraction of Paolo?

The answer was *both*. Plus, this intrigue was the only thing really interesting in her life right now.

She flung her covers down. *Must be eighty-five degrees in the house*. Angelo would crank up the heat and Elsa would slap it back down. They usually confined the duel to daytime and early evening, but now...She heard a harsh rasping beyond her door, a chair grating on tiles, which meant Angelo was in the kitchen and had turned up the heat. Erika clicked on her night lamp: three-thirty. She puffed out a sigh of resignation, kicked aside the remaining covers and left her bed.

In the morning her head pulsed with fatigue. And yet the night hadn't been a complete bust. While Erika drank mineral water and Angelo espresso, she learned about the widow Matilde Fassino. After the war, her banker husband had been indicted for extorting money from Jews but had died of an aneurism before justice could run its course. He was also alleged to have reported Jews to the Nazis for deportation to Auschwitz. "Not a couple who were universally loved," Angelo had commented in his sarcastic growl. "His widow still isn't." When Erika returned to bed at five o'clock, her thoughts were busier than ever.

After lunch she took the train to Turin and then the tram to meet Paolo at two o'clock. Standing in front of the building with the mansard flat for rent, she checked her watch—she was early. Her gaze swept up via Garibaldi: only a few short blocks to Piazza Statuto. Paolo said she should see the infamous square in daylight, however a feathery mist had returned to blur the narrow street. She decided to walk to the square anyway.

Once more she craned her neck to examine the statue of the black angel. Through the mist she identified thick wavy hair, a bare chest, and robes falling low around a muscularly defined abdomen. As the mist shifted she focused on his face, which expressed neither the serenity she'd seen in the eyes of stained-glass angels, nor the rapture of those in museum paintings. This dark angel frowned into the distance, fierce and foreboding, a harbinger of something dreaded. His wings stretched high, the pentagram spiking between them atop his head. He didn't look diabolical, despite the talk of crucifixions and black magic the night before, but rather youthful. Youthful and portentous. Once more she felt a slight chill. She glanced back towards Piazza Castello, on which the angel fixed his defiant stare. According to Paolo and Nadia, Piazza Castello harbored *white* energy, and yet Erika had felt a similar sensation of unease while standing in front of the Janus-like medieval castle...

She exhaled an impatient breath—*nonsense*—and stood back to appraise the monument as a whole. Her eyes moved from the angel, who held a feathered pen over something written on a stone, down to the sculpture below him—the mountain of rocks, to which clung marble effigies of those laborers who'd died digging the historic tunnel through the Alps to France. Their loins were also barely covered, and apart from that similarity, Erika could see no correlation between those tortured slaves of industry and the lofty defiant angel. That they shared a monument seemed another of Turin's schizophrenic wonders.

She looked around the rest of the square. A set of stunning buildings in red and ochre brick bordered it. At their base, stone arches provided access to porticoed shops, their roofs sporting dormer windows like the mansard flat she would visit with Paolo—once more, the contrast of the splendid and luminous with the dark and uncanny...

Paolo was waiting on the sidewalk when she got back to the apartment building. She reached to shake his hand, but instead he leaned in and brushed cheeks with her, the way friends and relatives greet one another in Italy. "You don't mind, do you?" he asked.

Should she? Accepting the gesture meant they were now friends. "Not at all," she said, and pointed to the building. "Can we go up? I told Nadia we'd meet her at two-thirty."

"Right. One thing I have to tell you about the flat...the owner, Eugenia Sillano, added a small kitchen and bathroom to the space...it's not quite legal without a permit."

"...Oh." Erika eyed Paolo, then shrugged. "As long as the place doesn't collapse on me."

"It won't." He drew himself up. "I supervised the work."

A corner of Erika's mouth twitched in a smile. "Why mention it then?"

"Well...it would just be better that you don't tell anyone there's a bathroom. None of these old mansards were built with them."

They headed to the entrance, Erika grinning to herself at the charm in Paolo's discomfort. He pressed the buzzer next to the name Sillano, and after a few seconds the large wooden door clicked open and they climbed to the third floor. A woman well into her sixties, wearing a wool sweater and skirt, stood waiting in a doorway, her legs clad in thick stockings, her grey hair pulled back in a tight bun. With a faint smile she brushed cheeks with Paolo. Once Erika and Signora Sillano shook hands, the signora suggested they go straight up to examine the fourth-floor mansard. "Then I'll make coffee," she added, her tone mild and reserved.

The signora, short and sturdily built, like country folk, led them up a set of stairs to the landing at the top of the building. They followed her past a large utility cabinet before arriving at the door of the dormer apartment, the only residence on the floor. The landlady plucked a long, old-fashioned key from a bulging leather key wallet and unlocked the door, opening it to a furnished space that included a sofa, tables, and a wardrobe. Paolo sat at the kitchen table while Erika and Signora Sillano made their rounds, the signora explaining the corner kitchen and transformable sofa bed. The bath, the only separate room, was a tad small, with barely space between the phone-booth sized shower and the toilet; although once the signora pronounced the rental sum, about forty dollars a month, Erika responded with a firm *sì,* and they shook hands.

"You won't mind not having a telephone?" asked the signora, her expression and tone doggedly neutral.

Erika glanced at the empty table next to the entrance, where Italian telephones usually sat. "No, no problem," she said. The price was fabulous and she could always use public phones.

"Fine. You can give my number as a contact in case you need a message delivered to you. Shall we go downstairs for coffee?" she said, a slight lift to her voice at last.

Paolo checked his watch. "Another time, Genia, we've got one more appointment."

The signora nodded impassively, then turned to Erika. "You can move in whenever you'd like."

"Thank you—tomorrow would be perfect."

As Erika and Paolo descended the stairs, Erika swelled with pleasure at her impending move. That this autonomy hinged on two slightly illegal situations caused her an instant of discomfort that lasted about as long as a mosquito prick. If the Manhattan Institute and Signora Sillano didn't worry about trifling illegalities, why should she?

11: The Revelation of Fog

Erika toyed with other thoughts as she and Paolo turned into Piazza San Carlo and parked the car. This was the square where she had lunched with Nadia and afterwards learned of Paolo's communist leanings. As they exited the car, headed for the arched stone porticoes, she observed him out of the corner of her eye. His jaw muscles rippled as he chewed the mouthpiece of his spent pipe. When he caught her watching him, he removed the pipe and flashed her that sparkling smile which continued to throw her. He didn't look like a criminal—he was even friends with an older lady whom he helped—and yet those very eyes betrayed him as the thief of Matilde Fassino's handbag.

The question that remained was *why*.

"Are you cold?" he asked her abruptly, as they strolled past shops toward Caffè Torino, where Nadia had suggested they meet.

He must have noticed her tightening her scarf. "The fog makes it chillier," she confessed.

"Yes, it's the humidity." He cleared his throat and hooked his arm in hers. "How do you say...the heat of bodies helps?"

She laughed and gave his forearm a squeeze. "I do come from Southern California, which makes the weather here hard to get used to."

"Blond California girl!" He stuffed his pipe in his pocket and pulled her closer in a sign of solidarity against the cold. A tickling ran through her.

"But are you a hippy girl or a rich girl?" he asked.

She gave him an annoyed look and loosened the hold

between them. "Neither. My father's a building contractor who thinks making money is supreme, and he doesn't give me any, which is fine with me. And hippies, by the way, are out of fashion."

"*Calma!*" Paolo objected in Italian. He halted and patted her hand. "I was joking," he resumed in English. "But you don't go along with your father?"

Erika shrugged herself completely free and slowly started walking again. "It's not that we don't *get* along, I just don't have much in common with him."

"How do you mean?" he asked.

She turned to look at him, at his warm inquisitive gaze.

"My father doesn't care about Italy and I'm just the opposite...I'd rather not talk about it."

Paolo cocked his head. His lips parted, then closed. They walked the remainder of the way in silence, Erika wondering how Paolo had provoked such a spontaneous reaction from her. Partly his touch, his concerned look, the intimate aroma of tobacco about him; all had invited her confidence, and she wasn't sure her response had been wise...

When they entered the café, Nadia was at the bar, waving them over with a bright grin. She wasn't alone. Next to her stood Flavio Moretti.

"You all know each other," said Nadia amid greetings and handshakes. "Let's get a table."

Erika wasn't surprised that Paolo knew Flavio, what with Nadia as a link, and she didn't mind Nadia taking the liberty of inviting the quiet dark Roman. She was keen to observe all three of them.

As they picked their way towards a free table, Erika's eyes lingered over the décor of Caffè Torino. According to Paolo, the café dated back to the turn of the century. It was rich with wood wainscoting and veined marble floors, and sculptures and inlays displayed the rampant bull, Turin's ancient emblem. In short, the café oozed aristocracy. For "aristocracy," Ivan would have substituted *history, culture,* and *heritage*. Erika imagined he might feel offended at being left out of this gathering and wondered whether he and Nadia had had further contact after the weekend in the country.

Nadia spoke to her in an aside as they settled into a peripheral table. "I hope you two don't mind Flavio coming—he called right after you, so I invited him."

Erika glanced at Flavio. He seemed to have heard Nadia and gave Erika a casual smile.

"Good to see you both," he directed at Paolo. "I first met Erika during one of Nadia's crazy parties. I think we might've gone overboard with the politics..." His sharp green eyes shifted back to Erika, watching her, considering her.

For an instant she held his gaze, then said, "Of course you didn't, it was great fun. Besides, I'm no lover of the Right Wing."

Paolo gave her an approving smile, extending it to Flavio and Nadia. "Erika and I exchanged a few words about bourgeois America before we got here. She seems to despise those values as much as we do."

"What kind of values don't you like?" Nadia asked Erika.

Erika was silent for a moment. She had questioned the venting about her father; now she realized her complaint might have come in handy. She had all but called him a bourgeois materialist. Now she assumed a studious frown and said, "Money guides everything in America, Big Business drives U.S. foreign policy." She paused, shifting in her chair, thinking through what to say next. "Overthrowing Allende in Chile, supporting death squads in Central America...the Vietnam disaster. You name it."

Paolo nodded at her. Then Flavio leaned in. "What about policy *in* the U.S.?"

Erika drew a silent breath, recalling a film she'd seen

last year in San Diego. She had studied the McCarthy era, but Woody Allen's *The Front* made the human suffering of the right-wing senator's witch-hunt more vivid. "I hate America's irrational, paranoid attitude towards communism," she said. "All those lives ruined in the fifties, people blacklisted and forced to leave the country, the ones who committed suicide." It wasn't hard to get carried away with the subject, for she was sincere about all of it, including her distaste for U.S. intervention in the Third World. But Italy was different. Italy had democracy, and armed terrorists threatened to topple it. She was just as opposed to the Red Brigades as she was to right-wing death squads south of the U.S. border. She wondered how she would have reacted if the CIA had hired her and sent her there.

"You should come to one of our soirées," said Paolo, putting a hand on her shoulder.

Nadia blinked when Erika looked at her. "Yes," she agreed. Flavio said nothing.

"I'd like that," Erika replied, noting Nadia's hesitation.

"I wonder where the waiter is?" said Flavio. "We'll never order drinks at this rate."

"And we've been chattering non-stop about politics again," said Nadia, "putting Erika on the spot. Time to change the subject."

For the remainder of the time they talked about Erika's move to Turin and all the seductions of the city. Paolo reiterated an offer to help transfer her things once she was ready, and when they finally rose to leave he proposed giving her a ride to the train station.

"I've got to help my father this afternoon," he said with an apologetic smile.

"We've got to run too, *cara*," said Nadia, "but we'll meet again." Her enthusiasm bursting to the surface again, she brushed cheeks with Erika. Flavio limited himself to shaking her hand.

They all walked to the exit, Nadia and Flavio backing

out of the door uttering "ciao." Everyone had somewhere to go but Erika. She felt a bit bleak as she turned to Paolo.

"I'm really sorry I can't stay," he said, as they exited onto the sidewalk beneath the porticoes.

"No problem." Erika glanced at her shoes.

"But I will be in Asti tomorrow to help you move," said Paolo, reaching inside his coat pocket and pulling out a pen and a scrap of paper. "What's your phone number? I'll call you tonight and we can establish the hour."

Warmth crept back into Erika as she gave him Elsa and Angelo's number.

"Now I'll drive you to the station," he said.

"No need. I'd like to stay in the city for a while."

She thought he was moving to press cheeks with her but instead his lips grazed hers. "Until tomorrow," he said. Erika nodded, a warm current rippling through her.

She watched him leave the portico for the parking lot, hands in his coat pockets. Then his dark form dissolved in fog that had thickened while they were in the café. For a moment she stared after him, reliving their tentative kiss. She heard no sound of a car engine starting, so she took a few steps into the parking lot to watch him get in and drive away. She got close enough to see his car then stopped, embarrassed he might notice her watching him. But he wasn't in the car. Through a wispy partition in the fog she spotted his navy blue overcoat—he was walking across the square.

So he wasn't headed home to his father...not yet, anyway.

On a whim she began to follow him.

He slipped in and out of traffic, making his way briskly out of the square. Erika quickened her stride, at one point breaking into a trot to keep him in sight. Heads turned as she whisked by in the floating mist.

A right turn down narrow via XX Settembre. The mechanical rumble of an approaching tram slowed her.

Instinct made her check her feet on the sidewalk and when she looked up, Paolo was crossing in front of the tram. She swore, then crossed behind the tram.

She followed him into via Pietro Micca. Under the street's low wooden porticoes the fog seemed more dense, claustrophobic. Erika bumped past people, spotting Paolo just as he opened the door to a store and stepped inside.

Tabaccheria, read the sign—a tobacco shop. She backed up and positioned herself in the alcove of the storefront next door, surprised to find her heart thumping, her neck hot under her wool scarf. More than anything she felt exhilarated. The only thrill close to this was the one she experienced in fencing, when she launched through the air in a flèche maneuver, scoring her point on a startled opponent. *Electrifying*. For an instant her eyes closed as she savored the frisson.

Then they snapped open. If Paolo were buying tobacco he wouldn't be long. She inhaled deeply. Her pulse slowed. Then the door opened and she peeked out to see Paolo continue along his path, a bag swinging from his hand. She resumed the tail, letting other pedestrians jockey in and out between them.

A cat streaked out of a side courtyard, almost tripping her, causing her to collide with the man in front of her. She looked frantically beyond him, mumbling, "*Scusi.*" Paolo didn't seem to notice the ruckus and was turning back into via XX Settembre. She scrambled after him as he made yet another turn.

Erika now found herself in a lane so narrow she could hop across it. Dusk was starting to gather but the streetlamps hadn't yet switched on. Musty odors rose from ancient and decrepit buildings, their façades chipped and peeling. Here, no pedestrians shielded her from Paolo as he vanished and reappeared in the greyish gloom, like a will-o'-the-wisp. A shift in the fog's curtain, followed by a casual glance over his shoulder and she would be caught—spying on him. She considered giving up the chase, but the chagrin of having lost him in the fog that first time, along with Matilde Fassino's purse, spurred her on. She flicked each of her fingertips against her thumbs, and her thumbs against her index fingers for good measure, thankful for the silence of her crepe-soled shoes as she proceeded through the murk.

Alternating her pace, she kept Paolo's silhouette in view. Then the scent of strong perfume rose from the vapor. A form materialized on her left and she slowed in surprise. In front of a door next to the cobbles sat a woman on a three-legged stool. Her flimsy, frilly coat hung open, exposing a dress that revealed plunging cleavage and virtually all of a pair of parted thighs. Erika couldn't help staring—first at the woman's pale, blasé expression, barely enlivened by heavy mascara and lipstick, then at a wicker basket sitting next to her. It contained, of all things, a sleeping poodle curled up on a blanket.

Paolo's silhouette was becoming fainter so she sped up. Two other nebulous figures emerged from a side street and joined Paolo in his walk. All three halted in front of a building, forcing Erika to slink back into the recess of a short strip of storefronts. Slowly she peered out, and her brain was dealt a sharp, stinging slap. Paolo had lied to her, only to meet up once more with Nadia and Flavio. She retreated back out of sight, her breath coming fast.

A click-clacking of leather heels cut short her indignation. She plastered herself against the door just as a stocky redhaired man came into focus, trundling past carrying a leather briefcase. When she peered out again he had stopped to join Paolo and the others in front of the building. She couldn't make out their words but the animation in their voices indicated they all knew one another. Then Paolo, Nadia, and Flavio waited while the man unlocked the tall wooden door. He held it for them as they filed in, then he followed. The door slammed shut, its echo reverberating in Erika's ears. For a moment she stared at the building in hot embarrassment. Then she stalked away.

12: Ambiguous Awakenings

Erika left the house Sunday morning, her thoughts grinding out the same questions as yesterday afternoon. And the mill in her mind only accelerated as she reached her habitual café, the Reale. She was to meet Paolo there for the move to Turin.

When she walked in, he hadn't arrived yet, though the freckled waiter Massimo approached to take her order. She mused over Massimo's absence on that foggy morning a little over two weeks ago, which had led her to defect to the Cremeria. She was still reeling from the consequences.

"You haven't been in for a few days..." he said.

"I've been away." She smiled but offered no other small talk, and like a good professional he returned to the bar, leaving her at grips with yesterday's events. Paolo, Nadia, and Flavio: they had ditched her after telling her she would be welcome at their gatherings. With Paolo's lie about helping his father, all she could conclude was that their business with the ginger-haired stranger had to be private, maybe secret.

She thought of Paolo's kiss and could still feel a stirring from it. Was she developing a weakness for him despite the fact he was a thief, and now she could add, *a liar*? Once more indignation shot through her like an arrow. Then she cooled: *indignation*, but also *intense curiosity*. She thought of her successful tail of him. What professional could have done better? And if Paolo felt at liberty to lie to her, she could give back as good. As if the Matilde Fassino purse-snatching weren't consuming enough of her interest, now this new mystery presented itself. Could they be related...?

"*Prego*," said Massimo, placing her cappuccino on the table.

She had looked right through the waiter as he arrived but now forced herself to concentrate on him. "*Grazie*. It's nice to be back." He dipped his chin to her and moved on to another table. Erika observed his dark red hair, which in turn gathered her thoughts back to yesterday's stranger, whose short hair was more on the reddish-blond side. In his suit, and carrying a black briefcase, he looked like a banker next to Paolo and his friends, especially compared to Flavio who with his long bushy hair looked like a pirate in comparison.

She had almost finished her cappuccino, checking her watch just as the antique glass-and-wood door rattled opened. Paolo stepped in and after a brief glance around caught Erika's smile. She thought of the Cremeria, a few doors down the sidewalk, and now wished she had suggested they meet there.

"Ciao." He bent and they brushed cheeks. "A coffee," he called out to Massimo before turning back to Erika. "Sorry I'm late. I'll drink it at the counter, then we can go."

"No hurry," said Erika. "It's only a quarter past eleven. We could even take a walk around the square before we go." *Perhaps stroll past the Cremeria...*

A flash of uncertainty altered his gaze. Slowly he sat down and undid the top two buttons of his coat. "I thought we could arrive in Turin by noon, get you systemized in the flat and then go out to lunch."

She ignored *systemized* and instead said, "There are lots of nice shops here, under the porticoes. The fog's lifted, and we don't have to rush..."

He shifted in his chair, undoing a third button. "But there are many more shops in via Garibaldi where you will live. We can, how do you say, *gironzolare per Asti* another time."

"*Wander around Asti*," she translated, then shrugged.

85

"It's up to you. You're the one doing me the favor."

For an instant his brow creased. Then his espresso arrived and he downed it in three sips. He clinked his demitasse in its saucer and said with a grin, "Let's move your things and then we can have fun."

Her lips responded with a smile, which didn't quite reflect in her eyes.

"Do you know Asti well?" she asked, as they sped down the Asti-Turin motorway, her two suitcases in the trunk and a small box filled with paperback books and a portable transistor radio on the back seat.

"So-so." He shifted the black Alfa GTV into fifth gear to pass a small FIAT. Though the sky remained stubbornly opaque, at least the lay of the land was distinct.

"But do you know people there?"

"Yes—*you!*"

"Ha ha! I mean besides me."

"I have an acquaintance or two."

"Well, Asti's a lovely little town worth getting to know."

"I hope you don't regret moving."

"Oh no," she said in an airy tone. "I might miss my usual cafés—the Reale, the Cremeria..."

In the pause that followed, the car slowed almost imperceptibly. A couple of cars sped past, a grey Alfasud splotched with dust from last week's rain and a white Volkswagen Golf, neither of which could boast the power of Paolo's vehicle. The heater hummed cozily and from the radio came ABBA's "Fernando."

As if snapping out of a daydream, Paolo accelerated and roared past both the Alfasud and the Golf. As he glided back into the right lane, he said with nonchalance, "You'll like the cafés in Turin. They're much grander."

Erika considered mentioning that the Reale dated back to 1793, but instead chose to move the conversation forward in line with her agenda. "I'll look forward to everything new in Turin you can show me. You still intend to invite me to your gatherings with Nadia and Flavio, I hope..."

"Of course." With his free hand he patted her shoulder. "We'll meet them again soon."

She wondered if he was thinking about yesterday.

"Where do you all meet?" she asked, keeping her voice neutral.

"Depends...usually at Nadia's."

Really? Not in via Barbaroux at your redhead friend's place? The scene still mystified her. A lane appearing like a long crack between two city blocks, its musty smell wafting in the shifting, spectral fog. Her glimpse of the odd prostitute and her napping poodle, followed by the arrival of the stubby ginger man, click-clacking by with his briefcase.

"Who else attends these meetings?"

"For now just Nadia, Flavio, and I."

Nice formal English, Erika commented to herself. She didn't share the comment, and she didn't know what else to ask at the moment and so lapsed into silence.

When they arrived, an orange tram was easing away from its stop in via Garibaldi, clattering like a slow-moving rollercoaster. Erika gave a mental nod to the fact she would have convenient transportation to and from her flat. They parked and carried her things to the front of the building.

Signora Sillano buzzed them in and when they reached her landing she gave Erika a black leather key wallet. "Go on up and get settled. You can come down for coffee later if you'd like."

Up on the attic landing Erika unlocked the door, letting Paolo enter first with the luggage, which he set on the floor. She put the box with her books and radio on the kitchen table and stared around the room in satisfaction. "My own place—thanks in great part to you," she said with a nod to Paolo.

"No need to thank me." He approached her and lightly

stroked her cheek.

She lifted her hand to his and their fingers entwined. "You'll introduce me to new friends now that I'm here..."

"Certainly." His grip tightened as he held her close.

She brushed her cheek against his, whispering, "I'll expand my horizons."

He pulled her into a proper kiss, its heat traveling up and down her spine. Curiously she felt at once aroused and clear-headed. The heat at pelvis level seemed to ground her while she experienced an almost detached sensation in her brain—as if she were observing Paolo and herself from a distance. She started unbuttoning her coat. He did the same and they threw their coats on a chair.

For a few seconds they watched each other. "On my own in Turin," she murmured.

His voice was low and even. "But not alone."

"Sure, there's always Nadia and Flavio..."

"And me," he said, embracing her.

His chest heaved as they kissed, and again the electric current raced up her spine to her head. Then it seemed to break out into the air, carrying her thoughts in a stream of cool clarity. She moved her lips to his neck, and in between bestowing light kisses, said, "Nadia, Flavio, you, and who knows...maybe I'll meet Matilde Fassino..."

13: Eugenia Sillano and Matilde Fassino

Erika expected Paolo to tense at her words; instead he seemed to deflate. He took a step back, releasing himself from her. He searched her eyes and finally nodded, a smile lifting one corner of his mouth. "I've been expecting this moment."

Erika stared intently, her detached thoughts having rejoined her emotions in spasms of excitement and apprehension. She worked at keeping her feelings contained, and with a deliberate sway in her step walked over to the sofa, sat down, and crossed her legs. "So you suspected I knew all along..."

He conceded the point with a shrug.

"But you didn't avoid me—just the opposite. And now you don't deny it..." She patted a cushion on the sofa. "You'd better sit down."

The brownish-red tiles echoed as he crossed the floor to join her. Slowly he sat and faced her. "Why deny it?" he asked with a touch of flippancy. "That would not be sporting."

She gave a thin smile at his use of the term. "So it's been a game for you?"

His eyebrows arched. "Has it not been for you as well? You could have denounced me right away. Instead you didn't and we have begun to know each other. And, I might say, *like* each other."

Instinctively she glanced at the distance between them on the sofa, a full cushion-length separating them. Satisfied, she drew a contemplative breath. True, she had at first viewed Paolo as an intriguing challenge to her pride, and yes, she found him appealing. But now that he'd confessed in so many words, and so offhandedly...

"Did you think I'd want to become intimate friends with a purse-snatcher?" she asked.

He sighed and sank back against the cushions. "There is much you do not know. It's not just robbery..."

"That, I figured—an architect stealing an old woman's purse?"

He shook his head. "You'll never figure out why I did it, so why don't we have lunch and I'll explain."

The color white was nearly all that registered in Erika's mind about the restaurant—tablecloths, napkins, the waiters' aprons—her thoughts absorbed in checking her burning curiosity with analytical coolness.

After an indifferent scan of the menu she ordered a plate of gnocchi with pesto. Paolo asked for a Milanese cutlet with a side of potatoes. Simple fare, thought Erika, to accompany a complex conversation.

"A bottle of Dolcetto too," he told the waiter, who nodded and strode off. "It will aid me to tell my story. *In vino veritas*, you know?"

"Whatever helps." Erika shrugged, sat back, and waited.

"*Matilde Fassino*," Paolo pronounced, frowning at his steepled his fingers. "You know her name, but do you know who she is?"

The waiter returned with the bottle of red wine and Paolo sat back, seeming to appreciate the reprieve. Impatiently Erika flicked her fingers under the table as the waiter performed his ritual and Paolo finally nodded his approval of the wine. As soon as the waiter left she leaned in and fired off: "Matilde Fassino, the widow of a war criminal who could have been prosecuted for stealing from the Jews if he hadn't died first."

Paolo's eyes narrowed and his voice hardened. "Not only did he steal from Jews, he was involved in *deporting* them to Auschwitz. Do you understand what that means?" He took a brusque swig of wine and glowered at her.

Of course I do, Erika almost said, but sensed she should tread carefully. "It was a horrible thing, I know, but—"

"Why do I take it to the heart? Is that what you want to ask?" He lowered his eyes, laying his napkin in his lap. "My mother was Jewish. Matilde Fassino and her husband stole everything she had and tried to have her shipped to Auschwitz. If Eugenia Sillano, your new landlady, had not helped, they would have succeeded."

Erika's thoughts raced but her speech was stymied. "I'm sorry," she finally offered. "Your mother survived the war, then."

"Thanks to Genia Sillano and her husband, who is now deceased. For a year they hid her in the cellar of their house in the country. Yes, she survived, but twenty years later she died of *tubercolosi*. When I was thirteen."

"Tuberculosis," Erika murmured.

"She was never well after that experience."

The waiter returned with their meals and Paolo's gaze shifted to his plate. He picked up his fork and knife.

For a while Erika kept quiet, picking at her gnocchi. Eventually she said, "You hate her, I understand."

He smirked. "But why steal her purse, you ask? Well, we don't like people of her category. We fight them in any way we can." He brushed his wavy bangs away from his eyes, revealing deep lines in his forehead—grooves of worry for a man she had learned was only twenty-six.

Slowly she leaned forward and asked in a gentle voice, "Does *we* refer to your communist friends? Nadia and Flavio, and others you said I'll meet?"

Paolo nodded. "If you'd still like to meet them..."

"Yes, even more after hearing this. I just wonder if stealing purses is, um, your friends' focus. Seems kind of..."

He sat back and sighed. "*Immature*, I know. That trick was my idea, not theirs. I just wanted to humiliate her. I didn't even take her dirty money—I threw the purse in a trash bin." Suddenly he seemed weary, almost irritated. "Let's just lose it for now."

She didn't correct "lose" with "drop," and they went on to eat in silence. When they finished Paolo took out his pipe and she her Marlboros. She had been smoking more frequently, partly out of habit, partly to sharpen her senses after a night of insomnia. She preferred the smell of Paolo's smoke, and as he tapped the loose tobacco into the bowl of his pipe she was again reminded of Bruno's lean, muscular hands. She had a good memory for such details.

When they got back to the flat, Paolo cut the car's engine and for a moment stared thoughtfully at the street in front of him. When at last he turned to her, he looked vibrant again. "Shall we get your things in order upstairs?"

This was the Paolo who had attracted her from the beginning, mirth and mischief dancing about him like leprechauns. "Sure," she said. "I can be pretty indecisive, so if nothing else, you can tell me what to put away first."

Inside the flat they spent a moment observing the room. "I don't have much," said Erika, unbuttoning her coat. "Most of it can go in the armoire. But my books..." She looked around, draping her coat on a kitchen chair.

"I should build you some shelves," Paolo said, laying his coat on hers.

"You do woodworking?"

"One of my hobbies."

Maybe that's why his hands resembled Bruno's. "My father loves woodworking too, but other than that I don't think he and you have much in common. Anyway, I've only got eight books, so they can go in the table-cupboard next to the couch. But I don't feel like unpacking right now; let's see what's in the kitchen."

They found plates, glasses, silverware, two pots and a pan, a pasta strainer, a Moka coffee pot. "All the basics," Erika said, pleased. "I'll only have to buy food."

"I knew Genia would provide for you," said Paolo. "She's been good to me all my life." His voice trailed off, and Erika watched him with a mixture of compassion and curiosity.

"Let's sit," she said.

The tinkling of the tall radiator coils communicated warmth as Erika and Paolo moved to the sofa. "Considerate of the signora to have the heat on when we got here, said Erika."

"She's generous in many ways." Paolo looked pensively across the room.

Erika turned to face him more directly, lifting her knee onto the sofa. "Awfully brave of her to hide your mother. Must have been a horrible ordeal."

"Passing the winter in a cellar, actually a sub-cellar below the main one, with dirt walls and floors...the cold...the damp...always listening for foreign sounds."

He hadn't moved his eyes; it seemed he'd formed and recited this description long before this day. Erika grasped his arm. "I can't imagine going through that or having anyone I love experience it."

"You don't need to pity me," he said, frowning.

Erika glanced down at her lap, then said, "I just want you to know I really do feel sorry about your mother...and if you'd like, we could try to be the way we were before I mentioned Matilde Fassino..."

He squeezed her hand and she nestled closer to him. As they kissed, the tingling in her combined with that sensation of clarity, like sparkling water that tickled and aroused her while filtering her thoughts. He pulled her tighter and she rubbed against him. He slipped his hand between their bodies and let it slide over her abdomen, down between her thighs. She gave a slight gasp and broke off. Wide-eyed, they watched each other. Then Erika asked, "Do you think Signora Sillano provided sheets for this sofa bed?"

"As you say in English," Paolo replied, "*I would lay money on it.*"

14: The Ginger Man

For a long while afterwards, they lay naked and quiet on top of the bedding. Eventually Erika started to curl up. "I'm getting cold," she whispered, and slipped under the covers.

Paolo followed suit, and enveloped in the flannel sheets, he stroked her hair and repeated his earlier observation: "Blond California girl!"

"The blond comes from my father's side," said Erika with a little laugh." What about your relatives?"

He shrugged. "Everyone says I look like my mother."

"Is your father Jewish?"

"No. The racial laws ended after the war, and some years later they met and married." For a moment he paused, appeared distracted. "I was born in May of '51."

"My grandparents brought my father here to visit in 1950," Erika offered, but Paolo was still looking away, so she asked, "Do you consider yourself Jewish?"

He lay on his back, eyes contemplating the ceiling. "They say if your mother is Jewish you are Jewish. Still, I was baptized Catholic. My father thought I would have better opportunities that way, but I don't really consider myself anything."

Erika propped herself on one elbow. Her voice came soft. "Do you mind telling me what happened between your mother and Matilde Fassino?"

His eyes remained fixed on the ceiling, his tone detached. "My mother never wanted to talk about it but I've heard the accounts. She couldn't get a proper job as a secretary because of the racial laws, so she worked as a domestic in Matilde Fassino's home. She also did secretary chores for Fassino's husband who was a banker in Turin. When the deportation of Jews started he promised to protect her...for a price."

Paolo paused, then in the same steady voice he went on. "She became his mistress, and when Matilde discovered this she went to the authorities and denounced her. To calm Matilde, her husband agreed to take all my mother's savings which were in his bank and transfer them to his accounts."

"So she was practically a slave to them," said Erika, resting on her side close to him. "What happened next?"

"Her husband, how do you say—*ha fatto una soffiata a mia madre...*"

"Tipped her off."

"Yes—tipped my mother off before the authorities got involved. She ran from shelter to shelter in Turin, until she ended up in the countryside where Genia Sillano hid her until Mussolini fell. *The end.*"

Paolo suddenly rolled over to face Erika. She feared what expression he might present and was surprised to see bright curious eyes. "Now it's your turn," he said. "Why do you not like your father?" In the room's growing penumbra, he watched her expectantly.

She turned onto her back and inched up the mattress to lean against the back of the sofa, pulling the covers with her. "I've already told you," she said, looking straight ahead. "I don't *dislike* my father. We just have different lifestyles and values."

"You said you don't like his bourgeois life," said Paolo, sitting up next to her.

Erika shrugged an assent. She didn't want to go into anything personal about her father.

Paolo, on the other hand, had no problem elaborating about his personal situation. "I am not satisfied with my father either. He shows no appreciation of what I do."

"But you still live with him..."

"Not for long, I hope. You said your father builds things?"

"Bruno's a general building contractor, he constructs mainly custom homes."

"*Custom?*"

"Tailor-made for people."

"That is fantastic, I wish my father did that."

"It's a bourgeois trade."

"*No*, it's a type of *artigianato*." He looked to her for a translation.

She stared back, toying with whether to ignore the silent request and continue the argument. She decided to cooperate. "Artisanry," she attempted, unsure whether the word actually existed in English.

"Thank you. But I don't mean to quarrel." He smiled in an apologetic way. "You call your father 'Bruno'?"

"Bruno Alan Rivoli." He goes by Alan, though, because it sounds American. Paolo looked confused. "Never mind," she said. "Calling him Bruno is just a little joke between us." She was getting sidetracked. She needed to find out why Paolo had lied to her yesterday about going home, when he instead met the ruddy man in via Barbaroux.

"You said your father came here in 1950?" asked Paolo.

"Yeah, but I guess he didn't much care for Italy—never came back and never talks about it. He's not in touch with anyone here. I'm the only one who *is* in touch since my grandparents died."

"Well I'm glad you are!" Paolo grinned and fluffed up her hair.

The gesture did not please her. She smoothed down her hair and said, "I'm going to hold you to your word about introducing me to new people in Turin."

"Certainly," he said, peering at her, subdued.

"I'd like to branch out, you know. I think your group of friends would suit me nicely."

"And I will see to it." But he seemed distracted again,

reaching across Erika for his wristwatch on the end table. "It's getting dark, I can barely see the time. Better to get up."

The strawberry-blond stranger: *will you introduce me to him as well?* The man seemed officious, with his swinging briefcase, important even. So different from the others...

"Shall we pay Genia Sillano a short visit before I leave?" Paolo was out of bed and retrieving his clothes.

"Maybe another time," Erika said, hot under the collar again at having been lied to and ditched the day before.

"All right. Stay warm in bed for a while."

She didn't. She rose and dressed to see him out. Then she combed her hair, collected her coat, and left the building to look for a café.

She chose the closest place, the Déjà Vu, across the street from her building. It held only a half dozen tables, all of them dark red like the counter behind which a woman took Erika's order for tea. When the woman arrived with a tray bearing pot, cup and saucer, Erika noticed she looked middle-aged but youthful at the same time, wisdom etched in lines at the corner of eyes that radiated enthusiasm as she smiled. Erika thanked her and resolved to return another time. Then she sat back, poured her tea, and prepared to make another move.

Paolo's history both touched and intrigued her, no doubt about it. Despite her irritation, she liked him, maybe a little too much, which made her even more determined to discover what he kept secret—first and foremost, what lay behind the illustrious Ginger Man. That's how she pictured him, some kind of elder, important player in their cause. She took a sip of tea, her resentment of Paolo, Nadia, and Flavio's deception still simmering in her, only to be cooled by reliving the thrill of tailing Paolo and discovering them all.

And that clinched things for her.

Monday morning Erika rose early and set straight out for via Barbaroux, located (she had learned by following Paolo) parallel to her own via Garibaldi. No fog hindered her this morning, and yet when she arrived in the Ginger Man's lane she noted that its sheer narrowness condemned it to permanent shadows. The building fronts were grey at ground level, some granite, others cement stained with damp. The brick of the upper floors seemed ancient, on the verge of crumbling. Many of the wooden doors were scratched and marred. Nothing in the lane looked like regal Turin of the high arched porticoes and sculpted balconies, yet it was only a five-minute walk from that sector to this one.

As Erika studied her way along via Barbaroux she saw no sign of the woman with the pet poodle—hers, no doubt, was an evening occupation. She approached the strip of businesses in whose recess she had flattened herself while spying on Paolo and the others. Large spools of colorful yarn sat in one store's display window, a collection of stylish dolls, both cloth and porcelain, in another. These shops were far from eerie or rundown. Erika passed them, and then another doorway, until she arrived at the Ginger Man's building. Its façade was cleanly painted beige, its entry door polished and framed in granite. A cut above the rest in the ancient lane.

Having located his building she now had to choose somewhere to wait for him to come out. She glanced at her watch: seven-thirty. It was a workday and he should eventually exit, if he hadn't already. Kitty-corner across the street she spotted a café, and in three steps she crossed the cobbles to peer through its narrow glass door. Three tables—smaller than the Déjà Vu—and the one next to the window sat vacant.

Quickly Erika entered and claimed it. She ordered a cappuccino and a brioche, paying for them straight away. After a couple of swallows of hot frothy coffee, her headache, stemming from a night of stalled sleep in her new home, began to lift. Bites of brioche helped as well, and when she finished she sighed contentedly, sat back, and continued her surveillance.

She checked her watch again: almost eight o'clock. *Would he be going to a job this morning?* She watched the intermittent passersby, their collars turned up, white breaths pluming in the still-pale morning light. She was the only patron in the café, with only a jukebox occupying the corner of the room. She got up and fed it some coins, eyes darting to the street, then returned to her seat.

Eight-thirty. People now came and went in the café, mostly drinking espresso at the bar. Her jukebox songs exhausted, Erika now puffed on a cigarette. Chin resting on her fist, she had almost fallen asleep, and though the cigarette tasted stale this early it kept her alert. She stubbed it out three quarters of the way spent and folded her arms. The warmth of the café was insidiously caressing. Across the street an orange cat sat in front of the Ginger Man's building, cleaning its fur. Erika smiled hazily, her eyes feeling weighty again, her neck beginning to bend...

She jerked awake, glimpsing a flash of reddish-orange swish across the street. *Not the cat.* The Ginger Man was on the move and she had almost missed him. With a stifled gasp she was on her feet and out the door, striding after this man with a barrel-like body, his buckled briefcase swinging next to him, a wool scarf flapping loose atop his overcoat.

He wouldn't recognize her, she told herself, and yet she should keep a discreet distance between them. His steps were short but swift and he appeared to be heading towards Piazza Castello. Then he turned into via XX Settembre. She squinted and followed. When he next turned left, she didn't know where they were in the maze of the historic center. He sped up, like a stout hamster pedaling its wheel, and she had to hustle. *Where the hell was he headed? To his office...or somewhere else?*

Finally he slowed, and she was able to examine the buildings around her, tall, brown-bricked, and immaculately kept. They reached another intersection and a street sign appeared—via Accademia Delle Scienze. There the Ginger Man transferred the briefcase to his left hand before stopping in front of a door flanked by dark Doric columns. He entered, leaving Erika to catch up. When she did, she found herself facing a sign: MUSEO EGIZIO. Her eyes swept the modest façade. So this was Turin's renowned Egyptian Museum. But what was the Ginger Man doing here at only eight fifty-five a.m.? She opened the door and stepped inside, halting when the door closed behind her with a cavernous echo. In the dimly-lit foyer a receptionist sat behind a counter, sifting through some papers. As Erika approached, the woman peered over her glasses. "Excuse me, but the museum opens at ten o'clock." She aimed a hawkish glance at the entrance.

"Sorry," said Erika, "the door was unlocked."

"A mistake—no doubt on the part of our assistant curator." She looked behind her with a pinched expression.

"Did someone mention me?" The Ginger Man stepped into view and gave the receptionist a lopsided smile. "The door was already unlocked. But have no fear, I'll lock it up tight."

At Erika he cast a full smile, blue eyes crinkling at the corners. "I'm Matteo Mattei—I do hope you'll come back when the museum opens." His arm swept wide to encompass an entrance hall filled with giant Egyptian statues. "There are mummies and all sorts of interesting artifacts upstairs." He turned a sharp look on the receptionist. "*Where*, by the way, I'll be spending most of my time today."

Erika gazed around: the ground floor alone was filled with display cases and large rock structures. And those towering statues. She wasn't sure what disappointed her more, being forced to leave this marvelous place or having to truncate her encounter with the Ginger Man.

"*Oh*, I'll be back," she said.

15: Masons, Alchemists, and the Great Mother Goddess

Outside, on the sidewalk, Erika marveled at having so effortlessly met the Ginger Man—*Matteo Mattei*—a professorial type with a blocky head and tweed suit.

And he had invited her back.

She shivered from the cold, but also from excitement, and looped her long scarf around her neck, flipping the ends back over her shoulders. The museum doors would open in an hour, yet she didn't want to seem too eager and rush back. Since she was scheduled to work from two to eight in the evening, she would first buy food for her flat. New to her neighborhood, she figured she could consult Signora Sillano, her landlady, about shopping possibilities. A coffee invitation from the terse signora still stood...but there was also the Déjà Vu located across from her building, with its cheery lady barista. She would ask her.

Erika found the same woman behind the counter, and the way she worked at rearranging bottles and making notes indicated she might be the owner. Streaks of grey in her long dark hair hinted at someone aged forty-plus, but when she smiled at Erika, her lively brown eyes seemed to reverse the count by a few years.

After downing her espresso at a table, Erika picked up an abandoned issue of *La Stampa*, the Turin-published newspaper Angelo always bought. Weather page up, she checked today's predicted high: 3 degrees Celsius, not much above freezing. The winter beast was amassing more and more muscle while sharpening its teeth.

A half hour later, Erika checked the red-rimmed,

white-faced wall clock, which matched the rest of the café's scarlet appointments: the museum would be preparing to open. The Ginger Man would be busy at work on the upper floor.

Again she questioned Paolo's silence concerning the man she now knew as Matteo Mattei. With no answer presenting itself, her thoughts wheeled back to having slept with Paolo, the first person she'd made love with since the fencing accident back home. It had felt right, almost like a type of healing. But what of that momentary state of both arousal and detachment? Never had she experienced the like; the fencing accident might have something to do with it as well.

Her thoughts swung back to Matilde Fassino. Erika understood Paolo's hatred of the woman, yet why steal her purse and risk getting arrested like a common criminal? Paolo's claim of immaturity just didn't hold up in Erika's mind. She wondered if Nadia and Flavio were aware of this juvenile antic.

And the Ginger Man: how did this museum curator fit into their circle?

Erika put him at about thirty-five years old—much older than Paolo and Nadia, both in their mid-twenties. Perhaps Flavio was closer to his age, though Matteo Mattei, with his short hair and stuffy tweeds, looked his elder as well. Still, all three had met in his building. She rubbed her forehead with the heel of her hand, deciding to shelve her speculations and speak to the woman at the counter.

"Would you like anything else?" the woman asked as Erika approached.

"My name's Erika Rivoli—I just moved in across the street."

"Then welcome! I'm Fausta, the owner here. If you need any pointers, just ask."

"As a matter of fact," Erika said, encouraged by the woman's friendliness, "if you know of somewhere to buy groceries..."

Fausta recommended an *alimentari* around the corner. Erika thanked her, began to take her leave, then stopped, frowning at the café radio behind the bar. Both she and Fausta listened keenly. A young, dark-haired man, seated at the nearest table, set down his newspaper to lend an ear as well.

"*Who* died?" asked Erika.

"The journalist Carlo Casalegno." Fausta shook her head bitterly. "After days in the hospital."

"The Red Brigades," said Erika, frowning at the radio again. "I read how they shot him in the face at the entrance to his home."

Fausta nodded. "By your accent I can tell you're a foreigner, so I won't rant too much. But all these militants do is kill. They can't even make their goals clear."

"I'm American but I have cousins here who say the same thing. But the Red Brigades don't want a communist state like in Russia..."

"Exactly, the hypocrites. Chaos is all they create and DIGOS can't seem to stop them."

"DIGOS?"

"The acronym for our internal spy agency. Don't get me started—they do nothing but pocket taxpayers' money."

Fausta looked around her café in barely restrained disgust. The man with the newspaper glanced at Erika before returning to his article. "I liked the color red before all this," Fausta said. "Now I have a mind to have the whole place redecorated."

Erika noted the calendar on the wall behind the bar: 29 November. She'd been in Italy only nineteen days and already there had been two shootings in Turin. She wondered whether the CIA liaised with DIGOS; if so, she would probably be doing the same—*if* she'd been hired. But she hadn't been and she couldn't change that fact. Her thoughts revolved back to the Ginger Man, Matteo Mattei.

She would head back to the museum now and shop later.

Within fifteen minutes, she was standing in front of the Museo Egizio's doors, flicking her fingers against her thumbs.

The museum welcomed her in full illumination. Zoo-morphic deities, human from the shoulders down, along with kings and nobles formed phalanxes on the ground floor, some statues almost as tall as the immensely high ceilings. Awestruck, Erika filed past them, feeling privileged but also a bit strange at being the only visitor in the hall. She made her way upstairs and there finally encountered a handful of other patrons, though she didn't spot Matteo Mattei. At the moment she didn't mind, for the room, filled with sarcophagi protected by glass, enthralled her. The rich reds and turquoises painted on the wooden coffins seemed to have diminished little over their thousands of years of existence, unlike the shrunken, wrinkled brown mummies inside them. Yellowed papyri, also behind glass, papered the upper half of the walls. Thousands of inky hieroglyphs transmitting hundreds of ancient messages about a mysterious civilization that made Erika quiver with fascination. She moved from one glass showcase to another, examining tweezers, razors, combs, everyday objects as modern now as they were three thousand years ago.

She strolled into a side room containing even more evidence of ancient Egyptian life: a rickety wooden bedframe, low to the ground and interlaced with ropes that probably once supported some sort of mattress. At the head of the bed jutted a crescent-shaped wooden support. Who knew its purpose?

She turned to another glass case filled with petrified food. She had just begun to read, "loaf of bread, dates..." when a form flashed its reflection in the glass, then disappeared. In Italian she heard, "Carlo, is everything cleared up in there?" followed by a distant response she didn't understand.

Then the Ginger Man walked into the room. "Well, hello there." He scanned the small space, then crossed to a corner to squat and pick up a screw. "You've come back," he said, smiling at Erika as he straightened and dropped the screw into his jacket pocket.

Erika's pulse quickened. "Everything's impressive. It's my first time here and I had no idea there was so much..."

"The biggest collection next to Cairo, over six thousand artifacts on display. Glad you're enjoying it."

"So many things I had no idea they used back then...like this bed," she added, hoping to keep the Ginger Man in her conversational clutches. "How did Turin come by it all?"

"Ah, it's a long history, Turin's love affair with Egyptology. The collection goes back well before Napoleon's time and that's just part of the story."

"Oh?"

"If you can wait a moment I'll tell you more." Matteo Mattei stepped out into the main hall where Erika could hear him giving orders. When he came back he reengaged her with a squinting smile. "Let's see, Turin and Egypt, where to start? Have you heard of Eridano?"

Erica shook her head.

"There's a legend about the ancient Egyptian prince who left his homeland thousands of years B.C. due to religious intolerance, and settled here because the Po River reminded him of the Nile. By the 1600s A.D. Turin was amassing everything Egyptian it could get its hands on: artifacts, obelisks..." He paused to look at his watch. "Do you have time for more?"

Yes she did. "I'm interested in all aspects of Turin's history. I've had fascinating discussions about the occult here..."

Mattei tilted his ginger head and scratched it with the buffed nail of his middle finger. "Well, if you're interested in those matters you might like to know a little secret about the church called La Gran Madre."

"*The Great Mother*," Erika translated absently to English.

"I thought you might be American," he said, drawing himself up as if pleased with his observation.

"My grandparents were born here."

"Ah, then you might have an Italian surname..."

"Rivoli, Erika Rivoli." She wondered whether she was doing the right thing, revealing her identity; but better to be honest, in case she might have more to do with the Ginger Man later on.

"A nice name," Mattei said. "Italian flavored with Scandinavian—much more interesting than mine, which in English I believe would be *Matthew Matthews*. Banal to say the least."

Erika smiled. "And what were you saying about the secret of La Gran Madre?"

"*The Great Mother*, as you correctly translated, refers not to the Virgin Mary as many surmise and as the religious hierarchy insists, but to Isis, the Great Mother Goddess of the ancient Egyptians. The church was commissioned in 1800 by the royal family who, like many of the rich and powerful in Turin, dabbled in the occult—alchemy, masonry, every one of these activities forbidden by the Church."

"The Church was powerful then..."

"Yes, but *The Great Mother*," repeated Mattei in English, before returning to Italian, "is an appellation open to interpretation. The church operates like a normal Catholic place of worship and the Catholic Church calls it *The Great Mother of God*. Still, they know they've been hoodwinked. Everyone knows. You only have to look at the church's porch, where there's a statue of a woman holding the Holy Grail—another manifestation of the Masons' influence."

"The *Grail?*"

"That's right. It's reputed to be hidden somewhere in Turin," Mattei confided with an avuncular chuckle. "The Masons revere it along with what they call the sacred Egyptian geometry. The marks of the Masons are subtly present all over the city's historical center. Their symbols"—Mattei raised an instructive index finger—"were once a secret way of communicating."

Mattei, having rocked onto his toes, now settled back on his heels. "Of course in America freemasonry was never prohibited. One only has to look at your dollar bill. The eye and the pyramid—classic masonic symbols."

Erika nodded appreciatively, not wanting to admit her ignorance of that matter.

"You must come back when there's more time," he said, consulting his watch again.

In a burst of spontaneity she said, "I wouldn't mind working here, learning something fascinating every day."

His smile was wry. "As a foreigner that could be difficult, admirable as is your enthusiasm."

"Or even volunteer?"

The wryness turned to condescension. "Of course—volunteering is pervasive in American culture. A sort of luxury you have in which to *fulfill* yourselves."

Erika's gaze sobered.

"Excuse me," he said, "I didn't mean to offend. It's just a perception we have here of the American: ever passionate to perform and accomplish. Enviable in a way, though here on the Old Continent we see 'volunteers' as those who would replace salaried workers."

"I already have a job teaching English," she asserted with an edge to her voice. "Like you, I just have a strong interest in all of this." She waved a hand in indication of the museum.

"Rightly so, rightly so." He lowered his eyes as though newly humbled. "Do come back later and we can talk more."

Erika paused to consider him. His comments about 'workers' was definitely revealing, and the haughty pride in his position seemed ironic, considering much of the grand European collections had been looted from Egypt. She wanted to follow up on that and almost asked when she should return. But she hung back, loath to appear the ever-eager American. *Arrivederci* would do for now.

She made her way downstairs, glad she had acted nonchalant towards Mattei's invitation to return. Right now the museum's air was stifling hot. She felt flush with success and just wanted to exit for a gulp of fresh air.

In the lobby she noticed an increase in visitors. Her eye alighted on a man with dark, almost black hair and mustache, who was studying the remnant of a rock tomb. Hadn't he been reading his paper in the Déjà Vu earlier this morning? Coincidence, she thought, as she headed towards the exit. She passed the ticket counter and was almost to the door, when she looked back and caught him eyeing her. Yes, it was him. She turned back to the door. Then slowly, as she opened it, she glanced back again. He was gone.

16: Quick Silver

The next morning Erika sat in the Déjà Vu, reviewing her visit to the Museo Egizio and her encounter with Matteo Mattei—a Communist like Paolo, Nadia, and Flavio, only clothed in the tweed of the Colonialist? Matteo Mattei seemed yet another of the riddles Turin kept casting at her. Like the mystery man who had appeared in both the museum and the café. He had pointedly looked at her in the museum, and she also recalled him putting down his newspaper in the Déjà Vu to listen to the announcement of journalist Carlo Casalegno's death. Nothing unusual about the latter, and yet twice she remembered him glancing up from his paper, and that was because she found him good looking: about her height, with straight dark hair hanging just below his ears, both hair and mustache set against fair skin and a turned-up nose. Without the mustache he would look almost boyish. Still, the coincidence of seeing him twice in one morning made her uneasy. After the pointed look he'd given her in the museum she couldn't help suspecting that he'd followed her. He hadn't come back to the Déjà Vu today and she wondered whether he ever would.

Ten o'clock, and Paolo walked punctually through the door. "*Un caffè ristretto*," he ordered from Fausta as he passed the bar. After glancing around he gave Erika a peck on the lips and sat down. "Interesting place. All red."

"One reason I like it," said Erika. "Cheery, with all this grey weather around."

"Mm...*Déjà Vu*, a unique name."

"Lends to the atmosphere of mystery in Turin, don't

you think?"

"Like the things we talked about on the phone last night?"

"*Exactly*—I'd like to see everything the assistant curator at the Egyptian museum mentioned, and you *did* volunteer to be my guide. Did I tell you the guy's called Matteo Mattei?" she asked innocently.

"You did," Paolo affirmed, looking towards the bar, as if checking on the status of his espresso. The avoidance of her gaze recalled his brief silence when she'd mentioned the name on the phone the night before.

"Funny, huh? In English he'd be Matt Matthews."

"Right," Paolo said with a distracted nod.

Once Fausta delivered Paolo's coffee, Erika went on excitedly, "This Mattei fellow talked about secret signs of the Freemasons and the Holy Grail."

"Yes, you told me," Paolo reminded her with a tight smile. "Between what is hidden and what is bizarre in general, you would have to read a hundred books on Turin to learn it all. But at least we can explore some things together before you have to go to work this afternoon." He downed his espresso and flashed one of his mischievous smiles. "Are you ready for a long walk?"

She was, even though he still wouldn't admit to knowing Matteo Mattei. Paolo had assured her she would meet his friends, and now it would seem the appropriate time to reveal a shared acquaintance. So what was wrong with the Ginger Man that fed Paolo's reticence? He had owned up to the purse-snatching only to hide something else...

They left the café under a frigid white sky and trekked to the Po River, crossing the bridge that led to the church called La Gran Madre. Their backs to the river, they observed the round, domed structure and the marble statue of a gaunt woman seated on a plinth next to discolored Corinthian columns. "That's the statue of the Graal," said

Paolo, "our word for the Grail. See, that is what she's supposed to be holding."

The woman's eyes lacked pupils, seemed sightless...or maybe all-seeing, thought Erika—some kind of blind soothsayer. She was draped in heavy robes of an ancient classical motif and a veil covered part of her hair. Her right hand clutched an open book while her left was raised high, holding forth the chalice indicated by Paolo.

"They say she's pointing it towards the place where the Holy Grail is actually hidden," he said, breath billowing in the icy air.

"Where would that be?" asked Erika, still studying the statue.

"Who knows? Some say it's buried right here under the church." He shrugged, and Erika gave him a sideways glance.

"The museum curator says this church was secretly dedicated to Isis."

"True," answered Paolo in a casual, almost philosophical tone. Once more, with no acknowledgement of the Ginger Man.

"I'd like to see the inside."

"You will find it a typical Catholic church, but we can go in."

They walked up the steps only to find the doors locked.

Paolo turned up his hands. "What else would you like to see?"

"Well, Mattei—"

"How about the secret masonic symbols around the city?" The interruption seemed to dare her to call his bluff. With a broad smile, he added, "Even though they're not so secret anymore."

She might as well give the probing a rest. Let things develop gradually and successfully as they had with Matilde Fassino. "Sounds good," she said, taking his arm. He pulled her close and kissed her.

They resumed their jaunt, re-crossing the dark, meandering Po, Paolo steering them into a street where they came to a halt in front of a large, scarified oak door.

"It appears damaged, doesn't it?" he said of the door.

Erika nodded. "Definitely marred, like other doors I've seen in certain areas of town."

"Well, this one is not. Look closely." He traced his gloved index finger along a series of light grooves. "Can you distinguish the compass and the square? And there, the *livella*?"

She squinted. "The *level*, you mean. I can barely make them out."

"That's the idea. Masonic designs deliberately meant to look hidden. Come, we'll go around the block. There's something even more interesting there."

When they arrived in via Lascaris, he said, "This whole complex is related to masonry."

Erika studied the façade of one of the buildings.

"You're looking in the wrong direction," he said with a shrewd grin. "Look *down*."

As her eyes shifted to the sidewalk, another pair of eyes met them. Erika bent down in wonder. "Eyeholes," she said, "like the half-masks they wear for Carnival in Venice."

Paolo squatted next to her. "They are vents for the cellar below the building. The Masons made them like eyes, which are one of their symbols."

Eyes—like the eye on the dollar bill, Mattei had mentioned.

The eye-slits were curvy, their outside corners flaring up as if with eyeliner, their inside contours pointing down.

"What creative lengths people go to in order to hide things in this city," Erika said as she stood back up.

Paolo draped an arm around her shoulders and they continued along via Lascaris, where exotic eyes stared up at them from the sidewalk at regular intervals.

"I wonder if the Masons were also trying to outwit the

Church," Erika asked.

"Definitely. In Piazza Solferino too." Paolo stopped and pointed to a square at the opposite end of the street. "The Church was furious at the symbols of alchemy sculpted onto the statues there, but they are difficult to distinguish so we won't take time for it in this cold."

"The Catholic Church in the U.S. doesn't bother with Masons."

"In your country the Church doesn't have the power it has here. We have the Vatican, and masons and alchemists have always challenged its power. Even in modern times Masons keep a very low profile in Italy, although there is nothing illegal in what they do."

"Alchemy...I keep hearing that repeated."

"A part of the occult. Masons and the royal family were involved."

"But alchemy's not *real*, is it?"

"Alchemy is much more than transforming metals. Masons see it as a way to—how do you say—transcend the spirit?"

"Well said," Erika replied, impressed with both Paolo's knowledge and his use of English.

Paolo smiled at the compliment. "Let's move on. It's almost noon and I want to show you one more interesting construction."

Snuggling arm in arm, they forged on through the narrow, shadow-stippled streets of Turin's historical center.

"More defiance of the Church," Paolo announced, once they entered via Arsenale, where they stood in front of a stunning art deco building with geometrical wrought-iron trim.

"These balconies are gorgeous," she said.

"Look next to the gate," said Paolo.

"Winged creatures...dragons?" Erika guessed, examining the strange black images mounted on either side of a massive ornate iron gate.

115

"Devils," Paolo corrected. "They face the church across the street, and just beyond it is the Curia, the seat of the Catholic administration in Turin. This is what you could call a theme in the city: the profane, in some cases the Satanic, defying the sacred. Like the black angel and his pentagram—esoteric knowledge outside of the Church's reach." He paused, seeming to reflect on this anew. "Anyway," he resumed, "this building was the first RAI office, the Italian Radio and Television headquarters, although the television part came much later."

Granted, these iron devils were meant to thumb their noses at the Church, yet they seemed feeble, even though their skinny arms and legs did end in claws. "I still think they look like dragons," she said, extending and flourishing an invisible foil at them, adding a lunge for good measure.

Paolo slapped his hands on his hips. "You look like you know what you're doing."

"I do," she said with a shrug.

"So you do *scherma*?"

"Fencing, we say. But yes, I used to. Anyway, we'd better get going. You've given me a fabulous tour and I think we deserve a hot meal. There's a nice little trattoria near my building. I'd like to treat you."

"*Treat* me?" Paolo asked with a confused frown.

Amazing how he had mastered technical, even lofty terms, only to be stymied by ordinary vocabulary. But that was typical in foreign-language learning. "Yeah," she said, "I'm *inviting* you for being such an outstanding tour guide."

"It's not necessary."

"*Palle*," she said in Italian for emphasis, rather than *bullshit*. "Come on, my teeth are starting to chatter—*knock together*."

They lunched in a trattoria recommended by Fausta from the Déjà Vu and then returned to Erika's place. Paolo had pestered her off and on during the meal about fencing: the different weapons, her preference for the saber, swordplay in movies versus realistic fencing. She thought she had put an end to the discussion, telling him she had dropped out of the sport for a while, but once they were settled on her couch he pounced back with it.

"So why exactly have you quit fencing?"

She gave an internal sigh. "I injured my right foot."

"Did you do it in a match?'

"...Yes."

"Oh." He glanced at her foot. "It seems fine now."

"Well I'm in Italy, so for the time being I'll continue my break from the sport."

"But there is plenty of fencing in Turin." He shifted to face her. It's an important Italian sport and I'm sure I could find a club for you."

"You don't need to bother," said Erika, looking away.

"But I think it's brilliant that you do this sport, I would like to learn too. It might be expensive to buy equipment and to join a club—too bad you didn't bring your things with you—but I could help with the money if you need—"

"I don't," she said bluntly. "Let's just leave it."

He touched her shoulder and she almost jerked away. The *accident* was back. She had tried to suppress its crippling intrusion upon her thoughts while yielding to the nostalgia stoked by Paolo's questions about the various fencing weapons. Nostalgia rose in her for the days when she had excelled at fencing more than at any other physical endeavor. Now she was losing balance, and the accident ballooned in her mind:

They were fencing with foils, dancing up and down the fencing strip: parry-riposte, parry-riposte. Or rather, Erika danced and her opponent advanced and retreated in ponderous steps. He was a bulky young man, taller than she, but she was used to fencing with men—and besting them. She had already scored three touches against this adversary and his blade had only met Erika's target area twice. Two more touches against him and she would win the bout. She rocked back and forth, her free left hand dangling loose beside her waist.

She was getting too close, and took two steps back to avoid his long reach. She decided to compensate for their height difference by striking low. She took a quick step forward, dropped the point of her foil, and made one of the deepest lunges she had ever managed: her left leg so low it almost flattened against the strip; her right leg in such an extreme extension, she would never recover in time if his parry came through. But he wasn't fast enough and she didn't miss. The tip of her blade came streaking up to land on his white-jacketed belly. Touch number four. One more to go.

They retreated to face off again. Cool pleasure coursed through her. Time to shut him down with a flèche. With his slowness she wouldn't even need to apply a feint. She glided back and forth along the strip until estimating the correct distance. Then she sprang into a flying lunge, her left foot crossing her propelling right foot. Exhilaration surged through her as her foil tip caught the neck of his white jacket—touch number five.

A sharp metal snap pierced the air. She had flown past him, and when momentum finally allowed her to stop she checked her weapon. The tip was broken off, the blade jagged. And something that hadn't been there before—a red film.

Her opponent had collapsed, blood soaking through the white collar of his jacket. Other fencers in white scurried to kneel beside him. His body twitched and jerked as scarlet spread across his jacket. Someone lifted his mask away to expose a bleeding, gurgling artery. Another fencer whipped off his long glove and pressed it to the wound. Erika numbly followed suit, kneeling, her hands fumbling to remove her glove. She added it to the pressure, and both gloves became quickly saturated. Blood began dribbling from the man's mouth, and Erika fell back on her heels as a horrific tableau of red and white filled her eyes.

"What's wrong?" Paolo called to her.

Her head was hammering as she turned a blank look to him. As always she couldn't picture her opponent's face; the mere attempt increased the pounding in her head.

Finally she focused on Paolo in a quizzical haze.

"You've been sitting there like you've had some kind of attack," he said.

Her brows contracted. Her eyes glistened in pain.

"What *is* it?" he insisted, squeezing her shoulder.

His warm, concerned touch set her to shaking. She struggled to harness her tears as he grasped her other shoulder and pulled her close.

Her eyes welled. Gently she pushed him away. She felt a tear escape as she spoke. "I killed someone."

17: Surprising Encounters

As Paolo drove Erika to work, afternoon shadows encroached like low, sliding cello notes. Stark tree branches were etched against a pearl-grey sky, their dark designs inviting divination. By the time Paolo drove her home after eight, the mist had moved in, marbling the night, and once more the city closed in on itself.

They sat in her flat's kitchenette, eating bread and cheese, and sipping the mulled wine Paolo had prepared. Carefully he observed her, and once their small talk subsided, he pressed gently: "The accident—it must have affected you strongly."

Erika remained silent, gazing at the bits of clove floating like nail heads in her wine. After six hours of tutoring, the vivid memory of the accident had mercifully retreated back to its lair, where she wanted it to stay.

"You have done no fencing since?" Paolo continued.

She took a slow, deliberate sip of warm wine before answering, "That's right."

For an instant Paolo watched her. Then he placed his hand on hers across the table. "I'm sorry, I hope you will return to the sport one day."

"Maybe one day." She shrugged. "Right now I need to keep my mind occupied elsewhere."

"Well, I can help with that," said Paolo with a grin.

She thought of his evasiveness concerning the Ginger Man, Matteo Mattei. "Yes, you can," she said, as they rose to retire to the sofa. She had divulged a terribly intimate secret this afternoon and she expected Paolo to be forthcoming in return—*of his own volition.*

So, as they settled back against the sofa cushions she returned to her usual tack. "Speaking of keeping occupied, will I ever get to attend one of your get-togethers with the Comrades? You did say I'd be welcome, but so far we've only met that once with Nadia and Flavio."

Paolo's gaze took on a distant air before returning to her. "Why are you so interested in our cause?"

Her brow wrinkled as she once more found herself on the spot. If there was something to hide regarding the Ginger Man, Paolo had good reason to pose this question. But to hell with those in the CIA who had rejected her, to hell with the accident—this was *her* investigation and she wasn't giving up.

"It doesn't seem you want to answer," Paolo persisted in a quiet voice.

And it doesn't seem you're going to come clean yourself, so we'll continue facing off. "I told you, I'm sick of the U.S. I left for good reason. Especially..." She paused. "Especially after the fencing accident. I just want to leave all that shit behind and start over with something meaningful."

Erika's shoulders slumped at the truth of the statement. Paolo relented and pulled her close. He smiled and kissed her. "Of course you can meet the Comrades. I'll set it up."

That night when they made love, Paolo continued to show tenderness. Almost too much. His touch was tentative, as though he were afraid of upsetting a restored yet delicate emotional balance in her. She was not fragile, however, and to express this she slipped on top of him. They rocked rhythmically until they both sighed their fulfillment. She fell onto her back, and after a couple of deep, silent breaths, felt she was regaining equilibrium, her clarity of thought. She did like Paolo. He was kind, accomplished, and he was a lover deliciously disconnected from everything American she had left behind. But with those thoughts came a shiver, a reminder that she had revealed a painful truth while Paolo still held back about the Comrades.

The next day, under a chilly, whitewashed sky, Erika made her way to the Manhattan school, fatigued and preoccupied. She had slept worse than usual with Paolo in her bed, given his intermittent snoring and their occasional bumping of feet. Even amidst calm and quiet interludes, just the awareness of him beside her had kept her awake, reflecting.

She had planned to stop for coffee at the Déjà Vu on her way to school but was startled to find the café closed. A white paper sign hung on the door, its black, hand-written printing reading *Chiuso Per Emergenza,* which meant *Emergency Closure.* From the pharmacist next door Erika learned why. A Red Brigade group had robbed a mini-supermarket the afternoon before, only a few blocks away. As the group fled, firing, a ten-year-old schoolboy caught a stray bullet and died before reaching the hospital. The boy was the nephew of Fausta, the Déjà Vu's owner.

The further Erika dwelled on the calamity—Christ, it had happened not far from where she lived—the more she found it difficult to drag herself to the school. She needed both a respite and a pick-me-up, so she chose a café near the school.

Although her sugared espresso didn't give her an enormous boost of energy, it did make her feel a little sharper. She had barely finished the last drop when she stiffened to peer out the window. Mustache, turned-up nose, glossy dark hair and black ski jacket: was that the furtive man from the museum?

She stood and watched until he turned the corner. Thoughts racing, she contemplated dropping money on the table and rushing out after him to make sure she wasn't mistaken. But what would she do if she caught up and identified him? She couldn't accuse him of following her just because they happened to be in the same neighborhood. Frustrated, she paid her bill and left the café for school.

"*Jesus,*" she muttered about the situation, as she proceeded down the sidewalk. She looked behind to see if anyone had heard, then whipped her head back around. *Him again, walking behind the person in back of her!* She glanced back once more but his gaze was aimed beyond her.

A trickle of pedestrians accompanied them on the sidewalk. Emboldened by their presence Erika slackened her stride; a quick peek back revealed he had slowed to match her pace. His eyes met hers in an expressionless glance then shifted away. Did he not care she knew he was following her? Obviously not: he'd probably meant to bait her out in the open. Concluding as much, she sped up, turned a corner, and yanked open the door to the Manhattan school's building.

He must have jogged to catch up, for as soon as the foyer door slammed behind her, she heard it open again. She turned to face him—yes, the same man from both the museum and the Déjà Vu. This time she noticed his eyes were grey-blue, and grim. *Who are you?* she was about to ask, when he advanced and seized her by the shoulders, backing her under the staircase.

She gasped as she felt her spine touch the glass-encased mailboxes mounted on the wall. Her purse slid off her shoulder but she let it tumble to the floor as rage and instinct took hold of her. As if clenching a saber, her right arm shot up to swat his left hand off her shoulder. "*Chi diavolo sei!*" she demanded. *Who the hell are you?*

He dropped his other hand long enough to flick her a sardonic smile, then in a flash he grabbed a handful of her hair. "Listen," he said quietly, his voice firm, "keep out of politics that are not in your interest, and stay away from the Comrades. Understand?"

Erika's eyes grew wide, pain shooting through her scalp when she tried to recoil from his grasp. He seemed to take her discomfort for an assent, and before letting her go he pressed his lips against her ear. "Good. In that case, *ciao*...for now," he whispered, warm breath tickling her ear. Once his grip loosened she parried hard with the same saber-like maneuver, knocking his hand against the glass cover of a mailbox. She half expected more aggression, but he simply shook his head, the steel-grey in his eyes issuing a rebuke. "Stay away," he repeated, sounding impatient now, "for your own good." With that he turned and left.

Heart thumping, Erika remained rooted in place, well after the clunk of the entryway door resounded off the marble floors. Then anger engulfed her again, along with embarrassment. Whoever this mystery individual was, he had meant to intimidate her. She didn't know which unsettled her more, the clenching of her hair and the whispering in her ear, or the fact she had previously found him attractive.

Gradually her temper cooled to a smolder. She smoothed her hair and gathered up her purse, eyeing it ambivalently. Who the hell *was* this prick? And *who*, she asked herself, *knew* him? She thought of the Comrades. Somebody had to have unleashed this bastard on her. Flavio? Nadia? Matteo Mattei? The museum curator seemed a natural leader, a believable boss who might now know—through Paolo?—of Erika's interest in their group. She shuddered to think that Paolo may have called Mattei yesterday while she was at work after their tour of Turin. *Tender, affectionate Paolo*. She pressed her forehead with the heel of her hand, then flicked her fingers.

And if she went to the police? She would have to report a man following her, aggressively warning her off his Red associates. Erika could predict the volley of questions and suspicions she would encounter, the extent of her involvement with Paolo and his connection with the others. They might even ask her about her job—her *undocumented* job. No. For now she would reserve that option and concentrate on Paolo and what she could figure out.

Calmly she began her climb up the stairs to the Manhattan Institute. In this tangle of live wires, one thing remained certain: she would not be frightened off.

The following morning Erika found the Déjà Vu open again. The gurgling and hissing of the espresso machine seemed harsh in the subdued atmosphere. Erika drank her coffee at the bar to show solidarity with Fausta whose eyes looked weighed down with their dark circles.

"Right now, I wouldn't mind seeing the Fascists wipe them all out," Fausta said, bracing herself on the low sink behind the bar as she faced Erika.

Erika waited a moment, then voiced quietly, "The Blacks wipe out the Reds?"

Fausta grunted an assent. "Obliterate them from our neighborhood, from the city, from the world." Her voice rose to match the anger in her eyes. Then slowly her expression relaxed, in resignation to the reality of things. "But they're all alike, aren't they? Reds, Blacks, all ruthless murderers. They can't even tell you what they want for this country. Nothing but misfits looking for an excuse to commit violence—to kill..." Her shoulders slumped. She stifled a sob. "Simo was just a little boy coming home from school!"

Erika reached across the counter and touched her arm. Fausta nodded acknowledgement. "Excuse me," she said. She dabbed her eyes with a tissue from her apron pocket then cleared her throat.

"He was a dear boy," said Erika, gravely recalling the time she met the ten-year-old Simo in the café. She didn't know what else to say, so she asked, "When is the funeral?"

"Next Monday at ten o'clock. At San Dalmazzo."

"I'll be there."

"You don't have to, but *grazie*." Fausta managed a painful smile. The streaks of grey in her long dark hair struck Erika as more prominent than usual, though her grieving eyes looked calm now. "I used to take a certain pride in Turin, its beauty, its legends," she said with a far-off look. She shrugged. "Now I think it's cursed."

On her way out Erika glanced at the calendar—2 December. The attack killing Simo had taken place the very day after journalist Carlo Casalegno had succumbed to injuries inflicted by the Red Brigades in a different neighborhood of Turin. She thought of the jerk who had menaced her just yesterday, of Nadia, Flavio, and Paolo going to their sneaky little meeting with Matteo Mattei, and of Paolo's stubborn silence regarding the Ginger Man. Next time she saw Paolo she would ask him where he stood on Red terrorism and collateral killings, which were now carving their way into her neighborhood. And she would demand a meeting with the Comrades.

"*Nel nome del Padre, del Figlio, e dello Spirito Santo...*" At Father Elio's pronouncement Erika automatically began to cross herself, then halted and returned her hand to her lap. She rarely went to church. The last time had been for the funeral of the fencer, the young man who had fallen under Erika's own unwitting blade. That service had felt like torture.

Now, once more, she had to listen to blather about God calling home his dear deceased to be with him in paradise. Well, that might sell for the death of an old person, but not for the murder of a little child, who had barely started life only to be struck down and probably die in pain.

And what of those left behind? If this was God's will (and wasn't everything, either by commission or omission?) then he had abandoned his faithful. Left them, for the rest of their lives, to deal with the crushing aftermath of barbarous, indifferent "Chance." Bleakly, Erika pictured herself (and everyone else in the church) at the mercy of a chaotic universe of harrowing proportions, battling to exert what little control they could over life with *no one* in charge.

For a moment she glared at the priest behind his pulpit. *We're all sitting ducks, regardless of Free Will.*

Erika's gaze turned back to the small, polished wood coffin, graced with a spray of yellow gladiolus and white lilies. She pictured the curly-haired Simo drinking his Fanta orangeade through a straw, pausing to chat merrily with regular customers of the Déjà Vu. Her thoughts veered to her younger brother Keith at the same age. Laughing as he played at pro wrestling with his friends, launching dropkicks in his black, high-top tennis shoes, his mop of brown hair flopping over his eyes...

She shook herself, her eyes smarting with tears. She felt an arm encircle her. Paolo, who had insisted on accompanying her to the funeral, squeezed her shoulder and handed her a packet of tissues. But was she tearing up over Simo or Keith? *How strange*, she thought.

Solemnly they filed out of church along with everyone else. There would be no post-funeral reunion, no comforting of one another with food and drink and company, as was the custom of Italian-Americans in the U.S.

"Here, it would be inappropriate," Paolo explained.

"Well," replied Erika, "without meaning to be rude, *I* could sure go for some food and wine."

"Certainly, it's past noon. Shall we go to the *trattoria* near your building?"

As they walked back to via Garibaldi, Erika watched Paolo keenly. He had condemned the Red Brigade attack that caused Simo's death, but Erika felt he hadn't gone far enough. Instead of categorically denouncing leftist violence, he instead referenced the clashes between Red and Black militants, stressing how the Reds kept the Blacks in check. "Otherwise," he said, "we would have the kind of state that tried to exterminate my mother and her people, and deprive all Italians of freedom—they are new Fascists but with the same goals of Mussolini."

"So, in your opinion, not all Red militants should be treated as outlaws?" Erika asked with skepticism.

"Correct. And not all Reds are violent. In fact, you will be able to see for yourself how our own peaceful group operates." When Erika's eyebrows rose, he added, "I am inviting you to our meeting tomorrow evening."

Despite her appreciation of the long-awaited invitation, she wasn't convinced of the entirely peaceful intentions of Paolo's Red cell. He still hadn't acknowledged knowing Matteo Mattei, and now this Mustached Man had come on the scene. Someone in Paolo's circle must be acquainted with the bully and she was determined to discover who that was.

The thought was never far from her, like a harrying wind that precedes an ominous storm. Erika and Paolo made love again that night, and as they kissed and embraced and turned in her bed, the Mustached Man reappeared in her mind, taunting her with his handsome smile, his warm breath in her ear, his hands pushing her back against the mailboxes. One of the Comrades had sicked him on her, someone who'd been told of her interest in their affairs. *Someone...*

Suddenly her fingers were yanking Paolo's hair.

"What's wrong!" he exclaimed, jerking free and rolling away from her.

Erica gulped a breath then exhaled in a nervous spasm. "Sorry..." she muttered, shocked at herself.

"What was that?" he demanded, rubbing his head then clasping her hand in a firm grip.

"I...I don't know. I just kind of spazzed out..."

"*Che diavolo* is *spazzed out*?" Paolo was angry, and his resorting to Italian in frustration showed it.

Erika didn't know how to translate the slang expression and didn't really want to, considering her embarrassment. "It means to sort of get carried away," she mumbled. "I don't know what got into me." And she really didn't. Any one of the Comrades could be responsible for the Mustached Man's aggression. Why take it out on Paolo when he had invited her to their meeting?

She edged closer to him and brushed her cheek against his. "I haven't been sleeping well. Forgive me?"

She felt his muscles relax as he kissed her, murmuring, "The fencing accident?"

She slowed, pulled slightly back, stroked the hair on his chest. "Sometimes it's not easy," she said, leaving it at that. As a distraction she slid her hand farther down his torso, and he arched and drew her against him. She had never used the fencing accident as an excuse for any type of sketchy behavior on her part. Just allowing Paolo to believe that the trauma had led to her pulling his hair irritated her. Firstly, it wasn't true, and secondly, it wasn't her style to exhibit that kind of weakness. On the other hand, she couldn't very well have disclosed her frustration regarding the Mustached Man; Paolo had yet to come clean even about the Ginger Man. Therefore, *so be it for now.*

The next evening they parked in Piazza Vittorio, near Nadia's flat in via Po. The square overlooked the Po River, and the reflection of city lights danced off the water, pricking the dense, cold darkness. As Erika and Paolo walked under the low porticoes of via Po, Erika noted the metal stands of sidewalk booksellers, shut and padlocked for the night. The neighborhood radiated a youthful, scholarly ambience, even if such coziness couldn't fully distract Erika from her concerns about meeting the Comrades. Who all would be there (Paolo wasn't sure), and would she have to take some kind of oath of secrecy?

She flicked her fingertips as she and Paolo arrived at Nadia's building, were buzzed in, and climbed the two flights of stairs to the flat. Nadia opened the door and swept them in with smiles and kisses on the cheeks. The moment all three arrived in the sitting room, however, Nadia's expression turned sober. Meekly, she withdrew behind Erika and Paolo as the latter two took in the scene. Though three people sat at a round table in the corner, one large blockish face filled the room. With narrowed eyes and a twist of his thin lips, Matteo Mattei smiled at Erika. After what seemed a condescending few seconds, he rose to greet her, followed by Flavio Moretti and Ivan Rivoli. *Ivan.* And yet, the surprise appearance of Erika's cousin and the Ginger Man was at best anticlimactic. Erika wondered at the meagerness of the group. *This was it? And the Mustached Man?* In Erika's mind his absence loomed as large as the Ginger Man's presence. But had she really expected to see the bully here? All things considered, his emergence from the shadows would have been the greatest surprise of all.

18: A Cryptic Chessboard

Erika scanned the cast of players grouped in Nadia's sitting room. Though Erika was acquainted with every one of them, by now they had all (including Ivan) become arcane chess pieces to her—arrayed in shades of muted greys and moving on a board with blurred boundaries. She knew neither their true intentions nor the sides each took.

"Erika!" Matteo Mattei clasped her hand with a firm, muscular grip. "I've told everyone we've already met."

"Yes," said Erika. She turned to Paolo and pointedly reminded him: "We met at the Egyptian Museum."

Paolo gave a faint nod and glanced away.

"Of course you also know our two other guests," said Nadia, finally stepping forward though in a strangely formal way.

Ivan advanced with a reserved smile and brushed Erika's cheeks with his own. She hesitated, then indicated Paolo. "You two might've already met..."

Both men gave quick nods before stepping back to let Flavio move in.

Though he and Erika had met three times before, Flavio continued to simply shake her hand—no chummy kisses. He appeared less the Caspian prince this evening, his blue eyes distant, his posture stiff and in sync with the tone of the room.

Only Mattei expressed any animation to speak of. "Shall we sit?" he said, with what struck Erika as a crocodilian grin, narrow-eyed and self-satisfied.

He indicated Nadia's clean-lined, Scandinavian-looking table with its modern, plastic orange lampshade hanging above. Nadia pulled an extra chair from next to a matching credenza while Flavio retrieved another from the kitchen. Erika's glance lingered on the long, blond-wood credenza, on which sat a television and a few knick-knacks, including a picture of a beaming Nadia flanked by two middle-aged people who could have been her parents.

"Sit where you'd like," Nadia said, "I'm going to get drinks."

Erika and Paolo took chairs side by side at the round table. *Was there equality here at what seemed Mattei's court? Did some, like her, have a personal agenda?*

Nadia returned with a tray of bottles and glasses. "Help yourselves," she said before setting it down and taking her seat.

Flavio reached for a .75-liter bottle of beer. "Would anyone like some?" he asked. Ivan raised his finger. It seemed to Erika that the two men locked eyes before Flavio filled Ivan's glass and then his own.

"I'll stick with Coke," Mattei told Flavio, while keeping a smile trained on Erika. The Ginger Man wore the same tweed suit Erika remembered from the museum, so incongruous compared to the others dressed in jeans or corduroys, and bulky sweaters.

"What will you have, Erika?" he asked her.

"The San Pellegrino orange. I'll get it," she added, and Flavio sat back.

"No, allow me," said Mattei. As he reached forward, his bulk strained the seams of his suit. He glanced at Paolo, who with a polite nod (and a smile of deference, Erika could have sworn) accepted a glass of orangeade as well.

Nadia poured her own glass of sparkling mineral water, leaving Erika to further speculate on the pecking order of the group. She watched her hostess take a sip, then settle back demurely. *So, any bubbliness this evening would be restricted to her beverage.* When Erika looked around again, she noticed that everyone at the table was eyeing her,

Mattei overtly, Flavio aloofly, Ivan sideways...all except Paolo whose gaze remained fixed on the bottles on the table.

Then Mattei began his interrogation. "So, Erika, I hear you're interested in our humble little cause." He sat relaxed, his barrel shape straining against the buttons of his tweed jacket. They all waited for her answer, Flavio watching her impassively from under long dark eyelashes, Ivan giving her a quizzical smile when her gaze crossed his.

How easy to merely affirm her interest and desire to join their group. But she would have to offer a motive. She replayed in her mind what she had told Paolo, Nadia, and Flavio before—trite though seemingly effective—and now voiced the litany: her disillusionment with life in America, her bourgeois, materialistic parents; the disgust she felt with her government and its military ventures to boost Big Business. She drew on emotion and hoped it didn't ring too clichéd.

"I can attest she's sincere in this," Paolo said when she'd finished.

Erika glanced at him in surprise. She swallowed and flicked her fingers under the table. "I support socialism," she went on, emboldened. "Both in my own country and here, but Ivan says the government in Italy is so corrupt that it'll take communism to put things right." She gave her cousin a quick glance and saw he was blushing. "I've been with Paolo for some weeks now. I know about this country's fascist past. I understand why you're Communists, but how do you want to go about things?" She let out a long silent breath and eased back in her chair.

Ivan was now staring at his hands, Nadia picking a piece of lint off her sweater. Flavio's bland gaze remained steady.

Slowly Mattei started to nod. "We have our own special niche, Erika. We all want a fair government and maximum empowerment of workers vis-à-vis *Big Business*, as you put it. So we support the communist party in any way we can.

We write pamphlets, distribute leaflets, help organize rallies, et cetera. Does that type of activism interest the girl who wanted to *volunteer* at the museum?"

At best Erika found Mattei's smile disingenuous, his tone echoing the condescension displayed in the museum when she'd first brought up the subject of volunteering. She could feel the heat rising to her face in what was already an overheated room. Everyone was staring at her now, as if she were some exotic species.

It irked her. "Your work does interest me," she said, "but so far all I've heard about is Matilde Fassino."

The temperature in the room seemed to undergo a reversal. Shoes shuffled beneath the table. Nadia and Ivan straightened from their slouches. Paolo stiffened next to Erika. For their part, Mattei and Flavio hadn't budged at all, Flavio's eyes still expressionless and Mattei's smile more lopsided than ever. He sighed. "Ah, Paolo's tragedy."

Paolo met Mattei's glance and fired back an immediate response. "I told Erika about my childish prank in snatching her purse, my immature, revengeful moment after all she did to my mother during the war."

Erika peered at him. He seemed to have recited on cue.

"Well, we do like to support one another," Mattei replied. Observing Paolo's discomfort he added in a sympathetic, paternal tone, "And we certainly understand our friend's 'immature' moment."

Paolo had lowered his eyes. Nadia was drumming the table, her gaze following her fingers. Ivan slipped a surreptitious, red-faced glance at Erika.

What had she stirred up? Erika couldn't decide which response to her mention of Matilde Fassino had been more strange—the collective, silent recoil, or Paolo's hurried attempt to explain the obvious. Once more she took to examining them one by one, until Mattei leaned forward and slapped his hands on his short, beefy thighs. The loud clap turned heads back to him. All heads but Flavio's:

thoughtful, cool and silent as a blanket of snow, he sat watching Erika.

"Do you have any other questions for us, Erika?" voiced Mattei.

The servility of everyone, except Flavio, further emboldened her. "I find it strange," she said to Mattei, "that you're a Red. I figured you for a sedate, conservative type in your curator job at the museum."

For the first time Mattei leaned in and folded his hands on the table. "Erika," he began, his tone indulgent now, "do you remember our talk about Egypt and the Freemasons? I'm not *only* a lover of Egyptology, I'm...how can I say...a spiritual alchemist, seeking to bring about purification in myself and the world around me. In that capacity I have ties with the Masons, although I like to keep that confidential. You'll keep that secret, won't you?"

Erika gave a shrug, then a nod.

He returned a knowing smile. "As well as anyone, I'm aware of what you've described as a weak and corrupt Italian government, and more disturbingly, a growing neo-fascist movement. This sickness in the state has to be healed, the fascist malignancy excised, the whole of the entity purified in order for it to evolve in an enlightened manner. I do whatever I can in my humble way." He spread his hands, sat back, then looked around at the others. "Now, does anyone else have a question for Erika?"

Flavio sniffed and scratched his head. "I'm wondering what Erika thinks she can do for us?"

Erika breathed in, then drew herself up. "Give me time, I'll think of something."

And think she did, after Paolo had dropped her at home, explaining that he'd withheld his connection to Mattei *and* Ivan pending permission to reveal them from Mattei.

From what she had gleaned so far, Erika summed the Comrades up: Ivan, a fashionable Red, perhaps resentful of what he didn't have; Paolo, loathing the Fascists for their crimes in the war; Mattei, who aspired, like all of them, to change the government, but as part of his "spiritual alchemy." Erika didn't know what to make of that. She recalled the gleam in his eyes, almost exultation, as he'd expounded on it. Mattei could be many things, but his own term *humble* didn't quite describe him. He was the boss of a little Red unit, seemingly innocuous, and he enjoyed his role. Erika couldn't help wondering how that could satisfy his ego and ambition. Then there were Nadia and Flavio, no longer a couple, it appeared. Fashionable Reds, as well? Nadia, maybe. Flavio, Erika couldn't peg. Although to his credit, he had asked a valid question: what *could* Erika offer the group? Especially, thought Erika with a grimace, a group in which at least one member, if not more, wanted her sidelined, and had made that perfectly clear through a menacing messenger.

The group had done nothing the rest of the evening but prattle on about the virtues of a communist though non-Stalinist Italy. No mention of violent means, let alone of the Red Brigades; only the power of the press and the ballot box. The rest of the evening, Mattei directed the conversation towards the trivial, until things came to a natural close. Erika had learned nothing about the Comrades beyond their banal business of helping to organize rallies and dispersing propaganda. Hardly anything spectacular, though she told them she was eager to help. Then again, that might have been the point of the meeting—to discourage Erika's further interest due to the group's sheer boringness.

True: their declared activities didn't interest Erika at all. *Matilde Fassino*, on the other hand...that gaping silence following Erika's mention of the woman still echoed in her head (if silence could do that) along with Paolo's drawn-out justification for the purse snatching: "my childish prank...my immature, revengeful moment after all she did to my mother."

Why recount what Mattei already knew—and so mechanically? Perhaps another attempt to divert Erika's speculation? Or maybe not...

At any rate, she'd had a good night's sleep alone in her bed, a nice chat with a recovering Fausta this morning at the Déjà Vu, followed by a relaxed day at school, without Paolo scheduled in the afternoon. Perhaps this Comrade business might just resolve itself on its own, she mused as she left work that evening at eight-thirty.

On her way down the sidewalk she noted three people next to the pole of her bus stop. Two young girls stood chattering and laughing, primed for a party, it appeared, in heavy make-up and spiked heels punctuating their long wool coats. One performed a twirl and the other clapped and tried to imitate her friend. Erika didn't notice much about the man whose back was to her until she reached the stop and he turned to face her. Bundled in his black ski jacket he met her eyes with a neutral gaze, his familiar dark mustache twitching as though in a subtle signal to her. Alarmed, she looked to the girls who were now practicing a dance step.

"*Uno, due, cha-cha-cha; uno, due, cha-cha-cha.*" One slipped and they giggled, hanging on to each other. "*Scusate*," they apologized for the disturbance.

The Mustached Man glanced idly at them then turned studious eyes back on Erika.

"You're fine," Erika told the girls, her nerves on fire. "Learning the cha-cha?" Her eyes darted to the Mustached Man and back. "I took lessons once."

Erika's heart beat fast as she slid first her right then her left foot to the side. "You have to do this first or you lose the rhythm." Then she demonstrated the steps, her gaze clinging to the girls.

The show netted applause. "*Brava*," they giggled. "*Grazie!*"

By the time they had practiced the dance, the bus arrived and they all climbed on. The girls made their way to the back, Erika sat towards the front near the driver, and the Mustached Man plopped doggedly down behind her. As the bus trundled on, her mind scrabbled for a way out. She couldn't get off at her stop—too close to her building. She didn't want him following her home, although she suspected he already knew where she lived. She could barely concentrate, could virtually feel his whispery breath on her neck. She pictured his almost sensual bullying of her, and her fear now turned to slow-burning anger. Soon she felt calm enough to develop a plan.

At each stop she took note of who got off the bus. Finally she said *arrivederci* to the dancing girls as they jabbered their way down the aisle and off onto the sidewalk. The bus heaved forward, swaying and rattling as it banged over the cobblestones, until it finally pulled up in front of Porta Nuova train station. Erika watched passenger after passenger descend; then, before the doors closed, she leaped up and hopped off.

She strode rapidly into the station, weaving through the lobby, past the ticket-sales windows, finally into the space where trains stood lined up next to their platforms. He had probably followed her so she didn't bother looking back. The resounding voices of the crowd, the public announcements, the whistling of conductors gave her a sense of reassurance; he would find strong-arming her a challenge here.

She approached the station café, slowed, and at last looked over her shoulder. Their eyes met—he was close enough to lay hands on her. But he didn't, and she continued into the café.

She chose a table where she could face the glass door to the station's foot traffic, commuters hustling to their trains or stopping to make a last-minute purchase.

Without hesitation he straddled a chair across the table

from her. Neither of them said a word. He didn't remove his jacket and she left her coat on too, poised to make a rapid retreat if necessary. Lips tight, eyes flickering about the room, he sat with his hands in his pockets while Erika continued her silence. *Let him explain himself.*

Then his eyes settled on her and he offered a strained smile. "You know, Erika, you're trying the Comrades' patience."

The sound of her name gave her a start. "So you know my name. What'll I call you?"

"...Gino."

Probably a phony name, she thought, but at least it was something. "You must be one of the Comrades who's losing patience. Are you their spokesman? *They* haven't asked me to leave."

Gino's hands left his pockets and landed on the table with a bang. "You're American, for God's sake," he said in exasperation. "You can't possibly believe you can be part of this group!"

"*Signori!*" a cheery waiter interrupted.

"Coffee," Gino grunted without looking at the man.

Erika's eyes latched onto the waiter's: *someone to fall back on, an ally if things go south...*

"Two," she said to him, feeling more confident. After yesterday evening, she sensed the Comrades didn't want her, but this "Gino" seemed willing to talk, and she was eager to learn what she could.

He sat back again, contemplating her, lacing his fingers, turning them outward and stretching his arms. Then he leaned in, and with a blade-like glare said, "Get out of this before you delve so deep you drown. Or get drowned," he added with a genteel smile. "This isn't your war and you're not cut out for it."

A chill rippled through her but her eyes didn't shy from him. *How would he know what she was or wasn't cut out for?* "The war," she repeated, "the communist struggle, you mean?"

"Not a game—and certainly no place for an American." He leaned in further and lowered his voice just as the espressos arrived. "The Comrades *do* want you out," he said, as if confirming her thoughts.

"*Prego*," announced the waiter, setting their coffees on the table then departing. Erika's eyes tracked him.

"*Which Comrades?*" she insisted.

"Everyone. And they'll be especially unhappy when I tell them you tried to join the CIA. And I can toss in the little secret about your brother to boot...Get out, before everything becomes common knowledge."

With that he rose, dug a couple of banknotes from his pocket, dropped them on the table, and with a curt nod, walked out without touching his coffee.

Erika stared at his retreating back, then at the money on the table. She had hoped to learn something from this man but could never have imagined his parting words.

19: The Second Accident

Erika peered at the light seeping through the crack in her curtains—finally daybreak—and returned to her musings.

Luigi—Luigino—Gino: if *Gino* was truly his name, she found it much more street-worthy than either of the names from which it derived. Especially *Luigino*, a name that made her picture a dancing bear in a circus. Phony or not, 'Gino' suited him; he had graduated from bully to blackmailer and she again felt embarrassed that she'd once found him attractive.

How had he discovered her connection to the CIA? And her brother—what did Keith have to do with anything? It seemed the CIA psychologist had also mentioned Keith months ago, but she couldn't remember why.

She frowned and rolled onto her back. Certain memories were sketchy after the car crash, which had followed soon after the fencing tragedy. She had distractedly run a red light and been broadsided, resulting in no harm to the other driver, but a serious concussion and ensuing hospitalization for her. For days after her release she was unable to lay her head down and serial headaches continued thereafter, especially when she recalled the details of the fencing accident.

She tried to concentrate on Keith and what he could possibly have to do with the CIA, but she could bring nothing into focus. She insisted, pressing her brow with the heel of her hand, which only brought on the beginning of another headache. She stopped. A cold fear slithered through her like a snake in winter: a snake that was confused, lost, unable to find a place to hibernate.

She shivered, gathering the covers to her as she sat up. The morning light seemed to pose a question that for the first time Erika felt like entertaining. *And if she quit everything and went back to San Diego?*

"Welcome to Paradise," was how her father always greeted their visitors. Sea, palm trees, and perpetual sunshine, Bruno meant, though the latter wasn't always the case. In spring, rain could drum down for days, and many an afternoon Erika had lain on the beach under overcast skies. She actually found that soothing: dozing off in La Jolla Cove or on the beach of the Hotel Coronado, the sun's sting buffered by hazy clouds, her senses teased by the lazy squawk of a seagull gliding overhead, the lull of waves rocking in rhythm.

Simpler days, the ones before the fencing accident. Before her estrangement from Bruno and her failure with the CIA. *Simpler*—had the past *really* been simpler, or was she now looking back at a mirage?

Italy: it teemed with the beautiful, the bad, and the bizarre, and at least she had begun a different life here. Work, Paolo...*the rest*. She emitted a nervous laugh: she had, in fact, launched the espionage career denied her by the CIA. Complex, even sinister, considering Gino's threats and Paolo's secrets. Did Paolo *know* Gino...and was Gino privy to Paolo's fixation with Matilde Fassino?

Everything seemed to revolve back to the old woman, and this filled Erika with a surge of excitement. This morning she would take further action on the Fassino matter.

By the time she shut and locked the apartment door behind her, thoughts of San Diego had evaporated with the lingering beads of water in her freshly washed hair.

By now Erika was enjoying occasional breakfasts at Fausta's Déjà Vu. A croissant or brioche and a cappuccino, plus casual conversation with Fausta, made for a stimulating and cheerful start to the morning. But today would be slightly different, she knew, as she crossed via Garibaldi to the swishing-spraying sound of tires gliding over wet pavement. She hadn't heard it rain during the night and now the sun was playing tease, winking at her through greyish clouds.

She cozied up to the Déjà Vu's bar, finding Fausta's assistant Mara sharing the workload in the busy café. When a gaggle of customers scuttled out the door, Mara went to clear their tables, and Erika delicately asked Fausta how she was getting along.

"Better," she answered with a soft smile. She glanced at the calendar. "December eighth. Almost a week's gone by, though it doesn't feel like it. By the way, thank you for coming to the funeral, Erika—Paolo too."

"You're able to keep busy," Erika observed, as Fausta twisted off an espresso-machine arm and disposed of its grounds in the trash.

"It helps." She refilled the arm's cup, screwed it back on, and set the machine to dripping. Mara came to retrieve the newly-filled demitasse and take it away on her tray.

When the businessman standing next to Erika left and no one took his place, Fausta at last exhaled a *whew*. "Your usual?" she asked Erika.

"Thanks, and a croissant this time." As Fausta prepared Erika's cappuccino, Erika casually said, "You know a lot about the history of Turin, I think."

"Not really, I'm just one of many who like to pass on the tales." She cast Erika an affectionate smile, which lent relief to her drawn features.

"Well," said Erika, her breakfast now in front of her, "I've learned some interesting things from you, like the burning of heretics in Piazza del Municipio, not far from here."

"Oh, everybody knows that!" said Fausta with a mild

laugh.

"You natives, maybe. I've still got lots to learn. Lately I've been thinking about World War Two..."

"Another tragedy."

"I wouldn't blame you for seeing everything here as cursed."

"I haven't gone completely dark and dour, Erika. I didn't lose anyone in the war. I just have to learn to come to terms with...with what happened now."

"Of course." Erika took a sip of cappuccino and dabbed her lips with her napkin. "The reason I mentioned the war...Have you heard of Matilde Fassino?"

Fausta's brows slowly rose. "Now that's not a question I expect to hear from a foreigner."

"Probably not," Erika agreed with an amiable shrug. "But I know of someone who worked for Fassino."

"Not a pleasant experience, perhaps...Excuse me a second." A young woman had strolled in and parked herself at the end of the counter.

Erika observed her while Fausta made her a cup of tea. The woman was shorter than Erika but looked fit and athletic in her snug bellbottom jeans and tight leather jacket. Maybe she worked out, thought Erika, though not many Italians frequented a gym, particularly not women.

When Fausta returned, Erika continued her probing. "No, not a pleasant experience. Matilde Fassino and her husband stole this woman's savings and almost got her sent to a concentration camp."

Fausta shook her head and sat on a stool behind the bar. "What the Fascists did can never be truly righted. The problem is that Red militants use those crimes as one of their excuses to overthrow the government—to get rid of Fascists still in parliament under new names. Only the Reds have nothing legitimate to propose in return. Of course the Black militants are no better with their Molotov cocktails and car bombings. Many even defend criminals like Matilde

Fassino."

"Disgusting," said Erika. "And I guess she's rich too."

"Filthy rich. Got away with it all during the war. Sits up there in her villa on Superga with her hidden hoard of diamonds." Fausta left her stool to pick up a sherry-sized glass and fill it from a bottle of sparkling mineral water. "Well," she said, before taking a sip, "that's the urban legend, anyway."

"Diamonds?" Erika repeated, placing both forearms on the counter to lean in. She gave a quick glance down the bar. The athletic-looking woman was gazing out the window as she sipped her tea.

"Part of what she and her husband supposedly looted during the war," said Fausta.

Erika turned her head. With a click, the woman at the end of the counter had placed her cup in her saucer and was reaching into her pockets to pay. Strange—no purse.

Erika waited for the woman to settle up with Mara at the cash register and leave before turning back to Fausta. "So Matilde Fassino might have a cache of diamonds?"

"Only a rumor, but it would befit her."

"And they'd be in her villa?"

"On Superga. Have you been to the top of that hill? You can spot its baroque church from practically anywhere in the city."

"No," Erika replied distractedly.

"You really should visit it. On a clear day you can see the entire Alpine arc. Not that we've had any days like that lately. But the church really is magnificent. Have Paolo drive you up some time."

Paolo: surely he was aware of the rumored diamonds, which could only compound his resentment of the horrible old woman. He picked Erika up the following Friday night after dinner, and at half past nine they went out to a discotheque, where they sat on a yellow vinyl couch in the semi-darkness of the club. The whole complex was subterranean, and dim, sparse ceiling fixtures drizzled light into a cavern-like setting.

As she sipped sweet vermouth, Erika watched Paolo anxiously, unable to divert her thoughts from the baffling encounter with the Comrades and the cryptic, mustached Gino.

"I enjoyed our evening at Nadia's," she finally said. "We could have asked some of them along tonight."

Paolo interrupted his sip of beer to give her an enquiring look.

"Well," Erika specified, "Nadia, Flavio, and Ivan, anyway. From my talk with Matteo Mattei at the museum, I can't really imagine him—"

"Right. Sorry again about not mentioning him earlier." His expression was weary, a mixture of contriteness and a pinch of impatience.

"Yes, you were sworn to secrecy until Mattei released you from your vow."

Paolo shifted uneasily and turned to stare at the dance floor. Speakers trumpeted "Never Can Say Good-bye," while dancers, one couple deft at disco, swung to the rhythms.

"Sorry," said Erika, her voice raised to compete with the music. "I don't mean to make fun of you. I only wonder who else you haven't introduced me to."

"Of the Comrades? No one." He took another swallow of beer and returned his gaze to the dance floor.

Maybe he wasn't lying. Still, she couldn't ignore that someone in the group knew Gino, and that Gino knew about her and the CIA, plus some clueless "secret" regarding her brother Keith.

After Gloria Gaynor finished, Lucio Battisti took up the relay. The room pounded with strident electric guitar and booming bass, the Italian singer wailing "*Dio mio no!*"

There was no solving anything tonight. Erika grabbed Paolo's hand. "Come on, let's dance."

He shot her a wry wink. "The best thing I've heard all evening."

They slipped in among silhouettes gyrating across the shadowy floor.

After Battisti, Donna Summer kicked in. "Ooh, it's so good, it's so good, it's so good..."

Erika felt the electric rhythms pulsate within her, enlacing her in the magic of the intense beat and Summer's spiraling voice. She danced harder and harder, she and Paolo fixating each other as though hypnotized in a snake dance. Despite his deceptions, Erika still wanted him, craved his touch. And his eyes looked hungry too.

"I feel luh-uh-uh-uv..." resounded in her head when she and Paolo collapsed dizzily onto their backs on Erika's bed. Spent, they lay in silence, the electric sorcery of the dance floor still sparking between them. When the pounding inside her at last began to recede and she felt the room's chill, Erika sought to reclaim her thoughts; to relax and release them into the crystal ether of rationality. Only now she felt tethered to confusion—Gino, the Comrades, Matilde Fassino and her reputed diamonds. And *Paolo*. She reached to touch his arm and a tingling current licked her.

He stroked her belly with light fingertips and she gave a little gasp. Was she really falling for him? If so, she needed to get a grip on herself, for whatever she felt for Paolo was at this point fluid at best—slippery as an eel, transmutable as the mythical salamander.

20: The Sacred and the Profane

Rain drizzled off and on the next day as Erika and Paolo speculated on what to do with a lazy Saturday.

"I have an idea," said Paolo. "There is something I have meant to show you and it's indoors; it's one of the buildings I'm studying that has a bit of a mystery." He grinned at Erika's inquisitive frown. "I am not going say another word until we get there."

That afternoon, under a shared umbrella, they made the fifteen-minute walk to the square housing the Royal Palace of the bygone dukes of Savoy, who would be the future kings of Italy. The palace had all the trappings of a royal residence, including huge wrought-iron gates with bronze equestrian statues on either side of the entrance and immense gardens in the rear.

"I know you've already seen this palace," said Paolo, "but perhaps you haven't made a visit to the church of San Lorenzo." He pointed to a building next to the royal complex, then directed her to its tall, ordinary-looking wooden door, topped with a sculpted cherub.

"This is it? It doesn't look like a church," said Erika as she scrutinized the building's plain, sand-colored façade. Its upper-floor windows had shutters but lacked balustrades and could not compare to the elegance of many churches in central Turin.

"I know the exterior isn't grand," Paolo said, pulling open the heavy door. "But that is part of what makes it interesting."

The rain had stopped just as they entered the dim vestibule, and Paolo propped their umbrella in a corner.

Erika could barely make out columns and pews. As they advanced, dark colors began to materialize in a pale light filtering in from the windowed cupola above. An odor of must tickled her nose and the damp made her shiver and wonder what purpose this visit served.

Then, as if someone had flipped a switch, sun rent the low clouds, sending light cascading into the nave. Marble pillars with flowery Corinthian capitals flared a dark pink. A spattering of gilt appeared on the altar and elsewhere. Statues and oil paintings took form. Erika gazed in amazement at the cupola, discovering sculpted, interlacing stone interspersed with tiers of windows.

She turned to Paolo. "This is what you're studying? It's almost magical."

"We've been fortunate the sun came out. But look what else," he said, indicating the cupola's windows. "On each, how do you say, *equinozio*...?"

She thought for a second. "Equinox."

"Right. On the days of the autumn and spring equinox, the sun shines through the cupola at noon in a way that illuminates *that* particular fresco—he pointed to a wall. "It's called 'Dio Padre,' and without this light it would remain in the dark. Really, the process is more complicated but difficult to explain in English."

"You've done a pretty good job as it is!" She grasped Paolo's arm. He really was a student of curious architecture—in this he was truthful.

He squeezed her hand and continued. "Guarino Guarini designed and built San Lorenzo in the seventeenth century, a time when architects were more than builders. They didn't just put up a building, they added their genius. Architects were not just mathematicians, some were astronomers, astrologers, alchemists." His hand swept the air for emphasis, his eyes gleaming. When he noticed Erika watching him, he relaxed his posture. "Anyway, I'm studying how Guarini accomplished this effect of light."

Erika nodded at the church's baroque splendor. "It really is marvelous. Might it be a *coincidence* that your last name is *Lorenzi*? Is that another reason you're studying the church of San *Lorenzo*?"

"Maybe." He pulled her to him, nuzzling his face in her hair. "But Matteo Mattei would say there are no coincidences."

Erika stiffened but didn't comment. The mention of Mattei had instantly shattered her generous mood. Once more her thoughts flew to secrets Paolo shared with Mattei and the other Comrades. Mattei, as leader, could easily be behind the bully and blackmailer, Gino.

Paolo, apparently oblivious to Erika's change of humor, had pulled away and wandered towards the altar to continue his description of the church. "There's a passage behind there that is connected to the palace. That way the royal family could enter in private. They sat in special...*logge*." He squinted at her.

"Loges," she translated coolly.

Then, as if a power from above had changed its mind, the clouds closed ranks, plunging the nave once more into eerie shadows. The cramped, heavy ornamentation in the church now felt oppressive to Erika. The religious passion in the subjects of the oil paintings seemed almost sinister. She pressed her forehead with the heel of her hand.

"Is something wrong?" asked Paolo.

"It's just dark again."

"Right," he agreed with a sigh of disappointment. "We can leave and come back another time, if you'd like."

That remained to be seen. Right now San Lorenzo gave Erika the creeps and reminded her of the caginess of Mattei and the other Comrades, including Paolo himself.

They stopped for a bite to eat near the square, Paolo continuing to expound on the church and Erika slipping him sidelong looks. When Paolo again mentioned Mattei, quoting the Ginger Man's shared interest in the church of

San Lorenzo, she finally claimed a headache as an excuse to call it an afternoon.

Back at her building Paolo retrieved his car and Erika proceeded to climb the four flights of stairs to her attic flat, thoughts of the Comrades and their enforcer Gino trailing along like a ball and chain.

She was still brooding when she got to her door, absently pulling out her key and twisting it in the lock. She had barely got the door open when a massive shove from behind sent her sprawling onto the tiled living room floor. When she rolled to look back, a short, athletic-looking woman glared at her from the doorway.

The woman dove for Erika, landed a punch to her mouth that split her lip, then gripped Erika's coat lapels and slammed her head against the floor. When the woman drew back to cock her fist again, a dazed but conscious Erika lifted her knee and rammed it against her chest. The woman gave a short gasp, disengaging herself and scrambling to her feet. In a flash Erika felt a kick to her neck, and with a groan, rolled desperately away and staggered to her feet. The woman was waiting with an angry sneer, feet planted solidly apart, fists displayed. "You were told to stay the hell away from the Comrades," she snarled. "Now you'll have to be taught."

The words were like another punch in the teeth, one that this time ignited Erika's instincts. She thrust her right arm out, mimicking a saber, and parried a series of blows from the woman. With her left fist she delivered a jab to the woman's chin, only to receive a kick to the knee from her aggressor's hiking boot. Erika swallowed the electric pain then shot forward, head-butting the woman's belly and sending them both tumbling to the floor. With punches, the woman battered Erika's ribs, all the while grunting. "*You going to learn?*"

Despite the fire in her side Erika fought herself free, dodging towards the sofa, then feeling strands of hair ripped from her head. She let out a blunt cry but managed to scuttle to the back of the sofa. She had scarcely got to her feet when the woman hopped onto the sofa and vaulted over it. Erika parried another punch, then retreated towards the floor-length glass doors that opened onto the roof. She felt a tugging at her throat, the woman had caught the loose ends of the long scarf wound doubly around Erika's neck. Erika fumbled at the door handle. The woman yanked harder. "*Do I have to strangle you!?*" she panted.

With her left hand Erika pulled at the scarf around her neck; with her right she grasped the handle and twisted it, then hurled herself back as she yanked open the door. Pirouetting, she kicked the woman in the stomach and advanced onto the roof, her scarf now dangling freely behind her. The woman followed, keeping one hand anchored to the opposite window-door that remained fixed in place. Her dark eyes blinked rapidly. She couldn't seem to let go.

The rain had cleared but the roof remained slick, and for the first time Erika could feel her heart thudding, all her senses surging. Pounding burned her ears, scorched her throat, yet one thing floated crystal-clear in her mind—the woman was unsure of the roof, while Erika had ventured onto it before, getting a feel for her footing as she'd checked to see whether the door could be opened from the outside. It could not.

Erika let her knees flex, delicately shifting from foot to foot. The woman took another step forward, the fingers of one hand still clutching the doorjamb. In a flash of spontaneity, Erika whipped off her scarf and flung one end towards the woman, who instinctively caught and squeezed it. Erika yanked her end and the woman lost her balance, falling to her knees on the red tiles, scrabbling as she began sliding downward, her momentum stopping right before she reached the gutter. Swaying precariously, Erika managed to keep her balance. A hand reached for her ankle;

she sidestepped it, plucked up her scarf, and retreated back into her flat.

At last, able to breathe smoothly, she watched the woman start to creep, white-faced, back towards the window. "Who sent you!" Erika hurled at her. "Why do the Comrades want me out?"

No response. Only a pause as the woman shoved the bangs of her short brown hair away from her glowering eyes. In that moment Erika recognized her—the woman sipping tea at the counter of the Déjà Vu while Fausta spoke of Matilde Fassino's reputed diamonds. It enraged Erika that she had once more been stalked. "Who *are* you!" she shouted again. The only sound from the woman was her panting, as she continued to creep up the roof. Realizing she would get no answer from her stalker, Erika spoke with deliberate sarcasm. "I don't know if there's a way off these roofs—you might try crawling to another mansard and begging them to let you in." With both hands she clenched her scarf in front of her and snapped it taut, maybe to show the stalker she'd won, maybe to feel her own strength. Then she shut the door and twisted the handle into the locked position.

On her hands and knees, the woman continued to scowl at Erika through the mansard's window-doors. Finally she tottered to her feet and studied the window. Erika sucked in a breath, stepped back. The woman's glare had intensified. *Would she dare try to crash through the glass?* To break through she would have to take a few steps back before charging. But her hands were braced against the jamb. She was afraid of heights. And after spitting a final curse at Erika, she again lowered herself to her hands and knees and began a delicate trek across the tiles towards the mansard next door. As soon as she was out of view, Erika allowed herself a deep sigh.

21: The Comrades, One by One

Erika remained at the window, half tempted to open it to see where the ghastly woman had gone. Caution kept her rooted, however, with a new rush of fear hitting her as she licked blood from her lip. Once more she thought of contacting the police, and again balked at the idea of explaining her association with the Comrades, especially now that she'd expressed her wish to join them. The police might not take kindly to a foreigner associating with possible criminals. And then there was Paolo...She flicked her fingers—for now she would leave the police out of it. After drawing the floor-length curtains, she went to close the door to the flat and check herself in the mirror next to it. Her lip was swollen and bleeding on the inside, her hair and clothes a mess. She got cleaned up and threw on her coat. She needed to get out of the flat.

Outside the building, she gave a good look around. No sign of the woman who'd attacked her. She wouldn't dare return to confront Erika in broad daylight on the street. Avoiding the Déjà Vu and anyone who might comment on her fat lip, she ducked into a café she had never before patronized.

"Vecchia Romagna," she ordered, looking sideways at the serving girl. Another advantage to an anonymous café: no one would speculate about her ordering brandy in the middle of the afternoon.

The girl nodded and turned to leave, though not without glancing at Erika over her shoulder. Erika turned away towards the window. In general she found classic Italian café-bars, where you could order anything from coffee and sandwiches to a martini, stylish and open to a more varied possibility of encounters. This afternoon, however, she pictured the advantage of slinking into a dark American bar.

The cold fear she had earlier felt now mutated to hot anger, which finally gave way to complete perplexity and dismay. She massaged her aching side and fingered her sore, puffy lip, still tasting the acrid blood. When her brandy came she swirled the first sip around her mouth, wincing as it stung her cut, but grateful for its bracing properties and its masking of the unpleasant taste of rust.

So, setting Gino against her hadn't been enough for whoever they were. *And who the hell were they!?* Her right fist tightened as she took another swig of brandy. Gino's hectoring and threats of blackmail hadn't worked, so now they were unleashing a Doberman on her.

She shuddered and swallowed the rest of her brandy, which made her feel calmer. Matteo Mattei and Flavio Moretti—they were the wild cards in this twisted business. Next to Nadia, Erika knew the least about them. Or could she truly say she knew any of them...*especially Paolo*? He had refused to acknowledge Mattei until his hand was forced. Could he be also holding back about Gino and now this Doberman enforcer?

She sat back, her eyes almost glistening with frustration. She wanted to give Paolo the benefit of the doubt, yield to her feelings for him. But how could she, unless he *freely, and of his own initiative,* told her about everyone and their plans. She would not ask again and risk being lied to. She would not be played in this way by Paolo, particularly when he acted like he cared for her. *He had to come clean.*

Every path her thoughts took led to an impasse. She needed some air. She paid for her brandy and left the café.

A clear sky met her gaze, needles of icy air pricking her face as she looked up via Garibaldi towards Piazza Statuto.

Absently, she headed that way. She passed corso Valdocco, the ancient "Valley of the Killed," and shivered as she imagined ghosts clinging ethereally to time and space. When she reached the monument of the black angel she stopped and stared intensely. Twilight was claiming the late afternoon but she could still make out his grim expression and the black pentagram atop his head.

What do you think? You, who represent the genius of mankind, the triumph of human will over nature, the power of esoteric knowledge. But the youthful face with the stern eyes remained frozen, guarding its secrets.

She gazed at the naked trees in the square, their branches like black lace against a darkening sky. The air seemed to vibrate with electricity, rarefied and charged with something she ought to be able to see. Her thoughts turned back to the five Comrades, each like a single point of the angel's pentagram. She would engage them separately, she decided, each apart from the closed ranks of the herd.

The easiest to start with would be Ivan. Tomorrow was Sunday and she would request they meet in Asti, where he lived.

Clu-clung, Clu-clung. As the train rocked through the winter-brown hills toward Asti, humming its metal tune, Erika thought over what she had told Paolo the previous afternoon; that she could not see him the next day due to a family lunch with Elsa and Angelo. It seemed lying now came easily to both her and Paolo; unavoidable, the way things stood. Then again, hadn't their relationship begun with lies and omissions?

On the walk from Asti's station to the Cremeria, she let her thoughts drift back to that fog-soaked November morning: a stroll just like this one, from the station to Piazza Alfieri, a newspaper under her arm at the time, then her decision to go to the Cremeria instead of the Reale. That initial encounter with Paolo, the purse-snatcher, had been the first of the deceptions. Since then, the Cremeria had revealed much, and Erika thought it fitting to meet Ivan there. Maybe, one-on-one, he would open up to her.

"What happened to your lip?" he asked, once they were settled in with their drinks.

"The worse cold sore I've ever had." Another facile lie.

He squinted. "I've never seen one that bad."

"Right. So what've you been doing these days?"

Ivan shrugged. "Work."

"That's it?"

He gave her a bored nod. "What about you, are you still with Paolo?"

"Yeah...why, have you heard otherwise?"

"No. But you never know with people."

"I suppose..." She studied him as he twisted his cigarette in the ashtray, methodically tapping off its ashes. "You and I haven't hung out in a while," she said.

"...I've been so busy."

"Busy with the Comrades?"

His brows rose, a curious but guarded look.

"I was glad to finally meet them," said Erika. "What do you think of Matteo Mattei?"

"Mattei? Seems a typical boss type."

"When did you meet him?"

Ivan looked thoughtful. "...Sometime after the party at Nadia's."

"He seems fairly taken with himself. And what about that huge silence when I mentioned Matilde Fassino?"

Ivan sat back, took a long pull on his cigarette. "No idea," he answered through a stream of smoke. "Seems like Paolo's the one who has the problem with her."

Erika wanted to point out how all the Comrades had gone icy at the mention of Fassino, but she sensed he might get defensive; he was already looking around the café as if tired of the topic.

Erika took out a cigarette of her own. "Speaking—"

"How's—"

Their interrupting each other produced mutual smiles, with Ivan granting Erika his first genuine grin of the afternoon. "Go ahead," she said and lit her cigarette.

"Just wanted to know how life in Turin's coming along."

"Not bad—teaching, of course. That's how I met Paolo, and through him the Comrades." She paused for a drag from her cigarette. "Seems it's a pretty small group. No others besides you four?"

"No, I don't know of any others," Ivan said, stubbing out his cigarette with meticulous care.

It sounded believable. Erika couldn't imagine Ivan rubbing shoulders with either Gino or that Doberman woman. "I wonder when we'll meet as a group again?" she asked. "I'm kind of itching for an assignment. Have they given you one?"

Ivan rotated his glass of Bourbon on the table, giving the ice a jiggle. "One day I passed out fliers in Piazza Alfieri. Nothing important."

Maybe not. Still, a troubling idea occurred to her. Unwittingly, he may have helped the Comrades in more than distributing fliers. Back when she was a candidate, the CIA had told Erika they would be conducting a background check of her, and they could have easily investigated her family here. Could Ivan have found out about their inquiries? Maybe have told Mattei, who then could have set Gino to work on her?

No, she was leaping the lines of logic. The CIA would never have identified themselves as *CIA*.

"Well," she said to Ivan, "maybe they'll call us soon for another meeting. Who usually contacts you?"

For a moment Ivan paused to observe her, then said, "Nadia and Flavio. But I don't know when we'll next be contacted." He downed the rest of his Bourbon.

We? The only contact Erika expected was more visits

from the hound-emissaries. But she didn't comment, perceiving she would get nothing more from Ivan.

She went on to bring up family and friends she had met during summers spent in Asti. This seemed to cheer him a little more. "What about Luciano?" she asked.

"I never see him. Remember what a smart-ass he was?"

"Yeah," she agreed with a short laugh. "And Patrizia?"

"She moved to Genoa. Too bad—I liked her."

"Remember that summer in Pautasso, when we took all those pictures together in the field behind the church? When we used to hang out in the café all day?" A warm current of nostalgia flowed through Erika, paired with a fleeting sense of hope for the return of the old Ivan.

"Sure, that was fun," he said, wistfulness playing in his eyes. "But I don't see any of them anymore." And the wistfulness was replaced with a tone of finality, the thud of a closing door.

Melancholy filled her as she observed the youth she had known since her adolescent years. They were teens when they first met, and all that concerned them during those languid summer days was whiling away the afternoons in cafés and dancing away the nights at discos and country festivals. Only six years ago, but it felt like sixty.

When she suggested they pay a brief visit to their mutual cousins, Elsa and Angelo, he declined. It was almost dark when she left the Cremeria. December eleventh, and minutes of light were dropping from each day like the last brown leaves from the trees. Time wasn't the only loss she felt.

22: Taking Stock and Buying Insurance

Late Monday morning found Erika walking down via Roma, her mind abuzz. Without Ivan she had made more of her visit with Elsa and Angelo yesterday than a simple family chat. Had Elsa and Angelo heard of the diamonds secreted in Matilde Fassino's villa on the mount of Superga? Yes, they had. Many people said they'd been looted from the Jews, though Angelo and Elsa expressed skepticism that they existed at all.

Even so, the simple mention of Matilde Fassino had knocked the Comrades onto the back foot. Paolo hated the woman for personal reasons. But what about the others?

Matilde Fassino represented fascism and it was no coincidence that Erika had chosen via Roma for her walk. The street was the most famous upscale thoroughfare in Turin, regarded as a showplace of fascist architectural style when reconstructed in the 1930s. Dark-grey columns with severe Doric capitals lined the porticoed sidewalks, the latter stamped with marble geometrical designs; the whole of the street was illuminated at night by decorative lamps suspended between the columns. Elegant and linear, the street projected clear right angles for a no-nonsense right-wing regime.

As she approached Piazza Castello, Erika looked up to see the tip of one of the most famous buildings in Turin. *Infamous*, rather, one could say of the Torre Littoria, or Lictor Tower. Popularly called the Duce's finger, it symbolized Mussolini's fingerprint on the city. Erika could in fact imagine a digit pointing skywards. She'd never heard fondness expressed for the Torre Littoria, but it was the first

Italian building erected with skyscraper technology and therefore too innovative to warrant tearing down after the war. Erika thought the plain glass-brick structure stuck out like a sore thumb next to the splendid Baroque buildings around it; or rather, as the tallest building in Turin it thumbed its nose at the others.

Every fascist architectural detail about via Roma she had learned from Paolo the Red. Red versus Black, that's what this whole conundrum had come down to: the Comrades against Matilde Fassino and her ilk. Still, what could be so gravely at stake that now Erika was being stalked by *two* hounds, one threatening to reveal her connections with the CIA? And how did the thug Gino find out about that? *Somebody* had obviously betrayed her. Her thoughts jumped back to her visit to Elsa and Angelo. She had asked her cousins if they'd received any visitors a few months ago who might have inquired about their politics, couching her question in terms of the U.S. government considering her for employment. Yes, Angelo had replied, a man had approached him in the Cocchi Bar, a pollster surveying political persuasions; an Italian, though. Erika had let the subject drop, thinking the man could have indeed worked for the CIA, considering the agency employed retainers all over the world. The same man, or another agent, might have moved on to "survey" Ivan's family. But she wouldn't ask Ivan; given that banal encounters with political pollsters occurred as commonly in Italy as in America, her query would only invite questions of his own.

It was clear that the Comrades were hiding something. At the meeting at Nadia's, the room fairly reeked with obliqueness and obfuscation. Nadia and Flavio practically acted as if they didn't know each other, when a short time earlier they had played passionate lovers. *Acted, played.* Nadia, all sweetness and light and bubbles up until the meeting, had barely said good evening to Erika in the presence of Matteo Mattei. And Mattei—turning out to be an alchemist freemason!

So who would be the most likely candidate to have unleashed two hounds on her? Surely not Ivan, so new to the organization; not even Nadia, so deferential to Mattei. And God forbid it was Paolo, a prospect that chilled Erika to the bone. That left Flavio and the Ginger Man Mattei himself. Supposedly Flavio worked with Nadia in import-export. Yet at this point he seemed more an unknown quantity than Mattei. Either one of them could have sicked Gino and the Doberman on her, although Mattei made more sense as the hounds' master—Mattei, the chief of the Comrades.

She stood in Piazza Castello now, facing the schizophrenic castle-palace, its dark medieval towers glowering down at her. She felt a sharp tinge of nausea at the thought of Gino and his "secret" about her brother Keith. It maddened her that she couldn't remember what the CIA had said about Keith and her family in one of the interviews. Could Keith have somehow interfered in her recruitment? The idea seemed ridiculous. She didn't view her brother as a threat, if she discounted his hogging of their father's attention when they were children. No reason why he would want to sabotage her chances with the CIA. Nevertheless, as she gazed at the tops of the towers, where long ago stood guards in chain mail, her chest contracted with anxiety. The old pressure mounted in her head, dark heavy bricks, like those of the castle walls, piling on her brain.

She walked on, squeezing her eyes shut against the pain, clipping a woman's shoulder as they crossed paths. "*Scusi*," she said with a weak smile. The woman gave her a curious look then strode on, not bothering to respond.

Erika ducked into a café, sat and ordered a "long" espresso, hoping the extra dose of caffeine would calm her pulsating head. Not having slept for a second night after the

Doberman woman's attack didn't help matters either. Events and coincidences whirled in her mind, shards of a mosaic that refused to be glued into a comprehensible design.

She pulled out a cigarette and lit it. *They all might be against me*, she muttered to herself with a grimace. She inhaled deeply and released a long, steadying stream of smoke. She could tolerate the idea of Flavio and Mattei wanting her out. Even Nadia. But Ivan and Paolo?

Ivan had not acted normal when they last met, though she could imagine, for now at least, that he knew nothing about the Hounds. Paolo, on the other hand...Her thoughts drifted to the smooth firmness of his naked back, the concrete-hardness of his thighs, the silkiness of his freshly-shaven cheek. She wanted to let herself relax about him, so caring did he seem, so interested in her accomplishments. How impressed he was that she was a fencer, and what tenderness he had shown when learning about the fencing accident. Yet sitting here, finishing her cigarette, she bridled with mistrust. For when it came to matters relating to the Reds, Paolo's first inclination was to lie or dissimulate, acknowledging the truth only when caught out. He had canceled his session at school yesterday, Erika only finding out through Brigida, the secretary. Signora Sillano said he hadn't even called in the evening.

She stubbed out her cigarette and flicked her fingers—things would have to change drastically for there to be any future with Paolo.

She sat back with a sober sigh. At least the nicotine-caffeine cocktail had eased the pressure in her head. She looked at her watch: eleven-thirty. Soon she would have to return home, eat something, and get ready for work. The thought made her inhale sharply and straighten in her chair. Ever since the Doberman incident, anxiety accompanied her each time she climbed the stairs to her flat. Granted she hadn't seen the woman since, but she had to assume the bitch had somehow gotten off the roof; only when Erika was safely locked inside her flat did her nerves relent.

She lit another cigarette with the lighter she'd bought on a whim in a tobacco shop—the shop Paolo had entered that time she'd followed him. She had returned to the vintage *tabaccheria* at another time to buy a lighter. The shop's rich cherry-wood counters and shelves exhaled aromas of gentle ageing and woody tobacco. She had spotted Paolo's brand; "Clan," it was called, its package sporting a Scottish plaid. She'd told the shopkeeper she needed a lighter and perused a display case of various sorts of knives as she waited: penknives, woodcarving knives, hunting knives, and—something that piqued her interest— a stiletto.

Her thoughts back in the present, Erika expelled a series of reflective smoke rings: *yes, it was just what she needed*. She picked up her purse, paid her bill, and left the café for the tobacco shop.

Weapons interested Erika, especially those with élan. In storage, in San Diego, she kept her fencing weapons, a saber and two foils. Now she stood once more before the glass display case in the fragrant *tabaccheria*, eyeing the stiletto. The shopkeeper watched her impersonally, every now and then gnawing his mustache.

"Could I see this one?" she asked, pointing to the specimen with the pearly-white handle.

The man removed the stiletto from the case, turning it in his hand for her appraisal. He closed the blade, then pulled it back open with his left fingers, his right hand producing a whipping motion so that the blade flew fully extended and locked into place.

Other than its shiny handle, the knife wasn't fancy; more important was its approximately three inches of gleaming blade, which ended in an extremely sharp tip, Erika learned when handling it herself. She examined its stainless-steel, offset guards. Her fingers felt comfortable against them. The weapon felt comfortable overall. With a prick of excitement she rotated it with nimble fingers.

"Press the knob at the base of the handle to retract it," said the shopkeeper in a professional tone.

Erika did so, then pushed the blade back into the handle, registering a click as the blade locked shut. She pulled it back open, inserting her thumbnail in the designed indentation on the blade's ridge, and flicked her wrist. Nothing moved.

The man gave a faint frown. "Try opening it a little more."

She pulled at the blade and tried again. This time the whip of her wrist produced a solid click as the blade achieved its extension. She rotated it again, smiling to herself at its glinting silver. "I'll take it."

The clerk nodded impassively, taking the knife back to complete the sale. As soon as she paid, Erika wanted to slip the stiletto into her coat pocket but decided it best not to appear too enthusiastic. She let the man box and bag it, though as soon as she entered her building and began the ascent to her flat, she released the stiletto from its packaging, gripping it as if she were shaking hands with a partner.

Inside her apartment she began a tactile inspection of her new acquisition. She fingered the stiletto's handle— knobs, screws, guards. This time she flicked it open on the first try. Yes, the weight and balance felt right. Although she really only knew fencing blades, instinct told her the essence was in the finger-play, as in the manipulation of a foil. How familiar to have a weapon in her grip again—good and natural, a logical extension to her hand.

She let her knees flex into *en garde* position, she practiced her parries with the stiletto, advancing and lunging, the thrill of confidence and empowerment sweeping through her like a musical symphony; such *vitality* after those months of...she stopped. As quickly as she had swelled inside, deflation followed. Her arm dropped and her eyes closed as the fencing tragedy bullied its way back into her thoughts. Slowly she folded the stiletto's blade back into its handle: *self-defense—she'd simply bought herself an insurance policy.*

23: Love and a Touch of Black

Paolo finally got in touch with Erika and came to her flat that evening after dinner. Regarding his canceled session at school the day before, he explained, "I've had an interview at an architectural firm." He looked preoccupied, eyes bloodshot and flickering, and Erika wondered what else might be consuming his attention.

She turned on the radio to blunt the tension fraying her nerves. It wasn't easy standing there facing Paolo, with the Doberman and Gino on her mind. Even tutoring, a job she could practically do in her sleep (*when* she could sleep), seemed oppressive these days, as she remained ever watchful for the reappearance of one of the two hounds. Paolo took a tall bottle of beer from Erika's half-size fridge and poured out two glasses.

She accepted one, eyeing him carefully as he sat beside her on the sofa. His lips parted, she waited for something to come forth, but instead he brought the glass to his mouth and guzzled a good portion. A sigh of fatigue followed as he set his glass on the floor and got up to retrieve his pipe from his jacket. As he settled back down and packed it with tobacco from the plaid pouch labeled Clan, she thought of the *tabaccheria*...its pungent though pleasant scents...her stiletto, nesting in the drawer of the end table next to her.

"What are you thinking about?" he asked.

She blinked at him and lit a cigarette, placing the ashtray on the floor next to their glasses. "Just wondering about your decision to get an actual job."

"I've told you, I don't plan to live with my father forever."

"I understand—in America you'd be well on your own at twenty-six."

"Like you at twenty-four...do you ever miss your parents?"

"...Sometimes." Watching Paolo smoke his pipe reminded her once more of Bruno. Tonight she saw her father not only in the way Paolo's lean hand held his pipe, but in his tired features, a vulnerable look. When Erika was small, Bruno's occasional haggard countenance worried her, filled her with an irrational fear that something bad might happen to him. She felt a confused urge to kiss Paolo's fatigued brow and eyes. Instead, she shook herself and took a drag from her cigarette.

As she leaned down and placed her cigarette on the ashtray, she saw Paolo's pipe joining it. He put his arms around her. "I'm glad you're not living with your parents, or with your cousins in Asti."

She inhaled a mingling of spicy smoke and fresh aftershave. She hugged his shoulders, and as his mouth slid toward hers, she turned her lips to his ear. "Is this the *only* reason you're glad I'm on my own?" she whispered.

He loosened his embrace and frowned at her. "Do you believe I'm profiting from you?"

"No," she said, slightly amused at his direct translation from Italian. "I don't think you're taking advantage of me."

"I love you," he said.

She stared at him in masked wonder. The lines on his forehead had deepened and she read concern in his eyes. He was worried she had misunderstood him, which made her loosen her guard. "I love you too," she replied before she could check herself.

He took her in his arms again and held her so tightly she could hardly breathe. Her side hurt where the Doberman had pummeled her, and in an urge to release herself she bumped her glass with her foot. "Whoops," she said when it rattled on the tile floor.

They pulled apart. "*Whoops*—I like that expression!" Paolo said, laughing as he rose to remove both their glasses to the kitchen.

She stood up and replaced the ashtray on the end table. She needed air and space. When he returned he cupped her face in his hands and kissed her. "*Davvero, ti amo*," he emphasized in Italian—*truly, I love you*—looking more vulnerable than ever.

"*Sì*," she answered numbly, confusion causing her thoughts to gyrate in dizzying loops.

Paolo hugged her again, this time more gently. She ran her fingers along his back. Fingers were intelligent; if only they could fathom what was going on here.

"Shall we?" he said, glancing at the sofa waiting to be unfolded.

"I'd like to just go to sleep tonight. Do you mind?"

"No...I'll sleep beside you."

They released the bed from the sofa. Erika changed in the bathroom, so Paolo wouldn't see the bruises on her side. She lay on her unbruised side, staring into the darkness as Paolo breathed behind her. *I love you, truly,* echoed in her head. *Truly,* she would need convincing of this.

In the morning's early hours, Erika could doze no longer. The pale light of another overcast day filtered through the crack in the drapes covering the long window doors. She wished she could go back to sleep, postpone thinking of what she would say if Paolo, who was still slumbering, were to insist he loved her in the stark clarity of day. First and foremost she would have to demand he come clean about the Comrades.

By the time he woke, Erika was dressed and sitting at the kitchen table with the radio on low.

"You're up early," he said with sleepy irritation.

"Did the radio wake you?"

He rubbed his eyes. "No, I don't think so. It's okay,

anyway."

Once the coffee was made they sat down at the table. "We could go for a drive before you have to be at work," Paolo suggested as they dipped biscotti in their caffè latte.

"We could go anywhere, see anyone we'd like...we haven't gone out with friends lately..."

Paolo drained the last of his coffee and rose. He walked around the table and bent over next to her ear. "Or, we could pass the day on our own—only us, here," he murmured, kissing her neck.

"Hmm...You know, it's been a while since I've seen Nadia and Flavio on their own. I'd like to maintain my friendship with them."

Abruptly he turned away and went back to his chair. "I'm sure they are working."

"True, but I was thinking of Nadia mainly. She's almost always available for lunch and she's got a long lunch hour. Or we could call and arrange to meet them both for dinner one night this week..."

Paolo frowned at his empty cup. "They aren't a couple, you know."

Exactly. So what are they, and who are they? Erika restrained herself. "Oh," she said, faking surprise, "then I really should get to know each one separately."

"Erika," said Paolo, shifting in his chair, pushing his cup and saucer aside. "I'm becoming less and less convinced of the Comrades. I'm not sure what they do will lead to anything productive."

Erika stared at him, this time in authentic surprise. "But we've had a meeting, and I told them I want to get involved. I'd like to meet others—"

"There *are* no others. And I don't believe that getting involved is a good idea at this point. You're a foreigner and you could get into trouble—even end up deported, and I couldn't stand that."

No others? What had transpired since she'd last seen

Paolo? The Doberman visit, for one thing. Erika studied him as he frowned and fidgeted with his napkin. "What about you, are *you* splitting from them?"

"...Probably." He lowered his gaze to examine his hands. "It may take a little time, but yes, I'm looking for a serious job and I shouldn't be associated with them."

This didn't ring right. What were his real intentions regarding the Comrades other than getting her to back away? Which would make sense now more than ever if he knew about the Doberman's attack. A chill grazed her spine. The coincidence of his telling her he loved her, followed by his fear for her deportation...were they real?

A subtle smile creased her lips. "Well, Nadia's my friend and Ivan's my cousin. Why should I drop them?"

"See them as friends but stay out of their communist affairs. Can you do that for me?" His eyes were pleading. "Can you trust that I love you and want to keep you safe and happy here?"

Love, safety, happiness...just twisted words. Entwined with *suspicion*, *disappointment*, and *mistrust*, they hung in the air above Erika like some kind of crazy Gordian knot. A knot she longed to slash with a saber. Her smile remained frozen in place; faintly she nodded at him.

"Good!" he exclaimed, as if all was now settled. "So what shall we do today?"

Erika continued to stare at him, marveling at his perky tone, at how he had changed the subject as though by decree. She struggled over what to say next, when an announcement came over the radio:

An explosion in Turin at a small newspaper press called Il Cardinale; one man killed and one injured; the offices ablaze; Molotov cocktails suspected.

Paolo had leaped towards the radio, turning up the volume before the bulletin ended. "*Cristo Santo!* Giorgio and Franco run the *Cardinale*—I know them! I've got to go there."

Erika gaped, as his panic obliterated her own concerns. "I'll come with you."

They couldn't get near corso Regio Parco where the newspaper *Il Cardinale* was located. Emergency vehicles and police had the road blocked and officers were waving traffic away. Smoke still curled into the sky, vicious and acrid, while the din of horns and shouting and whistles suffused the air with frenzy. Paolo found a side street where they parked and began striding towards the police barricade.

"I can't believe it—one of them is dead!" he repeated in Italian.

"Could someone else have been working there?" Erika asked, as no names had been revealed in the broadcasts they'd followed on their way over.

"No. They work alone."

So which of Paolo's friends had died in the blast and who were the perpetrators? On the ride over, Paolo had suggested Black terrorists. "If it's Black terrorists," asked Erika as they approached the smoking offices of the *Cardinale*, "would there be one group, or a variety like the Reds?"

"They are many," he replied, shaking his head.

A swarm of reporters with cameras, notepads, and handheld recorders were milling at the barricade. As Erika and Paolo wormed their way through, camera flashes and shouting erupted around them.

Two *Carabinieri* of the police branch of the military kept the crowd back. One shoved the palm of his grey-gloved hand at Erika and Paolo before they could touch the police tape. "Keep back," he said. Taller than Erika, he was imposing in his black knee-high boots and gleaming helmet. His black uniform had a red stripe down the trousers and grey goggles hung from his neck. She took a step back.

Paolo stood his ground and argued. "But my friends are

inside!"

The officer's eyes turned back to the reporters, a handful of whom had started to barge forward again once they noticed the attention given to Paolo. "The injured have been taken to the CTO. That's all I can tell you," he said, waving Erika and Paolo on their way.

Paolo grabbed Erika's hand. "We'll have to go to there, it's the hospital that specializes in burn injuries."

In the car they heard the confirmation on the radio: *a neo-fascist group is being sought for the firebombing of Il Cardinale newspaper offices.* Paolo gritted his teeth and clenched the steering wheel. Erika flicked her fingers, her pulse racing.

24: Confusion in the Ranks

After speaking to admission personnel Paolo and Erika reached Giorgio Testa's room in the CTO hospital specializing in burn injuries. No patient called Franco Galli had been admitted and the admissions representative refused to comment further.

"Only the two of them worked in the *Cardinale*," repeated Paolo with a hollow voice and haunted eyes. "So Franco's dead, the radio just won't release his name yet."

Erika didn't reply. Concern for Paolo weighed on her as did an ever-growing alarm. Violence from the Reds had already erupted in her own neighborhood and claimed the life of Fausta's nephew, and now the extreme Right had attacked close to home as well. She wondered why Paolo hadn't told her about his friends, Franco and Giorgio, and their left-wing newspaper, *Il Cardinale*.

"We're here to see Giorgio Testa," Paolo announced to the representative at the entrance to the burn unit.

"What is your relation to him?" asked a middle-aged woman in lay garb.

"He's my friend."

The woman gave both Paolo and Erika a visual once-over before continuing. "He's been treated for burns. Have a seat and I'll tell the nurses you're waiting."

Paolo and Erika took a seat on a wooden bench in the hall. Forearms resting on his thighs, Paolo frowned at his laced fingers, while Erika watched white-clad nurses and doctors sail through the halls, clip clopping in their white clogs. At one point Erika put her hand on Paolo's back and felt it stiffen. He didn't respond further, and after a moment she pulled her hand back.

A nurse came out of Giorgio's room across the hall. "You can see him now."

Paolo was on his feet and moving before she could finish, Erika following him into the room with apprehension.

"Giorgio," he murmured, as they approached a man in one of six beds, three of which were not occupied.

Paolo reached out to touch him but distress contorted his face and he dropped his hand.

"Paolo," said the bandaged man, holding out his hand.

After giving it a delicate shake Paolo patted Giorgio's head where hair was exposed. "You look like a mummy," he said with a stiff-upper-lip smile.

"Beware of my curse." Giorgio allowed himself a muted chuckle, then regarded Erika.

"Sorry," Paolo apologized with a distracted look. "This is Erika, my girlfriend from America. She's living here now."

"Good to meet you, Erika." Half of Giorgio's right cheek was bandaged, though he managed a smile. "You've chosen a difficult moment to settle in Italy, but welcome, anyway."

Erika liked this man whose sense of humor seemed bigger than his ordeal. He was large in size, too, one of the heaviest men she had seen in Italy, whose combined humor and girth conveyed a strong confident presence. Rather than feeling fearful or uncomfortable vis-à-vis his injuries, she felt at ease.

"You don't really look like a mummy," she said, returning a smile. "Maybe just your upper arm and that side of your face and head." Short-cropped brown hair still capped the left half of his head, and both of his eyes were visible.

"I was lucky," he said, with a first hint of despondency.

"And Franco..." said Paolo.

Giorgio shook his head and shifted his bulk, causing the bedframe to groan. "The window shattered and the petrol bomb lit the stacks of newspapers on fire. Franco started pulling our record books off the shelf, one fell behind and he wrenched the shelf away from the wall." Giorgio gazed away before continuing. "The whole thing came down on him. He was unconscious and I tried to pull the shelf off him..." He looked down at his hands. "But I couldn't breathe, and then I couldn't see through the smoke."

Erika glanced at Paolo whose eyes looked sunken and lost. He swallowed. "There's nothing you could have done."

Giorgio gazed away again. Respectfully, Erika turned her attention towards the two other male patients in the room, both bandaged in various patterns, one sleeping, the other casting discreet glances at Giorgio, Paolo, and her.

"Who do you think did it?" asked Paolo.

Giorgio returned his attention to them, his eyes grim. "The Black Order. We've received anonymous threats." He leaned back against his propped-up pillows and glanced at Erika. "I'd invite you two to sit, but I don't think I can play the entertaining host for much longer." He barked a dry laugh and his eyelids began to flutter. "They've given me enough dope to bring down an elephant."

Paolo patted Giorgio's shoulder. "Get some rest, we'll talk later."

"Right...later," said Giorgio, and closed his eyes.

"Are you up to driving?" Erika asked Paolo as they walked to the car. "If you want, I can..."

"I'm fine," he replied with a glance at the cold, anemic-white sky. "Miserable bloody day."

As they pulled away from the hospital Erika pondered him, empathy for Paolo's present state of mind and an urgency to know his ongoing secrets playing tug-of-war inside her.

"Were you close to Franco the way you seem to be to Giorgio?" she asked him.

In an apparent burst of frustration he accelerated, passed a car and cut back in front of it. Steadying himself he said, "Both were my friends."

Both...Were. Erika waited and watched him.

"We broke a while ago," he explained.

"You broke off your friendship with them?"

Paolo rubbed his neck in irritation. "They didn't approve of the Comrades."

"Their newspaper the *Cardinale* is left-wing..."

"Yes," Paolo sighed, "but Giorgio and Franco are Socialists, not Communists...Franco *was*, that is." His eyes darkened and Erika touched his shoulder.

He gave a little flinch. "Giorgio and Franco thought I was becoming too extreme and so do I now. I've told the Comrades I'm finished."

Erika tilted her head in surprise. She didn't want to contradict Paolo in his grief, but just this morning he'd hinted he would have to back away gradually from the Comrades.

She took a different tack. "What's wrong with them if all they do is write tracts and pass out fliers?" She wondered how much the newspapermen, Giorgio and Franco, had known about Mattei and his group...*even* of certain individuals and their penchant for violence. Could that have pushed them to break with Paolo?

Those goddamned Hounds: Why was someone in the group, or all of them, taking such drastic measures to run her out? At this point she didn't know which maddened her more, Gino's bizarre attempt to blackmail her or the aggression of the Doberman woman.

And of course one couldn't forget Matilde Fassino and her reputed diamonds. Before Paolo could answer her first question Erika posed another. "The Comrades aren't up to anything illegal, are they? Nothing to do with Matilde Fassino...?" She longed for him to open up of his own accord and so stopped short of mentioning the diamonds.

"*Ma lascia perdere Matilde Fassino!*" Paolo tightened his grip on the wheel, his jaw clenched as firmly as his hands. "I've told you why I stole her purse and there's nothing more."

Her mind spun like a carnival ride. *Drop Matilda Fassino!* She didn't know how to respond and touched his shoulder again.

He pulled away and continued sternly in Italian, "I assure you that I don't know what the Comrades are doing now. I've already told you I've finished with them and you must do the same. Look what can happen to even peaceful Socialists in this city. The Black Order are fascist terrorists—they could attack *us* next. Do not ask me about the Comrades again." He ran desperate fingers through the waves of his hair.

All the same, his rudeness made her burn with indignation and she had to force herself to stay calm. "Listen," she said in English, as they neared her neighborhood, "why don't we stop someplace for a drink." She checked her watch. "It's not even too early for lunch. Eating would do you good."

"I can't eat anything," he responded in Italian. "I'll have to drop you off at home."

"You're not coming back with me?" she asked in Italian.

"I can't. I'll call you later."

He pulled in front of her building, foot holding down the clutch, unlike when he usually dropped her off and they loitered to chat, the car in neutral or its engine extinguished altogether.

She retrieved her purse from the floor, and keeping her voice even said, "Well, I guess we'll talk later."

"Sure." He parted his lips and took in a small breath but remained silent.

She opened the door, slid out slowly, and looked back. "Ciao, then."

"Ciao," he repeated bluntly.

For an instant she stood frozen. *If he doesn't reach out to me...*

But he didn't, and she finally shut the door.

Numbness seized her as she watched Paolo's car trail off down via Garibaldi. She looked up at her flat in dismay, then let her feet propel her across the street to the Déjà Vu. She needed to think but didn't want to be alone.

"Ciao, Erika," Fausta hailed from behind the counter.

Erika blinked distractedly before returning the greeting and sitting at a table.

"What can I bring you?"

Like Paolo she found herself neither hungry nor thirsty. "Just some hot tea, please," she told Fausta with a distant look.

Fausta eyed her, started to speak, then turned to address another customer.

Sitting with her tea, Erika stared at nothing while her thoughts grappled with everything.

After fifteen minutes she left the café for the Egyptian museum. If Paolo would not talk to her, not commit to seeing her, she would have to continue with her own plan. There would be no future for them until she discovered the truth. When she reached via Academia delle Scienze she inhaled deeply and entered the museum.

"I'm Erika Rivoli, here to see Matteo Mattei. I was here before and he invited me back at my convenience."

The receptionist scanned Erika briefly then, picked up the phone. "You have a visitor. Erika Rivoli—says she's already seen you and you said to come back."

Cazzo, Erika swore to herself during what seemed a long pause. *Come on, Ginger Man!*

"...All right." The woman hung up. "Wait here, he'll arrive shortly."

Erika stepped into the exhibition hall, pacing absently, until little by little she was once more seduced by the magnificence of the room: the polished-black statues of animal gods; towering kings and queens who smiled serenely. An old black-and-white movie she had seen as a child came to mind. In the film they were entombing a dead pharaoh in his pyramid, but somehow a live person had got trapped inside. Blocks upon blocks of enormous grey stone began to slide into place, imprisoning and suffocating everything inside. The scene had frightened her at the time, and now as she observed a monumental statue of the jackal god of embalming, a frisson brushed her.

"Anubis..." came a voice from behind her. Erika gave a start before turning to engage the narrow eyes of Matteo Mattei. "People find him one of the most fascinating gods," he said.

"I find this whole culture mysterious," she replied, steadying her nerves.

Though she exceeded Mattei in height by half a head, she felt the air of dominance in his barrel-like bulk, his wide-legged stance, his ironic smile. "Still interested in volunteering here?" he asked, sweeping the air in the room with his hand.

The patronizing comment made her bristle with renewed confidence. "Actually, I came here to discuss the Comrades. After my one and only meeting with you, I thought you understood I want to get involved." She spread her hands. "So far though..."

She caught a twitch at the corner of Mattei's mouth. He glanced at the noon crowd milling about the room. "It's almost time for lunch—why don't you come to my office."

He indicated a chair in front of his desk, then settled in his own leather chair behind the desk. Erika immediately sensed he held a kind of strategic advantage. Stacks of folders, neat piles of paper, and various knick-knacks formed a sort of barrier behind which he sat comfortably. The bookshelf behind him, laden with tomes, furthered Erika's image of him ensconced within his fortress. Casually he picked up a pen from the desk and placed it in its shiny brass holder. He sat back and laced his fingers over the vest of his dark-blue pin-striped suit.

Erika felt a bit uneasy across from him in her casual corduroys. She crossed her legs. Her eyes roamed over his desk and lighted on a small metal ashtray with twin cigarette holders in the form of crocodiles, their jaws open to lock onto a smoke. She pulled out a Marlboro.

"Sacred crocodiles of the Nile," she observed, reminded of Mattei's own somewhat crocodilian smile. She offered the pack to him.

Smiling politely, he waved her off and pushed the ashtray towards her. He picked up a heavy table lighter shaped as a hippopotamus, and once he'd lit her cigarette he sat back again. "So, Erika, you've been feeling neglected."

Erika drew on her cigarette, hesitating before placing it between one of the crocodile's jaws. The ashtray was spanking-clean. "Well," she said, "Paolo hasn't had any news since we met at Nadia's. I thought you might eventually have something for me to do."

He smiled at her cigarette suspended between the crocodile's jaws. It was almost as if the ashtray had never been used before and was being inaugurated. His smile slid back to her. "I don't know whether Paolo has told you, but we are toning things down for now. Events are inordinately in flux at the moment." He tilted his head and scratched a ginger sideburn. "Have you heard about the bombing of the *Cardinale* newspaper?"

Erika tried not to look surprised. She plucked up her cigarette and took a drag. The attack at the *Cardinale* had only happened this morning; the "toning down" of the Comrades' activities must have started earlier. "I'm aware of that attack," she said, curious as to whether Mattei knew about Paolo's ties to the owners. "I would think such a horrendous act against the Left would make you even more determined."

Mattei nodded soberly. "The impulse for revenge is understandable. Still, unwise is the man who rushes to reprisal. Seriously, we have to pause and reflect. *Lie low and regroup*, as you say in English. As a foreigner I would imagine you, of all people, would want to back away now."

Back away—just what they all wanted her to do. "Because of the *Cardinale*?" she asked. "One of Paolo's friends died there. I can't exactly feel indifferent."

"Mm," he reflected. "Tragedy has hit Paolo close to home once more. I'm sorry about that."

Mattei was mocking Paolo again, Erika was sure of it, and she had a mad urge to slap his fat pink face.

"I don't know how Paolo will proceed after all of this," continued Mattei, "but I, for one, plan to devote more energy to calmer pursuits for the time being."

"Like your involvement with the Masons? You know, that still puzzles me. You're a Communist, but aren't Masons supposed to be religious?"

"Ah, you presume I'm an atheist! In Masonry, it is understood that we all believe in a higher power, simply something greater than ourselves. Naturally we welcome all sorts of Christians, and even Jews. But we're not restricted to institutionalized faiths. I, for example, harken to ancient pagan beliefs and the energies of the earth. Remember my mention of the church of the Great Mother?"

Erika sat straighter in her chair. "Yes, and I went there and saw the statue of the Grail."

"Yes, one of its mysteries, along with its informal dedication to Isis, one of the manifestations of the Great Mother Earth goddess. Both ancient Egypt and the Holy Grail are important in Masonry."

Erika leaned forward and stubbed out her cigarette, intrigued in spite of herself. "So you believe in both Isis and the Grail?"

"Well," and here Mattei chuckled, "I can't confirm the Grail is hidden here in Turin, as the local legend has it, but

I believe in the Oneness of creation—that Isis, Ishtar, or however you want to call the ancient mother goddess-creator has not relinquished her power. Alchemy has followed, poles of energy have been harnessed...Christianity and the Grail, along with all religions, are merely different expressions of the ongoing fluxes of the universe. I only acknowledge that the ancient Egyptians achieved mighty accomplishments, aligning their pyramids astronomically to the constellations of Isis and Osiris, building the enigmatic sphinx...but you must understand me by now—look where I work and live." He grinned and spread his arms to encompass not only his office, but it seemed the entire museum and city of Turin.

Erika had to shake herself. She hardly knew where she was after Mattei's fantastical discourse. Understand him? He was a sphinx himself. But weren't they all: Ivan, Nadia, Flavio, Paolo. *Paolo*. She gritted her teeth at the sting of their parting.

"Oh, look at the time," said Mattei, nodding at a clock on the wall inscribed with obscure numbers. "Those," he pointed out, "are Hindu numerals, the original Arabic numerals, quite different from our modern ones. But I've held the stage far too long and forced you to be my audience. Let me accompany you out."

Before rising she inspected him one last time. Before he could reach her side of the desk, she said, "But do you believe in communism as much as...*this other thing?*"

He halted for an instant and leaned against the desk. "I'm a man of dichotomies like most of us," he said, gazing reflectively past her. Then he resumed rounding the desk and met her eyes. "But I find most things reconcilable to the whole, yin and yang, light and darkness, good and evil, and so forth. Of course I'm still devoted to the cause of the Left; my country is in a revolution." He patted her on the back. "And you'd do best to stay out of it."

She shrugged. "Maybe you're right."

As she stood on the sidewalk outside the museum, she felt a sense of dubious accomplishment. Mattei might think she was backing away, which could give her more room to maneuver...if only Paolo would call soon. She buttoned her coat up to her collarbones and sighed. Both her scarf and gloves now lay at home in her armoire, the former a proven hazard in her new life, the latter an encumbrance if she were forced to defend herself. She headed down the sidewalk, hunched against the cold, her right hand fondling the stiletto in her coat pocket. She had another meeting to plan before going to work.

25: Another Two Down

Tinkling came from the coils of Erika's tall grey radiator as she sat at her kitchen table. Normally she found the subtle noise soothing, associating it with warmth, like the sound of a crackling fire. This afternoon it reminded her she was alone on the day after the firebombing of the *Cardinale* and Paolo's retreat from her. He hadn't called, and yet three times he had insisted he loved her. Her eyes narrowed as she pictured him rudely ordering her to drop the Matilde Fassino issue and desist from mentioning the Comrades, lecturing her with his typical ambiguity, only now in Italian. Yes, the shift to Italian was symbolic, a signal that things had changed dramatically in their relationship...*whatever the hell it was.*

She had told him she loved him on impulse, and now her anger over his behavior muddled her thoughts on that subject even further. With a sigh of irritation she roughed up her hair and forced herself to think about the bigger picture. *Why* had Paolo so vehemently commanded her to drop Matilde Fassino and the Comrades? There had to be more to it than the attack on the *Cardinale*. Matteo Mattei had said the Comrades were going on hiatus: "Hasn't Paolo told you?" *No—on the contrary, he said you were ratcheting things up and he wanted out.* So who was telling the truth? *As usual, probably no one.*

She pushed away from the table and went to have a look out the glass doors that opened onto to the roof. Reminded of the Doberman woman, she crossed to the armoire to fetch her stiletto from her coat pocket. Flicking the blade open—practice was making her proficient—she wondered what the Hounds might be up to. Gino hadn't surfaced in a while, but had he made good on his threat to inform the Comrades of her association with the CIA and whatever her brother Keith was involved in?

Keith. She traded the stiletto for a Marlboro and sat on the sofa. Keith was four years younger than Erika and they had never been close. She hadn't talked to her brother in ages, couldn't remember when she had last seen him. Everything had gone south after the fencing accident, and the car crash hadn't helped her memory. She shuddered at that interval, short, thank God, when she was unable to speak due to the blow to the left side of her head.

She took a long pull from her cigarette and flopped onto her back on the couch, ever thankful she could lay her head down; for even after her release from the hospital, pain and nausea had kept her propped up while sleeping. She blew streams of smoke towards the old-fashioned light fixture on the ceiling, focusing on her next move: Nadia. Erika had called her yesterday after meeting Mattei, and made a date to visit her in her flat this evening after school. She would get what she could out of the loquacious Nadia. Then, if necessary, she would move on to Flavio, though that might prove trickier. *Much trickier*.

At Nadia's, Erika turned down coffee for a glass of mineral water. She'd hardly slept last night after the *Cardinale* bombing and didn't want to risk another "white night" by drinking coffee at nine o'clock.

"Not too tiring, I hope, coming by after work?" asked Nadia, sitting on the opposite end of the sofa.

"Not really. I haven't seen you or the other Comrades for a while, and I wanted to catch up."

At this Nadia offered a thin smile, and Erika wondered if her mind was churning with what she was allowed to say or not. Her auburn hair looked more tousled than usual, and over her jeans she wore a red, long-sleeved t-shirt, stamped with a large image of the brand Marlboro, in its signature red, white, and black. Erika had noticed it immediately upon entering and thought it a bit silly. Erika smoked Marlboros but wouldn't dream of advertising them. In Italy, on the other hand, the brand held cachet. (She smiled to herself at Nadia, the Communist, flashing a major capitalist brand.)

"It *has* been a while," agreed Nadia in a distant tone, kicking off her flats and curling up on the sofa.

"Since the meeting here," Erika reminded her.

"*The meeting*," Nadia acknowledged, looking away. "Seems eons ago."

"That's why I wondered what was going on—why no one's followed up..." She let her voice trail off question-like.

Nadia's Italian cigarettes lay atop a set of glass nesting tables in front of the sofa. She offered one to Erika, who accepted it willingly so as not to trot out her Marlboro pack with Nadia's shirt staring at her. Their cigarettes lit, Erika waited for a response. Nadia took her time, setting the lighter down and nestling back into the sofa. The smoke she expelled came haltingly as she chewed her lip. "Meetings aren't my call," she said at last. "Matteo's the one in charge, and what with the *Cardinale* being firebombed he's decided to put things on hold. You've heard about that attack, haven't you?"

Erika nodded stiffly. The *Cardinale* excuse was getting very irritating. Mattei had used it in the same way to further justify the group's going into hibernation. Erika wondered if Nadia knew about her visit to the museum. "One of Paolo's friends died in the bombing," Erika said, "and another ended up in the hospital."

"I'm sorry." Nadia shook her head. "Paolo called Matteo yesterday when it happened and told him he was leaving the group."

Erika's hand halted in midair, then slowly returned her cigarette to the ashtray. Paolo had given her two versions of his "rupture" with the Comrades: yesterday morning, before they knew about the attack on the *Cardinale,* he'd said he was *planning* to break with them due to their radicalization; when he dropped her at home, after their visit to Giorgio in the hospital, he said he told the Comrades he was finished with them. Now, according to Nadia, Paolo had reported to Mattei yesterday, whereas Mattei had already announced the group's "hibernation."

She tilted her swimming head. "So the group's closing shop because of the *Cardinale*? The bombing only happened yesterday."

Nadia considered Erika through a veil of smoke. "Matteo's been sensing that something like that was going to happen, the stepping-up of right-wing attacks."

Sensing: no doubt he believed in the Oracle at Delphi as well. Erika saved her sarcasm. "You'd think someone would want revenge against The Black Order."

"We would all like revenge but we don't have the manpower. Plus why feed a vicious cycle?"

Erika, slightly embarrassed at having twice suggested retaliation, went silent.

"You're right," she finally said, switching gears. "I guess after seeing Paolo's reaction to what happened to his friends, I've become kind of passionate about things."

"Have you met them, the guys from the *Cardinale*?"

"Just Giorgio, the one who survived."

"Is he all right?"

"He's got burns, other than that I don't know."

"But you talked to him..."

"With Paolo, in the hospital. Not for long, though."

"Well thank God Giorgio made it."

Her concern seemed genuine, though Erika wondered whether there was more to it.

"Are you sure you don't want something more to drink?" Nadia asked.

"No, no thanks, I should go. I haven't had dinner yet."

"*Poverina*." Nadia reached over to pat Erika's arm. "You must be starving. I should have invited you to have a bite here."

"I'm fine," Erika said, rising and retrieving her purse. "More tired than hungry."

Especially tired of getting nowhere.

She left the apartment, plunging into the inky night to wait for the tram under the low porticoes of via Po. With the varying versions of when and how and why the Comrades were retiring, she didn't believe they were retiring at all.

Nor did she believe Paolo had split from them.

Erika tossed her cigarette at a storm drain in the street as she hustled up via Garibaldi to her building. Nine o'clock the next night and still no news from Paolo since Tuesday. She had run the gamut of Comrades, save Flavio, whom she had no number for. Seeking him out through Nadia would raise suspicion, plus why should she think Flavio would give a straight answer when no one else had done so?

She reached her floor and was already unsnapping her leather key holder, when she halted—no need for a key; a sliver of light shone through a crack in the door. Her heart began to pound. Quietly, she placed keys and purse on the floor and pulled the stiletto from her coat pocket. She opened the blade, pulling it into the locked position as stealthily as possible. So much for all her practice at flicking it open. Her coat hung hot and heavy on her and she silently dropped it next to her purse. Engulfed by both fear and anger, she tried to control her breathing before nudging open the door another crack with the tip of her shoe.

The table lamp next to the sofa was on, emitting a dim glow. Instinctively she adjusted the stiletto to fencing parry-four position to protect as much of her torso as possible. Her heart thumped harder; she squeezed the knife's handle until she felt its tiny screw heads dig into her thumb and index finger. Slowly she advanced.

Her sofa came into view, a black ski jacket draped over its back. Her breath caught, the burning in her chest and throat rising to her ears. Another step forward and she saw the end table, and then he appeared: Gino, half sitting on the radiator against the wall.

His eyebrows arched at the sight of the stiletto, then he smirked and shook his head. "Aren't we overreacting?"

His derisive smile and tone of voice filled Erika with a sense of the familiar, and she eased her grip on the stiletto, letting her fingers do the work. "What are you doing here!?" she demanded, her wrist rocking, the blade bobbing up and down as if it belonged to her Spanish foil.

A slight frown replaced his smirk as Gino slowly slid off the radiator. "Would you mind putting that down?"

Free of his bulky jacket he appeared leaner, though a wiriness still suggested plenty of strength and his legs looked solid and hard beneath his tight jeans. Her gaze shifted back to his light eyes and pale skin, so sharply framed and contrasted by his dark glossy hair and mustache.

"Well?" he said, spreading his hands and taking two tentative steps towards her.

"Stop." She stilled her wrist and the stiletto froze, extended towards his chest. She tried to keep her voice as level as her weapon. "I'll put my knife away after you leave and I call the police. Now why did you break in here?"

He shook his head, giving her a smile that now looked surprisingly apologetic. "If you go to the cops they'll learn plenty about you too—your involvement in a communist cell, your plotting with the Reds." As Erika's eyes darkened, his gaze hardened. "I'll play everything up, including rogue CIA spying. You'll be lucky if all they do is deport you."

Erika squeezed the stiletto's handle again. She knew he wasn't bluffing.

"And of course the police would also learn you killed someone." He took a step forward.

"What?" She reddened. "Who told you that!"

"Never mind. Just know I'll sing louder to the cops than you ever could—my word against a foreigner's. I'll tell all this and more."

What more did he have to tell? Perspiration began its slippery escape, spreading now to her knife hand. "My brother...what do you know about him?"

Gino advanced another step. "Keith? Everything."

"What do you mean!"

He didn't reply. Instead his foot came up, clipping Erika's hand, her knife flying away to clatter on the tile floor.

They hit the ground together, scrabbling for it. She grabbed Gino's hair, yanked with all her strength. *Remember this?*

Dark silky strands ripped free. "*Cazzo!*" he yelled, and punched her on the cheek. Pain radiated through her brow and cheekbone but she managed to block his next blow with her left arm, then shove the heel of her right hand into his windpipe. He gasped, and for a moment he seemed paralyzed.

As she scooted away on her belly, a hand grabbed her foot. She turned and landed a kick to his head with her other foot, snatched up her knife and crawled away. As she scrambled to her feet and turned she heard a crisp "click," and her eye caught the flash of a another blade—his blade. Both shock and exhilaration filled Erika, her arm instantly becoming a right angle, the stiletto taut as a saber. Gino's blade dangled at thigh level, like a punk's out of *West Side Story*. She initiated her mental chess, flexing her knees, rocking from foot to foot.

"Seems you've done this before. *Stiletto*?" Gino pointed at her weapon with his knife.

She nodded, indicating his weapon, recalling how quickly his knife had sprung open. "*Switchblade*?"

"Too bad I've had to resort to it." He advanced a step.

Erika continued to rock, retreating two steps then advancing, her torso presenting a profile, her left arm balancing beside it.

He frowned at her and raised his knife. "Enough with the swashbuckling—about time you left your fantasy world, which includes playing James Bond with the Comrades."

But she had locked into her fencing persona, her thinking, her eye, her reflexes thoroughly trained and disciplined, resulting from years of practice. Again she advanced and retreated, posture straight, blade now rotating.

"Enough!" Gino shifted his weight, raising the switchblade higher in protest.

This was her cue, and she launched a flèche, her body an arrow. Her blade struck his aside, her momentum continuing towards him, the collision sending them sprawling to the floor. Gino's head smacked the tiles. After a stunned moment, he lifted it to find Erika's blade pressed against his groin. His knife lay next to him.

She drew a steadying breath. "Just lie still or my blade might nick an artery—*or something else.*" She scooped up his switchblade with her left hand. "I could have taken you out—don't know why I didn't. Now turn over slowly." Indeed, during a normal flèche she would have struck him with her blade and flown past, but something inside had stopped her.

So that he could turn, she moved off of him, keeping the switchblade trained on his side. With her stiletto pressing through the weave of his sweater, she said, "I want you to slowly get up, turn, and walk out of here."

Erika held her breath as he rose gingerly. He advanced towards the door, both knives brushing his back. He stopped at the threshold. "May I turn around before I leave?"

"No...but you can tell me how you know about me and what my brother's got to do with this."

He shook his head, releasing a weary sigh. "Believe me, if you don't get it now, you won't want to."

She pressed the stiletto's tip against his kidney area and pushed. He inhaled, muscles tensing, but said nothing.

Her hand was beginning to shake with rage so she pulled back. "Whoever you're working for, tell them to leave me alone!"

"Easy, Erika," he said in a quiet voice. "I can tell you're not a natural killer. But you have had accidents and I wouldn't want to be the victim of another one. So I'll be on my way for now."

She glared at the back of his head. "Go!"

He had stepped over her coat and purse on the landing and was heading towards the stairs, when he stopped and turned to face her. "Could you toss me my jacket at least?"

"What?"

"I left my jacket on your sofa." A helpless smile accompanied this.

Fuck your cazzo of a jacket! She would not risk turning her back on him, or even backing up to fetch it. Then again, if it contained important items, she didn't want him trying to break in for it later.

She drilled him with her sternest frown. "Leave the building. When you're out on the street I'll toss it down from the roof."

For a moment he seemed to weigh the offer, then nodded and turned to continue on towards the stairs. *Deliberately strolling.* Heart still banging, she waited for him to clear the landing, his shoes echoing on the marble steps. Then she grabbed her things off the floor, hurried back in, dropped them in a heap and locked the door. She left the knives on the entry table and strode to his jacket. She was lucky to have it, she realized, for in throwing it down to him she could verify he had left the building.

She picked it up. She would have to wait for him to get downstairs, so she decided to go through the black parka.

From an inside pocket she pulled out what looked like a dog-eared dry-cleaning ticket; in another interior pocket she found a comb. From the left outside pocket she extracted a pack of Muratti Ambassador cigarettes and a lighter; from the right, a transport pass with the name CLAUDIO VOGHERA stamped on it.

His true name? She considered the pictureless pass so long she almost forgot he would be downstairs by now.

She returned everything to its correct pockets, opened the glass doors, and almost giddily climbed out onto the roof. With balanced, methodic steps she gained the edge and peeked over. Gino was standing near a lamppost, just outside its halo of yellow light. She let fly the jacket and heard it billow, then rustle as it hit the ground. Once he picked it up he moved directly into the light and gave a military salute in her direction. She scowled back for an instant, then turned and headed back in.

She had no sooner got the window locked and the drapes drawn when a trembling took hold of her. She kicked off her shoes and sat on the sofa, hugging her knees. She started to rub her face but let out an "Agh!" Her cheekbone and the area under her left eye throbbed with pain. She went to examine the damage in the bathroom mirror and found a red swath reflecting back at her, encompassing her left cheek up to her eyebrow. Another sinister blotch to add to her swollen lip that was almost back to normal. The stark reminders that she had been attacked three times made her shiver uncontrollably. She retrieved the duvet, then returned to the sofa, wrapped herself in it and lit a cigarette. With each pull she felt calmer.

Gino, or Claudio Voghera, or whoever this bastard was, had probably left the neighborhood by now. Even if he were tempted to come back he would likely imagine her waiting hyper-vigilant with two knives at her disposal. Plus, he couldn't be one hundred percent certain she wouldn't call the police. And yet...

She rose, grabbed a kitchen chair, and wedged it under the door handle. Back on the couch she finished her cigarette, her mind now methodically sifting thoughts. She had to see Paolo, determine once and for all his role in this mess that was spiraling dizzyingly out of control. For the first time she bitterly regretted having no phone. In the morning she would go out to a phone booth and call his house. She would recount every calamity that had befallen her and hope he would respond with equal honesty; *and help her decide what to do.*

The pain in her face still pulsing, she went to look at her cheek again. It seemed the huge splotch had turned darker—a classic black eye. She took three aspirin...perhaps she should eat dinner; the thought left her nauseous. All she wanted was to lie down. She didn't have the energy or the inclination to unfold the sofa bed, she would sleep on it as was, in her clothes, just in case...

Which reminded her to deal with the knives. She picked them up, eyes flicking back and forth between them. She retracted the stiletto's blade and returned it to the end table drawer, her interest now piqued by Gino's switchblade. She sat on the sofa to examine it. On one side of its grey handle she found a small, smooth, silver button. She pushed it, simultaneously trying to retract the blade with her left hand, but the blade wouldn't budge. A different animal from the stiletto. Fingering the steel thumb guard she discovered that it moved; she smiled as she was able with one hand to unlock the blade and squeeze it back into its handle. She pressed the silver button again and the blade sprang open with a vibrating life of its own. She felt a pleasurable shudder. She would have to grip this new pet securely when unleashing it or it might just spring out of her hand.

She massaged the handle with probing fingers. Its tiny screws were smoother than the stiletto's; more advantageous all around, this switchblade. She practiced clicking it open a few more times, then laid it on the floor next to the sofa, blade open. The throbbing in her cheek had started to let up, but a cold, crippling fatigue now replaced it, as if she had fallen into an icy pond and been forced to drag herself, soaked and freezing, all the way home. Shivering again, she retrieved her pillow, turned off the table light, and curled back under the duvet. She reached down and gave the switchblade a final reassuring squeeze before collapsing into sleep.

26: Eugenia Sillano and Sara Lattes

Erika woke to pain pulsating through her left cheek. She turned over and groaned, not knowing which had shocked her awake, the pain or her disturbing dream. She had been dueling again, this time against Keith with Gino's grey-handled switchblade. Her brother had gained on her and she found herself on her back with his own blade pointed at her throat. As the tip began to dent her skin, Paolo suddenly appeared and pulled him off. They both hovered over her, Keith now wearing a mustache.

She sat up: nine o'clock. Amazing she had slept at all considering her battle with Gino the night before. She got up to pull the drapes back, then made her way to the bathroom where in the mirror she grimaced at a dark-purple eye and cheekbone.

She took more aspirin before downing an espresso. No time to eat—she had to contact Paolo—so she dressed quickly and headed out to a phone booth, heartburn clawing her esophagus, Gino's switchblade snug in her coat pocket.

"Signor Lorenzi?" she addressed a voice she assumed belonged to Paolo's father. "It's Erika Rivoli, Paolo's friend."

"Ah, Signorina Rivoli, it would be nice for us to meet sometime." The light-hearted tone was warming, though Erika wondered whether Signor Lorenzi suspected anything unorthodox about his son and his friends.

"Yes..." she replied, flicking the fingers of her left hand. "I hope it's not too early but I'm wondering if Paolo's home."

"Not too early, but unfortunately Paolo isn't here. He left a note yesterday saying he'd be out of town with friends for a few days. Didn't say where or for how long. I'll tell him you called, though, when he returns."

Erika clenched the receiver. She wanted to say it was urgent, that she needed to reach Paolo *now*. But if Signor Lorenzi himself didn't know where his son was…She took a calming breath and leaned against the cold glass door of the phone booth. "Thank you. If you could tell him to call me back…it's kind of important."

"Of course. He has your number, I assume?"

"Yes, he knows how to reach me." Erika drew another breath.

"Is there something else?"

She squeezed the receiver harder. "No…"

"Well," said Signor Lorenzi, hesitant, "good-bye then."

"Good-bye." The line went dead and Erika felt like banging the receiver on the glass. *Where the hell is he and who is he with?* The only "friends" of Paolo's she had met were the Comrades, plus Giorgio Testa of the *Cardinale*, the latter perhaps still bandaged-up in the hospital.

Out of town, Signor Lorenzi had told her. She pictured Paolo off with Nadia and the others in some big country house, perhaps the one belonging to Nadia's grandparents, all of them hunkered down in a clandestine retreat, debating, plotting, perhaps mulling over how next to deal with her. She trembled with resentment. She couldn't face fuming alone in her empty flat and instead decided to pay a visit to her landlady, whose phone number Paolo used to contact her.

Delicately she tapped her cheek, recalling the sidelong looks people had cast her on the street. She would have to invent something to tell Signora Sillano, she realized, as she exited the phone booth to return to her building.

The signora's eyes widened the moment she opened her door. "*Buon giorno*, Erika…what happened to you?"

Erika shook her head with disgust. "Like an idiot, I fell down the stairs and banged my cheek."

"*Poverina!* I hope you didn't break anything."

"Nothing broken. My face hurts, so I took some aspirin."

"Good." The signora ushered Erika in and took her coat. "That bruise will last a long time, though. I might have something you could put on it. Would you like a cup of coffee?"

"I'd love one."

"Have a seat at the kitchen table, I'll be right back."

She watched the back of the signora's heavy brown sweater, wool skirt, and thick dark stockings, as the woman shuffled down the hall on her felt runners. Then she released a long sigh and went to sit in the kitchen.

The cheery, aromatic room infused her with both warmth and sadness. Like Elsa's kitchen it reminded her of her grandmother's, overflowing with jars and wooden spoons and every other kind of cooking implement. A big pot simmered on the stove, exuding the fragrance of minestrone, a smell that used to swirl in the air at her grandmother's. For an instant, time and space seemed to collapse, and Erika was filled with melancholy.

"Here we are," announced the signora, discarding her *feltri* and setting a medicine tube on the table in front of Erika. "Lasonil—it's an ointment. Take it with you upstairs and dab it on the discoloration. The swelling will go down and the bruises won't last as long."

"Thank you," said Erika, glancing at the tube distractedly as Signora Sillano made coffee in her Moka pot. She brought a tray to the table, laden with demitasse cups and spoons, a sugar bowl, and a plate of biscotti. Erika eyed the biscotti. She should probably eat something, only her stomach felt queasy. Coffee, however, she needed, for she was starting to get a headache again.

Signora Sillano watched her with a slight frown as she waited on the coffee. "Ice packs will help your cheek too."

Erika gave an absent-minded nod, urgency to contact

Paolo rearing back up. "I've been trying to get hold of Paolo—it's important, but his father says he's away with friends and he doesn't know where, or when he'll be back." She realized her foot was tapping the floor in a nervous tic and stopped it.

The Moka's gurgling began, the signora filled their cups and sat down. "He left without telling you?" she asked.

"We haven't talked in a couple of days." Erika's voice trailed off as she let the signora sugar her coffee.

She had barely spoken to Signora Sillano since she'd moved into the mansard flat, had only received one call from Paolo via the signora, as Paolo and Erika usually arranged their meetings in advance. Now, though, was not the moment to stand on ceremony. "I was wondering," she said, "if you might know of any place out of town where he might have gone with his friends."

The signora brushed a crumb off the oilcloth covering the table before returning an impassive look. "I don't know Paolo's friends, except you. Is something wrong?"

"I just need to talk to him." For an instant Erika closed her eyes against the banging in her head, and when she opened them, the signora's expression had softened.

"I'd like to help but I rarely see Paolo these days, and he doesn't talk about his friends."

Erika let out a resigned sigh, staring glumly past the signora at the colorful wooden cuckoo clock on the wall. At that moment it went off, all bells and whistles, its silly bird springing at her ten agonizing times to squawk the hour. Her head throbbed all the more.

"Are you all right?" asked the signora. "You really don't look well."

Erika shook her aching head. "If I could talk to Paolo, things would be better."

"Have you been involved with Paolo's friends?" The signora was leaning in, frowning now, and Erika winced, feeling like she was being examined under a microscope.

The signora sighed and placed a hand on her arm. "I don't know them personally, but I've heard he's got caught up with some hardened Communists who may not be a good influence on him...maybe you already know this..."

The signora's hand was firm, her manner mild. Her lined face, made all the more stark with her grey hair pulled back in a bun, hinted that she knew suffering. She had endured World War Two's countless hardships. She had risked her life hiding Paolo's mother in her cellar in the countryside. If the Fascists or Nazis had caught her, she would have been sent to a concentration camp herself.

Erika relented. "I know some of his communist friends...his 'Comrades'." She paused, flicking her fingers again. "One of them actually did this to me." She pointed to her cheek. "I'm sorry I lied about it."

"*Oh, Signur!*" The signora's eyes filled with confusion and worry. "But Paolo ..."

Erika shook her head. "I'm not sure he knows about the violent element in his group. Two of them are after me, a woman who tried to beat me up and the guy who did this to me."

"When did it happen?"

"Last night, upstairs."

"In the mansard?" The signora blanched. "How did he get in?"

"I don't know but he was waiting for me inside when I got home."

"*Dio santo!* I won't have this—not from Paolo's group or from anyone! I'm going to have a long security bolt installed upstairs."

"Thank you," murmured Erika, surprised to hear a curse from the normally bland landlady, "but I hate for you to spend money on my account. They probably won't come back."

"Don't give it another thought—it's a good investment. I warned Paolo about radicals before I knew he was actually involved with some, but he's always carried such a grudge about his mother's treatment by the Fascists."

"He told me you hid her during the war."

"Yes, and as his godmother I've kept up with him since his birth. Then his mother died—Sara Lattes, though not of the Lattes publishing family. Paolo was only thirteen and we grew closer. Now I rarely see him. And to think he's mixed up with criminal types..."

"He told me he was breaking with them, but I'm not sure it's true. They might be plotting something."

"Well, when we call the police about your assault we can mention that too."

Erika's head hammered harder. "No...please don't call them. I mean, I'd rather get to Paolo first. Once I tell him what happened to me, I'm sure he'll break straight away from them. If the police get involved now, he might get arrested too." She held her breath and hoped her appeal, coupled with the signora's maternal feelings towards Paolo, would forestall things.

"But your injuries..."

"This is the only injury," Erika said, indicating her face again. "The rest have been mostly threats." She clenched her jaw: *especially Gino's.*

The signora raised a sharp eyebrow and Erika felt obliged to explain.

"The guy who attacked me threatened to tell the police about my entanglement with their communist cell, which doesn't amount to much, though he'll make it seem bigger so that I get arrested and deported."

Perhaps Erika's desperation had mitigated the signora's outrage, for her tone turned more skeptical. "What do you think they're plotting?"

"Something to do with Matilde Fassino. That's how they hooked Paolo in, I think—his resentment of her."

The signora nodded sagely. "Has he also told you what she and her husband did to his mother?"

"Stole her money and almost got her shipped to Auschwitz."

"Awful as it is, I don't think that's the only thing bothering Paolo these days." For a moment the signora hesitated, her gaze fixated past Erika. "He found out Signor Lorenzi isn't his real father and that's seemed to harden him further."

Lips parted, Erika stared back in wonder.

"I was the one who told him a couple of months ago," said the signora with a rueful shake of her head. "Considering what's happened I figure you should know. When you first came to live here, I wondered about you—whether you might be a radical as well—so I kept my distance."

"Well, I'm not," Erika maintained. "I'm trying to find out what these people are up to, that's why I've been threatened."

The signora nodded in a conciliatory way, thought Erika. But this business about Paolo's father...another secret of his. "So Paolo knew Signor Lorenzi wasn't his real father before I got here," Erika mused aloud. "I could tell he had issues with him...Do you mind my asking who his real father is?"

"That's just it—I don't know who he is. After the war Sara continued to live with me in the country for a spell. Then she found a job and moved back to Turin. All she could afford in those days of depression, even on a secretarial salary, was a *soffitta*. Not a decent mansard like yours, more of an attic next to other attics, with one bathroom at the end of the corridor. The insulation was practically non-existent and I remember visiting her in the winter, my hands and feet freezing. I tried to get her to come back to my home but she said she needed to get on with her life. I felt so sorry for her.

"Then she told me she met a young man, much younger than her, something considered unacceptable in the day since she was close to thirty. I might have been the only one she confided in about the affair. She needed to unburden herself but never went into much detail about the man. Only that he had a foreign-sounding name—English, I think, maybe American. Then she told me she was pregnant. The foreigner left Turin and Sara met Signor Lorenzi. Paolo was born after they married."

Erika felt she was watching a movie. "He could've been American, then?"

"Possibly. Sara wouldn't confirm where he was from."

"Did Signor Lorenzi know he wasn't the father?"

"Yes, but he gave Paolo his name and obviously kept the truth from him."

"*He never told me*," Erika said with a pained look. "Then again he was always holding back."

The signora placed a hand on her arm again and gently asked, "Do you love him?"

Her thoughts tangled and spinning, Erika didn't answer. "I've got to find him. If I tell him about these attacks on me, I'm sure he'll want to help me and maybe I can help him."

"Hmm," the signora responded in speculation. "You say he and his Comrades might be planning something that has to do with Matilde Fassino?"

"Yes! It started with Paolo stealing her purse, and I've been trying to figure out why. He said it was immature revenge for what she did to his mother, but I don't completely buy it. He got really angry when I mentioned Matilde Fassino the last time we saw each other, yelled at me to drop the subject for good. Then he left and I haven't seen him since."

The signora frowned. "He's harbored much hatred all these years, but purse-snatching doesn't sound like him. He must have had another motive."

"Exactly." For a moment Erika's spirits lifted. Perhaps she had an ally. "You've heard about Matilde Fassino's diamonds..."

The signora offered a wry smile. "Of course, but no one knows where they are or if they really exist."

"I think Paolo and his Comrades might know something." Erika took a breath: "They might be planning to steal them."

27: In Extremis

A sudden trilling broke the expectant pause. Signora Sillano leapt to go answer her phone in the entryway. Vaguely Erika noted the sprightliness of this woman who had to be at least in her late sixties.

She drummed her fingers on the table then stopped abruptly when the signora called her.

"Erika, it's for you," she said from the kitchen doorway. "A man—I was hoping it would be Paolo, but..." She shook her head as she moved to sit back down.

Erika gnawed the good side of her lip as she made her way down the hall. Tentatively, she lifted the grey receiver from the table. "*Sì?*"

"Erika—Flavio Moretti, here."

She sucked in a silent gasp.

"I don't mean to alarm you," he quickly continued, "but I need to meet you."

The shock began to dissolve. *How ironic that I don't have to seek* you *out.* "How did you know where to reach me?" she asked warily.

"I knew you were renting from Eugenia Sillano."

"I see...well, I'd like to talk to you too. Not in my flat, though."

"Agreed. I had some place more out of the way in mind. There's a street near Porta Nuova called via Saluzzo. Do you know it?"

"Um..."

"It's parallel to the station and intersects with corso Vittorio."

"Okay."

"There's a café there, almost at the crossroads, called Il Ritrovo. A bit shoddy on the outside but fine inside. How about today at two?"

"...All right."

After ringing off, Erika stood thinking. She asked permission to use the signora's phone again. "*Buon giorno*, Brigida, it's Erika."

"*Sì?*" replied the Manhattan school's secretary in the brusque, officious tone that grated on Erika.

"I'm not feeling good so I won't be able to make it in today." Erika touched her cheek and smarted in confirmation.

An impatient sigh came down the line. "All right, I'll alert the students. You'll be back on Monday, I assume?"

Today was Friday. "I think so," Erika said, wondering how her face would look then.

Another irritated sigh. "Then see you Monday."

"Right."

A click followed. *Cazzo, the woman had no sympathy.*

"Is everything all right?" Signora Sillano had stepped into the hall.

"Yes, I've just called work and told them I won't be in today." She pinched the bridge of her nose.

"I don't blame you."

"About that first call, the man who phoned is one of the Comrades. I'm going to meet him this afternoon. Maybe he can tell me where Paolo is."

"I hope that's wise..."

"He's all I've got left to go on."

Gripping the switchblade, Erika climbed back up to her flat and locked herself in. After checking the bathroom, the only separate room in the studio where someone could hide, she threw her coat over a kitchen chair. Fatigue crushed her, and as she sank against the cushions of the sofa she let her head fall back, and dozed off.

When she woke she was curled up in a ball, her knife next to her. She stretched and glanced at her alarm clock. "Quarter to one?!" she exclaimed, bounding off the sofa and returning the switchblade to her coat pocket. She rushed to take a shower and dress, then threw on her coat, reached for her purse, and stopped. After the various fisticuffs she had engaged in, including the first with Gino under the stairwell at school, she concluded her purse was a hindrance she could ill afford.

She picked out her money, keys, and a comb, and transferred them to the pockets of her sailor-style bellbottom jeans. She stuffed her cigarettes, lighter, and bus pass into her left coat pocket. Her fingers collided with a foreign object, the Lasonil tube, which she tossed onto the entryway table; it could wait. She locked the door, gave the switchblade in her right pocket a squeeze, and hurried to the stairs, coat swinging.

She caught the tram, and by one-forty was heading to the train station. Furtive glances at her bruised face followed her, which she ignored, so absorbed was she with why Flavio wanted to meet her. At Porta Nuova she waited to jaywalk across the street. Fog lights glowed dully in the smoky mist; the return of the fog seemed an uncomfortable omen.

She made her way over to via Saluzzo, stood at its crossroads with corso Vittorio, and looked down the misty street. Flavio didn't say on which side she could find Il Ritrovo but did specify it was near the intersection. She proceeded down the sidewalk, examining each storefront. She gazed across the street but could make out little in the thick soup. Checking her watch nervously—one fifty-five—she turned and strode back to the intersection to cross to the other side of the street.

She passed a bakery, a horse butcher's, a dairy shop...and there it was—IL RITROV. The final "O" was missing from the hanging sign, which depicted three men in caricature huddled over a pile of loot. DEN OF THIEVES, it signified. Erika checked her watch again: three minutes to two. She could wait another couple of minutes, but didn't like the thought of loitering on the sidewalk in the fog when someone could easily be following her. Slowly she entered, wondering what kind of café would be called DEN OF THIEVES, half expecting to see a bunch of stubble-chinned old men drinking wine from short stemless glasses.

That wasn't the case. She didn't spot Flavio right off but saw a young couple at a table drinking beer. In fact most of the people (granted there weren't many of them at this hour) were drinking beer. Erika advanced past the bar, glancing at its multiple taps.

On the other side of the bar she caught sight of Flavio, who beckoned her with a jerk of his head. Massaging the switchblade in her pocket, she made her way to him. He half rose before she sat; he was a gentleman at least, this most cryptic of Comrades, and her last hope of discovering some truth in this agonizing mess.

"No trouble finding the place?" His eyes examined her face with curiosity, though he made no comment about her bruise. That in itself seemed puzzling.

"No, but from the sign, I didn't know what to expect here."

Flavio gave a friendly chuckle. "It's a pub, or at least an imitation of one. Drink?" he asked, raising a glass mug of beer, his inquisitive gaze lingering.

"I'll have the same," she said, nodding at the mug.

"Ale?"

"Sure."

Erika watched him slide out of his chair and go to the bar. If she looked different today, so did he. He looked gaunt, eyes pouchy with dark circles. His hair seemed longer, which made his face appear thinner, and overall he struck her more as a decadent, turn-of-the century Bohemian than the gallant Caspian prince of Nadia's country party. Was he also under stress from the Comrades? She turned back to the table and lit a cigarette. Ale didn't exactly sound appetizing at the moment, but people tended to be more forthcoming with a drinking mate.

A bit of froth sloshed over the lip of the dimpled-glass mug as Flavio set it in front of her. "Sorry," he said.

Erika waited for him to sit again before taking a sip. Questions assailed her like a flight of arrows, but Flavio had to be the one to broach the subject of this meeting he had initiated.

He took a swig of ale, eyeing her over the mug's rim. "What's happened to your face, if I'm not being too forward?"

Forward? She felt an impulse to laugh. Flavio might very well know *everything* that had befallen her. She took a stalling drag of her cigarette then drawled, "I might have fallen down the stairs...then again..."

She let the unfinished phrase dangle between them as he watched her, evaluating her, it seemed; she thought she caught a spark of concern in his studious eye. "Did your *fall*, or whatever it was, do any other damage?"

"No, I was lucky."

"That's good," he murmured, his gaze turning neutral. "I know you've been making the rounds of the Comrades, asking why you haven't been invited to take part in activities..."

"And no one will give me a straight answer—just that the Comrades are shutting down, or going on hiatus, or regrouping, or whatever, depending on who I'm talking to."

"Well," Flavio responded with a shrug, "I can't speak for the others, but I'm getting out for reasons of disillusionment."

Really? That was a new one, or maybe Paolo had expressed something similar the last time she saw him. Who could remember? "What about Nadia?" Erika asked,

210

suppressing her cynicism. "You two seemed to be involved when I first met you."

"Mm...well, that's over." His eyes shifted to inspect the room.

"Something suspicious?" asked Erika, with a quick look over her shoulder. She felt vulnerable sitting with her back to the room.

"Just being cautious. You've heard about the firebombing of *Il Cardinale* newspaper...?"

"You've all mentioned it, and it's starting to sound like an excuse to scare me off."

Flavio leaned forward. "Will it work?"

Erika stared at him. Was that earnestness in his tone, and concern once more in his eyes? "Is that why you asked me here? Because I'm not backing off until I talk to Paolo. You haven't seen him, have you?"

"No." Flavio sat back and took another swig of ale.

"Happen to know where he is?"

"Now that's a tough one," he said, frowning at his glass. This time she was sure she detected a touch of sympathy in his voice. "Paolo's also left the group and doesn't want to be reached by anyone."

"But I need to talk to him, it's urgent."

Flavio stared hard at her. "What happened to you, Erika? And please skip the nonsense about falling."

She sat in suspension, not knowing whether to trust him. But what other option had she? Finally she said, "People seem to want me out of the Comrades' business, two toughs in particular—a jerk called Gino and a woman who's like an attack dog." She gave another glance around the place. "If one of them catches me here I might end up looking worse."

Genuine worry now shone in Flavio's tired eyes. "You're right. I asked you here to warn you away from the Comrades. If you back off, it's logical you'll be left alone."

"How do you know?" she demanded. "Do these Hounds

work for you?"

"No."

"For Matteo Mattei, or one of the others?"

Flavio shook his head. "Everyone has his own concerns, but it makes sense that if you contact Paolo, someone might come after you again. You have to wash your hands of this whole affair, Erika."

"I won't quit looking for Paolo." Erika could feel the tremor in her voice and swallowed hard. "And I won't back down from threats either."

Flavio took a breath and began to speak, but Erika bulldozed over him. "That thug Gino, or Claudio Voghera, or whoever the hell he is, is trying to blackmail me about..." She stopped short of naming the CIA. "...About my brother. If my brother's mixed up in something, I need to know what it is."

"You don't want to go there, Erika." Flavio shook his head again. "Trust me, you won't like the answers." He sat back. "This is a dirty business, that's why I've gotten out, and you must do the same. I'm watching my back and maybe I can help you watch yours."

So he wished to help. She felt her heart lift. "Will you tell me about my brother and Paolo?"

"I can't tell you any more than I have." He leaned in again. "But listen: I'll try to contact Paolo, tell him you're worried. That's all I can do. Now it's best I go."

"Wait," she said as he rose. "I need your number."

He plucked a pen from the inside pocket of his coat and scratched a number on a napkin. "Here, if you get into more trouble, call me."

For a few heartbeats he stood watching her, and she longed to plead with him again. Finally he nodded at her and turned away, weaving through the tables. She stared at him until he was out of view. Then she put her head in her hands and stifled a sob.

28: Sinking and Floating

Erika hauled herself up the stairs to her flat, feeling like a hapless surfer dragged down and ground by wave after tumbling wave. The meeting with Flavio left her exhausted, gasping for a way out.

On her landing, switchblade deployed, she checked the utility closet—no one there, as usual. Who knew whether the Doberman had hidden in it before springing on her? The mystery of how the bitch had crept up on her still made her head swim. And Flavio's hint that he knew about the Hounds caused her cheek and head to pulsate mercilessly. Time for more pain relief, and maybe she should try the Lasonil.

She went into the bathroom and downed two more aspirin while grimacing at herself in the mirror. As soon as she uncapped the Lasonil and squeezed out a dab, she wanted to throw up. The signora hadn't warned her about the ointment's disgusting chemical smell. She held her breath and rubbed it delicately on her left cheek and under her eyebrow. Her stomach lurched again and she felt light-headed. She realized she hadn't eaten in over twenty-four hours, instead reeling from place to place on sugared espresso, beer, and aspirin. She waited for the nausea to dissolve, washed her hands and went to the kitchen. What had her Italian grandmother—*Nonna*—told her to eat when she was ill? "Rice," Erika said out loud and pulled out a pot.

Blanketed by sadness, she sat on the sofa waiting for the water in the pot to boil and thinking about her grandparents. Her grandfather Rivoli—*Nonno*—had died in his sixties. *Nonna*, at seventy, had passed away at the beginning of this year, followed by the fencing accident, the car crash, and her rejection by the CIA. With the piling on of this Red fiasco, how could 1977 end any worse? And who knew what 1978 would portend? After all, it was right around the corner. Somehow the thought spurred another wave of nausea and she nixed the idea of eating rice. Instead she used the boiling water to make mint tea, which made her feel better. She sipped it on the sofa while ruminating over the enigma concerning her brother. Not only Gino, but now Flavio seemed to know something about him. *But what, Dio Santo?* Bruno had always encouraged Keith to do woodworking with him. They would tinker in the garage and Keith would help Bruno at his job sites. Then, after high school, Keith had gone to work for their father fulltime.

She sat up straight, running both her hands back and forth through her hair. Was he still working fulltime for Bruno? Keith was twenty, and something now told Erika he had moved on. When had she last seen him and what was he up to? Damn the car accident and concussion, she couldn't remember! The more she tried, the tighter her head felt, as if encased in an invisible vise. A chill slithered through her. *Could* Keith have interfered with her CIA background check? Why had Gino mentioned him? Might he be meddling right now, perhaps in concert with Ivan? Ivan had made that one trip to the States, four years ago. Keith couldn't speak any Italian, had never cared to learn, but he and Ivan communicated quite well in English. Then, for his eighteenth birthday and graduation, their grandmother had brought Keith to Italy for the summer. Ivan was twenty-two then and already tinged with Red...

Still, why would either of them want to sabotage her? If she could just relieve the pressure in her head. She got up, ate a couple of biscotti in the kitchen, then went to the entryway table where her mini address book sat. She needed to make a long-distance call.

The doorbell buzzed. She looked through the peek-hole

and immediately opened the door. "Signora..."

"I wanted to tell you that I've arranged for a locksmith to come this afternoon," she said. "When you go to bed tonight you'll have a very secure door."

Erika smiled warmly. "Thank you."

"You still look peaked. Have you eaten?"

"...A little, and now I have to go back out." She felt bad, brushing the signora off, sensing the signora wanted to know how her meeting with Flavio went. But she had to get to the telephone office.

"You can have dinner downstairs with me if you're home this evening...?"

"I'd like that," Erika said. "We could talk then...but I'm not sure what time I'll be back."

"I'm making polenta. Come when you can, it's easily warmed up."

As soon as Signora Sillano left, Erika gathered her coat, stuffed the little address book into her back pocket, and took off for the SIP. With the West Coast nine hours behind, she might catch Keith before he went off to wherever he was working now.

She entered the lobby of the telephone office. Still feeling fuzzy, she decided to read Keith's number carefully to the clerk behind the counter, so as not to mess up with her Italian and have to pay for two calls.

"Booth number 3," the lady told her, with a trailing look at Erika's face.

Ensconced in her booth, Erika picked up the phone. On the third ring a woman answered. "Hello?"

Erika gave a start. "Um...I'm looking for Keith..."

"No one lives here by that name," croaked the irritable, early-morning voice.

"Keith Rivoli. Is this 323-5279?"

"Yes, but—"

"This is my brother's number," Erika interrupted,

fumbling to check her address book again.

"Can't be, I've had this number for two months. Now if you please—"

"I don't understand..." Erika looked desperately through the glass window for a glimpse of the lady behind the counter.

"What's there to understand, this is *my* number. Now if you don't mind..."

"Sorry," Erika muttered. She was starting to feel a sense of dread.

She left the booth and returned to the counter, but the woman who had dealt with her was now facing another customer. Erika waited, flicking her fingers; she wanted the same employee. *Come on!*

At last the woman was free. "*Scusi*," Erika almost pleaded, "I just wanted to verify I gave you the right number."

The woman looked at Erika's address book and compared numbers. "Yes, that's the one I connected you with."

"But somehow it wasn't right..."

"I'm sorry," said the woman, frowning at Erika's face again.

Erika wished she could brush away the bruise like a stray hair. "Could I try another number, then?"

"Certainly, but you will be charged for the first call as well."

"Fine, let's try this one."

She was assigned booth 5, and this time when she entered she was almost shaking with frustration.

"Hello."

"Hi, Mom, it's Erika."

"...Well what a surprise, you've finally called."

"Yeah..."

"You never write."

"I know, I'll try to write more often. But I need a favor,

Keith's number. The one I have is wrong."

"Oh God, Erika, you're not going to start that again!" Cheryl's voice sounded desperate.

"What do you mean?"

Erika's mother sighed with what seemed fatigue and exasperation. "I'm not going there with you. How are you feeling?"

"Fine. Just help me out, please."

"I can't help you. You have to do it yourself, and you can start by stopping these delusions about your brother."

"What delusions? I haven't told you anything yet. I just wondered if Keith was still in San Diego—"

"Erika, I can't take this! You know he's gone." Erika held the phone from her ear. Why was Cheryl shouting? "I'm sorry," her mother resumed in a weary voice. "But I really can't deal with this now. Aren't there any psychologists in Italy you could see?"

"What? Why the hell should I?"

"Don't use that tone and language with me!"

"Sorry." Silence dominated the line. If Keith wasn't in San Diego then where was he? Erika was afraid to rile Cheryl again by asking. She heard a sniff...or was it a sniffle? "Listen," Erika finally said, "I'm paying a fortune for this call...I've gotta go."

"Do try to take care of yourself."

Was that sadness she could hear in her mother's voice? "Right..." Erika answered in complete bewilderment. She hung up and left the booth, shaking her head as she approached the counter where a male employee looked up her charges.

"Ten thousand," he said, tilting his head at her.

Erika blanched. Over ten dollars! She pulled the lira banknotes from her pocket with trembling fingers and set them on the counter. She caught the man's lingering look and wished the Lasonil ointment would start working.

Outside on the darkening steps, she looked at her

watch: four o'clock. Cold and stunned, she couldn't figure out what was going on with her mother. Accusing Erika of delusions about Keith, shouting and claiming that he was gone but not telling her where...

A wave of weakness washed over her and her limbs felt like rubber. Then she gritted her teeth, drew herself up, and went back into the SIP. She gave another number to the man and entered her booth.

"Ivan Rivoli," came the voice on the other end.

"Ciao, Ivan."

"Erika...you've never called me at work."

"Yeah, well, I've got something very important to discuss with you. Are you free after work?"

"Um...it's kind of short notice."

"Sorry, but it's urgent."

"...I suppose I am, then."

"Can we meet near your office?"

They agreed to rendezvous at five-thirty at a café called Da Mario, in corso Regio Parco. Erika remembered the street well, for the *Cardinale* newspaper office was located there—burnt out by the Neo-Fascist Black Order. She wondered what was left of the newspaper now and whether Paolo's friend Giorgio had recovered from his burns.

She caught the tram outside her building in via Garibaldi. The wired vehicle lumbered along its tracks, with a mechanical thrumming like the fuselage of an airplane. It stopped and started in controlled spurts of power but didn't bounce and bang on the cobblestones like the bus, whose standing passengers had to hang on tight to the bars when it turned a corner. The tram's relative sedateness soothed her, and for a while she sat staring mindlessly ahead, enjoying the respite of being chauffeured. When she finally noticed passengers peering at her black eye, she turned her head towards the window and thought about Ivan. She would ask him if he knew anything about Keith. Even if he lied she would force something out of him. And she would ask about Paolo. What did she have to risk if the others learned of their meeting, besides another beating from the Hounds? At this she chuckled, a weak, feckless laugh. The man sitting across the aisle from her glared, so she sank low in the wooden seat, arms folded, chin in her coat. She closed her eyes for an instant and breathed deeply.

By the time she reached her destination in corso Regio Parco she felt in control once more.

Studying the area, she realized she would have to walk a few blocks to reach the intersection Ivan had specified. Hands stuffed in her coat pockets (no gloves, no scarf, no purse anymore) she fingered the switchblade. At least the night had broken free of fog and she could see. With that second bit of reassurance, she headed up the street.

29: Ivan and Company

Erika's mind felt sharp as the point of her switchblade now. The icy air seemed to go straight to her brain, crispening her thoughts and injecting an exhilaration that sent her gliding through the darkness up corso Regio Parco.

The narrow street, like via Garibaldi, was striped with tramlines, and as she approached a building with a thick sheet of plastic covering its window, she stopped. A barely legible sign read IL CARDINALE, its little redbird logo blackened with soot. She wondered whether Paolo had visited his friend Giorgio again since the attack.

Paolo. She gripped the switchblade in her pocket. Ivan had to help her find him.

She reached the intersection at five twenty-five and spotted the café called Da Mario. Of all the people involved in this murky mess she felt she could be the most direct with Ivan. A rush of excitement lifted her even further when she thought of questioning him about Paolo. *Calm down*, she told herself and flicked her fingers.

She stepped into the café, her gaze sweeping the room. No Ivan. She would have to wait. Then a hand tapped her shoulder and she spun around. "You're here."

"Just came out of the W.C. What the hell happened to your face, I almost didn't recognize you?"

"I fell down my stairs. Let's get a table."

Ivan grimaced at her. "You need to watch your step, you could break your neck." He pointed to a table. "That one's free."

Erika smirked as she followed him. *Yes, she had twice nearly broken her neck, so to speak.*

"Any other harm besides your face?" he asked once they sat down.

"No, fortunately not."

"What's going on that's so urgent?" he asked, taking a look round the youth-dominated café. "When I first saw your eye, I thought you might want a recommendation for a doctor."

Erika contemplated him: the sarcasm, the darting eyes, the stiff posture—she expected lies. "I'm—"

"*Signori,*" interrupted the waiter.

"A hot rum punch for me," said Ivan.

"Coffee," Erika ordered, waiting for the waiter to leave before getting down to business. "I'm interested to know what's happened to the Comrades. Everyone says they've shut down."

Ivan cocked his head in casual curiosity. "That's about the extent of it."

"Hmm...prompted by the bombing of the *Cardinale*?"

"Yes, that was the final blow." A flitting, almost imperceptible smile crossed his lips, as if he had been offered a cue "So you've heard about it?"

"Of course. Paolo lost his friend Franco, but you might already know that."

"I...I'm sorry. I did hear that."

"Have you seen Paolo lately?"

"No, we've all gone our separate ways."

"So you don't see *anyone* anymore?"

"Erika, what's this about? You said something was urgent." His face was flushed.

"Listen," she said, leaning in, planting her forearms on the table. "I know there's more going on than either Nadia, or you, or Matteo Mattei says. You're up to something, I can tell by how you're acting right now—so what is it?"

He shook his head. "I don't—"

The waiter arrived and dropped off their beverages, giving Ivan time to stall. After that, Erika bore down hard.

"Ivan, I'm about that far away"—her fingers mimed an inch—"from going to the police and spilling everything I know about your Red group."

Ivan's blush now faded to a pallor of dismay. Erika took a sip of espresso, giving him an instant to squirm, then continued in a firm voice. "I mean it. No one will help me find Paolo and I've got nothing to lose at this point. Now, are you all planning to steal Matilde Fassino's diamonds?"

Ivan's eyes widened in outrage and disbelief. Erika could picture the pistons in his brain shooting up and down. "What are you talking about?" he demanded. "Those diamonds are only a rumor. We don't like her, of course— no one does—but Paolo's the one who's obsessed with her."

"And you? What's in it for you?"

"Listen," he said, arms crossed over his chest. "I'm not involved in any plot and neither is anyone else I know of."

For a moment Erika stared into the middle distance between them. When she returned her gaze to him, she calmly said, "You and I've been pretty close over the years, true?"

He searched her eyes. "Mostly from a distance, but yes. Only now it seems we know each other less and less." He took a slow swallow of his rum punch.

"Flavio said he might help me contact Paolo," said Erika.

"He did?" Ivan set his cup down. He looked confused. "You've seen him?"

"Mm-hm."

"Well, maybe Flavio knows more than I do." Ivan shook his head, almost in irritation, as if something was not going to plan.

"I wonder if Flavio was ever Nadia's boyfriend, or if it was all a show that night in the country. Maybe they were trying to lure you into their group little by little."

"I wasn't *lured* into anything I didn't want to join. Who says they didn't just break off their romance like you and

Paolo did?" He sat back and lit a cigarette, without offering the pack to Erika.

Erika reached calmly for her own Marlboros and lit one. Ivan undoubtedly felt insulted and needed to lash out about Paolo and her. But he *had* heard about Paolo's having left her. Erika drew on her cigarette, then set in it in the ashtray. She leaned in. "I'm going to ask you something, and if you still value our relationship at all, you'll be honest with me."

He eyed her with suspicion.

"Do you know if my brother Keith is in Italy?"

He gaped as if she'd suggested Martians had landed in Turin. "I have *no* idea. Why would you think he's here?"

"I have my reasons." She felt electrified again.

Ivan shook his head. "Why should *I* know anything? I've only seen him twice in my life."

"You got on pretty well when you were together."

"Why wouldn't we? We're as much cousins as you and I are." He shook his head, his eyes narrowing in skepticism.

"So you know nothing about his whereabouts?" she persisted, her pulse accelerating.

"Erika, what's all this about?"

"Interference with Paolo and the Comrades. Someone's meddling."

"You think Keith's *meddling*?"

"Maybe."

"He can't speak Italian, doesn't know his way around... sounds very unlikely."

Perhaps it did. The only people Keith knew here were their relatives. Still, he could be operating with Ivan, staying with him at his parents' place. He might even have got in touch with Elsa and Angelo...she hadn't seen them for a while. And, of course, Paolo, Nadia, and Flavio all spoke English. Erika could insist on that point, but clearly Ivan was refusing to give up anything more. She fumed in silence at once more getting nowhere.

In the meantime Ivan continued to observe her. "Erika, I really can't help you. I'm sorry about you and Paolo but at this point we're all confused about the political scene. We've each got to sort things out for ourselves."

"What do you mean, *you're sorry about Paolo and me?*" *Time to explain this.*

Ivan hesitated, blinked a couple of times, then said, "I mean I'm sorry for both of you...he did lose a friend at the *Cardinale*."

"But you just said, *I'm sorry about Paolo and you.* You know he left, so what's happened to him?"

"Nothing—nothing that I know of." Red-faced, Ivan rubbed the back of his neck. "I did hear you two had broken up, that's all. Paolo didn't hit you, did he?"

An urge spiked in Erika to launch herself across the table and shake Ivan. She didn't know which enraged her more, his toeing the Comrade line by giving her the run-around or his attempt to change the subject with this outrageous suggestion about Paolo. "That's all you've heard?" she demanded.

"Yeah. Nadia said that Paolo needed space to sort things out after the *Cardinale* bombing."

If she heard one more phony mention of that newspaper, she would slug whoever made the reference. *Including Nadia.* She tried to relax, mentioned it was getting late.

Ivan agreed. "My mom will have dinner going soon and I still have to catch my train back to Asti."

Out on the sidewalk Ivan asked Erika if she was taking the tram.

She looked up the street to the tram stop. "I guess, what about you?"

"I'll get the bus down at the intersection." He pointed in the opposite direction, towards the crossroads of corso Regio Parco and via Mantova. "It goes straight to the station."

"Then I guess we'll part ways here."

As they brushed cheeks, Ivan squeezed her shoulders. "Take care of yourself." Then he turned and left.

A sinking sadness came over Erika as she watched him head down the sidewalk. She pulled out a cigarette and wiped away a sniffle with the back of her cold hand. In her present state she felt in no mood to return home. She took a couple of puffs and sauntered Ivan's way towards the bus stop. Where she would go, she didn't know. She watched as Ivan approached the commuters at the stop...and walked right past them. Erika's cigarette froze in front of her lips. When he threw a quick glance behind him, she stepped into a doorway. As she peered out, he was briskly turning the corner. So much for going home to *Mamma's* cooking. She tossed her cigarette in the gutter and strode after him.

In corso Verona she slackened her pace, keeping a gap between them though she really didn't care whether he spotted her or not.

He took a right turn, then another right, and slowed. Apart from Ivan's presence, this street was deserted. Erika hesitated, peering out from behind a building at the corner. He walked on, then stopped in front of a doorway and pressed the buzzer next to an address. A faint voice croaked from the loudspeaker. Ivan identified himself and was buzzed in.

When the door thumped closed she jogged to the building to scan the list of residents on the aluminum plate. *Flavio Moretti*, read one of them. *Jesus*—had Ivan come to report on their meeting to Flavio?

Indecisive, she retreated a few paces, but when a click signaled the door's reopening, she turned and stared. A short, sturdily-built woman was leaving the building. She advanced down the sidewalk in Erika's direction, then slowed, sidestepped the halo of a streetlamp and stood facing Erika.

The Doberman. Erika backed up, turned, and broke

into a sprint. As she rounded the corner she felt her heart knocking against her ribs, heard the woman's boots thudding behind her. She looked back to gauge the distance between them, and her foot slipped off the dark curb. In the split second it took to right herself, the Doberman had dived at her, sending them both crashing to the sidewalk. Erika blocked blows to her face, but the Doberman got in a series of quick, potent jabs to her stomach, and for a moment Erika was left wheezing. She rolled over the curb into the gutter as the woman got to her feet. "Still haven't cleared off, eh? Are you looking to get shot?" The Doberman unzipped her jacket while Erika pulled out her knife. As the woman reached into her jacket Erika pressed the switchblade's button and rolled out of the gutter towards her. Just as she heard a light "click," she plunged the knife into the woman's left boot with both hands. A howl and a gunshot sounded above her head. Erika yanked her knife free as the Doberman collapsed to her knees. Erika parried the semi-automatic pistol the woman was re-aiming at her, slashing the Doberman's fingers just as the gun fired again. Erika sprang and shoved the woman onto her back, landing heavily on top of her. The gun's lumpy metal dug into her ribs. She gasped and pressed her knife to the groaning woman's neck. The gun rotated against her ribs: either the woman was trying to pull it free with her damaged hand, or she was twisting it to be sure its bullet struck Erika and not herself. Erika dented the woman's throat with the tip of her bloodied blade. "Stop—STOP!"

Once more the gun shifted, and Erika nicked the woman's skin. A trickle of blood appeared, and Erika froze. Her hand started to shake, her face twisted into a rictus, tears blurred her vision. *No, not again!*

Then frantic voices sliced the air. "What's going on!?" "Who are you!?" "We've called the police!"

The metal against her ribs stilled. Panting, Erika looked up. Points of light were flashing at her from the balconies.

The Doberman woman was watching too. "Get off," she grunted, "unless you want to deal with the cops."

During a couple of agonizing heartbeats, Erika considered it: a rescue by the police. Then she looked at her knife, a lethal weapon, and witnesses all around. The door nearest them began to creak open.

Erika's mind spun like a roulette wheel; she could handle no more. She rolled off the Doberman and fled. She allowed herself one look behind and saw the woman limp-running in the opposite direction. After which Erika ran for all she was worth, heart pounding in her throat so hard she thought it would explode.

30: The Slimmest of Threads

Erika squeezed the switchblade closed as she ran from the short lane back to corso Verona. When pedestrians started to appear she finally slowed to a walk and jammed the knife back into her pocket. A surge of heat hit her. Her scalp was damp with sweat as she walked, head down, eyes darting about. The cold air soothed her until she reached a bus stop where she started to tremble with cold. When the bus arrived she sank into the first empty seat, folded her arms tightly, and closed her eyes.

Her mind remained numb until at one point she looked up into the driver's oversized rearview mirror and caught him returning a curious frown. Hurriedly she smoothed her hair and brushed off her coat, cringing at the outright stares of other passengers.

When she got off at her street, light-headedness hit her again. The rumbling of passing cars grated on her ears. Images of blood trickling from the Doberman woman's throat threatened to stop her cold. As she approached her building she squeezed her eyes shut and then opened them to clear her head, reminding herself she had eaten only two biscotti in over twenty-four hours. She remembered Signora Sillano's offer of dinner and checked her watch: eight-fifteen—maybe she wouldn't be too late.

She climbed to her flat to wash up and was greeted by a shiny new lock on her door. Naturally she didn't have the key for it, so she pulled her comb from her back pocket and applied it as best she could. Another quick brush of her clothes and she headed downstairs.

"Come in, Erika." said the signora, peering closely at

her. "Have you used the Lasonil?"

"Yes, thanks. And I see you've already had the new lock installed—thank you for that too."

"A good, long deadbolt. I'll give you the key before you leave. And keep applying the Lasonil, you'll see and feel a difference." The signora continued to study her. "You look worn out. If you haven't eaten I've got polenta on the stove."

Erika sagged with relief. "I was hoping I wasn't too late. I've been meeting people all afternoon."

If shock had previously kept hunger at bay, now her empty stomach twisted and clamored to the point she thought she would collapse. She ducked into the signora's bathroom to wash her hands and comb her hair properly, then quickly joined the signora in the kitchen.

The signora piled her plate with polenta and stewed rabbit. "Some Barbera?"

Eagerly Erika held out her glass. "Gladly."

For a while they ate in silence. Erika didn't know which restored her more, the hot, creamy polenta or the robust Barbera, which seemed to cauterize her battered, shredded nerves. Nonetheless, when the Doberman popped back into her mind, Erika's fork went limp in her hand. If the woman had continued to jab her with her gun...And now the bitch was still on the loose...

"Are you all right?"

"Yes," Erika said, widening her eyes at the signora. "Fine." She took another swig of wine.

"How did your appointment go this afternoon?"

Erika picked through her thoughts. After the battle with the Doberman, her earlier encounters seemed the distant past.

"The man who phoned you here," prompted the signora, "did you meet him?"

Flavio, she meant, of course. "Yes," Erika confirmed, massaging her forehead. "He was pretty vague about Paolo, except to say he's gone underground and doesn't want to be reached." She sighed. "I also talked to someone else who says Paolo needs time to sort things out." *Ivan*, who had gone to meet Flavio.

The signora shook her head sternly. "Well I hope he sorts himself out soon. What about this diamond business with Matilde Fassino?"

"I don't know. I couldn't get anything out of either person. They both said the Comrade cell was shutting down, but that's what they all say."

"Then let's hope it's true."

Inwardly, Erika shook her head: *not likely with the Doberman bitch also visiting Flavio*. She didn't reveal those particulars to the signora; no need to alarm her and revive her urge to call the police. Let her hang on to her hopes for Paolo, since there was nothing she could do, anyway. Erika would have to see things through.

Letting herself into her flat, Erika gave a grim nod of satisfaction at the new lock, then closed herself in and exhaled a long sigh. She pulled the switchblade from her pocket, clicking it open to examine the smear of blood on the blade. God only knew what the Doberman's foot looked like. At least she'd trimmed the woman's wings, slowed her down if nothing more. With a full stomach and a clearer head, Erika could at least view the encounter both philosophically and practically. She moistened a paper towel and wiped the blade clean. The switchblade had served her well, she told herself as she folded the blade back into its handle, better than the slower-opening stiletto could have done. Thanks to Gino, she admitted wryly, it had saved her life.

Despite the day's ordeal, her fatigue did not translate to sleepiness. Her eyes ached, her muscles felt like rubber, but her mind rebelled by cranking out questions. She sank onto the sofa and lit a cigarette, certain the Comrades were still scheming and that Paolo could be involved, wherever the hell he was. Why else had the Doberman been to Flavio's building and then attacked her again? And Ivan—surely he had crossed paths with the woman. Did *both* Flavio and Ivan know the extent of the bitch's viciousness? The thought sent chills crawling over her scalp like a host of spiders. What kind of *help* had Flavio offered Erika?

She drew hard on her cigarette. And where was Keith? Not in San Diego, according to her mother, and not at Ivan's, if he was indeed in Italy at all. Ivan wouldn't have lied, knowing Erika had only to call his parents to verify. *Keith and Paolo: what was going on?* When Erika had asked if Keith was still in San Diego, her mother had replied, "You know he's not." But she *didn't* know! Then she shuddered. Something spectral was slithering through her, a type of misty ghost whispering something she should know but couldn't make out. She rubbed her hair back and forth, blunted her half-finished cigarette and got to her feet. After what she had endured today she just needed to sleep. The duvet, left the previous night after Gino's incursion, still lay in a heap on the sofa, along with her pillow. She changed into her pajamas and for the second night stretched out on the sofa rather than opening it into a bed. She wrapped herself in the duvet and switched off the light.

But she couldn't turn her mind off. Against closed eyelids she replayed her scuffles with Gino and the Doberman—two knife-fights within twenty-four hours, the second requiring her to defend her life against a gun. Yes, she had acquitted herself and hoped both the Doberman and Gino would take notice and tread carefully with her in the future. Naturally, she wouldn't count on it.

Little by little she drifted off. When she woke with a gasp, she didn't know how long she'd been asleep. Only that she'd dreamed of yet another duel. This one with a masked opponent in fencing garb, though like Erika he wielded a knife. She concentrated to remember more. He was tall and bulky, which allowed Erika to evade his lunges. Round and round in circles they moved, Erika fleet and agile, the man strong but ponderous. She had to keep him at a strategic distance, for if he got close enough he could crush her with his weight and then stab her.

In the dream she glanced at her weapon, the stiletto, but for some reason it was now closed. She pulled it half open and flicked her wrist but the blade wouldn't whip open. She finally deployed it manually, barely avoiding a nick by her opponent's blade. She danced out of reach and again he lumbered closer. Much closer. She remembered hearing his panting, and maybe smelling his sweat. His blade glinted and she parried it sideways, her blade looping underneath his, so its tip landed on his jacket. A pause followed, then he collapsed to the ground.

Blood pooled around him. When she touched it with her fencing glove, it radiated out like water hit by ricocheting stones. She yanked her hand back and stared at her stiletto's white handle protruding from his gut. She knew he was dead and reached for his mask. Just as she started to lift its bib the scene went black.

Erika's head was damp, her pajamas contorted in lumpy wrinkles. She threw off half of the duvet. She had wanted to see his face, for she sensed the man in her dream wasn't the young fencer who had died in real life. She closed her eyes, hoping to drift back to sleep, to continue the dream and unmask this new opponent. Instead, a buzzing began in her head, a subtle static she could both hear and feel. She sat up. Something else was strange about the dream: she and her opponent hadn't been dueling in the fencing hall, but outdoors amidst grass and large trees— somewhere familiar.

She rose in the dark and walked to the window, trying to clear the harrying clutter from her mind. And it worked, for when she pulled aside the drapes she discovered a luminous sky over Turin and a layer of snow on the roof. She had never seen a night sky like this, one that bathed the city in pinkish-yellow light almost as bright as day. She stood transfixed, thrilled at a phenomenon she surely would never have witnessed in San Diego.

And then it came to her, a glimmer of memory. *San Diego*...daytime in Balboa Park, the setting of the dream duel. Leaving the drapes open, she paced thoughtfully in the illuminated room. *Why had she been dueling in Balboa Park and why did it all seem familiar?* But nothing more would come to her and she finally gave up. She was getting cold and went to close the drapes, indulging in one more long, sweeping look at the enchantment outside her window. She turned on her table lamp—four o'clock—and decided to unfold the sofa into a proper bed. She tucked in under the warmth of the blankets and began taking a mental inventory of all the nature areas she knew in Balboa Park. She named every species of plant she could remember, one by one, until she at last dozed off.

Three fitful hours later, Erika rose, got ready, and downed an espresso. Before leaving the mansard she pulled some dollars out of the stash she kept in a corner of the armoire. The phone calls to America had almost cleaned her out and she would have to exchange money to pay for the train to Asti. At least Gino hadn't rifled through her place and stolen her cash during his intrusion. But then he really didn't seem the thieving type.

Her black leather loafers provided almost two inches of crepe-wedge heel in a layer of snow equally as deep. Shopkeepers were out shoveling. By the time the tram arrived at Porta Nuova station her feet felt icy. The sky loomed like whitewashed plaster; not the sunny relief that blossomed after a snowfall in the mountains of California.

In the station she made a call to Elsa, exchanged her dollars for lire, and bought a ticket for Asti. An hour later her feet were mincing through snow in the Asti gardens, on her way to Elsa and Angelo's apartment.

Elsa opened the door with a smile that immediately twisted into an appalled frown. "What happened to you!?"

"I slipped down my stairs." Her *stairs* story had become as handy an excuse as the *Cardinale* firebombing for the Comrades. She wiped her shoes a second time on the doormat and stepped inside.

"You didn't break anything..." Elsa said fearfully.

"No, I've just got this ugly black eye."

Elsa examined the bruise with a distasteful squint. "Have you put anything on it?"

"Only Lasonil."

"Good, keep it up. If you want to mask it somewhat, foundation will work."

Erika nodded. "I think I'd better take these off," she said, looking down at her wet shoes, the hems of her trousers soaked as well.

"Your feet must be freezing—no boots?"

"I didn't think to bring any; you don't need them in San Diego."

"Well, we're not in the tropics here," said Elsa, taking Erika's coat and hanging it up while Erika removed her shoes. "You don't have a purse today?"

"...I didn't want to deal with it in this weather."

Elsa gave a slightly curious look but asked nothing further. "I'm going to get you the brand-new pair of slippers I bought Angelo," she said instead. "Take your socks off too, I'll hang them to dry on the radiator."

"Sorry I called at the last minute," said Erika as they skated down the hall to the kitchen on their *feltri*.

"I'm glad you did, gives us a chance to see you. Angelo's out so we'll have tea and then lunch when he gets back."

The kitchen was steaming with simmering pots, and its warmth, the softness of the new slippers, the familiar sedate atmosphere and fragrant food aromas, soothed Erika into semi-complacency. For a heavenly moment she felt like giving up the chase. But the purpose of her visit—the need to know—regained the high ground, and after Elsa brought tea to the table and they had finished their small talk, Erika began her enquiry.

"I know this might sound odd," she said, and sucked in a breath through her nostrils, "but have you seen any other American relatives lately or heard of any arrivals?"

"No..." Elsa drawled out, tilting her head and narrowing her eyes in curiosity. "Is someone supposed to visit?"

"Keith, maybe," Erika said after a studied pause.

"Your brother? We've only met him once. Is he visiting you for Christmas?"

Christmas: its imminent arrival hadn't been a solid reality for Erika. She'd barely noticed the sparse decorations about town.

"It's a week from tomorrow," Elsa reminded her. "If Keith is here you can both have Christmas lunch with us. But why are you asking *me* if I've heard anything?"

"Well, I don't have a phone..."

Elsa continued to stare quizzically at her, so Erika thanked her for the holiday invitation, though she could hardly see into this afternoon let alone next week. Her thoughts channeled back to the mix-up in the telephone office. If Keith had changed his number, her mother surely possessed the new one...so—

"What's wrong?" Elsa broke in.

For a moment Erika observed her cousin. Though Elsa and Signora Sillano were around the same age, Elsa seemed almost aristocratic compared to the signora: tall and stiff-postured, dressed in a cashmere sweater and soft wool skirt; her hair coiffed in short grey waves, her hands long, their skin smooth and unmottled. Unlike Signora Sillano, Elsa had been spared a hard country life. She had always lived in the city, minus the war years when she and Angelo ran an *osteria*, a tavern, in Val d'Aosta and made a fortune off the soldiers. Granted Erika felt more at ease at Elsa and

Angelo's, where she could open a drawer at will or turn on the television when she fancied; yet after all that had transpired since her arrival in Italy, her confidante would remain Eugenia Sillano.

"Nothing's wrong," Erika answered. "Because I don't have a phone, I wondered if you'd heard anything from America."

Elsa shook her head in consternation. "From which American besides you would I hear news? Your mother doesn't speak Italian, neither does Keith—"

"Bruno?" Erika suggested. Although she knew perfectly well her father never wrote or called anyone in Italy (he didn't even speak proper Italian) she still grasped at the slimmest of threads.

"We haven't talked to him since he was a young man here with your grandparents." She raised an eyebrow. "So might your brother be coming?"

Erika looked down at her tea as though the dregs might reveal a clue to this endless enigma. "I don't know." She glanced up at Elsa, staring through her, her mind already racing ahead to her next move.

31: Ally and Trickster

On her return from Asti, Erika found the roads plowed but the sky morphing into a glowering grey, threatening further precipitation. She went directly to the SIP, where she located the various phone books for Italy. She picked up Turin's and started leafing through the alphabet. *Testa*: the surname appeared a few times but there was only one *Giorgio* Testa. She jotted down the number, submitted it to the clerk at the counter, and was assigned a booth.

"Hello?" answered a man's voice.

"Giorgio Testa?" asked Erika.

"Who's calling?"

"Erika Rivoli, Paolo Lorenzi's friend. I met you at the hospital after the *Cardinale* fire."

"Yes, I remember you."

"You joked about looking like a mummy," Erika added. "I hope you're doing better."

The comment altered his tone favorably. "Ha! I am! I've shed my bandages and can no longer frighten my enemies into submission."

His humor buoyed her. She recalled the hospital scene, with Paolo patting Giorgio's head. She had come away with a good feeling about this man. Maybe he could help her.

"You know, I'm worried about Paolo," she went on. "I haven't seen him since the day of the firebombing and he won't get in touch with me."

"Have you tried his home?"

"Yes, I talked to his father yesterday. He says Paolo's gone off with friends—doesn't know where, or when he'll return." Erika searched for the right words. "Paolo was very upset at what happened to you and the *Cardinale*, and it seems things have gotten worse with him ever since."

In the silence that followed, she shifted nervously in the booth.

"Is he still with those Comrades?" Giorgio finally asked.

"I'm afraid so." Giorgio's mention of the Comrades encouraged Erika all the more. "They're extremely secretive," she said, "and I think he's in trouble...actually, I'm in a bit of trouble myself. I'd really like to find him so we can help each other, but I don't know what to do. I thought maybe you, being his friend..."

Giorgio let out a long, heavy sigh. "We used to be close, Erika, but I have no idea where he could be. We haven't seen much of each other since he joined that group."

"Oh..." Erika started to sink inside.

"But you say he's in trouble?"

"Yes—I think they're planning a crime. And these Comrades have thugs working for them who've attacked me."

"Attacked you?" Another pause. "Sounds serious...we could talk..."

"This afternoon or this evening?" Erika suggested, closing her eyes in hope.

"Late this afternoon. I'm dealing with the mess at the *Cardinale*, but I could meet you around five."

"Thank you. I'd like to meet somewhere no one will see me."

"You can come to my house. I live in the building to the right of my newspaper office. Do you know where that is?"

"Yes—corso Regio Parco."

"Ring, and I'll let you in—third floor."

Just before five, Erika approached the *Cardinale,* its windows still covered with plastic sheeting, its redbird emblem still smudged with soot: ironic and sinister, since the perpetrators were a right-wing militant group called The Black Order. Giorgio too had been a victim of violence, another thing that bolstered her sense of trust in him. On the building next to the *Cardinale* she located the plaque with the list of residents and pressed the buzzer next to his name.

"*Buona sera*," came the greeting. The door clicked open, Erika took a last look up and down the dark street, and ducked inside.

"Come in," said Giorgio, holding his apartment door open as she reached the landing. As she walked in past him, he gave her a sidelong look, and she knew why. "Let me take your coat." Before handing it to him she pulled her sweater down well over her back pocket where she had transferred her knife, a habit she'd quickly acquired when knowing she would have to part with her coat.

"Shall I make you coffee?" Giorgio asked, eyeing her face again before hanging her coat on a peg next to the door.

She knew she should explain her black eye, particularly since she'd said she'd been attacked. But first she wanted to find out how he was doing. He didn't look too bad, his burns resembling abrasions now. "Maybe just a glass of water," she told him.

"Have a seat on the sofa and I'll bring it."

Giorgio's flat was small from the looks of the sitting room and what she could glimpse of the kitchen. He probably put most of his money back into his business, such as it was now. Piles of newspapers, sheets of graph paper scribbled with notes, and a typewriter cluttered the small dining table that sat in a corner of the sitting room.

"How are you?" she asked as he arrived with a tray of glasses, a liter of mineral water, and a tall bottle of beer. "Your burns look like they're healing."

"They are. I still have to apply ointment, but I dispense with the bandages when convenient."

"I'm so sorry about your friend," Erika said, at a loss for

more original words.

Giorgio nodded his appreciation, clearing his throat and focusing on setting the tray on the wooden coffee table.

Erika saved him further discomfort by asking a different question. "And the *Cardinale*?"

"Now that's a big pain," he said, drawing himself up confidently. "I'm dealing with insurance red tape and the police, and it's like grappling with a hydra. I get one thing accomplished, and another bureaucratic head sprouts up to harass me. And I do have to fix that sign. The soot makes my redbird look like he's turning fascist."

Erika smiled at their shared observation.

Giorgio dropped onto the sofa with a weighty *thunk*. "Of course cardinals aren't native to Italy, apart from the princes of the Church," he said with a wink. "But I like your American redbird."

He was overtly examining her eye now. He appeared even bigger than when Erika had first met him in the hospital, when he was semi-cocooned in bandages and blankets. He wore his dark hair unfashionably close-cropped, which she deemed complementary to the kind of big-man-self-confidence he exuded: *I'm massive, I like my hair nice 'n short, and the hell with what anyone else thinks*. She figured part of his confidence also stemmed from his age. He had to be well over thirty. She started to speak, then looked away, uneasy about how to start with the whole saga. Plus, it felt so good to simply relax for a spell.

"There's beer too if you'd like," he said, indicating the bottle of Dreher lager.

Erika smiled politely and took the water. "This'll be fine, thanks."

"You mentioned Paolo is in trouble?"

Good, they were on. Erika launched into a summary ending with, "I'm sure Paolo and his Comrades are plotting something illegal, and I'm almost positive it involves Matilde Fassino." She took a sip of water and waited, reflecting on Paolo's snatching of Fassino's purse. Surely he'd been after some item in it.

"...I see." Giorgio scratched his temple in reflection before leaning forward to pour himself some beer. He gave a weary shake of his head. "Paolo would do anything to get back at that woman."

Erika nodded eagerly. "I know about what happened in the war. Have you heard the rumor about her diamonds?"

He took a swallow of beer. "Sure, but it's probably bullshit—excuse my language."

"No excuses necessary. Whatever the case, I think the Comrades plan to steal something."

Giorgio grunted and downed a good half of his Dreher. "I wouldn't put it past those idiots. You say you haven't heard from Paolo since the attack on my newspaper?"

"Right. Just before it happened he told me he was breaking with the Comrades. But I don't think that's true, I think he's with them now."

Giorgio finished his glass, refilled half of it, and took a contemplative sip. "I used to think Paolo had a sensible head on his shoulders, but he's turned out to be a moron. I told him these Comrades were asses. According to Paolo they dismiss my socialist newspaper as weak and cowardly—in other words, not red enough for them. Not that I give a shit about their opinions, but I do think one of them might have been involved in the firebombing."

"What? I thought the Black Order was responsible."

"They are, according to the police, and that's the mystery. I got a tip about a visitor snooping around the *Cardinale* about a week before the bombing. Supposedly she was connected to Paolo's Comrades. Around that time, the same person attacked Franco, my partner who died in the bombing. She crossed paths with him in the street one night and kicked him in the stomach with hiking boots."

Cazzo! Erika felt she'd been kicked in the solar plexus as well. "Was the woman short and stocky, with short brown hair?"

"Yeah, a truly nasty type."

"I call her the Doberman."

"You *know* her?"

"She and another thug have been hounding me for weeks, and I'm positive they're involved with the Comrades."

Giorgio lasered a sharp frown at her. "Did they do *that* to you?"

Erika blushed automatically. "Yes."

"*Cristo!* The same woman?"

"No, someone else."

"And Paolo's scheming to steal diamonds with these people?"

"At the very least I think they're going to do something to Matilde Fassino. Still, why would someone from the Red Comrades be associated with the Black Order?"

Giorgio squinted across the room. "It's what I've been trying to figure out myself. In any case, Paolo's got to be mad to stay with this lot." He looked Erika in the eye. "But whatever he's planning, unless he's lost his mind completely, he would not countenance an attack on you— not if he cares for you."

If he cares for me, Erika murmured to herself. "Well, I think he's out of control and in too deep."

Giorgio rubbed his sideburn and let out a sigh. He heaved himself up and went to look out the window.

"You don't see anything suspicious?" asked Erika.

He let the curtain flop back. "No, should I?"

"Well, the Doberman and that other thug have been following me."

"Do you have *any* idea where Paolo might be?"

"One of the Comrades, Nadia Regis, has a country house in the middle of nowhere. I went there once at night, and it was hard to find. Paolo could be holed up there with them."

"Nadia, eh? I met her through Paolo at a demonstration. She's one who always crows people aren't red enough."

"I'd like to check the place out," said Erika, "but I don't have a car."

"And you wouldn't want to just show up in a taxi." Giorgio gave a brusque laugh. "No, I'm sure they wouldn't take kindly to visitors. But...I could drive you tomorrow to see if Paolo's car is parked there..."

Erika felt a rush of enthusiasm.

"I'd even like to catch that bitch who helped kill Franco while burning down the *Cardinale*," he added. "Is Paolo still driving his Alfa GTV?"

"Yes!" Her judgment about Giorgio had proven good, and her spirits soared.

That night Erika again woke as if an engine was revving up inside her. She turned onto her back and drew calming breaths, all the while replaying in her mind a second dream-duel in as many nights.

Once more she had been fencing in Balboa Park, now near the Café Del Rey Moro. This time she and her nemesis employed proper foils, but that was the only thing normal about the encounter. In this dream her opponent had transformed into something grotesque. Short and slight, he pranced about like a court jester, wearing something like a carnival mask that hid his nose and eyes. He sneered at Erika, as though the match were a joke, making unruly and extravagant flourishes with his foil, which Erika parried with ease, then sniggering as he stepped back to take a dramatic bow.

Exasperated at this ridiculous theater, Erika finally lunged at his widely open target, tapping his ludicrous green-and-white striped doublet with the plastic tip of her foil. His mouth dropped open in surprise. His eyes, peering from the sequined, feathered mask, darted to his jacket whose white stripes now began to bleed red. Soon the entire jacket turned scarlet, his legs buckled and he fell to the grass, his foil landing beside him—*her* Italian foil.

She tried to reach him to lift his mask, but it was like plodding through waist-high water to get there. His lips were curled into a familiar grimace; she thought she almost recognized him...then the curtain descended and she'd woken up.

She sat up. Her head was starting to pound, her thoughts, her memory, screaming to break through and make sense of the dream. The hammering came harder, until she felt there was no room left in her skull for her aching brain. She threw the covers off as nausea clawed at her. She hadn't felt this sick from a headache since after the car accident and her concussion. Unable to hold off any longer she bolted to the bathroom and threw up. Not once, but a second and third time, as if she would eject her entire stomach.

On wobbly legs she pulled herself to the sink and rinsed her mouth, then splashed her sweating forehead with cold water. After a couple of stabilizing breaths she dried her face and staggered back to bed, collapsing on the duvet. The vomiting seemed to have released the pressure in her head, though she felt utterly spent and wasted. Starting to shake with cold, she burrowed under the covers, gazing into the black room. Narrow eyes gazed back at her. The eyes behind the carnival mask, the eyes she couldn't recognize, though she knew she needed to. The pain in her head ebbed further. The carnival mask began to fade, Masonic eye slits taking its place, those fanciful vents on the sidewalk of via Lascaris. In her mind she walked past them, counting them one after another, balancing on the edge of sleep, until she tipped into blackness.

32: Strange Medicine

Sunday morning after the night's ordeal, Erika woke sleepy and somehow rested at the same time, having slept straight through until nine o'clock. She met Giorgio at ten, in a café near neither of their neighborhoods and from there they drove to the countryside. The sky retained its stubborn pall and a vapory mist now rose from the snow, as they weaved through the hills around the village Erika knew to be near Nadia's house.

"I'm not sure," Erika repeated, as they attempted to vet country homes in the mist, cruising slowly in case they spotted Paolo's car. "It was pitch black when my cousin and I came here, and even with Nadia's directions we had trouble."

They returned to the village and stopped at a café.

"Nadia Regis?" responded the barman, as Erika and Giorgio stood at his counter sipping espresso. It was Erika's third coffee of the morning and she appreciated it heartily.

"I think she said her paternal grandparents own the house," Erika continued, "so Regis would be the surname."

"Don't know of anyone called Regis around here," said the barman, one hand resting confidently on his hip.

"You're certain..."

"I'm sure he's right," said Giorgio, returning his empty demitasse to its saucer and plucking a paper napkin from a holder to dab his mouth. "In a village everyone knows everyone, unless there's someone who purposely keeps to himself, and then he'd be known for that. We should move on."

"True," the barman agreed, eyes narrowed. "Which

reminds me of a house that's mainly empty. People've seen cars around the place but none of the occupants come into the village."

Erika looked hopefully at Giorgio.

"Where's the house?" he asked.

They took a different road out of the village, following the barman's instructions to stick to the narrow lane to the left of the village square as it led up a hill. On the right, as they neared the top, they would see the entrance to a long driveway that descended into a hollow.

Erika and Giorgio eased past the driveway and pulled onto a shoulder near the top of the hill, which was covered by a light crust of snow. According to the barman a farmhouse lay in the hollow at the end of the driveway, although nothing could be identified from the street.

"I'm going to turn the car around so we can keep an eye on the driveway."

Giorgio drove to the top of the hill, made a U-turn, then pulled back onto the same shoulder, where he shut off the car's engine and fog lights. For a moment they waited in silence, looking in the direction of the sunken hollow. "Shall we get out and have a closer look?" she said.

They both left the car and walked down a snowy slope, which ran down to more snow-encrusted grass. In the mist they could make out the side of a house and part of the driveway, but nothing more.

They glanced at each other. "I suppose you want to go down there," said Giorgio.

Erica nodded. The slope was neither very steep nor long, so they began their descent crushing the light layer of snow with careful steps.

At the bottom they crunched more frosty grass to reach the side of the house. Its windows were shuttered. Around the corner three cars were stationed on a large concrete courtyard fronting the house. Only one of the cars did Erika recognize, and it was Paolo's.

She flicked her fingers and gritted her teeth, thoughts vacillating between relief at finally locating Paolo and disgust with his lies about breaking with the Comrades, for surely this was Nadia's house. "He's here but what do we do?"

"As a journalist I wouldn't mind going up and ringing the doorbell."

Erika shot him an ironic smile. "Well, we could get a little closer and try to look in the window next to the front door. The shutters are open, and I could slip along the front of the house, ducking under the window."

"I'll follow you."

"Better not to risk both of us being seen."

Giorgio hesitated, his mouth twitching.

"If you wait in the car," Erika continued, "I'll be right back, and if someone *does* spot me we'll be able to drive away fast."

He massaged his chin, his gaze skeptical. "All right, but be careful. Notice the footprints we've left in the snow," he added, shaking his head. "Hopefully the snow will melt and they'll disappear.

Erika nodded, then waited for Giorgio to start back up the slope. She looked around the corner of the house again. Just as she did, the front door opened. She slipped back and waited, her back flattened against the spiky ridges of the stuccoed wall. The door shut with a thud, and heavy footsteps sounded on the concrete.

She peered back around. *Gino!* She recognized his glossy dark hair and ever-present black ski jacket as he made his way along the shoveled walk towards the opposite side of the house. She reached into her pocket and squeezed the switchblade she'd appropriated from him. As he turned the corner of the far end of the house, she walked quickly and quietly to the window. Just a glimpse inside, then she'd get out. Instead, she found the drapes drawn. She heard a car door open from the side of the house where Gino had disappeared. Evidently there was more space for parking. The car door slammed shut and its engine started up. He was leaving!

She sprinted back around the house and up the slope, slipping at one point and snatching at the icy grass. Reaching the car, she yanked open the passenger door and leaped in. "It's Gino, one of the Comrades who's been hassling me—he's leaving!"

"I heard the engine," said Giorgio, who had started his own car. "What did you see inside?"

"Nothing—the curtains were closed." She looked towards the hollow with a grimace. "Let's go before he sees us parked here."

As Giorgio's car passed the long driveway, Erika glimpsed Gino's car approaching the road. She looked back and saw it turn out behind them.

"We could follow him, find out where he's going," she suggested, stuffing her cold wet hands in her pockets. "He doesn't know your car..."

Giorgio glanced in the rearview mirror, nodding thoughtfully. "I've already planned that." He decelerated to twenty kilometers per hour, slow enough to make any driver lose patience, especially an Italian, thought Erika.

Gino ran up behind them, tapping his horn. As he gunned past in the oncoming lane, Erika hunched down. Then, allowing for a discreet distance, Giorgio accelerated. For once Erika thanked the gossamer fog, filmy enough to allow them to pursue Gino without his recognizing her in his rearview mirror.

"Ideally," said Giorgio, "I'd keep a couple of cars between him and me, but it's too foggy."

"You sound like you're practiced at this."

Giorgio returned a smug smile.

They passed through the village, winding along the narrow, wooded lane on its outskirts. The two cars then accessed a wider road. "He's heading for either Asti or Turin," said Giorgio.

Turin, it turned out to be. About forty-five minutes later they entered the southeast of the city, following Gino to where he finally pulled over next to the neon-green cross of a pharmacy. Giorgio stopped at the street's entrance, and he and Erika watched Gino leave his car and enter the pharmacy. "He's lucky to get that parking place," said Giorgio, scanning the street that was crowded with cars, some touching each other bumper to bumper.

"Can we wait here until he comes out?"

The question was answered by the blare of a car's horn behind them.

"*Cristo!*" Giorgio swore. "I'll go around the block."

"Let me out first, I'd like to see what he comes out with."

She exited the car to the reprise of the trumpeting horn, slamming the door as Giorgio drove on.

She slipped between parked cars, reaching the sidewalk and ducking into a cheese shop's recessed entrance.

Gino emerged from the pharmacy carrying a small package. He entered his car and pulled away just as Giorgio returned, complaining he'd been slowed by a car which had double-parked, just as they had done.

"Gino left the pharmacy with a bag," Erika reported. "Who knows where he's going next; maybe back to the farmhouse."

"No point in going back there unless we *do* knock on the door and ask for Paolo."

"True," Erika agreed. As they coasted past the pharmacy, a car zipped into Gino's abandoned spot. "Do you think we could find somewhere to park nearby? I'd like to check out that pharmacy."

"What'll you do there?"

"I don't know yet…"

Giorgio looked at his watch. "Then how about a bite of lunch first? It wouldn't do to rush into that pharmacy right after Gino left."

Erika bit her lip. Giorgio was probably right. "Do you know of a restaurant nearby?"

"I know the best dining spots all over town!" he said with a sonorous chuckle.

They settled into a small *trattoria*, much to Erika's relief, as *trattorias* were casual, moderately priced eateries.

"I used to come here when I was still in school," Giorgio told her.

Despite the no-frills simplicity of the place, Giorgio ordered a three-course meal: an antipasto of roast peppers and anchovies, a plate of tortellini, followed by a veal cutlet, accompanied by a plate of spinach. Erika would have been satisfied with a sandwich, yet ordered two courses at Giorgio's insistence. He was paying.

"So, the pharmacy," he said.

Erika frowned at her eggplant. "Gino's the one who slugged me and I'd like to know what he's up to."

Giorgio's fork and knife clanked against his plate. He looked angry.

"But I got the best of him in the end," Erika quickly added. She considered describing their blade-on-blade tango but decided against it.

"Even so," said Giorgio, "I'd like to take him aside myself—his knuckles wouldn't function the same afterwards. I'm ashamed of Paolo for associating with such a bastard. The only possible motive could be his hatred of Matilde Fassino."

"And I think the others are after something she's got, and if it's not the diamonds I don't know what."

"Who are the others, exactly?"

"Besides that jerk Gino, whose real name seems to be Claudio Voghera, there's Nadia, who you've met. Then there's this guy called Matteo Mattei, a curator at the Egyptian museum and a Freemason who's into Turin's occult."

"You're joking!" said Giorgio, wine glass suspended in the air. "Masonry and communism are mutually exclusive." For a moment he gazed past Erika in consternation.

"The only common motive they might have is money," offered Erika. "Plus ideology. Mattei has a justification for everything, though I can't picture him rallying in the square in his tweed suit."

"Anyone else?"

"A Roman named Flavio Moretti, a Communist who now claims to be a moderate. The problem is, I saw the Doberman, the woman who beat up Franco and attacked me, come out of his building recently."

"Jesus!"

Erika avoided mentioning Ivan. How could that help?

Giorgio wiped his mouth and set his napkin aside. "Anything else?"

"I'm sure something very serious is in the works. You should have seen Paolo's agitation when I last mentioned the Comrades and Matilde Fassino. He lied to me about breaking with the gang, and now we've seen his car at Nadia's house. Which brings me back to the pharmacy. The bag Gino carried out was medicine-sized."

"Something for himself, or maybe for someone in that house...?"

"Mm...If I could find out..."

"The pharmacist won't tell you outright," said Giorgio, pouring out the last of the carafe of Barbera. "Unless..."

Erika pursed her lips. "Unless I went in and told him that *Claudio Voghera* sent me back for something else."

"Mention that you don't want to pick up the wrong item..."

Their eyes locked and they nodded in unison.

Leaving Giorgio parked, Erika strode into the pharmacy, pumped-up with purpose. She spotted only one pharmacist, an elderly, spindly man with smudged bifocals and a dingy-white lab coat that she thought could use a dose of bleach. She approached him, projecting her most confident smile, which she hoped would eclipse her black eye, and placed her hands on his counter.

Once they'd exchanged *buon giornos*, and he had finished examining her bruise, she launched into her spiel. "A colleague of mine, Claudio Voghera, was here about forty-five minutes ago, but now he needs something else."

The pharmacist looked confused, his greasy lenses slung low on his nose. "He sent you here?"

"Yes. He's in a village half an hour away and I'm headed there anyway. He phoned me and said he needed some anti-inflammatory medicine as well."

The wizened man frowned sharply, eyeing her bruise again. "Tavor *plus* anti-inflammatories?"

"...Yes." Electric excitement shot through Erika at having so easily learned what Gino had purchased. Then the excitement flagged. She had no idea what Tavor was, and who knew what effect the combination of the two medicines would produce.

"And the anti-inflammatories are for *him?*" The old man seemed muddled.

Erika took a bracing breath. "Yes."

"I see," he muttered. "What is your name, signorina?"

For a heartbeat Erika's breath caught. "Nadia Regis," she uttered, stomach muscles tightening. "I'm just doing a favor."

At last the old man's confusion seemed to give way. "No matter. I can give you a non-prescriptive anti-inflammatory." He turned to a shelf behind his counter. "Cibalgina should help."

Silently Erika exhaled, then drew herself up to extract money from her pocket.

The pharmacist quoted the price and wrapped up the Cibalgina, taking her money while still hanging onto the package. "What did you say your name was?"

"Nadia Regis." Through the pleasant smile she maintained, a prickly heat began to sting her underarms, her neck...She hoped she wasn't turning red.

Slowly he handed her the package.

"*Grazie*," she said, forcing herself to gently accept it and to not back away too quickly. "*Arrivederci.*"

"*Buon giorno*," he replied, brows and nose twitching.

"It worked," she announced, yanking open the door and sliding into Giorgio's passenger seat. "Gino bought something called Tavor."

"And I see the pharmacist sold you the anti-inflammatories," Giorgio answered, glancing at her package and hoisting himself up. "*Brava!*"

"Thanks, but what is Tavor?"

"A drug for insomniacs, though my mother took it for years for anxiety."

"I can't imagine Gino needing it. He's about as cool and collected as they come."

They gazed at each other. Erika ticked off the names of the Comrades. "Who in the hell could it be for?"

33: An Unexpected Surfacing

I really hope it's not Paolo who needs the Tavor," said Erika, as she and Giorgio fell back to regroup over coffee.

"If it's for Paolo he would have picked it up himself," Giorgio pointed out.

"If he's okay..."

"Whatever the case, I can't imagine his needing a tranquilizer."

Erika fell silent, doubt about the pharmacy encounter creeping into the forefront of her thoughts. "You know, the old pharmacist seemed really confused at first—letting on about the Tavor, and all. But then he started getting suspicious and asked me my name twice. I gave him Nadia's."

Giorgio drew sharply on his Gauloise cigarette, squinting through the smoke. "He could be in league with Gino...Tavor's a prescription drug, so either a doctor prescribed it, or—"

"Or Gino got the pharmacist to give it to him," Erika finished. "In that case he might tell Gino that *Nadia Regis* came in."

"Then it wouldn't be much of a leap to figure out it was you."

"True: black eye, foreign accent...I've got to reach Paolo somehow!"

"On the other hand, the pharmacist might already know Nadia's name and not do anything." Giorgio gave her a sympathetic frown. "If you're worried about retaliation you could stay at my place for a while. I've got a sofa bed."

"I'll keep that in mind. Thank you!"

When she returned home, Erika found a note on the floor just inside her door. She scooped it up, read it, then quickly closed and locked the door before heading downstairs.

"So he's called!" she said, as Signora Sillano ushered her into her kitchen. "When?"

"Not more than half an hour ago. Put your coat over that chair and sit down," said the signora, retrieving a piece of paper from the counter.

"And he wants to meet me?"

"Yes. He said he could only make this one call, so you would have to either show up this afternoon or not. These are his instructions." She placed the sheet of paper in front of Erika and sat down. "I tried to get more out of him but he wouldn't say anything else."

Erika scanned the note. "Thank you, Signora, maybe he'll tell me what's going on." She checked her watch and got up. "I'd better get ready to go."

The signora rose to fetch Erika's coat from the chair and something clanged on the tile floor. She stared as Erika quickly squatted to collect the switchblade. The signora continued to stare. "This is worse than you've led me to believe."

"It's just insurance," Erika said, tapping her bruised cheek. "Once I talk to Paolo things should settle down."

"I'll tell you again to be careful," the signora said, looking both grave and earnest. "But if this goes much further and Paolo doesn't come to his senses, I'll have to call the police." That said, her eyes softened into a bleak smile.

"Thank you, Genia. I appreciate all your support. And I'll let you know how it turns out."

Erika hurried back up to her flat, heart thumping. She felt flushed, and in front of the full-length mirror in the entryway she gave herself a good checking over. The bruise still looked brutal, though it was now a lighter purple. On second thought, it could be an asset for now—let Paolo witness the full consequences of the company he kept.

She went into the bathroom, combed her hair, and put on some lipstick. Paolo had set their rendezvous in Porta Nuova train station in the same café where she had forced Gino to confront her; where he had revealed knowledge of her involvement with the CIA and hinted at some secret about Keith. She still wondered who else might know about her dealings with the agency. As for Keith, all she could do was hope for some further revelation from Paolo.

Entering the station, she cleaved through the bustling foot traffic, then slowed as she approached the café. The coincidence of Paolo's calling not long after she left the pharmacy had ridden with her all the way to the station. Had Gino found out about her visit and told him? Was that why he had surfaced? She longed to get a look at him before they spoke but couldn't spot him inside. She studied the crowd around her, let the hubbub of echoing voices and PA announcements wash over her, and then walked into the café.

After passing the bar she spied him, hidden in the back from passersby. She stopped to observe his profile as he produced a couple of short, reflective puffs from his pipe, his wavy hair looking longer than she remembered.

Then he noticed her. For an instant all she could see was shock in his eyes as he rose; then the exhaustion in his expression, the dark circles under his eyes, the rumpled clothes.

"What happened to you!" he asked, embracing her.

Erika remained silent, watching him until they both sat down. Then she broke the pause. "I've been looking for you for days."

"But your face!" he insisted.

"Doesn't look good, does it?" she said with a bitter smile. "Know who did it?"

"*Signorina*," interrupted the waiter.

"A coffee," said Erika, noting that Paolo had already ordered one too.

"Who did it?" Paolo demanded once the waiter loped off.

"Someone by the name of Gino, or Claudio Voghera, or whatever *cazzo* his real name is."

A shadow passed through Paolo's eyes, his jaw tensing. "I was afraid of something like this, that's why I told you to cut loose. Did he do anything else to you?" he asked in a wary voice.

"No, not him. But this"—she pointed to her cheek— "isn't all. A vicious woman, another Comrade, I suppose, attacked me yesterday. I could have been killed. Is this the crew you left me for?"

A grimace clung to Paolo's face. "I know Claudio Voghera but I've never heard of a woman like this. But I'm going find her and put a stop to both of them!"

Erika shook her head. "Things are beyond that, Paolo, unless you're their boss."

"Ridiculous!"

"But you know Claudio Voghera. And you said you left the Comrades, or were leaving them—I don't know what to believe."

"I'm sorry, I did lie, but I was trying to keep you away from them."

"From them and from what? What are you plotting with them?"

Paolo leaned over the table and took her hands, his expression pained but firm. "I can't involve you. Please understand it's because I love you."

"What kind of love are you talking about, when you don't trust me enough to tell me what you're involved in?" She pulled herself free. "What kind of future can that hold?"

Paolo sat back and rubbed his face as if trying to massage some kind of solution from it. The waiter dropped off Erika's coffee, giving them a hesitant look before leaving.

Erika glanced down at her cup and shook her head.

When she looked up, Paolo was surveying the room. "We can't stay here long. But I don't want to leave you alone. Not with whoever attacked you out there."

"Listen, I've defended myself against three attacks. Besides leaving the Comrades I don't know what you can do for me."

His face looked even more drawn and fatigued after the intense massaging he'd given it, and once more she saw her father—the bloodshot eyes and dark circles of an exhausted Bruno, the fragility that she both feared and wanted to love. An uncanny coldness crept through her.

Paolo was now staring at his hands now resting on the table, his spent pipe propped in the ashtray. "I'm afraid it's too late." His voice rang helpless and hollow. "They wouldn't let me."

"So the Comrades are threatening you as well?"

"They don't know I'm here. They think I'm checking in with my father; that's why I can't stay..."

His eyes wouldn't meet hers, and she could only sit back and stare at him. "Well, I guess I'm on my own then."

"I said I would deal with Claudio."

His gaze finally locked with hers, but she could only return a cynical smile. "And I told you I can handle myself. Plus I have Giorgio Testa on my side."

"What?"

"He's been helping me. He's also concerned about the mess you're in."

"What have you two been doing?" he demanded.

A coolness came over Erika. A splash of icy water that dispelled any further delusion. She was almost certain Paolo knew she'd been to the pharmacy, though naturally he wouldn't reveal it. And if he was privy to that, he probably suspected she had found Nadia's country house.

"I had to talk to someone," she said, spreading her hands. "God knows, you haven't been around."

Paolo sighed and rubbed his face again.

"And I need *someone* in my corner," Erika continued, "in addition to Signora Sillano. They both care about you, you know?"

Paolo's hands dropped to his lap. "You haven't brought *her* into it...?"

"*You've* done that by sending me messages through her. What do you expect? You run off, telling me you'll call and then don't..."

"I'm sorry." His eyes softened and he held out his hand. "But the fact that I love you means I can't risk involving you—"

"*No!* We're going round in circles!"

He withdrew his hand. Red-faced, he asked, "So what does Giorgio say?"

"He told me I could stay with him if things got rough. And I really appreciate that!"

For a moment Paolo gazed past her. Then, leaning in and reaching out to touch her, he quietly said, "Let me see your face." She let his fingers reach her chin and tilt it delicately to get a closer look at her left cheek and eye. "This can't happen again," he said with stone-like resolution. "Have you gone to Giorgio's yet?"

"I'm considering it. Claudio Voghera or that woman might come after me again and I don't want to make myself an easy target, since they both know where I live. They don't know about my link with Giorgio—unless *you* tell them."

Paolo's hand slid past her chin to caress her hair. "Don't say that. I would never put you in harm's way." Her eyes flashed and he immediately dropped his hand. "I've failed you, I know...my poor Erika."

Erika didn't reply. It was too depressing to affirm what he'd said. As for *poor Erika*: what did that mean?

"Let me come with you to Giorgio's," he said, hopefulness ringing in his voice.

"I haven't even told him I'll go."

"I'll call him. We can spend this evening together there. I'll call the Comrades and tell them my father's not well and that I have to stay with him. Then I'll call you at Genia Sillano's to confirm everything."

Erika's eyes narrowed and he blushed. His priorities were twisted and he knew it. He first had to account to the Comrades and then invent an excuse to be with her. *What a farce.* Still, with more time tonight, she might pry the Comrades' scheme from Paolo and maybe convince him to back out of it. What was there left to lose?

34: Beneath the Masks

Upon returning to her building, Erika went straight to Signora Sillano's, but the landlady didn't answer her door. Hoping Paolo hadn't called while the signora was out, Erika continued upstairs, flicking her fingers repeatedly until she reached her door. Inside, she almost slipped on a piece of paper on the floor. Another note from the signora: Erika was to meet Paolo at Giorgio's this evening. She squeezed the note tightly, crumpling it in combined eagerness and frustration.

When she got to Giorgio's flat, Paolo hadn't yet arrived.

"He said he had to check in with his father," Giorgio told her. "And he'll probably have dinner with him."

"Oh," said Erika, trying to check her disappointment. "His message said I should come at eight o'clock."

Giorgio gave a helpless shrug while Erika heaved an internal sigh. "You know," she said, "I appreciate what you're doing tonight, not to mention driving me around today."

"Not at all," Giorgio replied with a dismissive wave. "Maybe between the two of us we can straighten out our fickle friend."

"I hope," she said. "If he comes."

"Listen," said Giorgio, his smile encouraging, "I was just about to make myself a couple of sandwiches for dinner. Just prosciutto and cheese—haven't had time to shop—would you join me?"

Giorgio shoved his typewriter, newspapers and files to a corner of the dinette table so they could settle in. Once Erika began eating she relaxed a bit, though she couldn't keep her eyes off her watch. It was almost nine o'clock when they finished.

Giorgio gave in to the contagion and checked the clock on the wall behind her. "Maybe we need a little something strong while we're waiting. I've got some *genepì*. Have you tried it?"

Erika nodded absently.

"An excellent digestive," Giorgio went on. "The herbs that go into it come from our northwestern Alps."

Erika cared very little about *genepì* at the moment, yet she didn't want to disappoint one of the only two people now helping her.

Giorgio rose and returned with the bottle and two liqueur glasses. "Wish I had some dessert to share. When all this blows over, you and Paolo must come for lunch or dinner so I can treat you to my culinary skills."

Another time...who could guarantee that? Giorgio was keen to support her morale, although she sensed a hint of pessimism in his tone.

"I hope so," she said.

For another half hour they sipped their *genepì* and made small talk until Erika could no longer contain her worry. "I don't know why he's so late."

"I guess a number of things..." Giorgio muttered, offering her a cigarette.

"Hopefully not the Comrades." Erika politely declined his proffered pack of Gauloises—the French cigarettes smelled almost as strong as cigars—then went on to explain, "Gino could have followed him, especially if he's on to me from the pharmacy. I wouldn't put it past him to—"

The interphone buzzer cut her off. She stiffened.

Giorgio raised his eyebrows in expectation and hoisted himself out of his chair. He picked up the receiver. "*Sì?* Okay." He tapped the phone's button. "He's on his way up."

Exhaling heavily, Erika sat back.

Giorgio had the door open by the time Paolo reached the landing.

"*Grazie!*" Paolo said, giving Giorgio a strong, sustained handshake. "You look much better than you did in the hospital," he added, with a slap to Giorgio's back.

Erika sat with her arms folded as she watched the exchange in the doorway. Paolo seemed just fine; he'd made her wait so long, she would not get up to greet him with a hug.

"Sorry I'm late," he said to her, discarding his coat on the couch.

With a tight smile Erika nodded. An uneasy frown darkened his eyes as he bent over to kiss her cheeks.

"Sit down," Giorgio insisted. "We're just topping off dinner with a *genepì*. I'll get you a glass."

Flippantly, Erika raised her own, to which Paolo returned a weak but hopeful smile.

Paolo and Giorgio sat down, and Giorgio filled the three glasses. "Well," he said, observing the taut silence, "*Salute.*"

Erika and Paolo sat facing each other on Giorgio's king-size bed, Giorgio having offered them the room for privacy.

"Could you trust me to finish this commitment?" Paolo asked. "*Please*, if you care about me, just wait a couple of days and then I'll leave the Comrades for good and we can be together."

His words rang flat and clichéd. "*Trust?* You don't even trust *me* enough to tell me what you're doing. You at least owe me that."

Paolo shook his head vigorously. "I won't put you at more risk. Plus"—he looked down at the striped bedspread—"you wouldn't understand."

"You won't give me the chance!" Erika edged slightly away from him. "You have no business talking about trust." She kept her gaze level as Paolo's eyes rose hesitantly to meet hers. "I know you're planning something against Matilde Fassino. Stealing her diamonds, maybe?"

Paolo stared at her in wonder. "How did you come up with *that*?"

"If I'm off base, then tell me the truth."

"Of course we're not planning to steal any diamonds," said Paolo, observing her thoughtfully. "You know, I've always considered you smart but never thought you'd pursue things this far...maybe you *ought* to be working for the CIA."

This shouldn't have surprised her considering Gino's threats, still she was indignant. "Did Claudio Voghera tell you this?"

Paolo continued to study her, his gaze turning cynical. "Obviously I'm not the only one who hides things."

"It's not the same! The CIA is in the past and has nothing to do with now, or with you." In frustration she sliced the air with her hand. "*You're* the one screwing up our lives with this Matilde Fassino plot!" Suddenly she stopped. Something had exploded into the forefront of her mind—an idea, from a clue she should have already linked to the puzzle. "You've got her, haven't you? You're holding Matilde Fassino until she tells you where her diamonds are, or something else of value. That's what the Tavor is for—to keep her calm." She drew herself up in triumph.

Paolo, on the other hand, went red with anger, his eyes flashing. "Why do you give a shit about that evil, criminal bitch? She and her husband stole every cent my mother had and almost got her deported to Auschwitz—do you *understand* what that means?"

He looked away with a gaze turning from rage to desolation. In the dimness of the room, lit only by the small lamp on Giorgio's nightstand, he appeared as dark and distant as the cold universe that seemed to surround them.

His attention slowly returned to her. "You've got to stop playing spy, Erika."

"This isn't a game, and I won't stop until I find out what's going on with my brother Keith and the rest of you. He—"

"Erika...you're never going to find your brother."

The utterance was almost a whisper, and she thought she might have misunderstood him. "What?"

A weighty sadness now filled Paolo's eyes, accompanied by a doleful smile which unnerved Erika.

"What do you mean, *I'll never find him,*" she said.

He scooted towards her and put his hands on her shoulders. "I..."

She shrugged them off. "Have you *seen* my brother?"

"No."

"Then what do you know about him?"

"Listen, Erika, I want to protect you, but some things...if you don't come to grips with them..."

"What are you talking about?"

His eyes narrowed cautiously. "Your fencing accident..."

"So? You're aware of that. You know it still bothers me. Who wouldn't be haunted by something like that?" She looked at the nightstand and its faint beacon of light. In an increasing tone of doubt she said, "Keith's been meddling..."

"No—listen to me!" Paolo gripped her shoulders again and she was forced to focus back on him. Something far in the back of her mind was pricking her, a strange presentiment trying to break clear of the debris in her head. Warily, she stared at him.

"Erika," he said, at a slow, measured pace, "the fencing accident didn't involve you and another fencer."

"What are you saying? How would you know anything about it?"

"I know, just as I know about your failure to get into the CIA. I never wanted to hurt you with this knowledge, never wanted to have to correct you, but everything's gone too far now."

She was tempted to fling his hands off again, but a subtle paralysis gripped her.

Paolo drew a shaky breath. "Erika, you didn't kill a fellow fencer, you accidentally...you didn't mean to...but it was your brother who died."

For a long moment she sat silent. Then static started up in her head, growing and mixing with the chaos that continued to swirl around and inside her. "Repeat what you just said."

He squeezed her shoulders. "The one you stabbed...it was your brother."

A pulsating in her head joined the static so that she could barely hear his words, hardly feel his touch. The blood charged through her vessels with appalling pressure, a horrendous hammering, worse than she had ever experienced.

She gasped, and clutched her head. Eyes squeezed shut, she let herself fall onto her side on the bed.

"Erika, are you all right?"

Gripping her head, she rocked on the bed. Faintly she felt his hands on her back.

"Erika!"

"Horrible migraine," she managed to utter, panting.

"What can I do?" His hand was stroking her.

She shook her head, the pounding now clanging like giant church bells.

"Some aspirin," said Paolo. "Giorgio must have some."

She was about to be sick and wrenched herself up and off the bed.

"Where are you going!"

Erika flung open the bedroom door and lunged into the hall towards the bathroom. Inside, she slammed the door.

Someone was knocking. "Erika!" came a plea. She heard it right before she dropped to the toilet and threw up. She vomited again, and when at last nothing was left, she fell back against the wall. Like an orchestra slowly being hushed by its maestro, the pressure and the clanging and the static all began to diminish, and she could finally breathe.

Over her flushing of the toilet she again heard Paolo. "Erika, I'm coming in!"

"I'm okay," came her shaky voice as the door opened.

Paolo stood on the threshold, Giorgio behind him in the hall. "What can we do?"

"Nothing. I'll be better now." She pulled herself to her feet, Paolo's hand on her shoulder.

After rinsing her mouth and face, she made her way back to the bedroom, crossing paths with Giorgio who entered the bathroom. After she'd collapsed onto the bed he arrived with a wet cloth. "Put this on her forehead and call me if I can help," he told Paolo, before stepping out and closing the door to a crack.

She rolled onto her back, accepting the cool cloth from Paolo's hands.

"Just rest," he said. "No need to talk."

Erika didn't respond, but her gaze met Paolo's as he slipped onto the bed next to her and stroked her arm. She closed her eyes. Before long, she entered the sleep of the dead.

35: Awakening

Erika woke off and on during the night, at times writhing from a dream. Each time, Paolo held her as she fell back to sleep, but when finally she opened her eyes to daylight he was gone. His coat lay on a chair in the bedroom. She had last seen it on the couch where Giorgio must have slept and felt a prick of guilt for taking Giorgio's bed.

Then she remembered. In last night's dream she had seen the individual behind the mask. This time he was no caricature or anonymous fencer, he was her brother Keith, and she had accidently stabbed him before her car crash. The two of them in Balboa Park. He had proposed trying his hand at fencing. and she had felt eager to demonstrate her skills.

So they had loaded Erika's gear into her car and driven to Balboa Park to enjoy the space and the outdoors. *And*, for Erika, the attention. She and her fencing companions had previously put on shows for passersby. Fencing could *feel* like acting, and as she lay quiet on Giorgio's bed she recalled the details of that day as if she were remembering a play. No, it was like a movie, for once it started to roll in her mind she couldn't stop it:

They parked near the Café Del Rey Moro and walked to a patch of even, grassy terrain. She let Keith wear her new fencing mask, jacket, and glove while she used her old, well-worn gear. When offered a choice between her new Italian foil or her old, heavily-battered Spanish weapon, he insisted on the flashy Italian model. She began teaching him basic parries and how to advance, retreat, and lunge.

But he grew impatient. "Let's just get on with it, I'm here to have fun." He was twenty years old but acted like he was fifteen.

She gave the command to begin and he started towards her, twirling his blade and extending it before he'd even reached her. She deflected it effortlessly, landing the plastic tip of her Spanish foil squarely on his white jacket.

"One point against you." She laughed good-naturedly as she pulled off her mask. "Not as easy as you thought, eh?" A couple of people had stopped to watch, placing her in the limelight.

"We'll see next time," Keith said firmly, positioning himself to start again.

He charged down the grass again, at one point hopping from side to side as if he were playing basketball.

"Watch yourself," Erika called through her mask. "Keep your feet on the ground and your target area covered. No sweeping slashes like in the movies."

He lunged at her, and again she flicked his blade aside and scored.

Applause rose from a growing pocket of spectators. She removed her mask and took a bow.

"Why don't you ever attack?" Keith muttered.

"Don't need to—just have to wait and take advantage of your obvious moves." She winked at the crowd. "But if you'd like to see an attack..."

At that, the little audience clapped harder, and Erika grinned before hooking her mask back on. She let Keith bound around a bit longer, swatting away his blade until a decent distance separated them.

Then she launched a flèche, the plastic tip on her blade striking his jacket collar as her momentum sent her streaking past him. If it weren't for the sound of a metallic snap and the strange drag she felt against her foil, she would be preparing to answer the crowd's applause with an even deeper bow.

But there was no applause...her blade had broken...its sheared metal penetrating Keith's collar and jugular vein. He lay on the grass face up, the life draining out of him. She collapsed next to him. Someone ran to the café to call an ambulance...

The film finally stopped. Breathing heavily, Erika sat up against Giorgio's headboard, covering her tear-streaked cheeks with her hands. How could she have blanked all this out?

The only explanation had to be the car crash, which followed on the heels of the fencing accident and after Keith's funeral. She had spent days in the hospital, mute and concussed. She had dreamed...just as she had dreamed of absurd, alternative fencing scenarios these last couple of nights in Italy. One particular dream, however—the one featuring the killing of a fellow fencer—must have got trapped in her mind, suppressing the true tragedy of Keith. She shook her tortured head in wonder as to when and how this substitution had occurred. She just didn't know.

Why did Keith have to choose the new Italian foil? The weapon had a pristine blade—versus the Spanish foil's old one—and would probably never have broken had Erika used it for her flèche.

She wiped her eyes with a tissue from a packet on the night table and stared bleakly at the window, wishing she could repel the intrusive light and retreat into a dreamless sleep.

The door creaked open. "You're awake." Paolo watched her for a moment before entering to sit on the edge of the bed.

"It's okay," said Erika softly. "I understand what happened. I'll be able to get up now."

He stroked her shoulder. "You don't have to."

"How did you find out?" she asked in a far-off voice, her eyes on the window again.

"About your brother?" Paolo looked down uncomfortably. "One of the Comrades."

"Who?" Erika demanded.

"Flavio. He has an informant in the security services."

"Flavio," she grunted, remembering their conversation in the pub. *So this is what he wouldn't tell her.* "But how would the Italian security services know about my brother?"

"I don't know, Erika."

"Has Flavio told *everyone*?"

"I don't know that either. He just recently mentioned it to me."

Erika gazed at him askance. *Why now?* But she didn't ask. "Evidently, Claudio Voghera knows too. Both he and Flavio warned me not to pursue the subject of my brother." *And now you enlighten me right after I followed Claudio-Gino to the pharmacy...*

Paolo stroked her hair.

She pulled away from him, swung her legs off the bed.

"You should rest!" he protested.

"I'm fine." She stood up and headed to the bathroom, leaving Paolo to stare after her.

Once the door was closed, it was Erika's turn to stare at the wreck in the mirror. New tears were sprouting from her swollen red eyes to join sweat-matted hair mashed against her bruised cheek. Another sob rose that made her throat ache. Gritting her teeth, she ran ice-cold water and splashed her face until it was numb. Taking a bracing breath and exhaling slowly, she dried herself and rinsed her mouth. She surveyed the bathroom counter. Giorgio's toothpaste and brush stood in a ceramic cup...if only he had an extra. Tentatively, she opened the drawers of a cabinet—no luck. She opened the cabinet above the sink and was relieved to see a bottle of mouthwash. She poured some into her cupped hand and dashed it into her mouth, grateful for the invigorating sting as she gargled. She reached for the comb in her back pocket, but it must have fallen out somewhere.

She reopened the drawer where she'd seen Giorgio's comb, extracted it, and tried to tame her tangled, blond waves. She checked the comb for lingering fair hairs, then returned everything to its place and closed the cabinets.

Paolo was waiting in the corridor when she came out and followed her through the living room into the kitchen where Giorgio was rinsing dishes. Giorgio paused, looking concerned.

"I'm okay," Erika assured him quietly.

"Sit, and I'll make you coffee and something to eat."

She eased into a chair at the short, narrow table that stood against the wall to allow for movement in the small strip of a kitchen.

"You too, Paolo," said Giorgio over his shoulder.

Paolo's gaze alternated between Giorgio and Erika. "Well, I've finished breakfast..."

"No matter, you can keep Erika company while she eats. There's only room for two at the table."

"*You* sit. It's your house and I've already taken advantage of your hospitality."

Erika blushed at her own embarrassing intrusion on Giorgio's tranquility.

"Well," said Giorgio, "if you're going to stand there, I'll have another coffee with Erika. What would you like to eat?" he asked her.

"Caffè latte's all I need."

"Nonsense. After the night you spent, you'll need more than that. I've got biscotti and yogurt. How about a soft-boiled egg?"

The night she spent. How much did Giorgio know? At any rate, she really was famished. She felt gutted, in fact. "Whatever's easiest," she offered.

"Bah," he said, "it's all easy."

As Giorgio busied himself at the counter, Paolo continued to lean against the doorjamb. After half a minute's more observation he said, "I've got to go out for a while. Giorgio, could you please look after Erika?"

Giorgio halted and turned around, his dishtowel hanging on one shoulder. Erika frowned at Paolo. "Where to?" she asked.

"Once I finish this business today I won't have to leave again."

"*What* business?" Erika demanded.

"Let's not start."

"Come on, Paolo," said Giorgio, his voice testy. "Hasn't there been enough damage?"

Paolo folded his arms and stared stubbornly back. "You two have your coffee. I'll be back before long."

He turned on his heel and left the kitchen, Erika scowling at his retreating back. For a moment he disappeared from sight, then he was back with his coat on, opening the front door.

She leaped up as it swung shut. "I can't believe this!" She turned to Giorgio. "Did he tell you anything about what he's up to?"

"No. Just about the unfortunate incident that happened to you. I'm very sorry," he said, looking away for a respectful moment.

Erika nodded her acknowledgement. So Giorgio knew. She didn't know what to say. She could barely digest things herself.

"The coffee's ready," he said, sparing her. "Why don't you sit down."

Giorgio put the two cups on the table but Erika remained standing. She didn't want to think about herself, continuing instead to focus on Paolo. "I know he's going back to that house." And, she added to herself, *he probably dropped that bomb on me last night in order to distract me.*

"And you want to follow him," said Giorgio. "I can tell."

"I'll take a bus to the village."

"Buses to villages are few and far between, and first you'd have to come by a schedule. Then, when the bus drops you off in the square, you'll have to walk the rest of the way to the property—it'll take all day."

Erika began to pace. It was Monday and she would have to call in sick to work again.

"Sit down and drink your coffee," Giorgio insisted, "and we can discuss a plan."

A spark of hope made her heart leap. She reined herself in and returned to the table, which Giorgio had laid with a tin of biscotti. He pulled containers of yogurt from the fridge. "I'll get your egg going," he said.

"Really, this'll be enough, thanks...I should leave soon."

Giorgio frowned at her as he sat down. "Erika, you had a terrible shock last night. Are you sure you're all right?"

She glanced away for a moment, steeling herself, grateful she still had her self-appointed mission spurring her on. "Yes. Don't worry about me. You have your own grief with Franco and the *Cardinale*."

He didn't comment. "What'll you do once you get to the farmhouse?" he asked instead.

"I'll look for Paolo's car the way we did before. If I can somehow stop him from committing a crime against Matilde Fassino...They're holding her—Paolo didn't deny it—and I think the Tavor's meant to keep her calm."

Giorgio observed her more closely as she dipped biscotti in her coffee. Gently he said, "You want to save people—Paolo, the old lady...makes sense, I guess, after what happened to your brother."

Erika considered Giorgio's words. Maybe he was right. She felt disconcerted, embarrassed that her psyche had tricked her so thoroughly. But more than anything right now she wanted to assert control. "Yeah, maybe. But I also don't want to see Paolo go to jail."

"Neither do I, yet he won't listen to reason when it comes to that woman."

Erika recalled Paolo's plea for comprehension as they sat on Giorgio's bed. *Couldn't she fathom Fassino's crime?*

He had asked the same question in the same accusatory way the first time the subject had been broached.

"He wants justice," she said. "I understand his motive, but not if it means torture or murder."

"Justice," echoed Giorgio. "In the form of revenge for unpunished war crimes—a slippery concept and rich fodder for an editorial."

"That's *your* field," she said, looking at her watch and rising from the table. "I need to go."

"But what do you plan to *do* there?"

"I'm not sure..."

"There could be a solution." Giorgio swallowed the last of his coffee and stood. "We could see if Paolo's car is there along with the others—then call the police."

Erika eyed him curiously.

"No matter what, Paolo's in serious trouble. If we get the police involved and stop things now, the law might go easier on him."

"So we're going to turn him in..." Erika said gravely.

"It's the only way to be sure the old lady won't be hurt, if she isn't already."

"But I might be able to talk him down."

"How? Do you think the others will allow you to interfere?"

Erika stared ahead. Paolo would probably get arrested no matter what, and maybe Giorgio's idea was a better way out for him. "Okay. So, were you thinking of driving me again?" she asked.

"Yes. Besides helping Paolo and catching the Doberman, if she's there this time, there could be a story to write in all this." He added a wry smile.

Before they left the flat she called Brigida at the Manhattan school.

"Sorry, but I won't be in this afternoon."

"Again?"

"I thought I'd feel better but I don't."

"You know, Erika, if you continue like this we may have to replace you."

Hot blood mounted to Erika's head but she made an effort to think ahead. Who knew what would happen at the farmhouse? In a level voice she said, "I understand. Please give me two more days."

36: An Unexpected Absence

They could easily know you're on to the house," said Giorgio, as they sped through the countryside towards the farmhouse.

"I know," she replied, reminded of Paolo's appearance after her pharmacy visit and his timely revelation about Keith. She frowned at the road in front of them. "Paolo told me that the Comrade Flavio has an informant in the Italian security services who told Flavio about my brother."

"And how could the security services have discovered that?"

Erika eyed Giorgio, then decided, *hell, it doesn't matter who knows at this point.* "I was a candidate for the CIA at one time...your security service DIGOS could have found out, I imagine."

A laugh rumbled from Giorgio. "This is getting more 007 all the time!"

"They rejected me. Probably because of what happened with my brother, though they never told me that." Her eyes darkened. A wave of sadness and dismay crashed over her, and for an instant she thought the surf might take her down again.

"Are you all right?" asked Giorgio, glancing at her.

"It's such a mess...my life..."

He gave her shoulder a gentle squeeze. "You've already faced up to things, and today you've decided to take action to get Old Lady Fassino out of harm's way and save Paolo a worse fate with the law. That shows you're strong."

Erika steadied herself, managing a modest smile and focusing on the road again. They were nearing the village and she now felt as if time was counting down to an explosion. "It's going to be hard calling the police on Paolo. They'll arrest him before I can talk to him."

"I know. But remember, it's better for him in the long run. If we see his car and the others, it'll mean they probably still have Fassino and could hurt her."

Erika answered with a bleak nod, giving in to a sense of fatalism as they drove through the village and on towards the house.

"You'd better park where you did before," she said as they neared the property.

I'll need to get back fast once I see the cars."

He slowed, pulled onto the shoulder they had occupied during their last visit, and jerked up the handbrake. "We're going together."

"I need to go alone."

"Out of the question!"

"Please. Stay behind the wheel, ready to take off to find a phone as soon as I get back."

"It's too dangerous, especially if that thug Gino's there again, and maybe the Doberman woman."

"I won't be meeting anybody. I already know the property's layout, and as soon as I see the cars I'll get out— *and I'm fast.*"

Giorgio drummed his fingers on the steering wheel, eyeing her. "All right, I know I'm fat but I'm not going to wait long. If you're not back in five minutes I'm coming down after you."

"Give me ten."

"Seven."

"Thank you."

Erika made her way down the grassy slope; it was still slick, though enough snow had melted that a glitter of green shone through. At the bottom she jogged to the side of the house and looked around the corner.

A Ford and a Lancia sat stationed in the courtyard,

neither of them Paolo's or Gino's, or even Ivan's. But they could easily belong to Nadia, Mattei, or Flavio, and she couldn't rule out more cars parked on the opposite side of the house. She would have to check for Paolo's car there.

She examined the walkway that led to the far side of the house. Above the ground floor of the main house hung a balcony, probably belonging to a bedroom. She had noticed it the first time and knew no one could see her from it as long as she proceeded along the walk, hugging the house's exterior wall. Attached to the main house, next to the door from which Gino had exited the first time, stood another building that she guessed was a barn, a typical architectural twinning in old Italian farm complexes. She would have to pass by it as well to reach the end of the structure, beyond which would lie the extra parking. She consulted her watch: time to move, or soon Giorgio would arrive.

She eased along the side of the house, the wall's rough beige stucco scraping her coat. Quickly she reached the window whose shutters remained open but whose curtains were closed. Crouching, she passed the granite sill, then stood and continued past the front door, past a bench, and on towards a set of rustic double doors that stood open. The barn, obviously. Slowing, she peered inside: worn, chipped brick walls, cobwebbed corners, dusty cement floors—no bellowing animals, and best of all, no people.

She rounded the edge of the building and encountered a concrete-paved clearing. Gino's black Opel was parked there along with a blue Mini. No sign of Paolo's Alfa GTV. Mystified, she turned to head back. Now she had to hurry.

Why isn't Paolo here? she repeated to herself, as she slipped past the barn again. *What can it mean?*

She had almost reached the front door when it rattled with the sound of a rotating key. She froze as it opened. Out stepped Gino in his black parka. She inhaled sharply as he spotted her and shook his head. He closed the door and stepped towards her. Erika reached for her knife. Two clicks sounded: the spring of her switchblade and the safety of the semi-automatic Gino had pulled from his jacket.

They stood staring each other down, an interlude that didn't last long. At this distance Erika knew she could not prevail with only a knife.

When Gino spoke, his voice seemed pinched with irritation. "Give it to me," he said, fingers motioning her towards him.

Slowly she obeyed, putting one shaky foot in front of the other, heart thumping in her throat.

"Close it first," he ordered, nodding at the knife.

The front door opened again. "Claudio!" came Flavio's voice from the threshold.

Instinctively Erika turned towards the barn to escape.

"Don't try it," Gino warned. "Now close the blade!"

Grudgingly she did so as he quickly advanced and snatched the weapon from her. He tucked it into his jacket pocket and said, "Get inside!"

Flavio glared at her as she approached the doorway, Gino shoving her from behind. Once inside, Flavio slammed the heavy wooden door and frisked her.

She squinted into the dark room, the back of which was anemically lit by a table lamp sitting on the credenza next to the tape deck: same furnishings, same furniture, same room she remembered from the November evening when she had danced drunk there with Nadia, Flavio, and Ivan; the only truly carefree moment she had experienced since arriving in Italy. So much had changed…

Nadia and Mattei stepped out of the kitchen, both registering indignant alarm. For the first time in Erika's experience Mattei wore not a suit but a heavy wool sweater and corduroys—no doubt, his country gentleman look.

Nadia spoke first, her tone derisive. "What are *you* doing here? And what have you been doing—fighting on the playground?"

It took Erika a moment to realize the reference was to

her bruised face. Mattei was scowling at her. "Your visit is inopportune, to say the least, Erika." He looked at his watch and sighed impatiently.

"Where's Paolo?" Erika demanded.

"Perhaps *you* could tell us that," answered Mattei. "It seems your boyfriend is unreliable on all fronts. But we don't have time to discuss it."

"What do we do with her?" asked Nadia, running a hand through her hair.

"I'll take care of it," said Flavio, stepping forward. "We'll put her in an upstairs bedroom for now."

Nadia moved quickly to the credenza, yanking open the drawer containing her cassettes, only this time extracting a long key. She extended it to Flavio. "Here, put her in the bedroom on the left. It's the only one left I have a key to."

Flavio took the key, and drawing a gun of his own, started marching Erika towards the stairs.

"What about Ivan?" Erika called back.

No one answered. They all stood glaring at her. All but Gino, who seemed to be studying her curiously.

On the way up the stairs, Erika's thoughts reeled to Giorgio; any moment he could walk into this trap. She could only hope he would somehow call the police beforehand.

Flavio opened the bedroom door and surveyed the room, his eyes pausing on a set of floor-to-ceiling glass doors like the ones in Erika's mansard. The drapes were drawn. He motioned her inside with the pistol.

"What's going on?" she whispered frantically to him. "You said you'd help me..."

Flavio shook his head, eyes hard, voice firm. "Just stay put," he said, indicating a set of twin beds. He closed the door and she heard the metal clang of the key turning in the lock. His footsteps echoed down the tiled corridor. Distantly she heard their creak on the wooden stairs. Then, silence.

Erika's first impulse was to rush to the door, but reason told her there was no use trying to open it. So she attempted to slow her breathing and force herself to concentrate on her situation. Everything had happened so rapidly, as though Nadia had popped another cassette in the player and hit fast-forward. The tape was accelerating furiously and all Erika could foresee at its end were Gino's and Flavio's pistols pointed at her—*what shall we do with her?* And where had Paolo gone? Was Matilde Fassino even here? She remembered Nadia's words to Flavio as she handed him the key to the bedroom: "It's the only one left I have a key to." So, could someone else be locked in another room?

She gazed from the room's twin beds to the long, draped window. With a flick of her fingers she strode to it, slid aside the drapes, and looked through the glass. Outside was the concrete-floored balcony she had seen from below. Slowly she eased one of the doors open. It gave a sharp grunt as it scraped the bedroom tiles, causing her pulse to jump. Another little pull and she managed to slip outside.

She crossed the balcony to look out over the railing. No one in sight. Once more she hoped Giorgio had driven straight to the village to call the police rather than approaching the house. She peered down again—she was only one story up, and if she climbed over the railing and hung from its base, she might be able to drop to the courtyard without getting hurt.

The sudden sound of an approaching car made her start. Then the crunching of tires on gravel. She retreated back into the bedroom, leaving the balcony door and its drapes open a crack so she could see out. A large black FIAT sedan came into view, stopping at the end of the driveway near the courtyard. Two men in dark overcoats climbed out and headed towards the house.

She went back to the door leading to the hall, absently tried its handle, then pressed her ear to the wood. Footsteps on the stairs made her jerk back. Muffled male voices and further footsteps in the corridor followed. She faced the window again. *If not now...*

Back on the balcony she checked the yard below once more before swinging one leg over the railing, and then the other. Toes balanced on the slim edge, hands gripping the top of the railing, she twisted to gaze down. On the concrete courtyard sat a large terracotta vase filled with the dregs of summer soil. She would have to swing out with enough momentum to miss colliding with it. After a preparatory breath she began to crouch.

A mechanical clicking sounded from the bedroom. The door opened and swiftly closed.

"What the hell are you doing!" It was Gino, charging towards her just as she prepared to let herself hang into space.

"Get back here! Do you want to break your neck?" The words rang so incongruous that Erika almost forgot what she was doing.

"Come on," he insisted. "Get inside before they see you."

She pulled herself up but remained balanced on the edge, the railing between them. He held no weapon now, yet with a shove he could easily send her plunging from the balcony...But he didn't, and after a couple of achingly slow seconds, in which she rapidly weighed her options, she climbed back over the railing, one eye firmly fixed on him. "Who the hell are you? What's going on?"

"Just follow me."

At the bedroom door they listened to heels clipping down the hall. "Wait here a minute," he said, heading back to the balcony.

Erika deliberated whether to obey or to flee the room. Then voices rose from the courtyard and she followed Gino onto the balcony.

"Get back in!" he hissed, waving her off.

She didn't heed and instead caught a glimpse of the two newcomers below. They were escorting an individual to their car, someone short who shuffled along, covered from head to ankles by a blanket.

Gino shot past Erika. "Stay upstairs!" he ordered, before yanking the door open and jogging down the hall.

She blinked at the empty corridor, then redirected her attention to the courtyard. One of the men was opening the FIAT's trunk while the other continued to steer the blanketed figure towards it. All Erika could distinguish was feet, dainty and high-heeled, but she knew who the blanket disguised.

She left the balcony and slipped out of the room, moving down the hall to the stairs. There she waited, listening to a mix of male voices wafting up from the ground floor, punctuated by shrill words coming from Nadia. The front door opened then shut, and Erika began descending the stairs on the balls of her feet until she could make sense of the words.

"Where have you got *Erika!*" thundered a man's voice, which she had no trouble identifying.

They had Giorgio! Erika took another step down, and the wooden stairs creaked. *Shit.* Instinct made her tighten her hearing against the telltale sound, but a tall man with a slightly hunched back appeared at the bottom of the stairs. "Get down here or we'll shoot your fat friend!"

Heart raging, Erika resumed her descent. The man waved her into the living room. She recognized him from the courtyard along with his partner, who now came into view. Conversely short and stocky, prematurely bald, he held a gun to Giorgio, who stood dabbing his bleeding nose with a handkerchief. *Why had she involved him!*

"*Cazzo!*" yelled Nadia, looking from Erika to Giorgio to the newcomers.

The tall man was pale and thin. He glared at Erika with a mixture of barely-restrained anger and suspicion. "We'll have to take her and the fat man too."

At that, Giorgio dropped his handkerchief. As he bent

to retrieve it he jammed a powerful elbow into the ribs of the bald man, who folded with a groan as Giorgio grasped at his gun. Erika charged towards them.

"Enough, or I'll shoot!" came the harsh bark of the thin man who had pulled out his own pistol. "Back away," he ordered Erika.

Slowly she stepped aside while the bald man straightened and re-aimed his pistol at Giorgio. What could she do? Two guns and she didn't even have a knife. She couldn't help Giorgio, nor could she stop what was happening to Matilde Fassino. *Christ*, she couldn't even save herself.

But where were Gino, Flavio, and Mattei? "Where are the others?" she asked.

Nadia shot her a look contorted with fury and frustration. "You just couldn't back off, could you? All the warnings—Claudio's, and even..." She trailed to a halt, glancing away nervously.

"That's enough," said the tall hunchback. He waved his pistol at Erika and Giorgio, then pointed to the door. "The others are keeping watch outside so we can take you away!"

His answer startled Erika, her thoughts having caught on Nadia's utterance. By *Claudio* she meant Gino, of course. But what did she mean by, *and even...*?

Even the Doberman, Erika's thoughts completed. She glared at Nadia, ignoring the hunchback. "*You* set that woman on me!" She turned to Giorgio. "Nadia knows the woman who attacked Franco and bombed the *Cardinale*!"

Giorgio's eyes drilled Nadia with rage. "I knew you were a filthy bunch!"

Erika glanced back at the hunchback, expecting him to cut them off with impatience. Instead he gazed coolly at Nadia. "Why bomb the *Cardinale*?"

Nadia blanched, her features contracting. "I...I didn't."

The bald man gave Giorgio a shove that didn't budge him a millimeter. "Get going," he insisted.

"No!" said Erika, pointing at Nadia. "Not until she tells us what she knows."

"I'd like to hear your version too," said the hunchback, frowning at Nadia.

Roaring car engines, their tires tearing up gravel, sounded outside.

"Don't move, any of you!" The hunchback went to the window and flipped the curtain aside. Brakes squealed and car doors thumped open. "Police!" he growled, stepping to the door to lock it with keys from the adjacent windowsill. "What the shit is happening!"

Nadia recoiled, eyes flashing. Erika, Giorgio, and the bald man stared at her.

"I don't know," she whined, and headed towards the window.

"Get away from there!" The hunchback now aimed his gun at her.

"How do we get out of here now?" asked the bald man, casting a helpless look at his superior.

"We use these three for leverage." Beyond the door, staccato male voices seemed to shout orders. The hunchback peered out the window again. "Mattei is in handcuffs and they're forcing our trunk open. Your two other friends are talking as if they're part of the operation," he added, rounding on Nadia again. "They're goddamn cops!"

"I don't know what's going on!" Nadia objected, her wild gaze searching the room. She pointed to the kitchen. "There's a back door through there."

"Can we be seen from the courtyard?" asked the hunchback.

"No, but we'll have to climb the hill to get to the road."

"We? Not in your dreams. You're a traitor."

He nodded to his partner. "You check it out. Make sure cops aren't up there too."

The bald man left through the kitchen. Erika and

Giorgio exchanged nervous glances as the hunchback's gun stayed trained on them.

The front door shook and rattled. "Unlock the door and stand down!" came Flavio's voice. "We'll break through if we have to."

"Down on the floor, all of you!" commanded the hunchback, wagging his pistol at them.

Once they had complied he squinted through a corner of the window not covered by the curtain. "Cops galore, and your pal Flavio the star," he snarled at Nadia. "I don't see the other guy." He moved back to the door and called out, "I've got three hostages in here—if you try to break in they're dead!"

"Don't get carried away," Flavio yelled back. "We've rescued the woman from the car. You can still avoid a murder charge."

So Matilde Fassino was safe. But had they caught the bald man? Erika asked herself as she sat cross-legged on the floor between Giorgio and Nadia. Giorgio scooted slightly forward.

"Get back!" the hunchback shouted at him. "And where's that other guy?" he whipped at Nadia, "the one you called Claudio!"

She shrugged helplessly, eyes continuing to dart about the room.

"And what do you know about the attack on my newspaper?" Giorgio demanded of her.

"Shut up!" said the hunchback. He returned to the window and shifted the curtain a couple of centimeters. A shot cracked the air, shattering the glass and spinning him around. The moment he fell to the floor the back door banged open.

Gino appeared from the kitchen, taking aim at the hunchback. Both guns went off. Erika saw Gino fall. Then a knife skidded across the floor to her from his crumpled form. The switchblade. She clicked it open and flew at the hunchback who sat slumped against the wall, panting and re-aiming. She kicked the gun from his hand and dropped to her knees next to him, blade at his throat.

His hand moved to his leg.

"Watch out," shouted Giorgio, "another gun!"

Erika tightened her grip and nicked his neck. "If you move again, I'll slice you."

"*Cristo Santo!*" cried Nadia, and raced for the kitchen.

"Keep the knife on that bastard," cried Giorgio, "I'm going after her!"

As Giorgio barreled out of the room, the hunchback continued to gulp breaths, blood darkening the sky-blue shirt collar protruding from his sweater. For a heartbeat Erika was back in a nightmare...so much blood from just a nick. Then she realized the bullet from the courtyard had struck him near the collarbone.

She turned to Gino who lay on his side, clutching his stomach. "Gino!"

His eyes were slits. "Just watch *him*," he breathed out haltingly. "The others'll be here soon."

The others—Gino's police backup. Erika barely had time to acknowledge this extraordinary twist when the stomping of boots sounded in the kitchen. Flavio and a uniformed policeman entered the room, guns drawn. Making a quick survey of the scene, Flavio waved the officer over to Erika then crouched next to Gino. After an exchange of a few words, Gino mumbling his part, Flavio went to unlock and open the front door. "All clear in here," he told the other police in the courtyard. He nodded to Erika. "I'm sending out a hostage. Time for you to go," he told her.

"But Gino...Claudio."

A siren pierced the air. "An ambulance is coming. They'll take care of him." Flavio pointed at her knife. "Put that away before you go out."

Outside, the cold air struck Erika's face with a resuscitating slap. Six uniformed police with machine guns stood next to their three cars.

"Erika!" said Giorgio, rising from the bench against the wall of the house.

"Sit there next to him," one of the officers told Erika.

Erika and Giorgio embraced. They had both survived. Before she sat, she took a long look at the police vehicles stationed in the courtyard and up the drive. Giorgio followed her gaze. "All the animals are in cages," he said with a bitter smile.

Mattei sat in the back of one car, his pink complexion now ashen. He glanced at Erika, shock and confusion in his eyes. Then he turned away. Nadia sat in the back of a second car, pinching the bridge of her nose; in the third, the bald man stared gloomily ahead.

The ambulance's siren became deafening as the vehicle approached, grinding the gravel of the driveway. "And Matilde Fassino?" Erika asked Giorgio.

"Another police car already took her away."

The ambulance halted, debarking four men in white. They carried gurneys over the gravel until they were able to roll them to the house. Erika moved automatically to follow them.

"Have a seat," the police officer repeated patiently but firmly, placing himself between her and the medics.

Giorgio guided her back to the bench. As soon as Gino was borne out, Erika rose again. A blanket covered him from the neck down.

Who *was* this guy who'd turned from menacing to concerned for her safety, and who'd finally elicited *her* help? *Who were all of them?*

37: Masks Continue to Fall

The more that came to light, the more that remained obscure about the Matilde Fassino drama and its players. Plenty to ponder as Erika sat in the Déjà Vu at ten a.m. the next day. It was the first "normal" morning she had experienced since last Thursday, when she had come home to Gino in her flat and all hell had broken loose. She rubbed her left cheek. The bruise there had paled markedly and she would have gone back to work this afternoon if she hadn't squeezed an extra day out of Brigida.

This morning she would meet Flavio here in the café. Before having given Giorgio and her permission to leave the farmhouse, he had made them sign a form requiring their silence about the Comrades' plot and all events surrounding it. She itched to know what today's meeting would hold.

Fausta arrived at Erika's table expressing an astonished frown. So much for her faded black eye. "I fell down my stairs," Erika announced before Fausta could ask.

"Oh *Dio!*"

"No other injuries, though," Erika hastened to add. She hoped to soon put this bothersome lie to permanent rest.

"Well, I'm glad you're back. Mara is too."

Erika caught the eye of Fausta's assistant behind the bar and gave her the kind of relaxed, unburdened smile that hadn't seemed possible during the last five days.

"You look tired," said Fausta. "Your usual cappuccino?" Erika nodded, and Fausta patted her shoulder before pivoting off to the bar.

She *was* exhausted. Although last night she slept free of bizarre fencing dreams, concern over real events had kept her awake. One thought she couldn't shake was about her mother. Cheryl had not been crazy in accusing Erika of delusions about Keith. She closed her eyes and shook her head.

As her cappuccino arrived, Erika thought about her car accident and the mysterious trick of transference that had followed in her mind. Many things begged explanation, she told herself, just as Flavio walked into the café and ordered at the bar.

"Thanks for taking time to see me," he said, sitting down with an officious sigh. Though his features were drawn, the spring in his step and his straightness of posture indicated he was satisfied by the arrests he'd made at the farmhouse.

"You ordered me to come," Erika pointed out with a half-smile. "Am I really in that much trouble?"

"No. As long as you're willing to testify and you cooperate in finding Paolo, things should go fine for you. Have you heard from him?"

Mara arrived with Flavio's coffee, which gave Erika a moment to contemplate her response. "Yes," she said in an even voice. "He called to make sure I was all right, but he wouldn't say where he was."

"When was that?"

"Yesterday afternoon, after the raid, when I went back to Giorgio's."

"When he calls again, tell him to turn himself in, that things will go easier for him if he does, especially since he didn't take part in the actual handover of Matilde Fassino."

"*Handover?*"

Flavio put up a hand. "Wait and I'll explain. Paolo *is* going to call back?"

"I don't know." Erika was tempted to look away but forced herself to maintain eye contact with Flavio. "He didn't say, and he hurried me off the phone."

Flavio leaned in, scrutinizing her. "I sincerely hope he

does call back and that you and Giorgio Testa understand what's at risk—for Paolo *and* for you—if you don't report contact with him."

"I understand, and I'll tell Giorgio." She felt uneasy and had to resist shifting in her seat. "What about Matilde Fassino's *handover*?"

Flavio sat back and lit a cigarette, took a long drag before answering, as if to remind Erika just who was in control here. "Remember," he said, "you've sworn to keep this business confidential." Once Erika nodded, he continued. "Matteo Mattei had contracted to turn Fassino over to the two Red Brigade operatives who came to the farmhouse—for payment, of course."

"Red Brigades..."

"Right. The two you ran into are fairly important fish we've been trying to catch. If they'd succeeded in taking possession of Fassino they'd have probably held her for a significant ransom. Having captured them both, we hope they'll have plenty to tell us."

"So are you and Claudio Voghera with DIGOS?"

"We're with the security services."

His stiff tone and stony expression seemed to discourage further questions on the subject. Erika asked instead how Claudio was doing.

"He's had surgery for his abdominal wound. He'll have you to thank for skirting a second bullet."

Erika took this as a compliment, probably the only one she would receive, considering she'd ignored all previous warnings to back out of the affair. Maybe Giorgio was right about her wanting to save someone. In the end it turned out to be Gino (the bully, of all people!), who in reality was Claudio Voghera, who in turn had tried to protect her. A bizarre turnabout to say the least! At any rate, the outcome left her feeling somewhat redeemed, even accomplished, and less hollow inside.

"How long did you and the Comrades keep Matilde

Fassino in that house?" she ventured to ask.

No answer, *obviously*, though he sat observing her for a moment as if there was something he was trying to decide. "Remember the secrecy document you signed..." She nodded. "All right then. We kept her for not quite two days. Just enough time to avoid dealing with a missing-person's report and to keep her from injury." Flavio tipped Erika an ironic smile. "By the way, we knew you'd been to the house the day before."

The pharmacist—of course. But she didn't need to go there. Instead, she recalled the hunchback's calling Nadia a traitor. "You know, I was suspicious of you and Nadia from the first time I met you. I understand *you* now but I don't get her."

"Nadia was a type of asset; turns out she's Black Order."

"A neo-Fascist. So you employ people like that?" Silence and an impassive gaze from Flavio.

"And you put her in the back of a police car. Was that for cover?"

"Not entirely. We've arrested her for involvement in the bombing of the *Cardinale* newspaper."

Satisfaction spread across Erika's face. *Finally, an honest reference to the Cardinale.* "And that thug-woman who attacked me—Giorgio thinks she was involved too."

"Liliana Pera—goes by 'Lily.' She's got a husband who's already in prison, and she'll be on her way there herself once we find her."

Lily: the nickname sounded like a little bell, tinkling light-heartedness and innocence. Erika would have laughed if she hadn't felt so indignant. "She was at your apartment last week!"

"She shouldn't have been involved. That was Nadia's doing, and because Nadia couldn't control Lily, she sent her to me to rein her in. We didn't know about her connection to the *Cardinale*, at the time, or I would have arrested her on the spot."

"Well, *Lily* didn't listen to you. She attacked me that night on her way out and almost killed me."

"I'm sorry, but you *were* warned to stay away."

Erika felt her face burn. "What about Ivan?"

"I convinced him to get out. He wasn't at the farmhouse yesterday. We're dealing with him, but that's all I can tell you."

"And Mattei?"

"He's got his fingers in many pots."

"Like freemasonry."

"That's a front. We've been tracking him in the involvement of a pagan cult having to do with ancient Egypt. He's been jockeying for leadership, and the money from the Matilde Fassino trade-up would have helped him."

Erika's eyes narrowed. With what she knew of Mattei, she shouldn't be surprised.

"Well," said Flavio, looking at his watch, "I'll be off. Remember our deal: you cooperate and you'll be fine."

Fine? Paolo would go to jail, maybe Ivan too. Keith was dead...how was that for *fine*? "You knew about my brother," she murmured before he could stand.

Flavio sighed. "I'm sorry. I tried to spare you that."

"Who told you—the CIA?"

He nodded. "We had to look into your background once you got involved in this affair."

"Who of the Comrades knows...about Keith, I mean?"

"Just Paolo. We finally informed him so he would tell you and hopefully get you to back off."

So her suspicions were confirmed. True, Paolo had shown tenderness when he told her, but his purpose, as usual, had been tainted with manipulation.

Flavio studied her dark expression. "Seriously, if you need it, you could get help while you're here...we've got decent psychologists in Italy."

She gave an absent nod.

"Remember, it's for Paolo's own good that he turn himself in," Flavio reminded her as he rose. He left his calling card on the table. "I expect your help in that."

After Flavio left, Erika sat mulling over Paolo and his prolonged games of obfuscation. Like all the other players in this mad drama he had sported one kind of mask or another from the start. And yet he insisted he loved her. Just one more guise?

In a surge of bitterness she was tempted to turn Paolo in straight away. And she had the opportunity since she would be meeting him late tonight. Paolo had called when she returned to Giorgio's yesterday afternoon, not only to check on her but to arrange to see her, something she had not told Flavio.

She allowed the bitterness to subside. No, she did not wish to be party to a setup in which cops would swoop brutally down on an unsuspecting Paolo. Not to mention that Flavio had manipulated her all too often himself; she felt she owed him only enough to keep herself out of more trouble. So she would go through with her plan to convince Paolo to turn himself in. She glanced at her watch. In the meantime she owed Signora Sillano a visit and an update regarding the last two days.

Before ringing the signora's bell, Erika slipped the switchblade into her back pocket. She had considered leaving it home, what with Operation Matilde Fassino wrapped up, but she was fond of the weapon. Each time she gripped its handle she felt a sense of confidence, something that could temporarily override those lingering dark thoughts.

And, lest she forget, Liliana Pera was still out there on the loose.

At Signora Sillano's kitchen table, Erika summarized the Comrades' plot to kidnap Matilde Fassino in order to sell her to the Red Brigades.

"Thank God Paolo came to his senses and didn't show up," said the signora. "But how do you know all this?"

Erika mentioned how she'd found out where the Comrades were holding Fassino and had gone there to get Paolo out. "The security services won't let me say anything more," No doubt she was sharing too much information for Flavio's liking, and yet the signora already knew a good deal of the background. "What's left now," Erika stressed, "is for Paolo to turn himself in."

"Of course, he *must*. You have to convince him, Erika, otherwise his life will be ruined for good. I'll try to do it myself if he calls. You have no idea where he is?"

Erika truly did not, and once more she remained silent about her meeting with Paolo this evening. The fewer people in the know, the better. "If he makes contact, I'll do everything I can," she replied.

"His father called me the day before yesterday. I didn't mention anything about Paolo's imbroglio—what did I know for certain? But Signor Lorenzi is worried."

"I wonder if Paolo has questioned Signor Lorenzi about not being his real father?"

"If so it probably didn't go well. When I first told Paolo he seemed almost vindicated that Signor Lorenzi wasn't his father. But he was already involved with these extremists."

"Yet he wanted to know who his real father is?"

"Of course. But I've told you there's very little to go on."

"Maybe some roads are best not explored," said Erika, a shadow darkening her eyes.

The signora watched her with curiosity. "Maybe, unless the truth can help you get on with your life."

Erika hoped that would prove true for everyone. "What did you tell Paolo about his father?"

"Only that I couldn't remember his name exactly, but that it sounded English—like Alec, maybe. I left out the part about his being much younger than Sara. Taboos of the time, you know. Not that they mattered to me, I was just glad this young stranger was able to distract her for a spell from the tragedy of her life. She lost her whole family in the War. And the attic she lived in was as humid and sweltering that summer as it was damp and icy in winter."

Erika remained silent for a moment in renewed appreciation of Sara Lattes' plight. When she resumed, she asked, "So it was summer when Sara met him?"

"Late summer, early autumn."

"*Alec*. It's a common name in America."

"Yes, American or English. Sara said he also had an Italian name but that he wouldn't reveal it. Evidently he didn't like it."

Erika's brows rose. "She didn't know his Italian name?"

"Sara said she couldn't get it out of him. All very interesting, but it's not going to help Paolo at this point."

Erika was now gazing past the signora. "How old was this man?"

"Nineteen or twenty—and Sara almost thirty."

"And what year was it?"

"1950. Paolo was born in '51."

Erika straightened and stared at the signora. 1950 was the year that nineteen-year-old Bruno Rivoli spent the summer and fall months in Italy with his parents. She had told Paolo this at the beginning of their relationship, and he had innocently dropped the fact that he was born in May of 1951. "Could his name have been *Alan*?" Erika asked the signora.

"Possibly—*Alan*, *Alec*, something like that."

"What did Sara say he looked like?"

"I don't remember, but Paolo looks like his mother. She did say he smoked a pipe—like Paolo." A nostalgic smile at the coincidence brightened her expression.

Erika, on the other hand, felt her insides turn to liquid. She could barely keep from gaping. "Does Paolo know all this?"

"No, only about the English-sounding name."

"I'd better get going, Signora."

"So soon?"

"I have to go to Asti today. I owe my cousins a visit."

The signora nodded with affection. "I'm glad you have some family here."

"One last thing," said Erika, as they rose and made their way to the door. "Remind me why you decided to tell Paolo about his father in the first place?"

"Oh," she answered wearily, "I just got fed up one day. He complained so much about Signor Lorenzi; that he didn't understand Paolo's politics or his passion for architecture, that he wanted Paolo to do something real and solid like join Signor Lorenzi at Lavazza, or at least get a regular job as a builder. I told him he should be grateful to Lorenzi since his real father had left before he was born. Maybe I also wanted to distract him from his radical thoughts, but that probably backfired."

"I remember that last part, but the first—I guess Paolo doesn't really have much in common with Signor Lorenzi."

Numbly, Erika turned to leave. Once Signora Sillano closed the door, Erika stood silent for a moment on the landing. *Paolo's passion for architecture*. She remembered he had coveted Bruno's work of creating custom homes. *They were even alike in that*.

She left the building and headed for the nearest phone booth to call Elsa. It was noon. Thank God she didn't have to teach today.

"Would you mind if I came by after lunch?" she asked her cousin.

"We could hold lunch for you..." said Elsa.

"No, please don't. By the time I get a train it'll be late. Thank you, but go ahead without me. I'll be there within a couple of hours."

"Come when you can. If you haven't eaten I can warm something up for you."

Erika thanked Elsa again and hung up. She wasn't hungry and couldn't imagine ever being hungry again.

38: Beyond Reckoning

Angelo was taking his nap when Erika arrived at the flat, which was just as well, for Erika preferred to talk to Elsa alone.

"We've finished lunch," said Elsa, "but I've got some zucchini frittata left over I can heat up for you."

On second thought, maybe she was hungry after all. "Thanks," said Erika. "I wouldn't have imposed like this if I hadn't needed to talk to you."

"Nothing's wrong? Your cheek looks better but you still look drawn and gaunt."

"No, nothing's wrong exactly..."

Remnants of lunch remained on the kitchen table—wine, salt, a dispenser of Parmigiano cheese. The table's floral-patterned cloth had been cleared of crumbs, however, and a clean dish, flanked by utensils and a napkin, sat at Erika's normal place. She slid hesitantly into her chair, thinking she should somehow continue to excuse herself. When Elsa put the pan of frittata on the table, Erika raised her hand and said, "Thank you, Elsa, that's plenty—just the frittata and maybe some bread."

"Are you still worried about your brother Keith?"

Erika stared mechanically as Elsa sat down and filled her plate. She could not bring herself to tell her cousin about what had happened to Keith. "No," she answered quietly, "that's been resolved."

"So he's not here, then?" said Elsa, pouring Erika some wine.

Erika shook her head without looking up, waiting for the quaking inside her to run its course. She hadn't touched

300

the frittata.

"Is everything all right?" asked Elsa, inspecting her.

"Fine—he just can't come." Erika swallowed hard. "Actually, I'd like to talk about my father, about when he spent time here."

"So long ago. He was only nineteen."

"He's never mentioned his time here. Did he go by Bruno, or Alan?"

"Bruno, in the family. But we know the name 'Alan' from your grandmother. You're not eating..."

Erika picked up her fork. "I'm just wondering about my dad's...um...romances here..."

"What makes you ask that?" Elsa shot her an amused smile.

"Well..." Erika took a bite of frittata. "I heard he might've had an affair with a woman in Turin."

"Ah..."

"Is it true?"

"Well, I didn't learn about it until long after he'd left..."

Erika set down her fork in astonishment. The pause lengthened excruciatingly as Elsa moved to pour her more wine. "Your dad liked to carouse, like young men do," she finally explained. "It was summer and he'd go out with Ivan's father and his friends—all single young men—and come home in the small hours. Bruno was an American with dollars, and dollars went far in those days. He liked to treat his relatives and friends."

"What about the woman in Turin?"

"I don't know much. It was Ivan's father who told me later. He mentioned some kind of secret affair with an older woman."

Erika's pulse was thumping in her head. "How much older?"

"I don't think I ever knew."

"What about her name?"

Elsa shook her head. "Sorry, Ivan's father might know

more.

Erika's appetite was on the wane and so was her patience. She needed the name or at least the age of this woman, but she wasn't going to go to Ivan's father, particularly in view of Ivan's present predicament with the law.

"I don't know how long the affair lasted," Elsa went on, "but then your dad returned to America with your grandparents. Your grandmother said he always wanted to be a real American, not an Italian-American. That's why he went by 'Alan' and married his Anglo-American girlfriend. He was born in America and that's where he wanted to make his life, which makes sense. Funny," Elsa added, smiling at Erika, "you seem just the opposite."

Erika fixated the empty, brown-vinyl seat in front of her as the train bore her back to Turin, its faithful *clu-clung, clu-clung* rocking her into semi-calmness. The easiest thing, of course, would be to simply call Bruno and ask him if he'd had an affair with Sara Lattes. But she shrank from such a conversation with her father, didn't want to deal with the embarrassment, couldn't face the possible ramifications.

Her thoughts swung back to Elsa who had brought up the subject of Christmas again. *Will you be coming next Sunday?* Today was only Tuesday, and in the same distracted manner in which Erika responded to everything unrelated to her immediate, clamorous concerns, she had agreed to come for Christmas lunch.

Opening the door to her flat, Erika spotted another note on the floor, illuminated by the landing light. Signora Sillano again, asking her to come down. She dropped her coat on a kitchen chair and headed downstairs.

"I've been looking through my box of old letters this afternoon," said the signora as they stood in the kitchen, "and I found this from Paolo's mother." She handed Erika a postcard. "They were at the seashore—go ahead and read the back."

Erika glanced at the glossy photo of palm trees, parasol pines, and an azure sea. Then she turned it over, and before she'd finished reading the note she felt her skin turn to gooseflesh.

Dearest Genia,
Alassio is a paradise in September. Few tourists, beach practically to ourselves and water like a cool bath. Alan's truly in his element, like a blond, bronzed god! And he finally revealed his Italian name—Bruno! Visited famous Caffè Roma and saw the young owner's paintings, lovely as Monet's. Alan said he'd buy me one but I couldn't accept that much from him. Taking the bus up the Riviera towards France tomorrow. Can't wait!

The signature *Sara* was crammed into the corner at the bottom.

Hands almost trembling, Erika returned the card to the counter, script down.

The signora was observing her with curiosity. "I'd forgotten about 'Bruno' on this card, but you were right about the name Alan. How did you guess?"

Erika's eyes remained fixed on the card's idyllic scenery. In her shock, a strange, distant sadness came over her. "Such a beautiful moment," she uttered in a thick voice. "So happy they seem. How could he not love Italy?"

The signora frowned. "What do you mean?"

"*Bruno*," Erika said without looking up, "also known as *Alan*, is my father."

The signora blinked hard. "Your..."

Erika nodded, still avoiding the signora's eyes.

"I...I don't know what to say..."

Erika spared her the discomfort. "Sorry, Signora, but

I've got to go."

On the way out, Signora Sillano placed a hand on Erika's shoulder. "Are you going to tell Paolo?"

Erika stared right through her. "You can tell him if he calls—it's his right to know—but I'm not up to it."

She staggered downstairs, feeling riddled with needles like a hapless voodoo doll. Outside in the dark, she hit a wall of frigid air. She had no coat and didn't care. Automatically her feet steered her past piled-up snow marbled with soot and dirt, across the street and into the Déjà Vu, where she bypassed Fausta at the bar and slumped into a chair at a table. Once sheltered in the heated café a paradoxical bout of shivering beset her.

Fausta eyed her inquisitively, leaving the bar to approach her. "Erika, you look frozen—where's your coat?"

"Left it at home," Erika muttered.

"Then how about something hot to drink."

"Yes, please, a rum punch."

Returning to the bar, Fausta glanced over her shoulder askance.

Erika sat hunched, with her elbow on the table, her forehead pressed against the heel of her hand. *What are the odds? What are the fucking odds?* The question tumbled mercilessly in her mind like an unlucky die. When Fausta returned with the potent grog, Erika barely murmured *grazie* before snatching up the cup and sipping eagerly. Fausta watched her for a moment, then went back to the bar.

As the grog cooled, Erika's sips became gulps until she finished it. She felt a touch light-headed but experienced no relief from the grinding gears of her thoughts. Catching Fausta's attention, she called for another.

Arriving with Erika's punch, this time Fausta pulled out a chair. "Mind if I take a little break here?"

Erika shrugged—"Go ahead"—and immediately started in on her second grog. When she looked up, Mara had arrived with a glass of sparkling mineral water for Fausta.

"Bad day?" asked Fausta. "No coat—two rums...or maybe it's not my business."

Erika tilted her head. Her body felt warm now, her mind tingling. She guzzled the rest of the punch and returned the glass cup to its saucer with a clang. "Sorry," she muttered, then turned to face Fausta. "I have a brother. A live one."

Fausta expressed a cautious smile. "I've got a brother too."

"D'ya love him?" Erika slurred.

"Of course."

Erika squinted at her. "Body 'n soul?"

"I love him like a brother," Fausta answered with a nervous little laugh.

Erika's eyelids sagged, her focus drifting from Fausta. "I used t' love my brother like that...but lots o' times we didn't get along."

"Well, that's how it goes with siblings."

"But did ya ever wish he wasn't around?"

"Sure, sometimes, but not for long."

"Eternity's long...too long." Erika rubbed her burning eyes. *God she was tired.*

"Erika, has something happened?" asked Fausta, leaning in close.

Erika's chest heaved as she breathed in. Images of Paolo with his pipe and Keith in her fencing garb crashed simultaneously over her like an enormous, fateful wave. She gripped the edge of the table until little by little the pounding surf receded to a steady lapping at the shore of her consciousness. "I should go home now," she murmured.

"Might not be a bad idea. Have you eaten anything this afternoon?"

Erika shrugged.

"Be sure and have some dinner, then tuck yourself in," Fausta said, patting Erika's hand.

Erika nodded dully, reaching into her pocket for money—

"No, it's on the house tonight. Come back tomorrow morning for coffee so we can see how you're doing. And don't go out without a coat anymore."

"*Grazie*," Erika managed, struggling against tears and a painfully tight throat.

She left the expansive light of the Déjà Vu for the solitary darkness of via Garibaldi. Her tipsiness buffered the cold, though by the time she crossed the street, the piercing air was beginning to clear some of the vapors from her mind. If she hadn't been so exhausted she might have been able to walk in a straight line. Fumbling with the keys, she entered her building. *Jesus, she looked forward to collapsing on her couch.* In a couple of hours she was supposed to meet Paolo. She closed her eyes...*if she decided to show up*. Right now she felt like she'd just clambered out of a derailed train, smoke obscuring her vision, noise and debris cluttering her other senses.

She had passed the first-floor landing, on her way to the second, when she heard a click at ground level, then a whoosh from the opening door, street sounds spilling in. She stopped to listen to footsteps echo on the marble stairs below, more than one pair it seemed, though her judgment could be off with all that rum. On the first floor, the clang of a key reverberating in a lock: one, two, three turns; the clatter of a door opening and shutting. She shrugged and continued her heavy-legged ascent.

She halted again, this time on the second-floor landing. Definitely a second set of footsteps. She patted her back pocket, an empty gesture since she had left her apartment with only her keys and money. Inhaling sharply, she accelerated her climb. The footfall below came louder, heavy and staggered as if someone were limping.

She passed the signora's third-floor landing and hurried up to her own. The steps beneath her quickened in turn, though they remained ponderous and uneven. Again she fumbled with her keys, plucking at the two needed to open her door. Whether she could get both locks open in time, she didn't know...Then she stopped, fear fading into a cloud of calm that had suddenly hovered over her. Slowly she turned and waited.

The steps resounded louder, clumsier, and in shaved seconds the top of a head of brown hair appeared, and then the face she had anticipated. Semiautomatic in hand, the Doberman had reached Erika's landing, sweating and breathing heavily. "Not going in?" she panted, her expression strained yet smug.

"Why?" Erika said bitterly. "So you can shoot me in the back?"

"Too easy. *Cazzo,* I watched you stagger home with no coat. Are you drunk?"

Erika sagged with weariness. "Liliana Pera, right? Or do you go by *Lily*?"

The woman measured her with a suspicious gaze, her mouth twisting in disgust. "You wouldn't back off, would you? Now you've ruined everything!"

"*I've* ruined things?" *What the hell was she talking about?*

Liliana Pera adjusted her pistol's aim. "It was supposed to be a smooth operation—your boyfriend's Red bastards taken down. But no, you had to go mouthing off and get Nadia arrested and the cops after me."

Erika leaned against her door. Sobriety had almost completely reclaimed her, yet she was so tired. "Yeah," she said, lifting her hands and letting them fall, "I figured you were Nadia's creature—Black Order girls. You shouldn't have bombed the *Cardinale*."

Hatred gleamed in the woman's eyes. She took two steps closer, pointing the gun at Erika's face. "You and that fat *cazzo*, Giorgio!"

Pricked by the insult, Erika drew herself up, her voice

taking on an edge. "Leave him out of it—Flavio already suspected you and Nadia in the bombing."

"Shut up!"

"First you beat Franco up, then he dies in the fire you cause. No wonder you're in deep shit, and personally I can't wait for you to go down and join your husband in jail."

"Don't you speak of him. I should have killed you the last time we met!"

But Lily had not shot her, perhaps because there were witnesses. And here in this building the noise of a gunshot would no doubt draw similar attention. Erika leaned back again and glanced at the Doberman's left foot. She recalled the dry "tumph" that night as her knife cut into the woman's boot leather, like the puncturing of a cardboard box packed with goods; then the woman's banshee scream as Erika extracted the blade. "I see you've replaced your boots."

"In time to kick the shit out of you."

"I don't blame you," Erika sighed. "The humiliation you must feel." She could barely keep standing she was so tired. Her mind, her muscles—neither wanted to labor anymore. Time to stop taunting the woman. She wanted to cease thinking altogether, to curl up anywhere and go to sleep. Still, she couldn't resist adding, "If you weren't a criminal with no conscience, I'd feel sorry for you."

Too much: Liliana Pera kicked Erika in the stomach with her right boot, and once Erika was doubled up she hammered her back with the butt of her pistol. Erika dropped to her knees and felt a kick to her side. She fell to the floor, eyes closed. "Why don't you just get it over with and shoot me," she groaned, slipping back into the blur of inebriation.

The Doberman's response came in a hiss. "Not when this is so much quieter and more satisfying." She kicked Erika in the side again and Erika thought her ribs would explode. She gasped and contracted involuntarily but didn't look up. At this point she didn't even acknowledge it was the

Doberman beating her. All she could sense was some kind of cosmic punishment that obliterated the greater pain of her newfound reality.

At one point she did look up and saw triumph in the Doberman's smile.

"Sick, cowardly bitch!" Erika uttered between groans of pain. She tried to rise but the Doberman kicked her again, and again. Erika's eyes closed, her breath was ragged, but she could still faintly hear the Doberman cursing. *Hearing*: wasn't it the last thing to go when you were on your way out?

39: A Taste for Oblivion

Erika woke to a pain so excruciating and searing that it sliced her breath. She lay absolutely still in the dark, hoping it would retreat. After a few seconds, her thoughts cleared and she marveled that she was still alive, considering the ferocity of the Doberman's wrath.

The bed she lay in was not her own, nor was the flimsy garment she wore. Alien tubing protruded from her: plastic chafed her nostrils, a needle stabbed her left hand, and when she moved her legs she felt what could only be a catheter. She must be in a hospital. Once her eyes adjusted to the dark, fractured by a small stream of light coming through a half-closed door, other beds came into view but she could make out no patients in them. Shifting, she groped for some kind of call button but immediately collapsed as pain lanced through her torso. "Agh!" she cried. Everything felt broken inside her—literally, this time.

"Erika?" came a whisper.

Without moving the rest of her body she turned her head to see a figure in silhouette getting out of a chair. A low light was switched on and Signora Sillano appeared, looking down at her.

"I dozed off," the signora said. "Have you been awake long?"

"No," came Erika's voice in a croak. "How did I get here?"

"You left my house in such a daze after the news about your father...I waited awhile then thought I'd check on you. When I stepped onto the landing I heard such a ruckus upstairs—yelling and swearing. I called out to you and

310

started up the stairs, but before I got to the top this woman came rushing down and pushed me aside so that I almost fell. When I got to you, you were unconscious." She shook her head in dismay. "I called an ambulance."

Erika clenched her teeth at the thought of the Doberman shoving the signora. "I'm sorry," she said hoarsely. "You could've been hurt too."

"I'm all right. But you—you've got a bruised kidney and a cracked rib. What in God's name happened upstairs?"

"The pain," Erika mumbled. "It's hard to talk."

"Of course, I'll get the nurse. Just rest."

"Thank you...didn't think anyone would come...thought it was the end of me."

The signora smiled gently. After she left the room Erika gazed in dismay at the ceiling. *Jesus, what a mess!*

Through the shadowy doorway the signora reentered...with an apparition in her wake, a rustling, flowing white figure. If an earthly clip-clopping hadn't accompanied the strange being, Erika would have taken it for a ghost, or an angel.

"Well hello, Erika," pronounced a quiet, affable female voice. "I'm Sister Maria Giulia."

Erika screwed up her eyes. A woman in long white robes and a huge white, winged hat loomed over her. A nun. She'd seen nurses in habits like this on TV but never in real life, not even in the hospital where Giorgio had been.

"I'm going to give you more pain medication," the woman said. "Do you know why you're here? Do you remember anything?"

Erika recalled all too well but didn't want to reveal the sordid business, especially to a nun. Still the woman kept looking at her as if Erika might not be right in the head.

"I got beaten up," she confessed at last. "Kicked." Her mouth and throat felt dry as the Mojave Desert and she had a hard time speaking.

The signora put a hand on her shoulder. "I told Erika

what the doctor said about her rib and kidney."

The nun nodded, seemingly satisfied that her patient didn't have brain damage.

"My mouth's really dry," Erika managed. "Hurts to swallow."

"Caused in part by the codeine we're giving you for pain," the sister said with a sympathetic smile. "I've got another dose for you." She helped Erika take the pill with water. "You'll need to drink lots of fluids. And I'll take your vital signs while I'm here. By the way, your call button's there." Erika turned her head to see a cord wound around one of the rods of the bed's metal headboard.

After the nun billowed out of the room the signora sat down next to the bed again. Erika gazed droopy-eyed at the friend who had rescued her; probably she should try to say something more to her. She tried...but her eyelids had a will of their own, and closed as if in veto.

Erika woke to Signora Sillano arranging her breakfast on her tray. The hall rang with chatter and movement. "*Buon giorno*," the signora greeted her with her characteristic mild smile. "Feeling any better?"

"Maybe a little," Erika responded in a thick voice. The pain in her torso, rather than searing now, was more a relentless, hammering ache. She did not attempt to sit up and let the signora pour her water and slowly crank up her bed.

"Hungry?"

"Mainly thirsty."

"Drink your water. How about a damp cloth for your face, then we can see about food."

Erika drank copiously, then released a heavy sigh, laid her head back, and surveyed the room. She was indeed the sole patient among the four beds. "Which hospital is this?"

"The Molinette."

Erika hazily recalled the nocturnal visit of the billowy

nun. "Are all the nurses nuns?"

"Mm-hm," said the signora, handing Erika a moistened cloth.

Erika gave her face a few feeble swipes. "Even hurts to do this," she mumbled. "Gonna ask for more pain medication."

"The day-sister told me she'll come with it soon."

Gingerly Erika fingered her rib, remembering the signora's report about it and her kidney. She drank more water, then murmured, "What else did the doctor say about me?"

"Only that there's some blood in your urine which should go away in time."

Erika cringed at the thought. She wanted to check the catheter bag but didn't dare lean forward. She handed the cloth back to the signora, thanking her. Signora Sillano had been with her all night and now the morning. "I hope you get some rest today," Erika told her. "Sitting in that chair, you probably slept less than I did last night."

The signora patted her shoulder. "Don't worry about me, I'll go home after you've eaten, then come back later. I have a brush for you—"

Clip-clopping sounded in the doorway and in came a nun pushing a cart, white clogs presenting a strange complement to her flowing, angel-like attire. She nodded to the signora and greeted Erika, one hand resting on her cart, the other on her robed hip. "Not very hungry, are we," she stated in a wry but perky voice, as she glanced at Erika's untouched breakfast. "I'm Sister Teresa. You were asleep when I brought it in but I bet you'd prefer your codeine now."

Erika nodded firmly, relieved to see the nun reaching for the prepared dose on her cart.

"How's the breathing?" she asked, handing the pill and cup of water to Erika.

"Wish I didn't have to."

"It'll take a while to resolve itself. Shall I remove the breakfast before it grows mold?" she quipped with a jaunty smile.

"Yes, please."

"Some tea or barley coffee, maybe?"

Erika hesitated, frowning at the cart. "Caffè latte sounds better."

"No regular coffee for a while, too irritating to the kidneys—pretend you're in the children's ward for now."

"I guess tea, then." Though exhausted, she tried to gauge the cheerful if somewhat flippant nun—fortyish, ready wit behind sharp, vivacious eyes. All things considered, this wasn't a bad way to be greeted this morning.

Sister Teresa emptied the abandoned breakfast into a trash slot in the cart and handed the plate to the signora, then she ladled pre-made tea from a container into Erika's cup. "Let us know if you need anything else," she said with a half wink before clattering out of the room.

Erika looked at her cup—Deruta ceramics, with the classic dragon design. She figured the signora had brought it along with the white plate since family traditionally provided place settings for relatives in the hospital. Signora Sillano had gone well beyond casual friendship, and Erika's feelings fluctuated from immense gratitude to unease at being reduced to total dependency. She was searching for something else to say when there came a knock on the doorjamb.

"Not disturbing, am I?" After poking his head in, Flavio whisked into the room without waiting for an answer. "Finished with breakfast?"

The signora narrowed her eyes.

"Flavio Moretti from the security services," he said to her, showing his identification.

"Eugenia Sillano. I'm Erika's landlady."

"Glad you're here; I heard you found her," he said, a

314

curt smile accompanying his handshake. "I'll just need to speak with Erika alone for a moment."

The signora glanced at Erika.

"It's all right, Signora, I know him."

"I'll be back later, then." Methodically she put on her coat, gathered Erika's plate and utensils and put them in a plastic bag, which she then transferred into a voluminous canvas bag she had brought.

"Signora, may I ask another favor? Could you call the Manhattan Institute and tell them I'm in the hospital?"

"Of course."

Erika thanked her. One more invaluable courtesy to be grateful for.

Once the signora was gone Flavio took the empty chair. "Go ahead and finish what you're drinking," he said. "We can still talk."

Her cup of tea was the last thing on her mind. She wished she'd had a chance to brush her hair when the signora mentioned it. At least her face was clean. *His* hair, on the other hand, was now much shorter, bobbing when he walked rather than swaying; she wondered if he'd visited a barber yesterday afternoon, his undercover activities at last wrapped up.

"So you found me..." she said.

"The hospital called the police when you were admitted, said you had a cracked rib and a bruised kidney."

"Liliana Pera, finally getting her revenge after I bested her when she left your building."

"We *will* catch her. And we'll get Paolo too. Heard anything from him?"

"No." Erika gazed past Flavio towards the door. *Was Paolo concerned that she hadn't shown up for their meeting? Would he call Giorgio or Signora Sillano?*

"Well," said Flavio, rising from the chair with a sober smile, "your injuries don't seem life-threatening and I'm glad for that. I'll be back to check on you tomorrow. In the meantime, take it easy and report anything to do with Paolo." Here's my card again. "Just in case in your scuffles you lost the other one I gave you."

She hadn't lost it. Now she had two calling cards plus the number Flavio had scribbled on a napkin the time they'd met in that English-style pub. He'd offered his help then, but she had no idea who he really was at the time. Now he wanted her to inform on Paolo.

Another knock at the doorway. "Signorina Rivoli?" A tall man in a long white coat walked right in. "Doctor Carrà—I'm in charge of your care."

He didn't seem much older than Paolo, no more than thirty, and he looked awfully tired: dark smudges under his eyes, strands of wispy hair dangling onto his forehead.

Delicately he shook her hand then looked her over with an earnest, professional eye. "Feeling horrible, I imagine," he said with an understanding smile.

"Yeah," she half chuckled.

"Let's have a listen." Stethoscope at the ready, he started his examination front and back while Erika gritted her teeth against the pain of having to turn her torso.

"I'm sorry," he said, "I won't have to do this again till tomorrow. Don't worry about not being able to take deep breaths. You've got a fractured rib and a bruised kidney." He paused with an inquisitive look. "You arrived unconscious last night. Still, we sedated you in order to take x-rays and so forth."

So, Doctor Carrà had worked all night and now today, the universal lot of a young physician. "Anything else wrong with me?" she asked.

"That's it. You had an elevated blood-alcohol content when admitted, and we did x-ray the left side of your face as well, although that bruise looks older..." He paused, perhaps waiting for some kind of elucidation. When none came, he asked, "Any idea who did this to you?"

Erika exhaled a silent, weary sigh. "Yes, and so do the

police."

When she didn't elaborate he gave his pronouncement. "The rib will have to heal on its own as will the kidney. You'll have blood in your urine for a while, and you'll have to use the oxygen until you can breathe deeply on your own." He tilted his head and gave a sympathetic shrug. "Which means you'll be here for a few days. Is the codeine keeping up with the pain?"

"Pretty much."

"Let the sisters know if it doesn't. I'll see you tomorrow."

She watched his white coat swing out of the room, then closed her eyes. She wouldn't be going anywhere soon, and that was fine. Try as she might (*and she certainly wouldn't*) she couldn't get out of bed; and here, at least, she wouldn't have to face Paolo. Even if somehow he knew she was in this hospital, it would be a monumental risk to show up with Flavio and his men on the watch. That is, if he still wanted to see her...

When she next awoke, lunch sat on her tray and Signora Sillano was pulling clean cutlery from her canvas bag.

"*Salve*," Erika greeted her, less groggily this time.

The signora returned her typical soft smile as she poured Erika's water. "I hope you've regained your appetite, the hospital minestrone smells good."

"*Grazie*, Signora—for everything. And thanks for bringing all this stuff. In America no one brings you nice plates and things when you're in the hospital. If I didn't have you..."

The signora patted her arm. "If you didn't have anyone, the hospital would provide it all. Feeling any better?"

Not really. Instead, she answered, "The soup'll help, I'm sure."

After lunch the signora helped her brush her hair and teeth, and Erika finally decided to open up to her friend and ally. "Thank God you came looking for me. I was in a kind of shock after I left your house yesterday. I went over to the Déjà Vu and when I got back, a woman who was mixed up with the Comrades attacked me. Kicked me over and over when I was down. Said I'd wrecked their plans."

The signora shook her head. "You could have been hurt much worse." She shifted forward, her gaze uneasy. "Listen, I wanted to wait until after you'd eaten to tell you...Paolo called this morning."

Instinctively Erika leaned forward, then fell back in agony.

"Be careful," said the signora. "Anyway, he was very upset when I told him what happened to you."

So, being stood up last night had worried Paolo. Erika wondered if he'd told the signora about their planned meeting. "Did he say anything else?"

"No. I mentioned your injuries and that you would recover. I also said he had to turn himself in, but he rang off right after." She let out a helpless sigh. "What about that dreadful woman who beat you? Could she come back?"

Erika had to drag her thoughts from Paolo. "Liliana Pera? She knows the police are looking for her. I don't think she'll come here."

Another tap on the doorjamb. They both looked up to see Giorgio. "Am I interrupting?"

"No, come in," said Erika, delighted to see him. "Signora, do you know Paolo's friend Giorgio Testa?"

"Eugenia Sillano," the signora said, shaking his hand.

"Who told you I was here?" Erika asked him.

Giorgio slipped Erika a furtive glance, but she told him to go ahead. "Signora Sillano knows everything." And to the signora she said, "Giorgio has nothing to do with those Comrades."

Smiling politely, the signora rose from her chair. "I've got some things to take care of, so I'll leave for a while and come back at dinner time."

Giorgio waited until she had gathered her things and left the room before plunking himself into the chair next to Erika. "Paolo called this morning," he announced. "Said he talked to the signora. Who did this to you—that Doberman bitch?"

"Exactly—Liliana Pera, she's called."

"*Cristo!*"

"Flavio Moretti and the police are hunting her. They're looking for Paolo too; watching the hospital, I imagine."

"And tapping the phones, Paolo suspects. He hung up as soon as he told me about the attack. What kind of damage did she do?"

Reflexively Erika felt her side. "A cracked rib and a bruised kidney. Hurts like hell to move or breathe—and especially to cough. Otherwise, the doctor says I'm okay."

"I've heard about broken rib pain," he said with a grimace.

"Listen, Giorgio, I'm sorry I got you mixed up in all this."

"Never mind. You're the one in the hospital, not me. Now, any more news?"

"Flavio came this morning and said they'll go easier on Paolo if he turns himself in, seeing as he didn't show up at the farmhouse."

"I wish I knew Paolo's plans," Giorgio said, his fingers drumming his thigh.

"Would you turn him in if you did?"

For a moment Giorgio contemplated her. "When we went to the farmhouse we agreed to call the police for his own good."

"Right. But it's one thing calling them because Matilde Fassino is being held. It's something else setting Paolo up with the cops." She couldn't tell whether Giorgio felt the same ambivalence.

In fact he changed the subject. "How are you holding up otherwise?"

Erika shrugged. "I'm almost glad to be here, drugged and sleeping the day away; easier not to think about certain things."

"Understandable. I felt the same way in the hospital after Franco died."

What didn't compare, of course, was the *other*, the revelation about Paolo and herself, which she had no inclination to share with Giorgio.

He leaned closer to her. "Just remember to keep taking small steps forward. Whatever you do, don't isolate yourself once you get out of here. I wonder if you'll be out by Christmas?"

Jesus, thought Erika, what day is this?

"It's already December twenty second," Giorgio answered for her. "Only three more days to go."

"I might be out by then," Erika said with a studied frown. "I don't know whether I'll be able to get around though."

"I'm sure the signora will look after you. I'm going to my parents' for the holiday. You can come with me if you're up to it."

Erika gave a little gasp. "I'm supposed to spend Christmas with my cousins in Asti. With everything that's happened I almost forgot!"

"Well, I'm sure you'll work things out."

Erika nodded absently. She would have to get hold of Elsa and invent yet another story. Now, however, she felt crushed with fatigue and couldn't help closing her eyes. She felt a pat on the arm and forced them open.

"I'll leave now. I know how it feels to be pumped full of pharmaceuticals."

Erika offered a slack smile. "You'll come back..."

"Tomorrow," he said, hauling himself out of the chair.

Erika's eyes closed again and she slid into blessed oblivion.

40: Night Visitor

That evening Erika woke to a thick wall of darkness, breached only by the trickle of yellow light from the cracked-open door to the hospital corridor. She felt sheltered in this mantle of blackness, shielded from people and questions and decisions, the silky cocoon of dreamless sleep ever ready to envelop her again—if only she could free herself from the assailing pain in her side. She shifted positions, groaning in frustration as she was reminded of codeine's role in her escape into oblivion. To return to that blessed dimension she would have to call the sister who would invade her refuge with light and chatter.

Then the door began to ease open, and Erika recognized Signora Sillano's silhouette. "*Salve,* Signora," she said, loath to leave her friend to grope around in the dark. She winced as she twisted towards the lamp to turn it on.

"I'm not disturbing your sleep?" the signora asked, softly setting her things down.

"No, Signora, I need to ask for more codeine."

As the signora hung her coat up, she said, "I think it's time you called me Genia, rather than *signora.*"

Erika thanked her. Having to return to the brash brightness of reality, it was just as well she did so via Genia Sillano.

"It's getting near dinner time," said the signora, pulling out a fresh dish from her canvas bag. She removed the paper protecting it and laid it and a copy of *La Stampa* on Erika's table. "Matilde Fassino has had a stroke," she announced, "and she's in this hospital."

Erika stared wide-eyed at the newspaper's headline.

"The story of her rescue on Monday is there too, though nothing too specific. It seems she had the stroke late yesterday...she may have been admitted around the same time as you. Go ahead and read."

Erika snatched up the newspaper, scrutinizing the article, which was accompanied by a photo of Fassino. The Comrades had kidnapped her at some time Sunday morning when her maid was off duty. So, Erika thought shrewdly, Fassino had probably been smuggled to the farmhouse not long before she and Giorgio arrived the first time to reconnoiter; then Gino had left to procure the Tavor. *Damn*, she'd forgotten to ask Flavio whether they'd used the drug to calm the woman, although he probably wouldn't have told her.

The signora was right about the article's vagueness. It referenced communist operatives, Red Brigade agents, the security services, and a shootout, but no names, and nothing about Flavio's undercover operation. *Flavio*: he must have known Fassino was in this hospital when he came this morning, yet he'd kept it from her; did he think she wouldn't find out?

Erika's eyes shifted back to the black and white close-up. At the farmhouse she'd only spied Matilde Fassino's two small high-heeled feet shuffling along under a blanket. Before that, Erika had encountered her just that one fleeting time in the Cremeria over a month ago. Still, she recalled her frail hands, her petite but straight frame, and her impatience as she sputtered over the coffee Paolo had tipped from the waiter's tray onto her. The newspaper photo highlighted the wan, bony countenance of an elderly woman. And, Erika noted, the flinty, unsmiling eyes of a war criminal. Or was she merely *reading* such a look into the close-up? She wanted to find out. As soon as she recovered enough strength to leave her bed, she would find Fassino's room and get a fresh look at her.

The signora poured water, this time from a bottle of Fiuggi she'd brought. "So you were there when all this happened," she stated, once Erika's eyes had left the newspaper.

"Yes, but at least Paolo wasn't. I wish I could tell you more, but the security services...the fellow you saw this morning is really strict about my having been sworn to secrecy."

The signora nodded. "You know," she said, "the head sister asked about notifying your next of kin when we arrived last night. I told them you only had your cousins in Asti and that I'd take care of it. Of course I don't have their number..."

Erika's eyes darkened. "I'd rather handle it myself when I get out." She thought again about the form Flavio had made her sign. Obviously she couldn't tell Elsa and Angelo why she was in the hospital. "Sunday's Christmas and I'm supposed to have lunch with them," she said aloud, more to herself than to the signora. She didn't know if she would even be up to traveling that soon once she got out of here. When she thought of her helplessness, her involvement in a debacle that seemed to sprout new complications every day, of what had led her to this point, she wanted to bang her fist on her table.

She looked at her landlady in frustration. "Signora—*Genia*," she corrected herself, "I'm getting better. You might not need to come so often."

She didn't know why she said this. It didn't help that she felt like someone was hurling stones at her side. Her right hand found her call button—*definitely time for more codeine.*

"You haven't been here even twenty-four hours," the signora responded with a patient smile. "Certainly I'll keep coming. I just wanted you to know I can relay messages, like the one to your school."

"Thank you," Erika murmured, her cheeks flushing.

She sought to change the subject. "By the way, what did they say at the school? Did you talk to a woman called Brigida?"

"It was the secretary, and I told her you'd had an accident and would be in the hospital for a while. Of course she said she understood."

"*An accident*—perfect, Genia!" Erika would have liked to hear the *kommandant's* tone upon learning Erika was institutionally laid up.

"You know," said the signora, "I could do the same with your cousins...I could be even more truthful and say a madwoman attacked you..."

Erika smiled with relief. If she didn't hurt so badly she would applaud the signora. "You don't know how much I would appreciate that—"

She was interrupted by the entrance of Sister Teresa bearing pain medication. After downing the codeine Erika said to her, "I've heard questions have been asked about my next of kin. Please pass on that Signora Sillano will notify them."

"Of course," answered Sister Teresa with a playful smile. "You're twenty-four years old and we've determined you're mentally capable of notifying whomever you'd like."

When the sister left, Erika turned to the signora. "She seems strange for a nun."

"Mm," the signora agreed with a curious look. "I wonder what motivated her to take the vows—can't imagine her complying when it comes to silent obedience."

Erika grinned. The mere act of ingesting the codeine was making her start to feel better.

"How was your visit with your friend Giorgio?" asked the signora, finally settling in her chair.

"He and I went together to the farmhouse to get Paolo out. He said Paolo also called him this morning, but hung up quickly because he suspects the phones are bugged."

"I suppose it's to be expected until they catch him. Lord knows where he's hiding."

"All the Comrades have been picked up. He could be in a hotel..."

"That would be a huge risk since desk clerks have to collect your identity card or passport when you check in, and the police then come by to examine them. Of course there are hotels that don't abide by the laws. Not impossible for Paolo to be acquainted with one, considering the company he's been keeping."

Erika pictured Paolo slinking in and out of some dive that had peeling paint and burned-out light bulbs, as he dodged the authorities. "He can't keep this up forever."

The signora's nod was weary. Once they had both relaxed in contemplative silence the signora began to doze.

After dinner Erika insisted Genia go home to her own bed. "Really, Genia, I'm getting more rest than you. I'll be fine tonight, I've already used my call button, and all I do is sleep, anyway. I wouldn't feel right about you spending another night in the chair."

The signora agreed to go home and return in the morning. With affection Erika watched her exit the room, bundled in her coat and laden with bags. Then she shut her eyes. Truly, Genia Sillano was the only person Erika wanted to attend her right now—not Elsa, not even her mother. Neither of them would be able fathom her situation, provided she had the energy and emotional will to attempt an explanation.

For the first time since her arrival in the hospital she was dreaming, this time of snow—smooth, slick, with explosive puffs of powder spraying her face. Belly down, she glided on a sled through the forest, the sky a golden blue, sunrays tickling her face as she broke through a thicket of spruce into vast, open whiteness.

She felt something messing with her hair. Wind? No, she realized, prodding herself fully awake and peering into the darkness. Whatever had touched her head had now withdrawn, but she could still sense a heavy presence. No light in the room, not even the stream from the hallway. Someone had shut the door.

Then a whisper. "Don't worry, it's only me."

Paolo! Erika jerked forward then fell back with a groaning gasp, hot pokers plunging into her side.

"Don't move. Let me find your lamp."

"I've got it," she said in a hoarse voice, suppressing another groan as she reached above her. She turned on the lamp and squinted. Yes, it was Paolo, looking down at her with apprehension.

"Go ahead and crank the bed up," she said, pointing toward her feet. "Slowly," she added, wincing. "How long have you been here?"

"Not long," he said, propelling her to a sitting position. "I slipped into the hospital earlier when it was busy—there are lots of entrances—then I waited in an empty room until things calmed down for the night." He glanced at his watch. "It's a little after two now."

Erika felt a knot of ambivalence contracting inside her as she continued to stare at Paolo. His face was drawn, his cheeks peppered with stubble. "You could still get caught," she said.

He wrenched off his coat and tossed it onto another bed. "Doesn't matter, I needed to see you," he said, taking hold of the hand unburdened by her IV.

Her pulse quickened yet her hand didn't squeeze his. Instead she gently freed it and indicated the signora's bedside chair. "Sit down, you look like you need a rest. Have you heard what happened Monday?"

Paolo remained hovering over her, his eyes fixed on her face. "Giorgio told me briefly on the phone. Why did you have to go back to that house?" he demanded.

Why did he think? Was she supposed to let a major crime take place? She shrugged. "Why didn't you show up?"

He hesitated and straightened before saying, "After all

we talked about the night before, I couldn't go through with it."

Couldn't go through with it: was it for the sake of their relationship? At this point she didn't want to ask, so grotesque was the notion of carrying on with him as before. "Well, I'm glad you didn't come. Flavio says you'll be better off for it, especially if you turn yourself in."

"I couldn't do that until I saw you." Paolo looked her up and down for at least the third time. "Genia said you weren't in critical condition but I had to check for myself—"

"I'm all right, just a few kicks in the ribs by that thug, Liliana Pera. The one you say you don't know..."

"*I don't*," he emphasized, clearly annoyed by Erika's insinuation. Then his eyes darkened. "I caught up with Genia earlier, on her way to catch the bus."

"So you two talked..."

"She told me everything...mentioned the postcard."

Erika looked away.

"I've thought about it all evening," he said.

Anxiety and embarrassment mounted in her, trapped as she felt by hospital tubes and pain. "I can imagine," she said.

"I still love you and want to be with you," Paolo declared. He kissed her forehead and buried his face in her hair, which made her stiffen in defensiveness. He stood back, his eyes glistening and desperate. A spasm of compassion shook her.

The door jiggled opened and a young nun stepped in. Surprised, she frowned at Paolo. "Who are you? No one is allowed in at this time of night."

"He's taking the signora's place," said Erika impulsively.

"But I've never seen him before and we only allow family overnight."

Paolo and Erika exchanged crooked smiles.

"I'm not leaving," Paolo said, dropping into the

signora's chair.

The sister reddened, glancing uneasily from Paolo to Erika. Then she turned and left the room, leaving the door wide open, her robes and the wings of her big hat flapping in her wake.

For a stretch Erika and Paolo remained mute. An occasional clip-clopping sounded beyond the door, otherwise the hall seemed conspiratorially silent as well.

At last Paolo leaned forward. Quietly he asked, "What's Alan like?"

Erika's defenses flared again as she observed the exhaustion in her half-brother's features. She wouldn't tell him of this particular resemblance to Bruno. The reminder unsettled her now more than ever, with the intractable image of their shared flesh and blood staring her in the face.

"He's fair and blue-eyed like me," she said. "Builds custom homes, as you already know." She noted his bewildered but expectant frown, and decided she owed him a little something more personal. "He used to smoke a pipe."

Paolo's eyes sparked with surprise and irony. Then they saddened, and their poignancy made her kindly add, "When he used to smoke it he held it the way you do—like a wine glass."

"Both his parents were from here?" he asked, after what seemed a melancholic pause.

"Yeah, from Pautasso."

"So those cousins of yours in Asti...and Ivan...they're mine too."

They were. And the immediacy of this now resounded in her mind.

"Is Ivan in jail?" asked Paolo.

"I don't know. Flavio wouldn't talk about it. But Ivan didn't show up at the farmhouse either."

Paolo accepted this with a distant nod. Then he turned to face her again. "You know," he said confidentially, "you and I are only half related, genetically speaking—no more than first cousins, really..."

She stared at him, wondering at the implications of his euphemistic slant on things.

Mercifully, she didn't have time to reply. The sound of heavy steps on the granite floors of the corridor reached her—more like boots than clogs, and more than one set.

Flavio entered the room accompanied by three uniformed police, pistols drawn. The four halted. Paolo slowly stood and with a helpless smile spread his arms wide.

"Time to come in from the cold, Paolo." Flavio's tone was wry, though Erika sensed something almost indulgent, paternal.

"I was waiting for you all," Paolo answered, as one of the police handcuffed and frisked him. "And you, a *cop*," he flung at Flavio.

"We'll say you turned yourself in," Flavio said, and then faced Erika. "We're going now; I'll be in touch later."

As they marched him to the door, Paolo twisted toward Erika. She met his imploring eyes and gave him a nod of encouragement. She started to extend her hand, then let it drop in her lap as he and the police disappeared through the doorway.

41: To Look Her in the Face

After the police escorted Paolo out of Erika's hospital room, the nurse came back wearing a worried frown. "Are you all right?"

Erika answered with a stoic nod. She felt drained dry and didn't want to be fussed over by this young nun, who could be no more than in her early twenties. "You called them..." Erika said.

The girl looked embarrassed. "I had to report him to my supervisor...she had instructions about a man of his description."

"Of course," said Erika. "But don't worry, he caused me no harm." Then she closed her eyes and the sister withdrew.

She was awake when Signora Sillano arrived the next morning. The paralyzing pain in her ribs had ebbed and she hadn't needed codeine since the previous evening. She sat slightly forward when relating the news about Paolo.

"So it's done," said the signora with a heavy sigh, as she dropped into her chair. "I spoke with Paolo last night when he intercepted me at the bus stop."

"He told me...he knows about everything."

"I just hope my meddling doesn't backfire again."

Erika gave a resigned shrug. "Will you visit him in jail?"

"As soon as it's possible."

Erika looked reflectively past her. "I'll go when I'm released from here..."

"And how are *you* doing?"

"I don't know, just glad I've finally stopped running round in circles." Of course things were not resolved with

Paolo, but at least she didn't have to deal with any of that while she was confined to the hospital and he to his jail cell.

Before either Erika or the signora could go on, Doctor Carrà walked in. "You're awake, good, since I'm early this morning."

The signora stepped aside as he started to pull the curtain. "You can stay," said Erika. "He just listens to me breathe."

After the exam Carrà scribbled some notes and said, "Since you're hurting less and breathing better, I'd like you to start getting up. Move around a bit, then sit in the chair for a while at least twice today. I'm ordering the catheter and IV removed; continue using the oxygen as you feel you need it and we'll see how you are tomorrow."

By afternoon Erika was sitting alone in the chair in her room, the signora having gone home after lunch. She'd had to take more codeine and avail herself of the sister to stand, but at least she had cast off two of the irksome tubes. She was planning an eventual stroll around the hospital when Giorgio came in.

"You're up!"

"Doctor's orders. Grab a chair from that other bed," she said, "I've got to tell you what's happened."

Erika's abbreviated account of Paolo's visit, including Flavio's acknowledgment of Paolo's surrender, made Giorgio chuckle. "Clever bastard, he's killed two birds with one stone. But seriously," he added with sympathy, "I'm glad he got a chance to see you. Your reunion can't have been easy."

If you only knew.

"By the way," Giorgio said, "I read that Matilde Fassino's in this hospital."

"Amazing, huh? She must've been admitted around the same time I was."

"Does Paolo know?"

"He might've heard, but he didn't mention it and I

didn't have time to tell him."

"Well, if I can visit him in jail, we'll find out."

Erika had already envisioned Paolo behind bars, a grill or glass between him and his prospective visitors—a barrier that didn't displease her. Distance—she needed it more than ever. She said to Giorgio, "Do you think the trauma at the farmhouse could have caused Matilde Fassino's stroke?"

Giorgio's look was shrewd. "It's definitely occurred to me. There could even be implications for the government, though I'm sure they'll release as few details as possible. Then again, it could somehow leak that the security services were involved in kidnapping her..."

"Would *you* write that? After the oath of secrecy Flavio had us sign?"

"Erika," he said, a corner of his mouth turned cynically down, "I was there, with *you*, to help free the old lady. It's an angle no one else will have exploited and I can't help at least contemplating it."

Well, thought Erika, he's covered himself, sort of. Still she wondered whether Giorgio might bring *her* into some possible story. And what about his perspective on Matilde Fassino's war crimes? The woman had eluded Nuremburg-like charges, and her kidnapping and stroke could be considered a kind of karma.

The idea preoccupied her off and on the rest of the afternoon and into the next day, redoubling her resolve to at least get a glimpse of the old woman whom Paolo had depicted as the bitch-monster who'd ruined his mother's life, and over whom he had ruined his own.

Doctor Carrà had freed her for walks without her oxygen. Bending at the waist was torturous and when transitioning to her feet she had to hold her side, but Carrà had judged that normal.

"Shall I walk with you?" asked Signora Sillano, helping her into her robe.

Erika pursed her lips and stepped into her slippers. She planned to go as far as the stroke ward and didn't want to test the signora's understanding of her urge to get a look at Matilde Fassino. "I'd like to try it alone. I'll walk until I'm uncomfortable, then come back."

"All right, I'll wait here."

Erika gripped her side as she shuffled to the office at the entrance to her ward. The door was open but she knocked anyway. "Could you tell me how to get to the ward for stroke patients?"

A nun doing paperwork glanced up under her winged hat, one eye assessing Erika.

Erika straightened painfully and let go of her ribs. "Doctor Carrà sent me out for a walk and I know someone there."

"You'll need to go to Neurology, then."

After receiving directions Erika gingerly exited her ward to the elevator. Once inside she leaned against the wall.

By the time she dragged herself to the Neurology station she was sweating and almost panting.

A roving nun stopped her. "Are you all right?"

With halting breaths, her right hand clutching her side, Erika managed a tight-voiced "Yes."

"You don't look well. I think you should go back to your room."

Erika waited for her breathing to stabilize, pain keeping her partially bent over. "Just been for a walk...doctor's orders...come to look in on a patient I know."

"Which patient?"

When Erika told her, the woman bristled. "She's *not* receiving visitors. Under no circumstances," she reiterated when Erika's lips parted.

Jesus, she had made it all this way for nothing. No matter, she couldn't stay on her feet any longer. "Okay, I'll rest on the bench there till I'm ready to walk back."

"You do that," said the sister, shooting Erika another frown before moving on.

When she bent to sit, pain kicked her in the side again. She rested the back of her head against the wall and closed her eyes. How in hell would she get back to her room?

When she opened her eyes the same sister stood in front of her with a wheelchair. "Shall we get you back?"

Erika nodded, but as she was wheeled out of Neurology she looked back down the hall in frustration.

When she came rolling into her room, the signora rose in alarm.

"Don't worry, Genia, I'm fine. I just walked a little too far."

The sister from Neurology put her to bed with her oxygen and sent for codeine. For the rest of the afternoon Erika dozed—not, however, without contemplating her next outing to Neurology.

The next morning Erika was surprised to feel no pain-hangover from her wobbly marathon. She took a short walk with Signora Sillano to the end of the ward and back, after which the signora went home. Erika was sitting in her chair in bathrobe and slippers, reading a copy of *La Stampa,* when Flavio walked in carrying a beige file folder.

"Making progress I see," he said with a crisp smile.

"You could say that." She looked him up and down. He was wearing a suit, and other than his light eyes and olive complexion, no trace of the Caspian prince remained.

"Hope your spirits aren't too low after Paolo's arrest."

Erika eyed his folder, then gazed away without answering.

"Anyway," he said, sitting in the well-used visitor's chair, "I thought I might find Eugenia Sillano here. I've got some papers for her to sign, of the same order I gave you and Giorgio at the farmhouse."

"Well you'll have to try another time, since she's gone

home."

"I will. I heard you might be getting out of here in a couple of days..."

Erika assumed a poker face to study him. Doctor Carrà had just told her the news this morning. Did Flavio have full access to her medical information? And still no mention of Matilde Fassino's stroke, let alone her co-residency with Erika in the Molinette hospital. If he was monitoring Erika, he no doubt kept Fassino under even stricter watch—had probably already been to see her this morning. Once again she felt at a disadvantage, having to engage him in her hospital garb while he sat serene in a suit.

"Good news, right?" he prompted.

When she answered with a neutral nod, he rose and said, "Just keep a low profile when you get out. Go back to tutoring at the Manhattan Institute."

Erika gave an internal start. But *of course* he'd discovered her job.

"Don't worry, my branch doesn't bother about work status. By the way," he added, "we've picked up Liliana Pera. You can rest easy on that score. Well, I'll be off to see if I can find Signora Sillano at home."

With that he breezed out of the room. She was glad to see him go. Not least because she felt ready for another stroll down to Neurology. If Flavio had been flitting about the hospital, nosing around about patients, Erika could continue to do the same.

She checked the travel clock Genia had brought from her flat. She would have to get going before the signora returned.

She rose stiffly, tightened the belt on her bathrobe, then slowly began her trek out the door and out of her ward. When she arrived at Neurology her right hand was again supporting her left side, though this time she felt more resilient.

She took a long look around the humming hall. No sign

of Flavio or the nun from yesterday. Though her breathing was a bit labored she continued on.

She poked her head into one room after the other, and by the time she had finished checking both sides of the hall she was once more lathered in perspiration. She leaned against the wall for a moment, then trudged on into a side corridor.

Immediately she stopped and stared. A young, uniformed policeman sat slouched in a chair outside one of the rooms, reading a magazine. He glanced up at her and she looked away. *Matilde Fassino's room?* Then a quick clacking of clogs sounded behind her. She turned to retreat, only to collide with a nun rounding the corner. Erika let out a loud groan and fell against the wall.

"I'm sorry!" exclaimed the nun, reaching out to brace her. "Are you all right?"

"My rib," Erika gasped. "It's cracked."

"Where were you going?" Erika didn't answer. "Shall I get help to get you back to your room?"

Though pain radiated up under her arm, Erika was able to stand on her own now. "I guess I might need help," she admitted.

The sister frowned and gazed behind her. "Shall I look for a wheelchair now, or will you be all right for a moment while I check on a patient?"

Before Erika could respond, the police guard approached. "Can I help?" he asked, looking alarmed at Erika's distress.

"Thank you, Nello," the nun said in a maternal tone. "I'd better see that this girl gets to her room, then I'll be back to check on our patient."

As her pain receded, Erika glanced from the nun to the guarded room. "I can wait for the wheelchair. Go ahead and take care of your patient."

"You're sure...?"

Erika nodded.

"I'll watch over her," said the guard. The nun seemed satisfied and continued down the hall, disappearing into the room now guarded by an empty chair.

"You can sit there if you'd like," said the guard, indicating his chair.

"Thanks!" Erika beamed a grateful smile; then breathing heavily and supporting her ribs with both hands, she limped to his post. Suddenly she doubled up, her face contorting. "The pain's awful, let me tell the nurse!"

Eyes wide, the guard looked at the doorway. "Only hospital personnel are allowed in there."

"I'm about to collapse!" Erika pushed open the door and staggered into the room. The light was dim, the curtains drawn; the nun was leaning over her supine patient. No one else occupied the room, nor did the young guard follow. The nun who was taking the patient's blood pressure glanced back at her.

"Sorry," Erika grunted, "I can't stand up anymore."

The sister looked peeved, but motioned to a chair across the room. "Sit there, I'll be finished in a moment."

Erika headed that way, then once the nun returned to her patient, edged quietly towards the bed. Matilde Fassino's face, white as her bedding, came into view. Erika stopped and peered hesitantly over the nun's shoulder. She couldn't decide whether she recognized the old woman from a month ago in the Cremeria, or even from the recent newspaper photo—too many tubes in her, and her eyes were closed. Still, what other old woman's room, besides Matilde Fassino's, would be guarded by police?

The nun turned around. "You're supposed to wait over there."

"Sorry," Erika repeated. Wincingly, she instead eased herself into Fassino's bedside chair.

The sister shook her head, then started writing up her notes. "I'm almost finished, then we'll get you back."

Erika's gaze settled on Fassino. The skin on her long,

bony face looked crêpey and friable as tissue paper, her sleeping eyes like craters in stony sockets, her hands splotchy and gnarled as old olive trees. Rather than Paolo's monster, Erika saw the inhabitant of a coffin.

And yet Fassino was breathing, and the faint lifting of her chest (she couldn't weigh more than ninety pounds) sent Erika's thoughts back to the farmhouse, to Fassino wrapped in the blanket while the two Red Brigade operatives pushed her towards the trunk of their car. That trauma, on top of her two-day sequestration, had obviously tipped the scales for her. If there was anything left of Paolo's monster, it had to reside unseen, relegated to the shadows inside her.

"Come now," said the nun, having finished, "I'll get you a wheelchair."

For the second day in a row Erika was rolled back to her room and put to bed. Fortunately, Signora Sillano hadn't yet returned.

Waiting for her dose of codeine to take effect, Erika lay musing. She couldn't imagine Matilde Fassino ever leaving the hospital. And Flavio: he must have known there could be a health risk to Fassino while he played along with her kidnapping. From the start, had he simply written her off as a war criminal, and therefore dispensable?

The bottom line was that all of Turin, Asti, and likely the whole of Italy, knew of Fassino's crimes. *And her deceased husband's*: the banker had blackmailed Paolo's mother into becoming his mistress—and who wouldn't have yielded to him under threat of denunciation to the fascist regime?—then appropriated her savings, while his wife went on to report Sara to the authorities out of jealousy. Which one of the couple was more villainous, Erika couldn't decide.

At least for now the old lady would not be sitting rich and smug in her lofty villa on Superga. If Paolo knew of her ruin, he no doubt deemed it just. And yet, if he could see her lying shriveled and still and white as death, might he feel a smidgeon of remorse at having had a hand in her brutal downfall?

Erika shook her head—some pieces of this puzzle just couldn't be forced into place. But at least she had managed a final glimpse of Matilde Fassino; stared into the face that had catapulted her into a life-changing odyssey. More than one life had been altered in this odyssey, but only Erika had escaped, if not unscathed, at least free.

42: A New Friend?

After almost five days in the hospital Erika went home on Sunday, Christmas Day. Dr. Carrà had instructed her to gauge her activity according to her level of pain, and Genia Sillano pledged to look after her. Classes at the Manhattan Institute didn't resume until after the sixth of January, so Erika had plenty of time to recuperate; she also had an extended opportunity to mull over her association with the Manhattan Institute. The job suited Erika for now and she thought she might consult Flavio about how to get legal work status. Flavio might even have an incentive to help her. As long as Erika stayed in Italy, there would be no risk of her contravening the state secrets form she'd signed; whereas, if she returned to America she could conceivably blab about her adventure and incur no negative consequences. As for the secretary Brigida's reference to letting her go, it would take only a counter threat from Erika citing their illegal hiring of her.

The signora had called Elsa before Christmas with the report of Erika's beating by a madwoman and assured her that Erika would be ready to receive a visit on the day after Christmas. Erika joined the signora for Christmas dinner, along with the signora's daughter, son-in-law, and granddaughter. The merrymaking centered principally on food and drink, with multiple courses and almost as many wines. Wrapped presents sat at each guest's place at the table. Signora Sillano, despite her diligence at the hospital, had found time to buy Erika a burgundy and blue wool scarf. "You need to dress more warmly." Erika blushed and smiled at both the irony of the gift and the generosity of the signora. This scarf would likely not come to any sinister use.

On Monday, the holiday of Saint Stephen, Erika began to use the stairs regularly, up and down for meals at the signora's. In the late afternoon Elsa paid a visit, which consisted primarily of Erika's answering Elsa's enquiries about the attack with feigned bewilderment and helpless shakes of her head. Elsa agreed that there were *many crazies out there these days, especially in a big city.* Tuesday, she decided it was time to get out of the building. Coffee in the Déjà Vu re-established her routine and satisfied Fausta and Mara that she hadn't descended into drunken delirium after her last visit. By all rights, a visit to Paolo in jail should have been in order as well. But while Erika was still in the hospital Flavio had found the signora, and in addition to obliging her to sign the state secrecy document he informed her that Paolo could not receive visitors. For now Erika felt relieved. On the other hand, paying a different visit had been floating in the back of her mind since she was hospitalized. On Wednesday afternoon she took the switchblade from the end table drawer and sat on the sofa contemplating it. She felt a certain triumph at having adapted her foil talents to it. The foil had taken a life, the switchblade had saved one, and she didn't want to give it up. Still, it belonged to Gino. She glanced at the pearl-handled stiletto, the knife she had bought, remaining in the drawer. It was hers and she would consider it testament as well to the ongoing skills and mettle she had developed along her bizarre journey.

She shut the drawer and brought the switchblade to the console next to the front door. For a moment she considered her purse, abandoned there for close to two weeks now. The period in which it had proved a handicap was over; time to reclaim it and transfer her things back to it. And yet, she had finally shed that naked feeling of leaving the house without it. She liked going about unencumbered—a sensation of lightness and freedom, of being prepared.

She left the purse and tucked Gino's switchblade into her coat pocket. She took the tram to the SIP where she called Flavio, who confirmed that Gino was still convalescing in Asti's hospital and was allowed visitors.

Asti's only hospital lay less than a fifteen-minute walk from the station. Erika had been able to rest on the train ride over and decided to walk to the hospital rather than wait for the bus. As she crossed the big market piazza, her face was warmed by the revival of sunrays glistening in an azure sky. Her lungs felt invigorated by the cold dry air and she felt stronger and very nearly mended.

By the time she reached the hospital, though, she had unbuttoned her coat and was holding her side and sweating. She lingered outside the entrance until her breathing stabilized and then trudged in.

She found Gino's room (Flavio had given her the number) but she stopped short of entering right away. She reached into her pocket and felt the switchblade, sliding her thumb to and fro along its handle, across the smooth, raised release button. The gesture had become intimate, yet it was time to let her gleaming friend go.

Gino was sitting up in bed and waved her in. "Come, have a seat," he said, apparently pleased to see her. He didn't look too bad apart from that classic rumpled hospital air. Erika could certainly relate to that.

She offered a tentative smile and took the chair next to his bed. "I didn't know whether I should come, but Flavio said it was okay."

"He told me you'd been in the hospital too. You look kind of pale."

At least the black eye Gino had given her was now gone, though he must have noticed it at the farmhouse. She wondered what he'd thought about it then. "It's my first day out and about," she said, stroking her ribs, "and still hurting a bit."

"Sorry we couldn't keep a shorter leash on Liliana Pera." He shook his head soberly.

"At least I heard she's behind bars now."

"Paolo too," he replied softly.

For an instant Erika avoided Gino's gaze, then turned the topic to him. "You seem okay."

"The bullet was a .32—nicked my stomach but that's all. And thanks to you I didn't catch a second one. So I'm all sewn up and waiting to get out of here," he concluded.

Erika's smile was modest. "I'm glad everything turned out all right. And speaking of that, I wanted to return something to you. I think I've *borrowed* it for long enough." She pulled the switchblade from her pocket. For a couple of seconds Gino contemplated it.

"Keep it," he said with a wry smile. "You've earned it, plus you could teach me a thing or two with it."

Erika shot him a grin. Her rib pain had all but vanished in this moment, eclipsed by his gratitude and his compliments...plus something else...

"It reminds me of my fencing days," she added, fondly rotating the knife's grey handle.

"Then I'd hate to take you on with a sword." Another amused smile.

The humor in his eyes now settled into a subtle stare. He seemed to be assessing her with more than just professional interest. "You could go back to fencing. Or you could take up spying. You're not bad at that either, although I did notice you following me to the pharmacy."

"You knew it was me all the way there?"

"I suspected someone was tailing me; couldn't make out who in the fog, then realized it was you later on."

"The pharmacist, right?"

"Sorry, can't talk about the case."

"I *have* signed the official secrecy papers..."

Gino folded his arms in mock severity and shook his head.

So much for verifying the use of the tranquilizers. Erika shrugged her shoulders. "A lot of grey area in the espionage business."

"Practically nothing's cut and dried in life, particularly intelligence work."

"Mn...I'm not even sure of your real name. Should I call you *Gino*?"

"No, my real name's Claudio."

"Like on your bus pass—Claudio Voghera."

For a second or two he seemed confused. Then he exclaimed, "Brava—you went through my jacket pockets that evening! See what I mean about your spy instincts?"

"You might be right about that." She didn't want to talk about spying, however. Instead she asked, "Have you heard about Matilde Fassino's stroke?"

"Yes...unfortunate."

"Some people might say she deserved it, considering what she did during the war."

Claudio relaxed back against his pillows. "Justice versus human rights, you mean? Paolo would definitely side with the former."

"He has good cause, don't you think?"

"I suppose, but I don't let my mind get tangled up in things like that. We captured two Red Brigade operatives and that will lead to more arrests. *Que sera, sera* about the rest."

Erika didn't want to let it go. "But would you have kidnapped just any rich capitalist to get your results, or was Matilde Fassino a special case because of her history?"

"If we had sequestered *just anyone*," Claudio replied, "we wouldn't have got Paolo to come on board and strengthen our credibility with the Red Brigades. The RB operatives trusted our motives largely because they knew how much Paolo hated Matilde Fassino."

Yes, that made sense, though Claudio had offered no opinion concerning the ethical question of the kidnapping in general. But why should she expect one? She herself couldn't judge whether Matilde Fassino's role as criminal trumped that of victim, or vice versa, one reason she would have liked to hear Claudio's point of view.

She asked, "Was Paolo with you when you picked her up?"

"Can't talk about that."

Erika wanted to blow out a frustrated breath. If Paolo had only been in on the plotting, he might have a relatively easy time in front of the judges. Practically a sympathy case, considering his mother's fate at the hands of the old vulture Fassino.

Claudio's gaze had strayed to the ceiling and Erika took the opportunity to observe him more closely. "I understand about the importance of the mission's success," she said in a philosophical tone. "You're not like the police, sworn to protect people and all. Still, twice you could have killed me, and the first time we met you did rough me up a bit." She felt flushed, recalling the frisson she'd felt with Claudio's warm breath in her ear. If she was blushing he didn't seem to take notice. In fact, she thought she detected a hint of pink in his own complexion, plus a kind of sympathy in his gaze when it returned to her—if not something more...

"Just as well things worked out the way they did," he said. "That you weren't harmed even more."

An indirect apology, perhaps? His eyes were fastened onto hers. Then the sympathetic look slipped away, and she found herself faced with eyes like those of the CIA agent who had interviewed her in San Diego. Eyes like windows that glinted with the sun but whose curtains were drawn behind them, shutting away secrets, hiding amorality. When that agent first told her that a field operative's priority was to use people and then leave them behind if necessary, she felt sure she'd be up to it. Now she was less certain. After everything she had experienced in the last two months, a kind of mist had lifted, taking with it the romance and cachet of espionage. And yet knowing what little she did of Claudio and Flavio, she suspected that at least some spies were not completely devoid of compassion.

"Obviously this work isn't for everyone," said Claudio with a shrug. "A better choice might be to wait for Paolo to get out and live happily ever after with him."

Erika flinched, and Claudio cocked his head. "Or maybe not..."

Other than Paolo, only Eugenia Sillano knew Erika's latest secret, and she intended to keep it that way. "When do you think he might get out?" she asked.

"Who knows? Justice works at a slug's pace in this country. You'll have months to think about your future with him before he even goes to trial...if there is a future."

"I doubt it very much," she said.

"I can understand, after everything that's happened." There was a hint of sympathy playing in Claudio's eyes again, along with the other thing...

"Yeah," Erika went on, "the Matilde Fassino business, my brother...I want to put it all behind me."

"Good," Claudio said in a firm voice. "You don't owe any other explanation, and you should reject all guilt. Life is one giant accident to navigate and troubleshoot."

If only he knew how right he was.

"Just three people in Italy know about Keith," she said. "In America everyone who counts knows—one reason I don't want to go back."

Claudio nodded, his sympathy evident now. "There aren't any clear-cut answers to life, and insisting on finding them can drive you crazy. So keep your secrets and don't worry about the grey areas. You can't change them anyway."

"Like the kidnapping of Matilde Fassino..."

He displayed his palms, then let them drop to his lap. "Exactly."

43: On a Clear Day

Throughout the ride back to Turin, Erika's thoughts vacillated from Claudio to Paolo. Claudio had said he would be in touch so they could have "a proper civilized cup of coffee" once he was released from the hospital. The thought sent a tingling sensation through her as she rocked along with the train—what more was there to Claudio than met the eye? As for Paolo, deceit and mistrust had thwarted their relationship from the very start. And now this latest thing—the *coup de grace*. At least she had moved past the mental shock and physical repugnance of the thing and could feel a certain calm acceptance of fate. As Claudio had observed: life itself was a big enough accident to navigate, without getting bogged down in guilt. What troubled her was Paolo's assertion that he still wanted to be with her. In what way did he reckon this possible? Well, for now, with him in jail, she really needn't consider it.

Or so she thought. The next day she received a call from Flavio, relaying a request from Paolo for a visit from her. A short, supervised meeting between them, Flavio had specified, with him present. Determined at last to get the whole business behind her, she agreed.

Two days later, on New Year's Eve, Erika got off the tram downtown in corso Vittorio Emanuele. The prison called Le Nuove loomed before her, practically as grim and foreboding as the medieval castle in Piazza Castello, with massive dark-brick walls and menacing guard towers. She drew a resolute breath and walked to the visitors' entrance on the side. There she found the steel door Flavio had described, rang its bell, and waited.

The door opened and a uniformed guard waved her in after matching her passport to her name on his list. She followed him to a room where she was frisked by a female guard, after which she was led to another room. The guard unlocked the door and there sat Paolo and Flavio at a rectangular table, the only souls in the small, spartan space. Paolo sprang to greet her, brushing her cheeks with his. Flavio rose slowly and pulled out another chair.

They all sat, Erika and Paolo on either side of a corner of the table, facing each other, Flavio across the table from Erika at the other end. "You're forbidden to discuss the case," he instructed, taking out a notebook and pen, "and you're to keep your conversation in Italian." Though Flavio knew English, Erika figured he wanted to be sure that no sensitive information passed between Paolo and her. As for Erika and Paolo, Italian was all they had spoken since their estrangement after the *Cardinale* bombing.

For a long moment they took stock of each other, Paolo's forearms on the Formica table, Erika's hands in her lap. Paolo looked gaunt. The navy-blue turtleneck sweater he wore with jeans enhanced the sallowness of his skin, and the length of his hair now framed his face in a way that made him look even more drawn and tired. She tried not to think of his resemblance to Bruno.

Finally Paolo shifted, placing a hand on hers. "How are your ribs?" he asked.

"Much better," she replied, grateful for the small talk. "Did you know Matilde Fassino was in the Molinette while I was there?" She glanced at Flavio who looked up from his notebook, watched them for a couple of seconds, then continued writing. "She's in bad shape."

Paolo shrugged. "I heard. She's alive and it's more than she deserves."

So, no grey area there for Paolo, even though his blind obsession about Fassino had achieved little more than getting him locked up. She thought of asking if he'd taken part in the kidnapping but noticed Flavio observing them again. "What about you?" she asked instead. "How are you managing in here?"

"Well, they're not torturing me," he said, tossing a sarcastic look at Flavio, who had gone back to writing. "I wanted to see you and at least they obliged."

"No bail?"

"We don't have bail in Italy, we have house arrest. But I'm denied that. I'll be in here for the long haul. But when I get out..." He squeezed Erika's hand. Flavio's head popped up, and Paolo waited for him to return to his notebook before finishing, "Maybe you and I..."

The gleam in his eye startled her. Carefully she freed her hand. "I've been thinking about that..."

"And I," he said before she could go on, "have come to the conclusion that we don't need to let on about...*you know*."

Erika glanced at Flavio and lowered her voice. "You mean that we're related?"

"*Partially* related," Paolo contradicted. "Only Genia Sillano knows and she's always been on my side. We could be together when I get out, maybe even get married. It'll keep me going in here, something to look forward to in the New Year."

Shocked, Erika marveled at the shades of grey in Paolo's thinking when it came to incest versus his black and white view of Matilde Fassino's brutal treatment. Again she looked over at Flavio, who had now stopped writing though he hadn't gazed up. If he was following all this, what was he thinking?

Her eyes returned to Paolo, and in the muddle of this surrealistic moment she decided to humor him. "It would be a dishonest life, no matter what."

"No." He took her hand again. "The lie would be denying our love. We won't have children. That should make you feel better."

Make her feel better? The thought of producing children with Paolo sent her recoiling back to reality. She had to end this now. True, she had once felt a desire for him verging on love, and she felt sorry that he now saw her as his only sustenance while incarcerated and his refuge upon leaving prison. But the way he compartmentalized things struck her as pathological. Time to set him straight.

Flavio was now watching them curiously, so she further lowered her voice. "I couldn't live with you as if I didn't know we're related."

Paolo sat back, gripping the seat of his chair. "You're an obscurantist...but then again maybe you never loved me," he muttered, defiance mingling with fatigue in his eyes.

"Listen," she whispered between clenched teeth, "you look like my father right now. There's no way I can go on the way we did."

For the first time during their meeting, Paolo's expression turned reflective, as though a fraction of thought had finally detached itself from his monomania and floated into a sphere of objectivity. "Well," he said with a faraway smile, "I guess my looks can't be helped."

"Exactly," she said coolly, "and neither can anything else as far as I'm concerned."

Flavio cleared his throat. He was returning his notebook to his jacket pocket. "Time to go," he said.

"Wait." Paolo held up a hand to him, then leaned towards Erika. "So you're turning your back on me—leaving me behind the way you will the year 1977..."

That was exactly Erika's intention at this point. Just like a good spy. Only this was no longer a case of espionage, and though Paolo's tone rang matter-of-fact, his eyes were pleading.

"If they let me," she conceded, "I'll visit sometime later on." *When I've got my head around this thing*, she wanted to say but feared he might misinterpret it and hold out hope they could be together.

Paolo's lips tightened before he yielded with a resigned shrug. Meanwhile Flavio pushed away from the table, the metal-legged chair screeching against the tiles and at Erika's nerves. She rose slowly.

After gazing at the table for a moment Paolo followed suit. Flavio knocked on a metal door at the opposite side of the room from where Erika had entered. They waited, Paolo now looking oddly aloof as he and Erika watched each other.

Finally a guard opened the door and entered. Paolo glanced at him, then turned a frown on Erika. Gingerly she reached for his hand. He took it and pulled her to him. Sinking under a wave of sadness she let him hug her hard.

Then Flavio stepped in to separate them. The guard motioned Paolo forward. Only once did he glance back on his way to the door, and then with a pained look. He crossed the threshold and the guard slammed the door behind them, its reverberations quaking through her. She stood staring at the gleaming metal barrier until she felt Flavio's hand on her shoulder. "Let's go," he said.

Crisp air pricked Erika's face and cleared her moist eyes. The sky shone a pale blue, another day without fog or mist; only some straggly clouds wafting to and fro in a high-altitude breeze, as if unsure of which way they wanted to go. She herself felt like those clouds as she stood outside the prison. She had forgotten to ask Paolo if there had been more to his snatching of Matilde Fassino's purse than the juvenile stunt he'd claimed, the fateful act that had both propelled Erika to him and contributed to their split. Flavio wouldn't have permitted the topic, most likely, and either way it didn't really matter. She doubted she would ever understand Paolo's reasoning. She was finding it hard enough to understand herself.

New Year's Day found Erika back in the Déjà Vu for a breakfast of brioche and cappuccino.

"Enjoying this dry weather?" asked Fausta from behind the bar, after offering New Year's greetings.

"Definitely. I feel I'm back in more familiar territory."

"Well, these blue skies won't last forever, so take advantage while you can. Have you been up to Superga yet?"

Erika remembered Fausta's first reference to the famous hill on which Matilde Fassino resided. No doubt she had seen the news about Fassino's critical condition. Erika was glad Fausta hadn't mentioned it.

"No," Erika replied, "I haven't had time."

"Well, with skies like these, you could have a wonderful view of the Alpine arc—sometimes you can see all the way to Monte Cervino. Better than in summer, with the haze."

Erika recalled that Monte Cervino was Italian for the Matterhorn, one side of which lay in Italy. "Is there a bus?"

"Take the Dentiera." Fausta looked out the window and drew a long, contemplative breath. "Maybe 1978 will prove luckier," she said, both melancholy and courage in her gaze.

Erika hadn't spoken of Fausta's deceased nephew since the start of her own overwhelming ordeal. But she understood, and nodded.

That afternoon, with Fausta's directions, Erika climbed aboard the Dentiera, a steep-grade tram transporting passengers up the 2,205-foot-high hill of Superga. At the top she made a quick tour of the enormous baroque church that housed the tombs of the dukes of Savoy, then went straight out to the scenic overlook. The city of Turin and the Po River valley lay below in a vast stretch of alternating buildings, houses, and countryside. During her ride up the mountain she'd wondered where Matilde Fassino's estate might sit. Now as she stood above everything, thoughts like those fizzled against the splendor before her. She was above and beyond all that.

The city's hilly panorama gave way to the titan Alps, jagged and frosty and shimmering in the day's brilliant clarity. She guessed at which might be the Matterhorn but wasn't sure, since everything was covered with snow. What felt important was that she could see for miles and miles across artificial boundaries into different lands and dimensions.

She thought of the youthful black angel perched atop his mountain sculpture in Piazza Statuto, wings aloft as he challenged the white energy of Piazza Castello. Once more she felt his shadow graze her with a whisper of things to come. With the arrival of the New Year she felt ready for a fresh challenge herself, thanks to her newfound understanding of past and present, which once more called to mind the double-faced castle of Piazza Castello. Yes, duality seemed omnipresent, and yet, didn't the two sides of the castle meet and share brick and mortar? Didn't black and white blend to grey? Grey, the color of Claudio Voghera's eyes. Like him, she wouldn't get bogged down by too many scruples. She would just try to do her best. She thought of the switchblade back in her flat. She looked forward to teaching Claudio a few of its tricks.

Acknowledgements

Many thanks to relatives and friends in Turin and Asti—Nuccia Rosmino, Francesco Brunetti, Iris Sardo, and Luisa Sardo—for lending me their deep knowledge of these cities. Although I lived two years in this part of Italy during the militant Years of Lead and have ever been a student of history, I would have remained in the dark about Turin's historical reputation concerning the occult and magic. As part of my research I embarked on a nighttime bus tour—"Torino Magica" ®—an up-close revelation of the city's renowned points of occult energy; part of Turin's history and charm, they fascinate, whether you're a believer or not!

Much appreciation, as well, to my critique-group partners, past and present, especially authors Paula Riley and the late Bill Kuechler.

And finally, I thank readers Angela Sell, Barbara Stefano, Lorena Merighi, Livia D'Andrea, Cora Robey, and Melissa Smith for lending another round of sharp eyes and valuable input.

Excerpt from *Snow Blind*, sequel to *Silver Blades*

Chapter 1

Erika Rivoli looked away from the Swiss psychologist, out the window into the late-afternoon gloom. This was her third session with him and she could no longer put off confessing her dream, not if she hoped to get help from this psychologist for her insomnia and intense headaches. Finally she met Dr. Betz's steady stare, her emotions repressed like packed-down snow, her voice even: "In my dream I sleep with my brother and I kill him," she uttered almost matter-of-factly.

The psychologist didn't flinch. And yet, thought Erika, *why should he*? Instead, as she had made him wait, he did the same with her. Then his head tilted a fraction and a faint smile crossed his eyes. The smile lingered before at last he gave a long professional nod and pronounced a bland: "Interesting."

How else should a shrink respond to a bomb like that—*fascinating...extraordinary?* Neither seemed suitable for 1980 when nothing seemed shocking anymore. His curiosity was piqued though, and whichever school of psychology Dr. Betz followed, she liked him. Then again, he was only the second therapist she had seen in all her twenty-six years of life and very *unlike* the pushy, presumptuous woman she had once seen two years ago in San Diego, where she was born and raised. *San Diego, USA, Turin,*

Italy, and now Bellinzona, Switzerland. And always, it seemed, on the run.

That, she hadn't told Dr. Betz—that she was on the run. No one must know. Erika had found Dr. Stefan Betz, chosen him at random on one of her walks through the city. A polished brass plate inscribed with his name gleamed next to the door of the five-story, terracotta-roofed building which his office occupied. Her insomnia and headaches had been surging like the surfers' waves at Mission beach. On top of that, now that winter had arrived in the Alps, with its three-pronged attack of wind, cold, and snow, she also felt lonely, and isolated. Still, what should she expect? She had chosen this bizarre path she was on.

Erika waited, studying Dr. Betz and his dark, sturdy looks, his sharp chiseled cheeks and nose that reminded her of a Medici bust she'd seen in a Florence museum. Maybe, as he gazed back at her own blond, blued-eyed looks, he wondered if she was lying about incest and fratricide.

"So that is the gist of your dream?" he finally asked, dark brows inching higher.

"*Già,*" Erika answered. *Right.* They were speaking Italian, the language of Switzerland's Canton Ticino. "Not your average recurring dream, I imagine." Her flippancy sounded phony to her, but it was the only way she felt comfortable expressing herself about the dream.

"Who can say what *average* is? And your headaches start when you wake up from these dreams?"

Erika nodded. "The dreams come right before I wake up in the morning, and sometimes in the middle of the night. Combined with the headaches they make me feel like I'm trying to pull myself out of a vat of cement in the morning."

Dr. Betz made a swift note on his pad and looked back up. "You're from California. How are you dealing with this severe winter month of January?"

Ah, he thinks the jolt from palm trees to pines sagging

with snow might have something to do with my condition. So far he hadn't asked what *brought* her to Switzerland, which was just as well, though she had a cover story for that.

"I'm used to the cold. I lived in Turin, Italy before I came here."

"Your Italian is very good."

She acknowledged the compliment with a slight nod which she hoped came across as modest. Her Italian was at least fluent. "My grandparents spoke the language." His Italian was good too. They both had accents, his German, from German-speaking Switzerland, no doubt.

"So how long have you been having these dreams and headaches?"

She made as if she were considering it, though the calculation was easy. "About two months." Since right before she'd fled Italy in November. She didn't reveal that connection. She just wanted help, relief, without telling her whole life's story.

"Can you describe the dream?"

Erika shifted on the corner of the brown leather sofa. She was comfortable, the room felt cozy, lit by a low lamp, tomes crowding cherrywood bookshelves, a heavy wooden desk covered with papers behind the doctor's swivel chair. Out the window, the light was fading, the gloam of an overcast sky. She felt even warmer looking out at the cold, the lonely cold, and didn't want to leave.

"Do you feel you can tell me?" he asked.

Of course he would want to know the dream in detail. His sharp, stony features seemed to demand it. Yet his voice was so mellow, a mild baritone, that the man channeled calmness. And unlike the pushy old shrink in San Diego, he was on the young side, maybe late thirties.

She drew a silent breath and began to narrate, once more as if there were kilometers between them, as if someone else was speaking. After finishing, she blurted with a half-mocking chuckle, "Is that Freudian?"

Dr. Betz returned a non-committal smile. "Oh, I think there's more to it." Outside, crooked tree limbs glowed black against a sky turning from white to grey. "Maybe you'll choose to share more about that at our next session."

Erika nodded a slow assent.

The train brought her to the base of an icy mountain, to the station of Cobbio, the village where she lived, in a house she didn't own—not a home, but a hideout. At least there was a twenty-minute train service back and forth from Bellinzona. If not she would feel trapped in this village of a few hundred people, caged in by hoary mountains. She hiked up the terraced hill that held the village, the cobbled roads and paths cleared of snow. No worries about slipping, for this was Switzerland: snow was plowed and shoveled practically before it hit the ground.

She let herself into the three-story, one hundred-year-old house. The owner, Romano Rosselli, lived in San Diego and had been a friend of Erika's grandparents. It was he whom she had contacted from Turin to ask if she could stay in the house. She wouldn't pay rent, they'd agreed, only utilities. His niece in Cobbio had given Erika the keys. What made the house a good hideaway, apart from its remote location, was that no one could trace her now that her grandparents were deceased, and Romano Rosselli was not a friend of Erika's parents or any other of her relatives.

She lit the kerosene stove in the kitchen, the only source of heat in the entire relic. Spacious as the house was, she lived in the kitchen next to the stove's radiant heat. It warmed her quickly, and she shed her coat and settled at the kitchen table to write a letter in Italian:

The translation into English of the exposé continues to go well and I can't wait until the story hits the press. I still haven't noted anyone I consider suspicious here in Cobbio. Of course, Bellinzona is different, with about 17,000 inhabitants, I was told, and all of them strangers to me. I haven't spotted any tails, you know how vigilant I am, but I imagine there will be one.